Ian Rankin is the multimillion-copy worldwide bestseller of over thirty novels and creator of John Rebus. His books have been translated into thirty-six languages and have been adapted for radio, the stage and the screen.

Rankin is the recipient of four Crime Writers' Association Dagger Awards, including the Diamond Dagger, the UK's most prestigious award for crime fiction. In the United States, he has won the celebrated Edgar Award and been shortlisted for the Anthony Award. In Europe, he has won Denmark's Palle Rosenkrantz Prize, the French Grand Prix du Roman Noir and the German Deutscher Krimipreis.

He is the recipient of honorary degrees from universities across the UK, is a Fellow of the Royal Society of Edinburgh and a Fellow of the Royal Society of Literature, and has received an OBE for his services to literature. In 2022 he received a knighthood as part of the Queen's Platinum Jubilee celebrations.

Website: IanRankin.net
Twitter: @Beathhigh
Facebook: IanRankinBooks

Ian Rankin
The Iconic Number One Bestseller

Also by Ian Rankin

IAN RANKIN

A HEART FULL OF HEADSTONES

ORION

First published in Great Britain in 2022 by Orion Fiction,
an imprint of The Orion Publishing Group Ltd.,
Carmelite House, 50 Victoria Embankment
London EC4Y 0DZ

An Hachette UK Company

1 3 5 7 9 10 8 6 4 2

A CIP catalogue record for this book
is available from the British Library.

ISBN (Hardback) 978 1 3987 0935 5
ISBN (Trade Paperback) 978 1 3987 0936 2
ISBN (eBook) 978 1 3987 0940 9

Typeset by Deltatype Ltd, Birkenhead, Merseyside

Printed in Great Britain by Clays Ltd, Elcograf S.p.A.

www.orionbooks.co.uk

In my end is my beginning

**Words Mary Queen of Scots had embroidered in French
on her clothing shortly before her execution**

This is my truth, tell me yours

Manic Street Preachers

Now

John Rebus had been in court plenty of times, but this was his first time in the dock. As the charge was being read out for the jury's benefit, he took it all in. Things hadn't yet recovered from COVID. Apart from the judge and Rebus, everyone was masked, and there were cameras and monitors everywhere. The jury were being housed elsewhere – a cinema on Lothian Road – as a health precaution. He could see them courtesy of one of the large monitors, just as they could see him.

He tried to remember his first time giving evidence in a case, but couldn't. It would have been the 1970s, not quite half a century ago. The lawyers, court officials and judge had probably looked much the same. Today Rebus was flanked by two uniformed guards, as would have been the case back then. He'd been in the witness box once when the accused had tried barging his way out of the dock to have a go at him, one of the guards hauling him back. What was the accused's name? Short and skinny, with curly hair. Began with an M, maybe. Ach, everybody's memory started going eventually, didn't it? It wasn't just him. An age thing, like the COPD that meant he was allowed to keep an inhaler in his pocket along with his face mask.

He wondered how his dog was doing. His daughter, Samantha, had taken Brillo to hers. Rebus's granddaughter doted on the mutt. He was glad the public gallery was empty – meant he hadn't had to fight with Sam to stop her attending. There was a simplicity to life in custody. Other people took the decisions for you. He didn't have to think about meals or dog walks or what to do with his day. Being an ex-cop, he even found himself popular with the prison guards. They liked to linger in his cell, sharing stories. They kept an eye open, too – not everyone inside would have his best interests at heart, which was why he had the luxury of unshared accommodation, even as HMP Edinburgh was bursting at the seams. Not that anyone outside of a few pen-pushers referred to it as HMP Edinburgh – it was Saughton, sited at the westernmost end of Gorgie Road. If you headed into town from there, you soon passed the Hearts football stadium and then Tynecastle police station. In a roundabout way, it was the latter that had brought Rebus here.

Malone, that was the skinny guy's name. A career housebreaker who didn't at all mind terrorising any occupants he found on the premises. One of his victims had suffered a coronary and died on the spot, which was why Rebus had made sure Malone wouldn't get away with it. That had entailed a bit of embroidery from the witness box, which was what had caused Malone to fly into a rage – and *that* never looked good to a jury. Rebus had tried to look shaken by the outburst. The judge had asked if he needed a minute.

'Maybe a glass of water, Your Honour,' Rebus had said, trying to summon up a few beads of nervous sweat. All of this while Malone was being taken from the courtroom, cursing Rebus and his corrupt kind to the rafters.

'The jury will ignore what they've just heard from the accused,' the judge intoned. Then, to the advocate depute, 'You may continue, if Detective Inspector Rebus is ready.'

Detective Inspector Rebus was ready.

He tried to recall the first time he'd set foot in Tynecastle cop shop. Would he have been a DI or a detective sergeant? Probably a DS. He had never been based there himself, though for a time he'd worked out of nearby Torphichen. But Torphichen was practically Edinburgh's salubrious West End. Tynecastle – Tynie to those acquainted with it – was a tougher proposition altogether. Rebus reckoned there was a thesis to be written about the proximity of football grounds to areas of high deprivation. The land around Tynecastle stadium comprised tenements mostly, separated by wasteland and industrial units. Further west the tenements gave way to estates such as Burnhill, with its ugly concrete blocks from the 1960s and '70s, whose condensation-heavy windows resembled cataracts in a crumbling face. For at least some of the people who lived their lives there, allegiance to the local football team provided distraction and even occasionally an all-too-brief euphoria.

Not that Rebus had ever followed any one team.

'Come on, John,' he'd often been teased, 'Hearts or Hibs, it must be one or the other.' To which he would always shake his head, just as he found himself shaking his head now as he happened to catch a few of the clerk's words. Seemed to be taking for ever to get through the charge sheet.

'You are indicted at the instance of . . . and the charge against you is that you did . . . on the fifteenth of . . . at . . . against . . . and did . . .'

Rebus was trying not to let the jury know he was absolutely aware of them. He knew which camera was trained on him and his eyes never met it. The polished wood of the courtroom; the slate-coloured carpet; the little ledge on which he could rest his hands – these were his apparent focus. Then there was the witness box. A screen stood near it – not a TV monitor, but an actual physical screen so that a witness could testify without eye contact being possible with the defendant. The whole thing was on wheels so it could be rolled into position as and when needed, rolled up the temporary ramp . . .

Hang on, why had it gone quiet?

Rebus looked to the judge, who was staring at his QC. The clerk of court was staring too, from above the charge sheet.

'Apologies, Your Honour,' the QC said, rifling through his papers.

The clerk gave a theatrical sigh. The whole thing was bloody theatre, something Rebus had come to realise all those decades back. Well, theatre to the various professions involved anyway. Anything but theatre to everyone else.

'This is the point in proceedings where you inform of us how the accused intends to plead,' the judge admonished the QC.

Rebus glanced towards his defence team – senior counsel and junior counsel in their daft wee wigs, solicitor in a dark buttoned-up suit. Senior counsel wore a gown of silk and a piece of neckwear Rebus now knew was called a fall, though no one seemed to know why. They looked to him like the relative strangers they were, though he'd met them often these past few weeks and days. Junior counsel's face was impassive, probably thinking about the shopping she had to do on the way home or the games kit to get ready for her kid's next day at school.

'Mr Bartleby?' the judge prompted. Rebus liked the look of the judge. He seemed the type who'd pour you the good whisky, no matter who you were. The senior counsel was giving a nod, satisfied with whatever he'd been checking.

He licked his lips.

Opened his mouth to speak.

Rebus couldn't help but mimic him, drawing in a lungful of sweet Edinburgh air . . .

Then

Day One

1

The pubs were opening again, and this time without the need to sign in and order from your table. Standing at a bar seemed a novelty, though you were aware of the bottle of hand sanitiser on the corner or over by the door, and the track-and-trace QR code or the old-fashioned clipboard on which you scrawled a name – any name, and contact number – any number. Rebus still hadn't a clue how the QR code worked. Now and again a savvier customer or one of the bar staff would try showing him, but the information was like a stone skimming across the surface of his brain, soon sinking, never to be retrieved.

The pub he was in today was on Brougham Place. He had walked Brillo across Bruntsfield Links in low winter sun, dog and owner casting long shadows. There was the usual traffic on Melville Drive and plenty of students using the footpaths. He supposed the university was back in business. Things had been very quiet for a while, Rebus confined to barracks with his COPD until the vaccine programme kicked in. But now he was a free man, and boosted to boot. No more distanced meetings with his daughter and grand-daughter, them one side of the garden gate and him the other, shopping left outside the door for him to collect. People could go about their lives again. He could give Samantha and Carrie a hug, though he sensed a reticence still in his granddaughter, who was yet to be jabbed. Were things really getting back to normal, or was there no longer any normal for them to get back to? The drinkers in today's pub still slipped their masks back on if they wanted to move about the place. They still twitched if anyone had a sudden coughing fit. Lockdown had offered Rebus the perfect excuse not to try seeing his doctor about the dizzy spells and chest pain. Maybe he'd do something about that now.

Aye, maybe.

For the present, he contented himself with the evening paper. There was a story about local businesses on the Royal Mile that felt under siege, shoplifters and addicts menacing them and taking from them with seeming impunity. Meanwhile in West Lothian a car had been vandalised with acid and a nearby house attacked with a petrol bomb. Rebus knew that probably meant a gang feud. Not that it was any of his business, not any more. When his phone pinged, a drinker at the next table visibly flinched. Rebus gave a slow shake of the head to reassure the man that it was just a normal text rather than a COVID alert. But when he checked his screen, he realised it was anything but normal, insofar as it was from a man called Cafferty. Morris Gerald Cafferty, known as Big Ger.

You not out with the dog?

Rebus thought about ignoring the question, but he doubted Cafferty would give up.

Yes, was his one-word reply. Cafferty's response was immediate.

How come I can't see you?

Pub.

Which one?

Why?

Are you on some sort of miser's contract that means you can only type three-letter texts?

Apparently not.

Rebus waited, took a sip from his pint, and waited some more. Brillo was curled at his feet, not asleep but doing a passable impression. Rebus rested his phone on the table and swirled the contents of his glass, renewing its foamy head. He'd been told once that he shouldn't do that, but he couldn't remember why.

Ping. *I need to see you.*

Ping. *Come to the flat.*

Ping. *No rush. The next hour will do. Finish your drink and take the dog home.*

He debated how to answer. Did he even need to? No, because he was going to go, and Cafferty knew he would. He would go because he was curious – curious about all sorts of things. He would go because they had history.

On the other hand, he didn't want to look too keen. So instead he slipped his mask on, walked to the bar and ordered another pint.

12

*

Cafferty's home was a three-storey penthouse in a glass tower on a development known as Quartermile. It had been the site of Edinburgh's old infirmary, and the original renovated buildings nestled between steel-and-glass newcomers. Rebus's own home was a ground-floor tenement flat on a quiet street in Marchmont, only a ten-minute walk away. The two were separated by Melville Drive. On Rebus's side sat Bruntsfield Links, where pitch-and-putt was played in summer months. On Cafferty's side sat a large grassy area known as the Meadows. There were usually plenty of joggers, cyclists and dog-walkers making use of the space. Rebus had to avoid a few as he walked towards Quartermile. He wondered if Cafferty was watching his approach. On the off chance, he offered a two-fingered salute in the building's general direction, earning him a quizzical look from a young couple seated on a nearby bench.

He paused for a moment outside the door to Cafferty's building, wishing he still smoked. A cigarette would have given him a reasonable excuse to delay entering. Instead of which, he pressed the buzzer. The door clicked open, the lift taking him up eight storeys to the top. The landing here led to just the one door. It had already been opened. A well-built young man was scooping up the mail that had obviously been pushed through the letter box earlier. He was fair-haired and had a build toned by regular visits to the gym. He sported what looked like a Fitbit on his left wrist. No actual watch and no rings.

'Who are you then?' Rebus enquired.

'Mr Cafferty's personal assistant.'

'Must be some job that, wiping his arse as and when. I know the way.' Rebus snatched the mail from the man's hand. He'd taken no more than two steps down the hall when a strong grip on his shoulder pulled him up.

'Need to pat you down.'

'You're joking, aren't you?' But it was clear from the look on the young man's face that he wasn't. Rebus managed a sigh as he unzipped his padded jacket. 'You know I was invited here, right? Making me a guest rather than a really shite ninja?'

The hands went around Rebus's ribs, up under his arms and down his back. When the man crouched to check the legs of his trousers, Rebus had a mind to plant a knee in his face, but he reckoned there might be consequences.

'I hope you enjoyed that as much as I did,' he said as the man rose to his full height again. Instead of replying, the assistant grabbed the letters Rebus had taken from him, then led the way into the flat's cavernous open-plan living area.

Rebus noted that the staircase had had a stairlift fitted, but otherwise the place was as he remembered it. Cafferty was in an electric wheelchair over by the floor-to-ceiling windows. There was a telescope there on a lowered tripod, just the right height for someone seated.

'I suppose you have to get your kicks somehow,' Rebus commented.

Cafferty half turned his head and offered a thin smile. He had lost some weight and there was an unhealthy pallor to his face. The eyes were still the same steely orbs, though, the large clenched fists a reminder of past, bruising endeavours.

'No flowers or chocolates?' he asked, looking Rebus up and down.

'I've a dozen white lilies ordered for when the time comes.' Rebus pretended to be interested in the view across The Meadows to the chimneypots of Marchmont. 'They still haven't found him, have they?' he mused. 'The guy who shot you? Thinking is, they never will.'

'Andrew, get John here a drink, will you? Maybe some coffee to counteract the alcohol?'

'What's the point of alcohol if you counteract it?'

'A whisky, then? I don't have any beer.'

'I don't need anything, other than to know what I'm doing here.'

Cafferty stared at him. 'It's good to see you too.' He turned the wheelchair and aimed it at the long glass coffee table across the room, at the same time gesturing to Andrew that he should leave.

'Which is he, carer or bodyguard?' Rebus asked as he followed.

Cafferty gestured towards the cream leather sofa and Rebus lowered himself onto it, moving a large cushion emblazoned with a saltire out of the way. The only thing on the table was the mail Andrew had placed there. Cafferty's gaze settled on him.

'How about you?' he enquired. 'Did you have a good pandemic?'

'I appear to have survived.'

'Sums up the pair of us, wouldn't you say? On the other hand, you probably feel it as much as I do.'

'Feel what?'

'Mortality, chapping at the door.' To reinforce the point, Cafferty rapped the knuckles of his left hand against the arm of his wheelchair.

'Well, this is cheery.' Rebus leaned back, getting as comfortable as the sofa would allow.

'Life isn't cheery, though, is it? We both learned that lesson long ago. And stuck here during COVID, there wasn't a hell of a lot to do except . . .' Cafferty tapped his forehead.

'If you'd asked, I'd have let you borrow a jigsaw.'

Cafferty gave a slow shake of the head. 'You forget that I *know* you. You're telling me you sat for weeks on end in that flat of yours, that living room, that *head* of yours, and didn't brood? What else would you do?'

'I had a dog that needed walking.'

'And you had your daughter and granddaughter take it for those walks – I saw them.' He jerked his head towards the telescope. 'And Siobhan Clarke too, sometimes. She could never get within a hundred yards of here without staring up. Staring, mind, not . . .' He raised two fingers towards Rebus.

'If you could maybe get to the point while there's still a bit of light in the sky.'

'The point is . . .' Cafferty sucked in some air and expelled it noisily. 'I've had nothing to do but think back on things I've done, people I've done them to. Not all of it strictly merited.'

Rebus held up a hand, palm towards Cafferty. 'I no longer take confession. Siobhan's the one you need to talk to.'

'Not for this,' Cafferty said quietly. 'Not for this.' He leaned forward in his chair. 'You remember Jack Oram?'

It took Rebus a few moments, Cafferty staying silent, content to let the synapses do their slow-grinding work.

'Another of your legion of the disappeared,' Rebus eventually stated. 'What was the name of his place – the Potter's Bar?'

'I knew you'd remember.'

'A pool hall where a cue could come in handy in more than one way. Oram's name above the door but profits accruing to the man I'm looking at right now. Oram starts skimming and pretty soon he needs more than a pool cue to save him.'

'I didn't touch him.'

'Of course you didn't.'

'He ran before I could. Turned into a missing person case. I've half an idea your old pal Siobhan worked on it.'

'So?'

'So I hear he's back in town.'

'And?'

'I wouldn't mind a word, always supposing he can be persuaded.'

Rebus gave a grunt. 'What are you going to do, have Andrew pat him down with a bit more malice?'

'I want to say sorry to the guy,' Cafferty stated solemnly.

Rebus made show of cupping a hand to one ear. 'I must have misheard.'

'I'm serious. Yes, he took what wasn't his, and, yes, he ran. He's been laying low the past four years, doubtless scared shitless. Probably only came back because he heard about this.' Cafferty thumped the arm of his wheelchair again.

'I'm still not sure I get it.'

'That's because you don't know what he needed the money for. His brother, Paul, died of cancer. Left a wife, two kids and precious little in the bank. Jack wanted to help, whatever it took.'

'Are you asking me to believe you've suddenly grown a conscience?'

'I just want to tell him to his face that I'm sorry for what happened.'

'So have your gofer go fetch him.'

'I could do that, but seeing how you're to blame for what happened to him . . .'

'What do you mean?'

'Four and a bit years back, you were drinking in some pub, got chatting to a guy called Eric Linn. Ring a bell?'

'I've met a lot of people in a lot of pubs.'

'The two of you had a mutual acquaintance, Albert Cousins, snitch of yours from back in the day. Linn asked if you still saw him. You said no, but you'd heard he was losing a bit too much at after-hours poker games in the Potter's Bar.' Cafferty broke off. 'Anything?'

'Maybe.'

'Well, Eric knew I had a stake in the bar and he reckoned I might be interested, which I was, because nobody had thought to tell me about these wee sessions. Jack Oram had been holding back, not cutting me in. That got me doing some digging, and it started to look a lot like he'd been skimming from the pool hall, too. Lucky for him, he got wind I'd be wanting a word.' Cafferty paused again. 'All because your mouth got a bit slack in a bar one night.'

Rebus was silent for a moment. It was true about Albert Cousins and his gambling. Rebus couldn't have known not to mention it in conversation. All the same . . .

'The streets have changed,' Cafferty was saying. 'I've not got the eyes and ears I once had.'

'Neither have I.'

'But you still know your way around, and you've got time on your hands.'

'I'm a bit long in the tooth to play Humphrey Bogart.' Rebus got to his feet and retraced his steps to the window. He heard the whirr of the wheelchair's motor as Cafferty followed him.

'I'm on the way out,' Cafferty said quietly. 'You noticed as soon as you walked in here. Those bullets did too much damage.' He suddenly looked tired. 'I just feel bad about Oram. I can't explain it exactly, why him and none of the others. And there's money in it, of course.' He was gesturing towards a wall unit. 'Envelope there with some cash in it. You wouldn't be Humphrey Bogart if you didn't take it.'

'Any chance of a femme fatale on the side?'

'No promises, but who knows what you'll turn up. It's got to be better than festering in that flat of yours.'

'I'm halfway through another jigsaw, though. Sergeant Pepper, a thousand pieces.'

'It'll still be there.'

Rebus turned and leaned in towards the seated figure. 'Whatever happened to Oram, I'm not to blame – you are. You'd have found out eventually, one way or another. Plenty chancers out there who'd be happy to track him down for you.'

'I don't want just any chancer, though – I want the biggest.'

Rebus gave a thin smile, almost despite himself. 'So what have you got, apart from his name?'

'Could be he's using an alias – I would, in his shoes. Last sighting was near Gracemount a few weeks back.'

'A lovely spot for an ex-cop to go walkabout. Is this you trying to get me bushwhacked?'

'He was coming out of a lettings agency on Lasswade Road.'

'Didn't you used to own a lettings agency?'

Cafferty nodded. 'It changed hands a few years back.'

'And that's his last sighting – a lettings office that used to be in your name?'

Cafferty offered a slow shrug. 'I know you'd rather it was a Hollywood mogul's house, but that's all I can offer.'

Rebus leaned down further, his hands gripping the arms of the wheelchair. The two men fixed eyes, the silence lengthening. Then he pushed himself upright and shook his head slowly.

'I'll think about it,' he said, walking towards the door.

Cafferty stayed facing the window. In around five minutes, he could place his eye to the telescope and watch Rebus heading back across the Meadows. He heard the front door close and sensed Andrew behind him, awaiting instructions.

'Tea, I think,' he said. 'Builder's strength.'

'I didn't like him,' Andrew commented.

'You're a good judge of character. But then you probably wouldn't like me either if I wasn't paying for the privilege. Though with what you're learning, maybe I should be charging tuition fees.'

Cafferty manoeuvred his wheelchair towards the wall unit. Rebus had taken the envelope, of course he had. Satisfied, he moved to the coffee table, reaching forward to sift through the mail. There was an A4-sized envelope with familiar lettering in the top left corner: *MGC Lettings*. The cheapskate bastards were still using his personalised stationery.

'Hell is this?' he muttered, opening the flap. There was a single sheet of paper inside, a printout of a grainy photograph. The profile of a man, taken through the doorway of a living room. Cafferty checked. Nothing on the back of the photo and nothing else in the envelope.

Andrew was standing behind him. 'Who's that?' he enquired.

'Not the faintest fucking idea,' Cafferty said. And he meant it. He didn't recognise the man at all.

The living room, though . . . Well, that was another matter entirely.

2

Detective Inspector Siobhan Clarke was in the CID office at Gayfield Square police station. She had been staring at her computer for almost five minutes, a mug of tea grown tepid beside her.

'I can make you another,' Detective Constable Christine Esson suggested. Clarke blinked herself back into the room and shook her head, then squeezed her eyes shut and arched her spine until she could feel the vertebrae click back into place.

'I'm going to guess Francis Haggard,' Esson went on, holding her own mug up to her face. Her dark hair was cut pageboy style and had never changed in the years they'd worked together. Her desk faced Clarke's, making it difficult to hide, though Clarke suspected her colleague could read even the back of a head.

'Who else?' Clarke admitted.

Haggard was a uniformed officer based at Tynecastle police station who stood accused of domestic abuse, 'abuse' being the current terminology. Previously it had been called domestic violence, and before that, domestic assault. None of the three, to Clarke's mind, came anywhere near defining the severity of the crime. She had encountered victims turned to husks; self-belief, trust and confidence scooped out. Some had suffered all their married lives – often physically, always psychologically. The abusers ranged across class and age, but this was the first time she'd had to deal with one of her own.

Haggard had fifteen years of service behind him. He'd been married for the past six, and according to his partner, the angry outbursts and gaslighting had started within the first eighteen months of marriage. Clarke and Esson had interviewed Haggard that very afternoon, not for the first time. He'd sat across the table from them, shoulders back, legs splayed, one hand occasionally cupping his groin. His solicitor, who'd had to slide his own chair further away to avoid their knees touching, had just about managed to hide his obvious disdain.

Haggard had complained about the presence in the room of not just one but two female detectives, turning towards the lawyer. 'You sure you're okay with this, Mikey? Couple of blokes might see things differently.'

The solicitor, Michael Leckie (Clarke doubted anyone else in his life ever referred to him as Mikey), had shifted in his chair, saying nothing.

'I see how it is,' Haggard had said, nodding to himself. 'Pitchforks are out and the pyre's nicely smouldering.' Then, turning his head sharply towards Leckie, 'Go on then, tell them what I told you to.'

At which Michael Leckie had cleared his throat and transferred his attention from the file of papers in front of him to the two detectives seated opposite.

'I suppose,' he said, spacing his words as if reciting a language he'd only recently learned, 'you will have heard of a condition known as post-traumatic stress disorder?'

'PTSD,' Esson had replied.

'PTS fucking D,' Francis Haggard had echoed.

'PTSD,' Esson said now, shaking her head in disbelief. Somehow, without Clarke having noticed, the tepid tea had been switched for a fresh mug. She lifted it and took a slurp. Esson herself only ever seemed to drink hot water, at least while on duty. 'It'll never fly, will it?'

'I don't know,' Clarke confessed. All Haggard had stated at the interview was that the job he'd been doing for the past fifteen years had left with him the condition.

'My client is unwilling to go into details at this time,' Leckie had commented, sounding as though he might not himself know too many of the particulars. Haggard had already been charged and was out on bail, with the stipulation that he not go within a couple of postcodes of his wife or their shared address. He'd been suspended from police duties, naturally, and interviewed several times as part of the investigation. Esson had been assigned to the case from the get-go, but Clarke had only come aboard when DC Ronnie Ogilvie, Esson's usual CID partner, had caught COVID, leaving him isolating at home.

'PTSD,' Esson repeated.

'I've been looking it up online,' Clarke said. 'It's for battlefields and terror attacks. Surviving a tsunami or childhood trauma.'

'He's going to say a priest fiddled with him after choir practice, and thirty years later he's battering his partner?' Esson sounded sceptical. 'Funny he's only just decided that's his mitigation. Pound to a penny some men's group online will have suggested it. We should check if it's been tried in the past. And we need to let a psychologist have a go at him.'

'There's a lot we need to do, Christine. Has he been stationed anywhere other than Tynecastle?'

'A few relief shifts down the years. But otherwise, no.'

'So this PTSD stems from working at Tynie.'

'The dreaded Tynie. Suddenly it begins to look more plausible.'

Every cop in Edinburgh knew at least one story from Tynecastle. Officers there had a reputation for overstepping the mark and getting away with it. Countless prisoners had tripped on their way to or from its holding cells, or fallen down stairs, or somehow lost their balance and ended up planting their face into a wall. CCTV wouldn't have been functioning at the time. Accusations of misconduct would be withdrawn or come to nothing. There were whispers, too, of larger misdeeds – manufactured evidence, cover-ups and bribes.

'Her name's Cheryl,' Esson suddenly said.

'What?'

'Cheryl Haggard. The victim. We shouldn't lose sight of her in all this.'

'That's a good point. If he's been suffering from PTSD, wouldn't she be the first to know? He'd have said something, wouldn't he? Or she'd have sensed him changing.'

'You've not spoken to her yet, have you?'

Clarke shook her head. 'I know you and Ronnie did.' She dug into the files on her desk, finding one of the transcripts. 'How's she doing?'

'She's got her sister looking after her.'

'Well, that's something. Who's the liaison officer?'

'Gina Hendry. She says she knows you.'

Clarke nodded. 'We go back a bit. I'll talk to her.'

'Tomorrow maybe, eh, boss?' Esson was holding up her phone, screen towards Clarke so she could see the time display.

'Already?' Clarke turned towards the window. Outside it had grown dark.

'Been a long day, and I think it's my turn to get them in.'

'You make a compelling case, Detective Constable Esson.' Clarke reached down to the floor for her shoulder bag.

Siobhan Clarke lived in a tenement flat just off Broughton Street, not much more than a five-minute walk from Gayfield Square. Esson had taken her to a bar on Leith Walk, where they'd shared some nachos to go with their drinks. Leith Walk itself was the usual mess, courtesy of the roadworks for the new tram line. Some sections of pavement were all but inaccessible, and the bar owner had hung a banner above the door to let potential customers know that *Yes We ARE Open – And Ready To Serve You!* Clarke wasn't sure how far a single plate of nachos and two rounds of gin and tonics would boost his coffers. As they'd left, he'd said he hoped to see them again soon.

'And bring a friend – bring *lots* of friends.'

With plenty of distance between them and the next occupied table, Clarke and Esson had found themselves discussing the case. They'd tried not to at first, but had soon run out of topics. Esson had swirled the ice in her glass as she started things off.

'The arresting officers, I could tell from their notes that they were trying to go easy on him. One of their own and all that. And there's Cheryl standing at the far end of the hall with blood pouring from her nose and tears streaming. It was the neighbours who called it in. Far from the first time they'd heard screams. They'd summoned us one time previously, but Haggard had talked his way out when the uniforms pitched up. I thought the days were past when we turned a blind eye to domestics.'

'Doesn't help when you're confronted by someone who carries the same warrant card as you.'

'Might have talked his way out again this time if he hadn't started mouthing off, then given one of them a shove. Have you seen the flat?' Clarke had shaken her head. 'I went for a look-see. New development in Newhaven, close by the harbour, views across the water from the balcony. The neighbours work in finance. They told me the wall insulation's really good, which is how they knew the screams were serious. You saw the photos of her injuries?'

'New and old, Christine. I've memorised the descriptions. I've read the interviews you did with her.'

'Sometimes being a spinster's not so bad,' Esson had sighed.

The two women had locked eyes and shared half-hearted smiles.

Walking home, Clarke considered the relationships she'd had. Plenty of them down the years, always spluttering to a halt like a car with a leak in its fuel line. She had come to the eventual realisation that she was fine on her own. She had her flat, music and books and TV. She had friends she could hang out with or whose dinner tables she could share. They had mostly stopped trying to pair her with eligible men (and women, come to think of it). Edinburgh wasn't the worst place to be single. She didn't look out of place at concerts or the cinema or theatre. Okay, she'd been bored for stretches of the COVID lockdown, but she'd also enjoyed the silent city and its emptied streets.

The flip side, of course, was that while some crimes had fallen off a cliff, others had increased, including incidents of domestic abuse. Relationships had become pressure cookers. With pubs and clubs closed, drinking took place at home. Tempers frayed; insults were hurled – followed by fists and whatever came to hand.

That was the card she'd been expecting Haggard to play when he sat down in the interview room. Not bloody PTSD.

She had reached her building and was fishing her keys out of her bag when she heard a noise behind her. She wedged one of the keys between her fingers, turning it into a short stabbing weapon, bunched her fist and turned, coming face to face with someone she recognised.

DI Malcolm Fox.

He'd been seated in what looked like a brand-new Mercedes. For once he wasn't in one of his many well-tailored work suits. His hands were deep in the pockets of a dark nylon puffer jacket. Noting the key Clarke was holding, he raised both hands in a show of surrender.

'Nice to see you too,' he said.

'You never call, you never write,' Clarke replied. 'It's almost as if the longer you're based at the Big House, the easier it is to forget all us little people.'

Fox worked at Gartcosh, Police Scotland's nerve centre. She wasn't sure why his career had taken off while hers was stuck in the bus lane, though her one-time colleague John Rebus had taken to calling Fox 'the Brown-Nose Cowboy', meaning he was a yes man, a willing and eager toady, and he looked good parked behind a desk in one of those suits.

'I'm here now, aren't I?' Fox gave a fulsome shrug. As well as the jacket, he was wearing blue denims and tan-coloured brogues, none of it quite working. His dark hair was cut close to the scalp, gelled at the front, and his cheeks gleamed as if they saw more of a razor than was strictly necessary.

'It's eight o'clock at night, Malcolm.'

'You weren't at the office.'

'I have a phone, though.'

He gave a twitch of his mouth. 'I wanted to see you in the flesh.'

'Why?'

He turned his head in the direction of Broughton Street. 'Grab a drink?'

'I've had a drink.'

'With Christine Esson – your front desk told me. I did look in at one or two places in the vicinity . . .'

'Still got a bit of the detective left in you.' Fox had worked CID and then Internal Affairs before the big move to Gartcosh's Specialist Crime Division.

His hands were back in the pockets of his jacket, as if to signal that he was feeling the cold. 'Maybe a coffee, then?' His eyes were on the door behind Clarke.

'I don't think so. I'm pretty exhausted.'

He nodded his understanding. 'The Haggard case.'

Clarke couldn't help her eyebrows going up. 'You're well informed.'

'He's playing the PTSD card, isn't he? Or hasn't he told you that yet?'

Clarke gave him a hard stare. His eyes were almost twinkling. He knew he had her.

'You've got precisely ten minutes,' she muttered, shoving the key into the lock.

They climbed the stairs in single file, Fox to the rear. 'Saw you clocking the car,' he said. 'I could probably get you the same deal, if you're in the market.'

'I'm not.'

'Well, bear it in mind. Is Rebus still driving that old Saab of his?'

'How would I know?'

'You don't see him these days?'

'Who I see and don't see is none of your business.'

'Just making conversation.'

'Well don't.' They had reached her landing. She opened the door

24

and stalked down the hall. A quick survey of the living room told her she had nothing to worry about. Relatively tidy and evidence-free. She draped her coat over a chair and sat down, facing the doorway, where Fox now stood while he examined his surroundings.

'Cleaner's week off?'

'Says the man whose best friend is a microwave.'

'I actually know a few recipes these days. I'll cook for you one night.'

'Is that a threat?' Fox just smiled and started unzipping his jacket. 'Hardly worth your while,' she added.

'So no coffee, then?'

'How the hell do you know about Haggard?'

'He's a police officer. It's my job to know.'

'In your past life maybe, but you're not Complaints any longer.'

'But I was – and my boss says that's what's important.' He gestured towards the sofa and took her stony silence as permission to make himself at least partially comfortable. 'We're a bit worried about this case, Siobhan. Worried about possible repercussions.'

'The bad publicity, you mean?'

'A rogue cop is never a good look.'

'Not the first time an officer's been done for domestic abuse, so I'm guessing it's not just that, meaning it's got to be the PTSD angle.'

'I worked Complaints for a number of years, Siobhan. Tynecastle was seldom off our radar, but we never could get anything to stick.'

'I'm still not sure how you know he was going to cry PTSD.'

'He told us.'

'What?'

'An email to the chief constable. He says talking about it will require him to detail a lot of incidents involving a culture of corruption within Police Scotland – I'm quoting verbatim.'

'Does he give examples?'

'No.'

'But you don't think he's bluffing?'

'My boss has no way of knowing.'

'Your boss being the chief constable?'

'In his wisdom, he passed it down the chain to the assistant chief constable.'

'Jennifer Lyon, right? And she gave it to you?' Clarke watched Fox nod. 'To what end, though?'

'We need to know more about this defence of his – what he's going to say, how much of it he can prove. Online news agencies and bloggers are already sniffing. They know Haggard means Tynecastle and Tynecastle is rattling with skeletons.'

'Well, I'll be sure to keep you posted.' Clarke brushed invisible flecks from her trouser legs.

'Will you, though?' Fox said into the silence.

'Let me think.' She cocked her head. 'You come skulking around here at night – that smacks to me of wanting things kept low-key.'

'I did try the station first,' Fox countered, but Clarke shrugged off the comment.

'None of this seems to be coming through proper channels. Did the ACC choose you for your background in Complaints or because she knows the two of us have history? Might make me a softer touch, happy to leak anything I hear in the interview room?' Her face stiffened. 'Why did Haggard send that email? He wants the case dismissed, doesn't he? To do that, he'll threaten whatever it takes, and lo and behold, he's already got you and your boss doing his work for him.' Clarke's voice was rising as she got to her feet. 'That's not going to be how it works, Malcolm. I can't believe you'd even try this on.'

'I did tell the ACC it was a big ask.'

'Does *she* want the case shut down?'

'She wants what's best for Police Scotland.'

'Fewer column inches, you mean.' Colour was creeping up Clarke's neck. 'Tell her I'll send her the photos of Cheryl Haggard's injuries. The photos *and* Cheryl's statement. I'll do it first thing.'

'She knows the details of the case, Siobhan.'

Clarke was signalling for Fox to stand up. She was already at the doorway. 'You can tell Lyon we spoke. But as long as I'm on this case, it *is* a case. And it *will* go to trial, I promise you that.'

'You're very confident. I've always admired that side of you. Other sides . . . maybe not so much.'

'Enjoy your shiny fucking car, Malcolm.'

She led him to the door, slamming it shut after him. Back in her chair, she called Christine Esson, but got no answer. Flicking through her list of contacts, she found a number for Gina Hendry and sent her a text: *I'm attached to the Haggard case. Want to speak to Cheryl. You okay to liaise? Would love to catch up anyway. It's been a while. S*

In the kitchen, she put the kettle on. A bottle of Edinburgh Gin, half full, stared at her from the worktop.

'Not tonight, Satan,' she cautioned it, reaching instead for the tea bags and a mug.

Day Two

3

Rebus was up before it got light, the usual full bladder to blame. Brillo looked keen, so they headed out to the Meadows. Rebus took a small hard rubber ball for the mutt to chase, though he'd drawn the line at those fling-and-fetch things most dog-walkers used. Instead, he scuffed the ball along the ground with the toe of his shoe, meaning Brillo never had to go very far to retrieve it.

After breakfast, he stayed at the table, looking over his notes from the previous night's internet search. He hadn't uncovered much. Jack Oram's disappearance had been flagged up in a few editions of Edinburgh's evening paper. His family had put together a Missing poster, which had found its way into one of the stories. Rebus had printed it off, along with a smaller picture of Oram on his wedding day. His wife's name was Ishbel. Rebus had a stack of old telephone directories in the cupboard and consulted one of them. According to the newspaper, the family home had been in Craigmillar, and this was confirmed by the directory. Would the phone number still be the same? He tried it but got the constant tone telling him no such number existed. Stood to reason – he'd almost ditched his own landline when he'd moved flats a couple of years back. If Siobhan Clarke had had her way, he'd have ditched the phone directories too.

So he had an old address for the Oram family, a couple of grainy photographs, and the fact that the Potter's Bar had morphed from pool hall to a pub called the Moorfoot. Not much to show for an evening, in other words. But then there was the lettings agency on Lasswade Road – if Oram needed a flat, did that imply that he was steering clear of his family? Did they have any inkling he was alive

31

and kicking? And suppose Rebus did manage to track him down, was Cafferty really about to offer an olive branch to the guy, or was it not far more likely he'd be tying a noose to that branch instead?

Rebus reached across the table and lifted the envelope he'd taken from Cafferty's flat. It was fat with twenties and fifties. He didn't know what he was going to do with it, but he wasn't going to keep it.

And he definitely wasn't handing it back.

He knew that Eric Linn, the man he'd told about Albert Cousins' poker losses, had died of lung cancer a couple of years back; he had heard as much from someone who'd attended the funeral. Cousins himself, one of Rebus's more reliable snitches in CID days, had gambled everything away, lost his wife and his home, and topped himself. There hadn't been more than a dozen people at the crematorium. When Rebus had chatted to Linn in the pub that night, had he known that Linn knew Cafferty? He didn't think so. Had he known that Cafferty was a silent partner in the Potter's Bar? Yes. But how the hell could he have known the poker nights were happening without Cafferty's knowledge? He looked again at the photos of Jack and Ishbel Oram. At the time, he hadn't given the story much thought. The past was littered with people like Oram who'd got on the wrong side of Cafferty and suddenly not been around any longer. There was no way he could have connected it to a few words spoken during yet another drinking session. It really wasn't his fault.

Brillo was lying curled in his basket. He gave his owner an imploring but resigned look as Rebus slipped a jacket on.

'A couple of hours max,' Rebus explained, thinking that it might even be true.

His Saab was waiting outside. It was a wrench to leave the prime parking spot by his front door. More usually he had to trawl the area for a reasonable-sized gap. When he'd first moved to Marchmont, more than half a lifetime ago, there had been fewer students and fewer cars. Now, the students owned cars and thought nothing of paying for a parking permit. Rebus himself qualified for a disabled badge, but he'd baulked at the idea. He was conscious that his Saab – which started at the third time of asking – was the oldest car on his street and was edging towards 'vintage' territory. The council had plans to stop petrol and diesel cars using the city centre, but vintage cars would probably be exempt. 'Just another year or two,' he told the Saab. Always supposing the specialist garage in Wardie Bay could keep performing their regular miracles.

The drive to Lasswade Road didn't take long. This time of day, traffic was mostly piling into town rather than out. Two-storey houses and single-storey bungalows lined the street, alongside a smattering of shops and businesses. Behind, only a short distance away, lay badlands not unknown to Rebus in his CID days. He parked outside a vet's practice, through the window of which he could see anxious owners seated with pet carriers on their laps.

The windows of the lettings agency – one either side of its door – were covered by vertical slatted blinds and details of a few dozen properties, giving Rebus little inkling of what might be happening inside. The door itself was part wood and part frosted glass, with a metal gate (unlocked during working hours) providing added security. He took a step back and looked at the signage above the façade: *QC Lettings Agency*. So he already had one question in mind as he pushed open the door. It gave a little tinkle, courtesy of an old-fashioned bell attached by a spring on the inside.

'Cute,' Rebus said as he approached the receptionist. The room wasn't large but there was a desk angled into one corner, a large plastic screen protecting the receptionist from visitors. 'Sorry, I forgot.' He dug in his pocket for the lanyard, which he slipped around his neck. A laminated card was clipped to it, giving notification that he was exempt from wearing a mask. 'My lungs,' he explained as he took in the rest of the room.

There was a two-seater sofa, a small occasional table, and a water cooler, plus an entire wall dedicated to more properties available to rent. The receptionist was a no-nonsense woman in her early fifties, hair tied back and glasses perched on her nose.

'What does the QC stand for?' Rebus asked.

'Quality Counts, I've been told.'

'Like the sherry?'

'Like the sherry.'

'Why do I get the feeling I'm not the first to have made the connection?'

She gifted him a cool smile and asked if he was looking to rent.

'Not today,' he apologised, bringing out the photo of Jack Oram. 'But I think this man was. I'm not sure exactly how long back. A few weeks, I think. He's called Jack Oram, though he might be using a different name.'

He was holding the photo for her to take, but she seemed reluctant.

'What's this in connection with?'

33

'He was reported as missing four years back, but he's been spot-ted coming out of this office.'

'It's not a very good photo, is it? When was it taken?'

'I'm not sure,' Rebus admitted.

'I've not seen him,' the receptionist concluded.

'Could anyone else have dealt with him?'

'There's just me.'

'I'm assuming you get a lunch break, though?'

'Twelve thirty on the dot, but I just nip over the road to the baker's.'

'Maybe you could check all the same, just to put my mind at rest?'

She gave him a stare and a sniff, then got busy on her keyboard. 'The name Oram isn't coming up.'

'Like I said, he might be using an alias.'

'Why would he do that? And what's it got to do with you anyway?'

'His family haven't given up hope. They asked me to do some digging. You can imagine how desperate they are.'

'I suppose I can,' she eventually admitted, half turning her head towards a closed door at the back of the room. 'If I do need to step out for any reason – say a dental appointment – I either lock up or Mr Mackenzie keeps an eye on things.'

'He's the manager?'

'He owns the firm, yes. Well, it's a family business – something QC prides itself on.'

'Do you think you could ask him?'

'He's in a meeting right this second. I'm not sure how long it'll last. If you leave me a contact number . . .'

She was interrupted by the closed door suddenly opening. It stayed open as a woman strode out. She was a decade younger than the receptionist, her high heels clacking on the parquet floor. Knee-length red leather skirt and a waist-length jacket of the same vibrant hue. Rebus was enveloped in perfume as she passed. Their eyes met for the briefest of moments. Hers were a striking blue. Plenty of make-up and all topped by thick black hair. He was reminded of Elizabeth Taylor in what he would have called her prime. The bell attached to the door quivered as she made her exit. Without waiting to be asked, Rebus entered the office, cutting off the receptionist's objection by closing the door once he was inside.

This inner office was half the size of the outer one. Just a single desk, bare apart from a small notebook computer folded shut and

34

unplugged. Behind it the narrow window had bars on the outside and offered a view of a patio enclosed by a high wooden fence. A drinks cabinet against the wall told Rebus that successful clients might be offered a glass to celebrate. The man sitting across the desk took a moment to realise a stranger was standing in front of him.

'Who are you?' he asked, not without reason.

'My name's Rebus. I'm here on behalf of Jack Oram's family.'

'Is that supposed to mean something to me?'

Rather than provide an immediate answer, Rebus sat on one of the two available chairs. The woman's perfume was even stronger in this enclosed space. Mackenzie was probably much the same age as her. He wore a white shirt and blue silk tie. Gold cufflinks at his wrists and a heavy-looking gold watch. His blue pinstripe jacket had been draped over the back of his chair. His hair was tousled and silvered and probably hadn't been restyled since he was a young man. It gave him a slightly unruly look, while taking years off him.

'Who was it that just left?' Rebus asked.

'Why do you want to know?'

'Thought I recognised her.'

Mackenzie glared at him. 'My wife,' he stated. 'Elizabeth. Where do you know her from?'

'It'll come back to me,' was all Rebus said. 'Meantime, maybe you could look at this photo.'

Mackenzie took the photo from him and studied it.

'He's called Jack Oram,' Rebus said. 'Though he may be using another name. Went AWOL four years ago. His family think he's reappeared, and he was seen leaving these premises.'

'I don't know the name and I don't know the face. Besides, Marion deals with the majority of the clients.' He gestured towards the front office. 'And an assumed name wouldn't get him very far – we require photo ID and bank statements.'

'As is right and proper.' Rebus took the sheet of paper back. 'Do you mind me asking your first name, Mr Mackenzie?'

'It's Fraser. And yours?'

'John.'

'And you're some sort of investigator? Paid a finder's fee by the family, that sort of thing?' Mackenzie's accent, which had started out as refined Edinburgh, was coarsening slightly, as if it had decided that Rebus didn't merit one of its performances. Rebus held up the photograph again.

'It could be mistaken identity, I suppose. Someone in here recently who looks like him . . .'

'Your guess is as good as mine.' Mackenzie made a show of opening his computer, as if readying to do some proper work. Then the phone in his pocket vibrated and he took it out, holding it away from him as he tried reading whatever was on the screen.

'It's vanity, you know,' Rebus said, getting up from his chair.

'What is?'

'When you need glasses but refuse to wear them. I'm just guessing it's down to vanity.'

'Not the worst sin, is it, Mr Rebus?' Mackenzie said with a smile.

'Not by a long shot,' Rebus was forced to agree.

He reckoned Brillo would be fine for another hour so drove from Lasswade Road to Craigmillar. He'd worked CID there for a spell, but the old police station on the main road had turned into some kind of Pentecostal church, albeit with metal shutters firmly closed. Its replacement was a short sprint away, a new-build reflecting changes in the area. Craigmillar and next-door Niddrie had kept the police busy in Rebus's day, crumbling housing and endemic poverty proving fertile soil for crime and criminals. Much of that had now gone. The up-to-date low-rise blocks and buffed-up facilities had altered the face of Craigmillar utterly. Rebus passed a shiny library and a busy-looking Tesco Express. He turned off the main road into the estate where Jack Oram had lived, pulled to a stop kerbside and felt able to lock his car without fearing it would be vandalised in his absence.

'Changed days,' he said to himself.

Hoardings advertised new developments further into the estate. The houses here were of a vintage, but roofs had been replaced and the double-glazed windows looked new. Gardens were tidier than would have been the case at one time. Oram had run a successful little business and could have afforded to live elsewhere in the city, but Rebus knew that a sense of community and belonging were sometimes more important. He'd known gangsters – in many ways Cafferty was an anomaly – who stayed in the same council houses they'd grown up in long after they'd amassed their fortunes. There was safety, too, in surrounding yourself with people who would look out for you. They felt you were one of them, long after this had

36

ceased to be the case, and a few quid handed round could always oil the machine of neighbourliness.

Rebus had the address from the phone book. It was at the end of a terrace, pebble-dashed like the others in the street. The front garden had been replaced by a driveway, though no car sat there at present. There was a garage at the side and hanging baskets, currently devoid of life, flanking the front door. The door itself looked new, dark varnished wood with a tall rectangle of stained glass above the letter box. The bell had a camera attached. Rebus pressed it and waited.

The woman who opened up rolled her eyes when she saw him. 'What's he done this time? I hardly ever see him, you know.'

'You think I'm the police?'

'You mean you're not?'

She was in her forties, dyed orange hair falling to her shoulders, and dressed for a gym she almost certainly never visited.

'Just to be clear, who are we talking about?'

'Maybe start with who you are and what you're doing here.' She folded her arms and tipped her head slightly to one side.

'You're Ishbel Oram, I recognise you from the photo.'

She narrowed her eyes. 'What photo?'

'Your wedding. You've hardly changed,' Rebus lied. 'And the reason I'm here is your husband, Jack. I've heard he's back in town and I'd like a word.'

'Back in town?' Her eyebrows rose. 'Who's saying that?'

'So you've not seen him?'

'I don't go to seances.'

'You reckon he's no longer with us?'

She stepped down from the doorway so she was level with Rebus. 'A man called Cafferty had him done away with,' she stated. 'I didn't used to think that, but I do now, though we have to wait three more years to make it official.'

'Presumption of death, you mean?' Rebus watched her nod. 'What makes you so sure Cafferty's to blame?'

'Jack got on the wrong side of him – that's something you don't want to happen. Then there's the envelope. Stuck through the letter box a few weeks past. No note, just five hundred quid. That's got to be him, hasn't it?'

Rebus thought of his own envelope, the sum probably identical. 'Cafferty, you mean? Why not Jack himself?'

'Dead men tend not to be earners.'

'Why wait four years to send it?'

She considered this. 'A guilty conscience sometimes takes a while.' She peered at him. 'What is it you wanted with Jack anyway?'

'Your first instinct wasn't far off – I used to be CID. There's a bit of unfinished business from back in the day, and I thought Jack could help, so when I heard he'd been seen . . .'

'Seen where?'

'A lettings office on Lasswade Road.'

Her face grew quizzical. 'Why would he be there?' Rebus didn't like to say: a fresh start, new identity, no family. 'Anyway,' she went on, 'I'm sorry to disappoint you.'

'So the person you thought I was here about . . .'

'Is sweet FA to do with you, mister whoever you are.' She began to retreat inside the house.

'Thanks for the chat,' Rebus said to the door as it closed. He walked to his car, thinking about the newspaper coverage of Jack Oram's disappearance. Yes, a son had been mentioned, described as a school-leaver, making him sixteen or seventeen then, early twenties now.

What's he done this time?

Well, yes, that was a good question.

He got as far as the main road, but when a parking bay presented itself, he pulled over. Among all the rejuvenation of Craigmillar, one row of unkempt shops remained. A newsagent/post office, bookmaker, laundrette, barber and nail salon. Plus, at one end, a bar with grilles over both windows and a sign that identified it as the Moorfoot. Aka Jack Oram's old place, the Potter's Bar.

'You used to do this all the time,' Rebus told himself under his breath. 'How hard can it be?'

Officers working on an inquiry used to joke that they kept shoemakers in business. You could wear out a decent pair while doorstepping a neighbourhood, asking the same questions at every door, facing the same sights and smells. Faces sullen or antagonistic; wafts of whatever was being fried in the kitchen; almost always a blaring television or growling mongrel. So Rebus wasn't exactly surprised when, pushing open the door to the newsagent's, a dog started alerting everyone to his arrival. It was the owner's German shepherd by the look of things, and its message to Rebus was: don't mess with my human.

The post office section of the shop was a fortress of security

38

screens and reinforced door. But there was also a counter nearer the front where groceries and cigarettes could be bought. The racks dedicated to newspapers and magazines were almost non-existent, reminding Rebus of the way tastes had shifted in a few short years. He grabbed an *Evening News* – the thing seemed to be on sale from dawn these days – and showed Oram's photograph to the woman at the till, who just shrugged and shook her head. He then queued behind a woman who seemed to be sending the contents of an Amazon distribution centre back to base, one box at a time. While he waited, he skimmed the pages of the newspaper. There was a follow-up story on the acid and fire-raising attacks in West Lothian, police apparently investigating a possible connection between the two.

'Consider me shocked,' Rebus muttered to himself.

The Royal Mile traders and their shoplifting woes also merited a follow-up, with fresh photos and interviews. The cops and the council came in for the usual drubbing, with a spokesperson from Police Scotland stating by way of defence that patrols would be increased in order to restore confidence in a street considered 'the jewel in Edinburgh's tourist crown'.

Having finished reading everything apart from the sports and small ads, Rebus stepped forward, interrupting the customer to ask if he could just put one really quick question to the exasperated-looking man behind the screen. Without waiting for an answer, he held up the photo, receiving another shake of the head. Nothing ventured, he showed it to the customer too, with the same result. He gestured towards her packages.

'You'd be quicker driving them to the warehouse yourself,' he suggested, leaving the paper on the counter and heading for the door.

He gave the laundromat and nail salon a miss, found the barber's closed, so tried the bookie's instead. There was only a smattering of customers, and again he was reminded that times were changing. Like the news, betting had moved online. As a child, Rebus had found betting shops intriguing and mysterious. His father would meet pals there and could spend half a Saturday studying form and listening to the races over a distorted loudspeaker, a stub of pencil in one hand, cigarette in the other. Rebus sensed that no one lingered long in this modern equivalent. There were no chairs and tables, no stove to keep the place heated. Just banks of TV monitors and a scattering of slot machines, plus a long shelf you could lean against while filling in a slip.

As he showed Oram's photo to the few punters, there were wary shakes of the head. No one asked him why he was there, because no one wanted to know. The female cashier, still in her teens, was equally dismissive, hardly raising her eyes from her phone. As Rebus stepped outside, he realised he only had one real option left. But before he could enter the Moorfoot, there were shuffling footsteps behind him. A small, hunched man had followed him from the betting shop, cheeks sunken and teeth largely absent from his gaping mouth.

'Might've seen him,' the man said, his voice croaky. 'Not for a month or so, though.' He looked around to check no one was unduly interested in him or the stranger he was talking to. 'Not calling himself Jack these days, though. Davie Loach, he's going by.'

'But this Davie Loach is Jack Oram – you're sure of that?'

'Looked a lot like him, that's all I'm saying. You're Rebus, aren't you?'

Rebus was beginning to think the man seemed familiar. He gave a slow nod.

'I'm Ralph. I used to work nights at the baker's on Nicolson Street. You'd drop by sometimes when the rolls were just out of the oven.'

Rebus couldn't help but smile at the memory. He dug a five-pound note from his pocket and pressed it on the man.

'No need,' Ralph said, not looking like he was about to refuse.

Rebus gestured towards the betting shop. 'Have a flutter on me.' Then, 'Davie Loach, you're positive?'

Ralph nodded definitively.

'Did you speak to him at all?'

'Always kept his head down.'

'And where was it you last saw him?'

Ralph gestured once more towards the door he'd just left. 'You need to give a name when you place a bet. I asked Debs what he'd called himself.'

'Debs being the cashier? And she just told you?'

'She's my granddaughter. Don't hold it against her that she didn't say anything. All sorts come round here. Usually there's money owed and a beating in the offing.'

Rebus nodded his understanding. 'You got a phone on you?' He proceeded to recite his own number while the man dabbed it in. 'If you think of anything else or you see him, it'll be worth your while.'

It was Ralph's turn to nod, after which he pocketed his phone and headed back indoors. Rebus had no memory of him, but that was hardly surprising. Hot night-time rolls would have been two or three decades back, and he'd have been well refreshed, as the saying went. Speaking of which, there was a bar waiting for him. A half couldn't do any harm before home.

The Moorfoot comprised a long, narrow room. Rebus could just about imagine a couple of pool tables fitting in. The bar itself took up almost no space at all, and across from it sat two betting terminals and what looked like a quiz machine. In place of piped music, there was a venerable Dansette record player behind the bar along with a selection of LPs and singles.

'Nice touch,' Rebus said, pointing towards it.

'A blast of Mott the Hoople helps clear the place at closing time,' the barman explained. He was tall and barrel-chested, and Rebus doubted he'd have too many problems with unruly clients, Mott or no Mott.

Rebus ordered a half of IPA, and the man turned to retrieve a clean glass. Rebus noticed that his belt had been tightened a couple of notches too far, which only served to highlight the flab around his middle. His polo shirt had a vodka manufacturer's branding on it, and there were a couple of faded tattoos on his arms. They looked home-made, probably stretching back to teenage years. There were only three other customers: a young couple glued to one of the machines, and an older man at a corner table, seemingly hypnotised by the near-empty glass in front of him.

Rebus had brought out a debit card, but the barman shook his head. 'Cash only.'

'Card reader broken?'

'What card reader?'

So it wasn't only the music that was vintage. He handed the man a ten. 'You been here long?'

'Long enough.'

'Are you Mr Crosbie?' He had registered the name of the licensee on a small noticeboard outside.

'I just work for him.' The barman handed Rebus his change – a good amount of it. When Rebus took a sip, he realised why. They should have been paying him to drink the stuff.

'Beer okay?' the barman enquired.

'Nectar. Have you happened to see this guy in here?' He was holding up the photo of Oram.

The barman's small, deep-set eyes moved from Rebus to the photo and back again. 'Can't say I have. Who is he?'

'Surprised you don't recognise him. He used to own this joint, back when it was the Potter's Bar.'

'Well before my time.'

'You'll have heard the story, though.'

'Got into trouble and headed for the hills.'

'Except it seems he's back on the scene and calling himself Davie Loach.'

'Is he aye?' The barman was pouring himself some lemonade from a nozzle. He set the glass aside as the young couple approached. The man wanted a note changed for coins he could feed into the machine.

'Losing streaks never last for ever,' the barman commiserated. The customer made a clucking sound. He noticed that Rebus was holding a photograph up for inspection, but quickly decided he could safely ignore it and its owner.

'Two more rum cola,' he said. His date was stroking the back of his neck and he turned to give her a kiss. Once their mouths had met, neither seemed in any hurry to come up for air, the barman watching as if he had front-row seats at the latest Hollywood block-buster. Rebus reckoned he was left with two options – finish the beer or walk over to the table in the corner. He opted for the latter.

The man seated there didn't look up at his approach, or even when Rebus held the photograph out in front of him. He lowered it a little so it rested next to the man's beer glass.

'Not ringing any bells?' he cajoled. 'Maybe the belfry's empty, eh?' The man looked up at him then, but his mind seemed to loiter elsewhere. Fair enough. Rebus would have been the same if the alternative was facing the reality of this soulless room. Contrary to the barman's words, here was incontestable evidence that some losing streaks were for life.

'You've been a wonderful audience,' he concluded, folding the photo back into his pocket.

'Missing you already,' the barman said as he made his exit. 'Bring some records next time.'

'Not sure I've got anything suitable for a wake,' Rebus retorted, giving the bar and everyone in it a final look before leaving.

4

Clarke was on her way to the interview room when her phone alerted her to an incoming call. When she saw Rebus's name, she almost didn't answer, but she knew he wouldn't give up.

'Everything all right?' she asked.

'Top of the world, DI Clarke. How about you – blood pressure higher than normal?'

'What makes you ask?'

'You sound like an elastic band that's about to snap.'

'You freelancing for NHS 24?'

'Just friendly concern. I take it you've a pressing engagement with a crime scene?'

'In a manner of speaking. I'm working the Francis Haggard case.' There was silence on the other end. 'He's a uniform at Tynecastle, but more pertinently, he thumps his wife – or at least he used to.'

'That's never good.'

'No, it's not.'

'So you're pretty busy right now, then?'

Clarke came to a halt and sighed into the phone. 'Of course you're not just calling for a catch-up.'

'Well, that too, of course.'

'But?' At the far end of the corridor, a door opened and Christine Esson's head appeared. Clarke signalled that she would only be a minute.

'Do you remember working a misper case four years back?' Rebus was saying. 'Man named Jack Oram. Lived in Craigmillar, owned a pool hall.'

'One of Big Ger Cafferty's men,' Clarke acknowledged. 'We did what we could until we started hitting brick walls.'

'Any chance of a look at the file?'

'Why?' She lifted a hand to her forehead and started rubbing it. Only John bloody Rebus could induce a headache so quickly.

'I'm just interested.'

'You're also a civilian – which means the answer is no.'

'Talk me through it, then. Maybe over a drink or a meal. I still owe you for what you did during COVID.'

'I took Brillo for walks and delivered some groceries. It wasn't exactly onerous.' When she glanced up, it was no longer Christine Esson's head at the door of the interview room but Michael Leckie's. 'I've really got to go, John.'

'Does that mean you'll think about it?'

'It means goodbye.'

'Hang on, there's something else. Oram's son. I think he's maybe not unknown to Police Scotland. Maybe add him as a postscript?'

'Goodbye, John.'

Clarke ended the call and dropped her phone back into her bag. She made her apologies as she entered the room. Esson had set up the recording equipment. Clarke looked everywhere but at Francis Haggard as she took her seat and composed herself. He was slouching in his chair, almost horizontal, elbows leaning on its arms.

'My client would like to thank you for seeing us at such short notice,' Michael Leckie said.

'We're always available to hear a full and contrite confession,' Esson commented. Finally Clarke's eyes met Haggard's.

'They've talked to you, haven't they?' he said. 'The brass, I mean?'

Clarke kept any emotion out of her voice and her face. 'Whether they have or not has no bearing on this case.'

'We both know that's a lie, DI Clarke. And the fact that they've been so quick off the mark tells me they're rattled. They *should* be rattled, too, because once I start telling my story, the walls come tumbling down.'

'Frankly I doubt you're that important.'

'In some ways you're right, of course. I'm a very small piece of the whole. But even the smallest part of a mechanism can be crucial, especially when it goes wrong. And it started going wrong for me very early in the game.' He hauled himself upright, leaning forward to ensure he had the room's attention. The crotch-cupping machismo of the previous interview had gone. 'First few weeks at Tynie, those are the ones you've got to get through, and it starts with your name. Me being Francis, that was all they needed to start the ball rolling. A Catholic name, apparently, so I became St Francis of Assisi, Hail Mary Haggard, Il Papa. As it happens, I *was* born Catholic, not that it was relevant. What mattered was that they had their pigeonhole for me.'

'Who's they?'

'I'm getting to that.' He paused before continuing. 'After that, they just kept probing, looking for weak spots. Everyone got the same treatment, and pretty soon I was one of the ones doing the needling, firing likely nicknames at the latest newbie. Is that bullying? Indoctrination, maybe? Because if you couldn't join in the banter, you might as well hand in your notice.' His eyes flitted from Clarke to Esson and back again. 'Women were slappers and sows, and if anyone didn't agree, they were poofs or wimps. So yes, my skin got nice and thick, and sometimes I even led the pack, eager to please the boss, that boss being Alan Fleck. He was our sergeant, and he would look out for us once he'd moulded us. He was always there, standing at the back usually, just watching and maybe drinking the whisky he kept in his desk.

'But he wasn't alone. Plenty of other officers from other stations knew what was going on. They'd be given a tour and get to watch us while we played. There was one I think you know, DI Clarke. Retired now, of course, same as Fleck. I'll be naming more names in due course, lots of them. But you know who I'm talking about here. The sarge loved him, loved the way he'd spent his whole career "getting away with it". He'd tell us all the stories – this was after we'd passed the initiation, of course. By then we were ripe and ready, ready to do whatever was asked. Fit somebody up? Alter evidence? Intimidate witnesses? All that and a lot more besides. Backhanders from criminals, sometimes even doing their dirty work for them. Perjuring ourselves in court – well, that became standard procedure. We were bad cops, and some still are. We know where the bodies are buried, and it won't be a pretty sight when they're dug up. All because we'd been made to feel that we'd get away with it. Go ask your friend – he got his fair share. He was wallowing, same as us. And you know what? The way the world's turning out, maybe that's the only method that makes sense. "Police hard," the sarge used to say. That's the culture I was introduced to. That's why I turned out . . .' He sought the right word, 'disordered.'

45

Silence filled the room as Haggard leaned back in his chair. Clarke turned her attention to the lawyer.

'This is what you're taking to court?'

The palms of Haggard's hands came down hard against the table. 'Nothing's going to court! The chiefs are going to shut you down!'

Leckie's fingers landed gently on his client's forearm. 'Francis, please.' Then, to Clarke, 'Mr Haggard continues to meet regularly with a therapist to try to deal with these issues. He is heartily sorry that his temper got the better of him on that one occasion with his wife.'

'A lot more than one occasion,' Clarke corrected him.

'You have no evidence of that.'

'Neighbours tell a different story, one they're willing to share from the witness box.'

'Those vegan arseholes,' Haggard muttered. 'They've had it in for me from day one.'

'Your wife's sister kept all the text messages sent to her about your abusive behaviour.'

'Nonsense, the lot of it.'

'The procurator fiscal doesn't think so.' Clarke turned back to the solicitor. 'This was a waste of our time, Mr Leckie. Do better, please.' She got to her feet, signalling the end of the meeting. Esson stopped the recording, following Clarke to the door.

'DI Clarke . . . please . . .'

Clarke stopped and turned to face Haggard. He seemed suddenly cowed and exhausted.

'Ask yourself why I'm doing this, burning bridges, turning friends into enemies.'

'You tell me.'

'It's because I need to. That's why I warned the brass – whether in court or on the QT, Tynecastle has to pay. Then maybe I can begin the process of forgiving myself. That's what my therapist says. I hate what I've become.' He had shifted his gaze from Clarke to Esson. 'What the job's done to me, I mean, what it's made me do to Cheryl. I'm just hoping it's not too late.'

'Whatever you're paying this therapist of yours,' Clarke stated, 'it's too much.' She tried to make eye contact with her colleague, but Esson seemed transfixed by Haggard's words. Rather than wait, Clarke made her exit, striding down the corridor and turning the corner, where she came to an abrupt stop, trying to control her breathing.

There was one I think you know . . .

'Bloody John bloody Rebus,' Clarke said in exasperation. She glanced up to see Esson approaching, looking thoughtful. 'Christ's sake, Christine.'

'What?'

'You're falling for it.'

'Says who?'

'Focus on what he did, not what he'll say in order to get off.'

'He's right, though, isn't he? About what the job can do?'

'He's an abuser, Christine, end of. The smart ones get away with it because they're plausible.'

'I'm not stupid, Siobhan.'

'Good, because that's the last thing you need to be right now.' Clarke broke off as Haggard and his solicitor turned the corner, heading for the front door. Haggard met her look, his face lacking obvious emotion, and not for the first time, she wished she could see inside someone's head.

Clarke and Gina Hendry had agreed to meet at a café bar on Corstorphine Road. Hendry had a latte in front of her but was perusing the wine list when Clarke sat down opposite.

'Shame it's too early,' she mused.

The first time they'd met, Clarke had asked the obvious question: how do you do it? To work domestic abuse liaison, you needed to be an ally to the victim yet at the same time maintain objectivity. You were part police officer, part psychologist, part social worker. Hendry had allowed her hair to go grey since they'd last met up, probably as a consequence of lockdown, yet still managed to look younger than her age, her face wrinkle-free, eyes lively, cheeks a natural pink. A waiter took Clarke's order of a double espresso and barked it towards the counter. Hendry had chosen a table in a dimly lit corner rather than the window. Clarke suspected it was because the women she helped had ex-partners, some of whom would almost certainly bear a grudge. Best not to be too visible.

'So he's got his defence strategy,' Hendry said without preamble.

'We'll have a clinical psychologist examine him,' Clarke assured her. 'But just to be clear, Cheryl's not mentioned PTSD to you at any point?' Hendry shook her head. 'Would it be okay if I asked her? Is she up to that?'

47

'She's a bit bruised – mentally, I mean – but her sister is being a complete bloody rock under the circs.'

'What circs?' Clarke nodded her thanks to the waiter as her drink arrived.

'Her name's Stephanie Pelham, Pelham being her married name. Ring any bells?' Hendry watched Clarke shake her head. 'James Pelham is a developer. Buys up derelict land and turns it into expensive flats and houses. He's also an angel.' She saw Clarke's look. 'Meaning he puts money into start-ups, hoping to make a killing down the line. Worth a mint, a good chunk of which Stephanie is intent on taking from him.'

'They're getting divorced?'

'After she found out he was playing away from home. So she's got that going on and now she's looking after her sister, too. There's only a couple of years between them and I get the feeling they've always been close.'

'And Stephanie lives nearby?'

'Hence the choice of watering hole.'

'You say Cheryl's bruised, but she's doing okay?'

'She's not falling apart, if that's what you mean.'

'And she's not going to change her mind about the court case? I know it happens.'

'All the time,' Hendry agreed. 'But I don't sense that happening here. Maybe if Stephanie weren't backing her one hundred per cent.' She met Clarke's eyes. 'The PTSD thing won't fly, will it?'

'I don't know.'

'And it's all down to his years at Tynecastle cop shop?'

'We interviewed him this morning, Gina. The way he spoke . . .' Clarke broke off.

'Christ, you think he's got a chance?'

'Look, we both know the culture. It's maybe not as widespread these days as it once was, but it's still there and plenty of our fellow officers insist on keeping their traps shut about it.' She gave a sigh. 'Christine Esson thinks maybe the job did play a role in altering his behaviour.'

'I don't buy that,' Hendry said. 'He's into coercive control and always has been. If he was an airline pilot or a minister of the Church, he'd be exactly the same.'

'But then there are the suits at the top,' Clarke added. 'They've hinted they want this particular case to just melt away.'

'They'd be better off taking a flamethrower to Tynecastle. Job done.'

'Something he said hit home, though – if he uses his defence, he's consigning himself to the wilderness. Seems like the nuclear option, no? Why take it that far unless you really feel the button needs to be pressed?'

'You're forgetting that prisons are not comfy places for cops, Siobhan. Added to which, men who're violent to women don't always go down well with the other cons. In his shoes, I'd do everything in my power to avoid that outcome.'

'You're probably right,' Clarke conceded.

Hendry glanced at her phone, checking the time. 'I said three thirty.'

'Am I giving you a lift?'

She shook her head. 'Mine's around the corner. We'll take both – trust me, parking is not going to be an issue.'

Stephanie Pelham lived in a large contemporary glass box with electric gates and a driveway twice the size of the car park at Gayfield Square police station. There was a yellow Porsche parked in front of a two-car garage. By the time Clarke and Hendry had parked, Pelham was at the front door to meet them. Wavy blonde hair, coloured nails, but casually dressed and probably sporting less make-up than if she were venturing out. The interior of the house as she led them inside was all pale wood and cream walls, with a floating staircase leading to the upper floor. She climbed ahead of them, explaining that the living area was upstairs to make best use of the view.

'It's beautiful,' Clarke said, meaning it. The heightened position of the house, on a leafy street by Corstorphine Hill, meant much of Edinburgh was laid out before them, thanks to a wall of glass sliding doors beyond which a deep terrace stretched the width of the building.

'That's why I'm getting it and he's not. No way I was losing this to the scumbag.'

'I believe he's some sort of developer?' Clarke enquired.

'Amongst other things. He did the apartment block that became Cheryl's prison – to be frank, that's how they could afford to buy.'

Pelham had picked up a wine glass, an inch of pale yellow liquid left in it. She pointed towards Clarke.

'I'm going to guess gin and tonic.'

'Maybe not while on duty.'

'And I know Gina is a red wine girl,' Pelham said, ignoring Clarke. There was a kitchen visible through a doorway, and she was making towards it. Clarke looked at Hendry, who gave a twitch of the mouth. This, she seemed to be saying, is the price of admission.

'Stephanie did the whole interior,' she explained. 'It's what she does for a living.'

Clarke nodded, as she felt was expected, though she harboured reservations about some of Stephanie Pelham's touches. Too many floor-standing sculptures and abstract wall hangings for her taste.

'Exotic,' she commented. The smile Hendry gave indicated that she wasn't exactly a fan either.

When the drinks arrived, they sat around a large wooden dining table. They'd just finished chinking glasses when they heard soft footsteps on the stairs.

'Ah, here she is.' Pelham got up to fetch another drink while Hendry made the introductions.

Cheryl Haggard had dark, sleepless eyes, bloodshot from recent tears. Her skin was pale, her hair straw-like. She was probably an inch shorter and four kilos lighter than her buxom sister.

'Thanks for agreeing to meet,' Clarke said as Haggard settled in the chair across from her.

'That's all right.' It was an automatic response. Cheryl Haggard looked far from all right.

'I think you've talked with my colleague, Christine Esson,' Clarke said. 'I'm fairly new to the case, so I thought we should maybe . . .'

Haggard nodded throughout without making eye contact. She wore a long-sleeved top with the arms pulled down so that her hands could disappear into them. She allowed her right hand some freedom when her drink arrived. Like her sister, she was on white wine. Clarke had sampled her own gin and tonic and was hoping she'd still be able to drive after finishing it.

'How's the case going?' Pelham asked.

'We're making progress. I don't suppose we could have a few moments alone with Cheryl?'

'Suppose all you like. I'm staying right here.' She reached towards her sister and clasped her wrist. Again, the look Hendry gave Clarke intimated that there'd be no getting around this, so Clarke yielded with a nod of understanding.

'Remind me how long you've known your husband, Cheryl.'

'Best part of ten years.'

'And you've been married for six?' She watched the slow nod.

'Thank Christ there are no kids, that's all I can say,' Pelham added.

'He never wanted them,' her sister said quietly.

'Any particular reason?' Clarke asked.

Haggard gave a shrug. 'The way the world was going ... he didn't want kids of ours having to live through it.'

'A bloody nonsense,' Pelham muttered.

'Had he always thought like that?' Clarke pressed. 'Pessimistic about things in general?'

'Job probably didn't help.'

'He talked to you about his job?'

'Not really. I mean, you don't, do you?' Her eyes went from Clarke to Hendry and back again, as if seeking acknowledgement of the fact. 'Maybe it would have done him some good to let it out instead of bottling it up ... I don't know. Most nights he was late home – a few drinks with the lads after work. His way of letting off steam.'

'The lads being his colleagues?'

'We didn't have other friends. It was always nights out with blokes he worked with and sometimes their partners.'

'You think the job got to him, maybe changed him?'

'Maybe.'

'I can't believe I'm hearing this,' Pelham snapped, glaring at Clarke. 'Sounds like you're defending him.' Then, to her sister, 'I warned you this would happen, Cheryl. Under the bloody carpet it goes.' Her phone rang and she answered it. 'I'll have to call you back, Melinda,' she barked. 'Later, sweetheart, mwah.' She tossed the phone back onto the table. 'Work,' she explained.

'The thing is,' Clarke pushed on, focusing her attention on Haggard, 'Francis is saying PTSD is to blame. In other words, the job. So I'm wondering if you think there could be any truth in it. Did his behaviour change down the years? Did he ever try to explain his fits of violence?'

'He was always a bastard,' Pelham said, but her sister was shaking her head.

'He definitely got worse over time. And PTSD – I remember him googling it. It was in his search history on the computer.' She narrowed her eyes to help her think. 'But that was after.'

'After what?'

'After the neighbours got the police to come. Not this time, but the time before, when they just talked to him and left.'

'You should have ditched him that same bloody night, Cheryl.' Pelham turned to Clarke, her eyes drilling into her. 'I told her to, but she wanted to give him another chance. How many chances does a wanker like that deserve?'

'Trust me, I'm on your side.' Clarke turned her attention back to Haggard. 'He became more abusive as the years passed, Cheryl? Just so we're clear?'

'It was words at first. He might not even raise his voice. I couldn't cook a proper meal, keep the flat clean. I didn't deserve him, he gave me everything. My clothes were never right, I was an embarrassment when we went out.' She paused. 'I had friends of my own, but he didn't like them, so they had to go.'

'Control,' Gina Hendry agreed, nodding.

'He couldn't push *me* away, though,' Pelham said. 'Eventually he stopped trying.' She touched her glass against her sister's.

'The first time he hit me,' Haggard said, lost in remembrance, 'was after a big dinner, some annual police thing. Black tie. He was given a bravery award for stopping a guy jumping off North Bridge. I hadn't been pleased enough. Hadn't smiled or clapped . . . He was halfway through getting undressed in the bedroom. He walked up to me and slapped me hard across the face. I spent the rest of the night locked in the bathroom. He bought flowers the next day. I think he might even have cried.'

'Like any crocodile,' Pelham said.

'How long ago was this?' Clarke asked.

'Maybe four years back.' Haggard was looking at her. 'He was already a cop when I met him, so I don't know what he was like before. When we started dating, he seemed nice. We fell in love . . .' Tears were beginning to trickle down her cheeks. Her sister gave her wrist another squeeze before rising to her feet.

'Top-up?' she asked. Clarke realised she had drained her drink without even noticing. She looked to Gina's red wine, only a sip missing from it. Cheryl Haggard had got up too, and was heading for the stairs. All three women watched her go. Then Pelham pressed her palms to the table's surface and leaned across it, her eyes once more meeting Clarke's.

'This is why he can't get away with it,' she hissed.

'He won't,' Clarke replied.

'Men are all the bloody same. I'm speaking from experience. You know how my ex got caught? Some website snapped a picture of him coming out of a hotel with the piece of skirt he'd been shagging. Almost young enough to be his bloody daughter, too.'

'Which website?' Clarke asked.

'Calls itself the *Edinburgh Courant*. Do you know it?'

'It rakes up the occasional police story.' Clarke shifted slightly in her chair. 'And we won't have that top-up, thanks all the same. We should leave you to get on with the rest of your day.'

'Well, we're here if there's anything else – I've put work to one side for as long as Cheryl needs me. I can't tell you how much I'm looking forward to seeing Francis in court.' Pelham broke off, running a finger down her wine glass before eventually rousing herself. 'You've got my deets, yes?' She watched as Clarke nodded. 'It was two other officers we were dealing with originally.'

'DC Esson is still involved,' Clarke explained. 'DC Ogilvie is off work at the moment. That's why I'm playing catch-up.'

'Have you met him yet?'

Clarke knew who she meant and gave a slow nod.

'Don't fall for it,' Pelham counselled. 'They're all actors, the bloody lot of them.'

Clarke was in her car, trying to decide whether to head back to the station or call it a day, when Christine Esson called her.

'What did you think?' Esson wanted to know.

'She's fortunate she's got her sister in her corner.'

'Stephanie's definitely a rock. Did she try kissing you when you left?'

'No.'

'I feel honoured then.'

'Just you, or Ronnie too?'

'Ronnie got the full mwah-mwah – both cheeks.'

'Lucky he didn't give her COVID.'

'Lucky he didn't give *any* of us COVID.'

'How's he doing anyway?'

'Says he's completed Netflix and is starting Disney Plus. You on your way back here or going home?'

'How much longer are you sticking around?'

'Maybe an hour. Gunshots reported in West Pilton. They need bodies to help with that. Not that there *were* any bodies. But I'm checking hospitals and surgeries in case any walking wounded emerge.'

'I've got one quick stop to make before I can be there. Should I bring supplies?'

'A cake wouldn't go amiss. Did Francis discuss PTSD with Cheryl?'

'Only after the first appearance of uniforms on his doorstep.'

'Could mean something or nothing.'

'Doughnuts okay, or do you need something stronger?'

'Doughnuts will be fine. See you soon. Mwah.'

'Mwah,' Clarke said with a smile as the call ended.

Stephanie Pelham was refilling her glass when the doorbell rang.

'Bloody cops,' she sighed, heading for the stairs. 'I'll get it,' she said at the sound of Cheryl's bedroom door opening. She undid the lock and turned the handle. 'Did you forget someth—'

The force of the door sent her stumbling.

'I want to talk,' Francis Haggard said. 'She's got time for CID, she can find time for me.'

He stepped over Pelham. Cheryl had slammed shut her own door with a squeal. Pelham was back on her feet. She grabbed a fistful of Haggard's leather jacket.

'Hell do you think you're doing, Francis?' She could smell the alcohol coming off him.

He ignored her and started slapping the bedroom door with his palm. 'Cheryl, we need to talk about this! I've said I'm sorry. I'm seeing someone about it, a therapist, I mean.' He pressed his forehead to the door, eyes squeezed shut. 'I'll do whatever it takes, sweetheart. You know I will. Things can go back to the way they were.'

'Francis,' Pelham warned him, 'I swear to God you need to leave right now.'

'I want to talk to my wife.'

'Look at me, Francis. Look at me.'

He turned his head slowly, eyes opening. Pelham had taken a couple of steps back. She had her phone out, held in front of her.

'I've already hit record,' she said. 'So unless you want to find yourself on remand, you'll walk out of here right now.'

'Cheryl,' he said to the door, his voice softening further, 'you know I love you. You know I do. We can sort this out. You and me together, put it all behind us.'

'Later.' The door's thickness muffled the single word. Haggard angled his head, the better to hear.

'What was that, Cher?'

'We'll talk later. Give me some time.'

'We *will* talk, though, yeah?'

'Still recording,' Pelham stated.

Haggard twisted his body in her direction. 'That goes nowhere,' he said, nodding at the phone. 'Or else . . .' He stabbed a forefinger towards her, even as she kept her attention focused on the screen. 'In fact . . .' He made a lunge, wrestling the phone from her grasp.

'Proud of yourself, are you,' Pelham spat, rubbing at her wrist. He pocketed her phone and pointed at her again, waggling his finger a little this time. Then he pushed past her and headed for the door.

'Call me when you're ready!' he yelled over his shoulder to the bedroom door. 'I'll be waiting!'

Pelham followed him down the hall, slamming shut the front door and making sure both locks were engaged. At the sound, Cheryl emerged.

'Are you okay?' she said.

'Bastard took my phone.'

She padded towards her sister on bare feet and held her in an embrace.

'You can't go near him, Cheryl,' Stephanie Pelham stated.

'I just wanted him to leave. It worked, didn't it?'

Pelham, her chin resting on her sister's shoulder, looked up towards a corner of the ceiling. The CCTV camera stared back at her. She managed a thin determined smile.

5

Rebus had just finished eating an early dinner of microwaved haggis when he heard the doorbell. Brillo trotted with him to the door. Siobhan Clarke was standing on the step.

'Well, well,' Rebus said, while Brillo's welcome was more effusive. 'In you come then.'

Rebus had been in his new home a while, but there were still boxes waiting to be unpacked. Clarke, who had helped with the move, noted them stacked in the narrow hall.

'I said I'd get round to it, and I will,' Rebus told her. 'On the other hand, if I've done without whatever's in them this far, maybe they don't need emptying at all.' He had retreated to the living room. A CD was playing, John Lee Hooker. He turned the volume down. Clarke was sniffing the air.

'Stovies?' she guessed.

'Haggis,' Rebus corrected her.

'With brown sauce, right?'

'Right,' he acknowledged. 'Join me in a beer?' Two empty cans stood on the dining table, with four unopened brethren lined up on the bookcase.

'I shouldn't.'

'Another way of saying you will.' He yanked the ring pull and handed her the drink. 'Not your first of the day?'

'Nor yours, despite doctor's orders.' She made show of sniffing the air again. 'No cigarettes, though, so that's something.'

Rebus sat himself at the table and gestured for her to join him. She slung her shoulder bag over the back of the chair.

'Haggard case getting to you?' he enquired.

56

'Just a bit.' She took a slurp of the beer. 'Any chance of a glass?'

'Makes for more washing-up.'

'Or else you've no clean glasses.'

'Busted,' he said, raising his can towards her in a toast.

'I remember I mentioned Haggard to you on the phone,' Clarke said. 'You made it sound like you didn't know him.' She watched Rebus nod while he drank. 'He seems to know you, though.'

Rebus took his time swallowing the mouthful. 'Is that so?' he eventually said.

'Every copper in Edinburgh knows Tynecastle is a cesspit and probably always has been.'

'I was never based there.'

'Your pal was, though – Alan Fleck.'

'Alan's long retired.'

'Only three or so years, actually. You used to pay him visits at Tynecastle. He liked to showcase the unofficial training new officers were put through. Lessons in racism and sexism, lying under oath, cooperating with criminals . . .'

'Hang on, Siobhan.'

'It's all going to come out, John, one way or the other. Malcolm Fox is in town, and though he's no longer working Complaints, he'd like nothing more than to hang a whole laundry's-worth of cops, serving and otherwise, out to dry. Either Haggard spills his guts to a jury, or else he gives it to Fox with the promise that a trial will at the very least go easy on him.'

'I told you, I don't know Francis Haggard.'

'Well, he's ready to drop you from a great height with no parachute.'

The silence lengthened between them until Clarke retrieved her bag and reached into it, bringing out a large padded envelope.

'The Jack Oram inquiry,' she said. 'Everything I could dig out. Talk to me and I'll hand it over.'

She drank as she watched Rebus weigh up his options. 'Oh,' she added, 'and I ran a check on Oram's son, Tommy.'

'Do I need to trade for that, too?'

'Not much to tell. Usual teenage misdemeanours. More recently there was an accusation of theft, but that didn't get anywhere.'

'What kind of theft?'

'He was working on the electrics in somebody's flat. Money went missing.'

'He's an electrician?'

Clarke shook her head. 'More of an odd-job man. Works for a lettings company. Something needs fixing in one of their properties, he goes in.'

Rebus's whole body seemed to have stiffened. 'Which company?' He watched Clarke shrug. 'QC Lettings?'

'That sounds about right. Looks like I've touched a nerve.'

'Their office was the last sighting of Tommy's dad.'

'So why are *you* interested? You were cagey when you phoned.'

Rebus had finished his drink. He fetched the last two cans, opening hers, giving her little alternative.

'I don't know what it is about Tynie,' he said as he sat back down. 'You're right that it's always had a smell about it. Not sure the blame rests with Alan Fleck or any other single individual. It's almost the building itself. When you walk in, you can sense an atmosphere. I'm not much of a one for the supernatural, but if you told me it was built on an old Indian burial ground, I'd be tempted to believe you.'

Clarke picked up her can, found it empty, and reached instead for its replacement. Beer on top of gin – her head would be pounding later.

'I'm not exactly sure,' Rebus went on, 'what stories Haggard will have on him. I very much doubt any of them will be corroborated by his colleagues.'

'Corroboration or not, if the stories are juicy enough, the media will run with them.'

'So Police Scotland have sent Malcolm Fox to initiate the cover-up? And first thing Malcolm did was ask you to suspend the inquiry? I bet that went down well.'

'As you can imagine. But the fact remains, Haggard is going to argue that PTSD is behind his violent outbursts. The stuff he's mentioned so far, however – lying under oath, even fitting up innocent people – none of that cries PTSD to me. There's got to be more, which is why I went looking online. Remember the Kyle Weller case? Arrested one night on the street, taken to the cells at Tynecastle, complained of feeling unwell . . .'

'Dead next morning when they unlocked his door.' Rebus nodded slowly.

'CCTV somehow wasn't working that night. A witness to the arrest changed their story. That's one of several cases that I should have remembered. They all involved Tynecastle. My guess is, they all feature Francis Haggard, too.'

'And he's going to spill the beans just to lessen a domestic assault charge?'

'Maybe he wants to atone. That's what Christine Esson thinks.'

'You're not persuaded?'

'Christine likes to see the best in people. I learned the opposite.' Rebus met her eyes. 'For better or worse.'

He stretched out his arms either side of him, palms turned upwards. 'What am I supposed to say, Siobhan?'

'I need to know if he has a chance of making any of it stick. I spoke with his wife today and came away more determined than ever.'

'Fair play to you, but I swear I've got nothing to hide.'

'In my experience, that would be a first. You're not even telling me why you're so interested in Jack Oram.' She was interrupted by her phone alerting her to a text. Her eyes widened, then narrowed as she read it, her lips parting to show her bottom row of teeth.

'Sounds like trouble,' Rebus commented.

'It's Cheryl Haggard's sister. Francis barged his way in earlier, trying to get to Cheryl. Left with one of the sister's phones because she'd been filming him.'

'Phones plural?'

'One for work, one for personal use, I'm guessing.' A second text had arrived. 'There are security cameras in the house, though. He's on tape.' Clarke let out a loud exhalation.

'I'd say he breached his bail conditions,' Rebus suggested.

'Absolutely he did.' Clarke was making a call, her phone pressed to her ear. There was a slight shake to her right hand, adrenalin coursing through her.

'Christine?' she said into the phone. 'We need to pick up Francis Haggard. He must have been watching Stephanie's house. Probably saw me and Gina leave and his hackles went up. He forced his way in.' She listened for a moment. 'They're both unharmed, but probably more than a bit shaken. Can you rouse a couple of uniforms and meet me at Haggard's flat?' She listened again. 'No, I'm in Marchmont, so maybe twenty minutes.' Her eyes met Rebus's. 'Yes, I'm at John's. Just a social call. Twenty minutes, okay?' She ended the call and stared at the beer cans. 'Christ, am I even under the limit?'

'I could give you a lift.'

'You've been drinking too.'

'But I'm a pensioner rather than a serving police detective – I've a lot less to lose.'

'I can't believe he'd do it. I really can't even begin to . . .'

'I'll drop you there. Squad car can take you home or bring you back here.'

'I can almost walk home from his flat.'

'I thought Haggard lived down in Newhaven.'

Clarke looked at him. 'He's not in his own place. He's renting on Constitution Street. But now I'm wondering why you would know where someone you claim *not* to know lives?'

'Oops,' Rebus said, sliding his arms into his jacket and picking up his car keys. 'Maybe save that for later, eh?'

'Just to be clear, you're dropping me off and then leaving.'

'Scout's honour,' Rebus said, ushering her to the door. As she preceded him, slinging her bag over her shoulder, he glanced back at the dining table. Yes, the Oram file was there, forgotten in all the drama.

He started whistling some blues as he took out his key and locked the door.

'Town's a mess,' Rebus commented as roadworks steered him down yet another long-winded diversion.

'This car's not much better,' Clarke said, studying her footwell.

'If you'd rather walk, I can drop you here.'

She mimed zipping her lips closed, but opened them again a minute later. 'Easter Road would have been quicker.'

Rebus took his eyes off the windscreen long enough to glare at her.

'You don't scare me the way you used to,' she told him.

'I'm rusty, that's all.'

'Did you hear about the shooting?'

'No.'

'Earlier today in Pilton. No casualties reported. Like you said – town's a mess.' She was lifted from her seat by a pothole Rebus hadn't spotted. He cursed and focused on the road ahead. 'So, Jack Oram,' she said into the silence.

'A spot of unfinished business, that's all.'

'Unless he's dead, of course.'

Rebus allowed the point with a shrug. 'I wasn't lying about Francis Haggard,' he said eventually. 'I barely knew the guy.'

'You did visit Tynecastle, though, watched the initiations?'

'Just games, that's all. Silly boys' games.'

'Even games can have consequences.'

'So one minute you're getting called St Francis, the next you're thumping your wife?'

'Wasn't just about the nicknames, John. It's everything that happened after.' She peered through the windscreen. 'Better to turn here and park on Wellington Place. Main road's blocked top and bottom for the tram works.'

'You're the boss,' Rebus said through gritted teeth.

She was right, though, and a couple of minutes later he was bringing the Saab to a halt as close to the cut-through as possible. Clarke thanked him and got out, then stuck her head back inside the car.

'Straight home,' she warned him.

'Yes, Mum.'

Then she was gone. Rebus let the engine idle for a couple of minutes, then turned off the ignition and got out. The evening was bitter, felt like some sleet blowing in. He fastened his jacket, started whistling softly again, and began to follow her.

One side of the pavement was out of use altogether, as was the carriageway. Two uniforms were waiting at the door to one of the tenements, along with Christine Esson. Rebus stayed back until they'd gained entry to the building. When he got to the main door, it had locked itself again. None of the buzzers had names next to them, just flat numbers. Two key boxes had been affixed to the door frame, a sign that there were short-term lets on the stairwell. He tried a buzzer at random.

'Fuck is it now?' a hoarse male voice crackled from the tiny speaker.

'Food delivery for your neighbour. They're not answering.'

There was another muttered curse, but the door clicked open and Rebus was in. He could hear noises from above, a fist thumping at a door. Then Clarke's voice: 'Definitely the right flat?'

'Well, he's either comatose or not at home,' a male voice replied. 'Want us to wait or what?'

'Could be anywhere between here and Corstorphine,' Esson then said. Rebus heard the clatter of a letter-box flap being closed. He guessed Clarke had bent down to take a look. She had, after all, learned from the best. 'Pubs will be open for a while yet,' Esson was saying. 'We could put out a description?'

Rebus had heard enough. He retraced his steps silently to the main door, pulled it open as stealthily as he could, and came face to face with Malcolm Fox. Fox eased his gloved hands into his coat pockets.

'Fancy seeing you here,' he said.

'I could say the same,' Rebus countered. 'But your bird has flown, so he won't be going to any safe house with you tonight, DI Fox.'

'Why am I not surprised you're so well informed? Though that does beg the question as to how. Did Alan Fleck send you?'

'No.'

'But he's a good friend of yours?' Fox gave a smile as cold as the sleet hitting both men's faces. 'I've been getting myself better informed, too.'

The door behind them opened, Clarke's face falling as she saw Rebus.

'It's making more sense all the time,' Fox commented.

'Straight home, you said.' Clarke's eyes remained on Rebus.

'Curiosity got the better of me.'

Clarke turned her attention to Fox. 'What brings you out this time of night?'

'Same as you, I dare say.'

'Not even close,' Clarke informed him. 'Haggard has breached his bail conditions, and now it looks like he might have done a runner.'

'Stands to reason,' Rebus said. 'He's bound to know custody awaits.'

Fox manoeuvred himself between Rebus and Clarke. 'Is there any reason why we're debating this in front of a civilian?' he demanded, turning as the door opened again, Esson and the two uniforms emerging. Esson was just ending a call.

'Word's gone out,' she assured Clarke. Then, recognising the other two figures, 'Hello, John. Malcolm, long time.'

'So do you need us to stick around?' one of the uniforms asked as his radio squawked.

A window above them rattled open. 'Any chance of moving the party on?' a voice demanded, sliding it shut again. Rebus recognised the voice from the intercom.

Clarke gestured towards the two uniforms. 'I want you back here every hour on the hour until your shift ends. You ring Haggard's bell, you knock on his door. Whoever takes over from you, same schedule stays until I say so, understood?'

There were nods of agreement as the two young officers headed off towards their patrol car and a bit of warmth.

'Is that us done?' Esson asked, keen to get back home.

'I need a lift,' Clarke informed her.

'I'm happy to . . .' The look Clarke gave him made Rebus leave the sentence unfinished. She turned to Fox.

'What are you doing here, Malcolm?'

'My guess,' Rebus butted in, 'would be that Malky comprises a one-man snatch squad.'

'More to the point, Siobhan,' Fox countered, 'is what *you're* doing here with a civilian who's been named this very day during an interview with an officer accused of domestic assault.'

'The only name I heard during that interview was a retired sergeant called Fleck.'

'You know as well as I do who else he was talking about, names or no names.'

'How did you get hold of the interview?'

'I thought I told you, I'm working directly for the assistant chief constable. That tends to open a few doors.'

'It would help if you didn't look so smug about it,' Rebus said. 'But then I'm guessing you look smug whether you're brushing your teeth or taking a dump.'

Fox ignored him, focusing on Clarke instead. 'He just gave you a lift here, didn't he? Probably means you were at his flat. I find that all a bit too cosy. Correct me if I'm wrong.'

'This is my case, not yours,' Clarke stressed. She could sense Christine Esson stiffening slightly. '*Our* case, I mean.'

'Christine's case actually,' Fox said. 'You'd be nowhere near it if COVID hadn't intervened. And I very much doubt Christine would have gone haring off to share news of what was said in a police interview. Christ, Haggard's defence will have a field day.'

'We didn't talk about the case,' Rebus interrupted.

Fox stared at him. 'Do you think my head zips up the back?'

'Makes it easier for your bosses to shovel their shit in.'

'I think we're in danger of losing sight of something here,' Esson said, raising her voice. 'Cheryl Haggard is a victim of domestic abuse. An hour or two ago her partner stormed into what should be a place of refuge. We need to protect her, and that means tracing him. Standing around here shouting the odds doesn't seem to me to be helping much.'

'Christine's right,' Clarke said. 'Everything else can wait.'

'Of course,' Fox said with a slight dip of the head. Clarke gestured to Esson, and the two women began hurrying away. Esson seemed to be complaining about the non-delivery of a promised cake.

'Plenty places open nearby,' Fox told Rebus, rubbing his hands together. 'A quiet drink and a chat, what do you say?'

'I say whatever it is you think you're going to accomplish here, you're wildly mistaken.'

Fox studied him. 'If this goes to court and Haggard tells his tale, that could end up bad news for people like your good friend Alan Fleck – him and anyone else in his orbit. Maybe you should think about that, John. Could even be some jail time waiting at the end of the process.'

'You'd come visit, though, wouldn't you?'

'I think I might, yes.' A smile spread across Fox's face. 'You never know, maybe I'd even enjoy it.'

Rebus took a step towards him.

'Careful, John. Wouldn't want your health taking a sudden turn for the worse. It's already on a shoogly enough peg, from what I hear.' Fox began to back away, turning his collar up. Rebus watched him go, the blood pounding in his ears.

6

Fraser Mackenzie was first to arrive at the restaurant. He liked it because the food was great and the tables nicely distanced. They kept the background music low, and the maître d' always offered a complimentary glass of fizz. He'd been there only five minutes, kept busy with the wine list, when James Pelham approached across the restaurant floor, his usual large strides seeming to eat up the distance. He was chuckling by way of greeting and flung a hand out for Fraser to clasp.

'How are you doing, pal?' he enquired, his free hand landing on his old friend's shoulder.

'I'm fine, James. Yourself?'

'Churlish to complain, business-wise.' He removed his cotton face mask and tucked it into his breast pocket. 'Lean times as you well know, but rapidly picking up.' He waited for the waiter to unfurl his napkin and lay it across his lap, opted for sparkling water over still, and rested his elbows on the table, noting that only one place setting remained.

'Gaby not joining us?'

'Paws off, James. I know what you're like.'

'Red-blooded, the same as you, though if bloody Steph gets her way, I'll end up gelded.'

'Hellish about her sister.'

'Bloody awful. Never liked the guy, if I'm being honest. Typical copper, always made you feel you had something to hide. Rubbed my bloody nose in it when Steph chucked me out. Can't say I'm disappointed to see him get what's coming to him.' He broke off to watch a slender woman in a clinging full-length dress being escorted to a table by her portly male companion.

'You're incorrigible,' Fraser Mackenzie said with a smile.

'Bit too bony, actually,' Pelham said, his eyes widening as he looked past Mackenzie's shoulder. 'Ah, this is more like it.' He began to rise to his feet, arms stretched out to smother Elizabeth Mackenzie in an embrace. 'Not that we're allowed any form of intimate contact these days,' he complained, finally releasing her.

Elizabeth had fixed a smile to her face, but it didn't reach as far as her eyes. She flapped open her own napkin before the waiter could do anything with it and waved away the offer of water.

'We were just talking about Francis Haggard,' Fraser told his wife. She raised one eyebrow but said nothing.

'You know Steph's erased me from her life?' Pelham continued. 'You probably see more of her than I do.'

'Been a while since we required her services,' Elizabeth stated.

'I know it's difficult for you both. You're my friends, but you're her friends too. I really appreciate you not taking sides.'

Elizabeth looked at him. 'Who says we haven't?' Then, to her husband, 'Is there wine on its way?'

As if on cue, a tray appeared, glasses of champagne transferred from it to the table. Elizabeth had already taken a mouthful when James lifted his glass and proposed a toast.

'To the bonds of friendship.'

She looked at him again. 'Friendship only goes so far, James. Is everything okay?'

'How do you mean?'

'Your marriage is crumbling, you stand to lose a lot of money to Stephanie, investors are bound to get the jitters when they see the mess the CEO is making of his life.'

Fraser reached a hand towards hers, but she shifted it further away. This was between her and Pelham.

'It's a limited company, Beth,' Pelham said. 'Nothing in my personal life can interfere with that. Your money is one hundred per cent guaranteed.'

'That better remain the case.'

'I'm almost insulted you show so little confidence. When have I ever given you cause—'

'Maybe when your company began to be investigated for furlough fraud.'

Pelham's Adam's apple bounced as he swallowed. He took a sip of champagne.

'How do you know about that?'

'The *Edinburgh Courant* – same blogger who papped you coming out of that bloody hotel with your latest conquest.'

'Unsubstantiated rumours.'

'You mean you're not being investigated?'

'I mean it's a simple admin error. The money will be repaid and no further action will be taken.' He looked to Fraser Mackenzie and attempted a conspiratorial smile. 'This is worse than that time in the bloody rector's office – remember?'

Elizabeth was not to be diverted. 'Your simple admin error could prove hellish costly in terms of both cash and reputation. And coming on top of the divorce . . .' Having stated her case, she picked up her menu and began reading. Her husband followed suit, but Pelham just stared at the pristine white tablecloth.

'I wish to hell I knew who it was,' he said in an undertone. 'That bloody internet troll, I mean.'

'I thought it was an open secret,' Elizabeth said without lifting her eyes.

'What?' Pelham looked to Fraser. 'Do *you* know?'

'Not the foggiest.' He turned to his wife. 'You're a constant source of surprise.'

'While you remain an open book, my love. Oysters, I think. Then maybe the venison. We'll need a good bottle of red.' She seemed only now to notice that Pelham was still staring at her. 'You really don't know who the *Courant* is?'

'If I did, I'd bash their bloody brains in.'

'Don't be stupid, James.'

'I'd pay someone then. A punishment beating.'

'You'd pay someone to beat up a stranger? Christ, listen to yourself.' She gestured towards their waiter, who, masked and visored, was hovering at a discreet distance.

Once the food was ordered, Fraser consulted the sommelier about the wine, eventually agreeing on a Barolo.

'An excellent choice, sir.'

'Better make it two bottles,' Pelham barked, pointing a finger at Elizabeth. 'I'm determined to loosen that tongue of yours.'

'You're welcome to try, as long as you're picking up the tab.'

'That seems fair.'

'I just hope they don't cut up your credit card when the bill comes.'

Pelham turned towards his old friend. 'What do you see in her, James? I'm serious – there must be something.'

'Not something,' Fraser said, taking his wife's hand in his and giving it a squeeze. '*Everything* . . .'

Pelham raised his champagne glass again. 'Then here's to those of us lucky enough to have everything.'

But when he went to drink, he found he was already down to the dregs.

Siobhan Clarke made the call from the comfort of her sofa. Laura Smith picked up after too many rings.

'You're busy,' Clarke guessed.

'I'm actually in the bath with a Maggie O'Farrell novel. That's why I thought twice about answering. But then I decided you wouldn't be phoning at this hour unless you've got something for me.'

'Which you, though?'

'To be honest, I'm not fussed. Either will do.'

Smith was the *Scotsman* newspaper's crime correspondent, but as newsrooms had shrunk, so she had been given additional remits, which hadn't stopped her considering other options in the freelance world. She had been well placed – in terms of contacts and experience – to start an Edinburgh blog. It had been slow to gain traction, but she had persevered, and now she could boast at least some income from advertising revenue. The *Courant* had been an eighteenth-century newspaper, which was why she'd chosen that name for her site. She'd also decided on anonymity, which left her free to publish stories a cautious editor might have spiked.

'I was talking to Stephanie Pelham earlier,' Clarke said. 'She was telling me how grateful she was for the blogger who outed her sleazeball husband.'

She thought back to when she'd first realised that a couple of details from a *Courant* story could only have come from a conversation she'd had off the record with Laura Smith over drinks in a wine bar. 'Don't worry, Batman,' she'd told Smith, 'your secret's safe with me . . .'

'I was hoping,' Smith said now, 'that you were going to tell me who's behind this string of attacks – acid and arson and now bullets. That can't end well.'

'Sorry to disappoint you.'

'What about the Haggard case, then? You'll have noticed I've been steering clear of it.'

'I'm sure the victim would thank you for not naming names.'

'You have to admit, though, there's plenty of justification to do just that. This is a serving police officer abusing his wife. The public has a right to know.'

'Come the trial, they will, but she needs all the help she can get right now.'

'Why? Has something happened?'

Clarke closed her eyes. 'No,' she said. 'I just meant in general.'

'Well, no promises, Siobhan. My fans have an insatiable appetite.'

'And bigger platefuls every time?'

'You better believe it.'

She opened her eyes again, staring at the fireplace in front of her and the sleeping TV screen to its left in which she could see herself reflected.

'It just got me thinking,' she said. 'Hanging around outside hotels with a camera – it's not your usual style. In fact, it's more something a private eye might do, employed by a spouse who suspected their partner of cheating.'

'You're good.'

'Stephanie Pelham had someone tailing her husband?'

'I can't possibly comment.' Clarke could hear the suds lapping around Smith as she moved position in the bath.

'Why would she give the photos to you, though?'

'To maximise the punishment, I'd guess, by which I mean his embarrassment. Coming back to these attacks, though – they've got to be connected, right? Our city's Mr Big has left the stage. Lots of second-rate actors thinking they have a shot at stardom. I don't envy you the job of sweeping the theatre clean afterwards.'

'Well, that's cheered me up. Have you been in touch with Stephanie about her sister?'

'I told you, I've been steering clear.'

'So nothing you can tell me about the relationship?'

'Between Cheryl and her abuser?'

'Yes.'

'Not a thing – is there something you're not telling me?'

'No.'

'Sure about that?'

'Moderately sure.'

'Then I'll leave you to it while I get out of this water. Just remember to nail him, Siobhan. Nail him to the wall.'

Clarke listened to the phone go dead. She knew she could make

69

another call, check whether Haggard had turned up yet. Or she could go there herself and sit in her car and wait.

'That's what you'd have done, isn't it, back in the day?' she asked, as if Rebus were standing in front of her.

It took her several minutes to decide that she would go to bed instead.

Day Three

7

Next morning, as he waited at a red light on his way to QC Lettings, Rebus texted Clarke to ask if there was any news of Haggard. When a message arrived, however, it was from a number he didn't recognise.

No winnings for me yesterday. Talked to a punter who knew Jack. He saw him across the road from his old house. Went to say hello but Jack ignored him and walked off. Says he was just staring at the house. Keep eating the rolls. Ralph

The ex-baker from the betting shop. So now he had two people who'd ID'd Jack Oram, alive and kicking. As he was parking on Lasswade Road, he got a reply from Clarke too, a single word.

Nothing.

He was hoping for better from QC Lettings.

The bell chimed as he entered. Marion looked up from her computer. Rebus gave a little wave and gestured towards the inner door. 'He's expecting me,' he lied, turning the handle.

Fraser Mackenzie was standing behind his desk and in the middle of a phone call. He kept talking, flapping his free hand to indicate that Rebus should wait outside. Instead, Rebus sat down, crossing one leg over the other, smiling up at Mackenzie, who seemed to be losing his train of thought.

'Look, Jimmy, I'll have to call you back. Is that all right?' He ended the call with a further muttered apology and gave Rebus a long, hard stare. It was a contest he was never going to win, and eventually he sighed theatrically and settled in his chair.

'Jack Oram has an alias,' Rebus explained. 'Davie Loach.'

After a bit more staring, Mackenzie opened his computer and

started typing. 'No record of him,' he said. 'A phone call would have done, you know. Marion could have told you.'

'Well, how about Tommy Oram? Surely you'll know the name of one of your employees.' Rebus watched Mackenzie shrug. 'He does repairs to your properties, general maintenance. There was an accusation he lifted somebody's belongings.'

Mackenzie gave a slow nod. 'Tommy,' he intoned.

'Tommy Oram, son of Jack.'

'I don't think I ever heard him called by his surname.'

'Not even when you took him on?'

'That was Beth's doing. She said he was a friend of Gaby's.'

'Gaby being . . .?'

'Our daughter.' Mackenzie was beginning to lose interest, busying himself with the trackpad on his computer. 'So you've not found this guy Oram yet?'

'Give me time. Have you got an address for Tommy?'

'Marion will know.' He glanced up at Rebus. 'We finished here?'

Rebus couldn't think of a reason to prolong the meeting, which was a pity, as he was enjoying needling the man.

'Ever hear from the old owner of this place?' he asked as he rose to his feet.

'Not a peep.' Mackenzie glanced up again. 'Different spheres, Mr Rebus.'

'Meaning you know his reputation. No qualms about taking over his business?'

Mackenzie leaned back in his chair. 'If you have a rental portfolio of any size, everyone assumes you're the new Peter Rachman. But the way I look at it, I'm helping people out in their time of need. A lot of them have problems and not much money, but they still deserve a roof over their head, same as you and me.'

'You're basically a Samaritan then, or some sort of guardian angel?' Rebus watched the man shrug, in what he guessed was supposed to be a show of modesty. 'Same as Cafferty before you?'

'I bought his business, not his morals.' Mackenzie leaned forward again, focusing on his computer.

'What did you do before this?'

'A bit of everything. Now if you'll excuse me . . . And best of luck with your search.'

A few moments later, Rebus was parked in front of the reception desk. Marion was taking down some details over the phone from a prospective client.

'That's a very popular area . . . you'll need to be primed to make a decision . . . I'm talking hours rather than days . . . Not if that's your upper limit, no. Piershill and Restalrig might be a better bet . . .'

Rebus had picked up a stapled printout of available properties. He'd heard that things were tough for renters, and looking at the monthly rates, he could believe it. People with deep pockets were buying as an investment, freezing out those with less in their war chest, who then ended up vying to rent in this heated market. His daughter, Samantha, had been lucky. He hadn't had to help her too much when she'd moved into town. She was in a double-upper in Currie, just west of the city. Rebus had joked that she'd bought a place with stairs to deter him from visiting.

Sixteen steps from main door to landing. So far, he'd managed them twice.

'He wasn't really expecting you, was he?' Marion said, having ended the call.

'Guilty as charged. But he did say I should talk to you about your handyman, Tommy, surname Oram. Son of the man I'm looking for.'

'I didn't make the connection.'

'You sure about that?'

Her face hardened. 'Are you accusing me of lying?'

'No,' Rebus replied, without bothering whether he sounded sincere or not. 'Your boss tells me Tommy is a friend of Gaby's.'

'I think that's correct.'

'How often is he in here?'

'I'm not sure he's ever crossed the threshold.'

'Really?'

'Why would he? He doesn't keep any tools here.'

'So if there's a problem with one of your flats . . .'

'The client lets us know and we message Tommy.'

'And where are the tools kept?'

The sigh she gave could have graced a theatre stage. 'In a lock-up.'

'Any chance I could have his mobile number?'

'Not the slightest.' Marion sniffed and kept her eyes on her computer screen.

'He still lives at home with his mum, doesn't he? In Craigmillar?' He didn't expect her to answer, which was just as well. But he re-membered Ishbel Oram's words: *What's he done this time?* He could hear close bonds in her tone and phrasing. Her son was someone she saw and spoke to every day.

'Always a pleasure, Marion,' he said, beginning to zip up his jacket. 'Oh, one other thing Fraser told me to check with you – he can't recall the precise date the previous owner of this place last paid a visit.'

She gave him a blank look.

'Morris Gerald Cafferty? MGC Lettings?' The prompt elicited nothing more than a shrug. 'Fraser told me the pair of them were close,' Rebus said, rubbing at his jaw.

'Funny, I thought he told you the precise opposite.' She paused, enjoying his reaction. 'It's not the most solid of doors, and Mr Mackenzie's voice does tend to carry. Goodbye, Mr Rebus.'

Christine Esson had given the neighbours her number, so it was her they called. They were waiting in the corridor outside the Haggards' flat when Esson and Clarke arrived. Their names were Anthony and Giselle Carrington, and they both worked in finance. Early thirties, casually but not cheaply dressed. Clarke could imagine them sharing yoga sessions and smoothies. They looked so similar, they could have passed for siblings. Giselle's arms were folded and she shifted from one foot to the other, signs that the break-in had unnerved her. Anthony gestured towards their neighbours' door. A tool of some kind had been used to prise it open.

'Did either of you go in?' Clarke asked. They both shook their heads.

'Came back with the shopping, found it like this,' Giselle said.

Clarke looked up and down the corridor. 'Any CCTV?'

'Just at the main entrance,' Anthony answered. 'We all have video monitors in our hallways. You can check who's outside before you let them in.'

'There's a concierge,' Giselle added. 'They're supposed to keep an eye open.'

Clarke nodded and looked at Esson.

'Scene of crime are on their way,' Esson confirmed, 'but it's a busy day.'

'We could maybe risk it.'

Clarke dug out the disposable gloves Esson had given her in the car. Esson had a pair of her own. They slipped off their shoes and Clarke pushed the door all the way open. A vase on a hall stand had been toppled and lay in pieces on the varnished wooden floor. The glass in two paintings was cracked. She edged into the open-plan living area. The crockery in the kitchen area was untouched, but drawers had been opened and emptied, making the floor treacherous. A wooden coffee table had been upended. The blinds in front of the glass doors leading to the balcony had been hauled down, and out on the balcony itself, flowerpots had been upturned, strewing soil and bulbs everywhere. Clarke paused for a moment to take in the view across Newhaven harbour towards the Firth of Forth.

'Cheryl doesn't have a job, does she?' she asked Esson.

'I think she'd have liked one, but Haggard wanted her at home.'

'Stephanie hinted that her husband gave them a good deal on the place. You knew this was one of his developments?' She watched Esson nod. 'Looks like she had a hand in the decor, too. Reckon anything's been taken?'

'Hard to say.'

They headed into the larger of the two bedrooms. Drawers had been emptied here, too, and the bedding tossed into a pile on the floor, clothes dumped from the fitted wardrobe, and the contents of the bedside cabinets dispatched across the mattress. Clarke noted two passports and some pieces of female jewellery. Esson indicated the carpet they were standing on. It was streaked with white powder. Clarke dampened one finger of her right glove and dabbed at it, transferring it to her lips.

'Not talc,' she confirmed.

The second bedroom was being used as an office. The computer now lay on the floor, along with the printer. More powder was scattered across the floorboards. In the bathroom, the contents of the cabinet had been scooped into the sink. Two large pizza boxes lay in the bath. Clarke picked one up and opened it. It was empty and unused. She shared a look with Esson.

'Talk to the concierge?' Esson suggested. Clarke gave a slow nod. 'Were they expecting to find anyone home? Got a bit fractious when the place was empty?'

'Looks more like a message to me,' Clarke replied. 'And not a very subtle one, either.'

'Tynecastle?' Esson speculated.

'Tynecastle,' Clarke echoed.

*

77

High End Motors belied its name by consisting of a concrete-walled and corrugated-roofed warehouse behind a high chain-link fence topped with barbed wire and motion-sensitive lights. The forecourt boasted so many potholes, Rebus wondered if the council's roads department had been involved. As he got out of the Saab, a middle-aged man appeared, dressed in a three-quarter-length black woollen coat and red scarf.

'Can't do you part-exchange on that,' he said, studying the car's bodywork. 'I've got the number for a good scrap dealer, though.' He broke into a grin and held out his hand. 'Good to see you, John. Or it would be, if I didn't know why you're here. Francis has gone and done it, has he? Always was a rash one . . .'

For as long as Rebus had known him, Alan Fleck had carried himself with the air of a confident salesman. He led the way inside the showroom, arms swinging as though leading a platoon. The flooring here was new and level, well-placed spotlights picking out the array of gleaming vehicles. Rebus identified a couple of Porsches, three BMWs, and something even lower-slung. Fleck tapped it with a finger as they passed.

'Ferrari. Goes like the clappers, but you want to steer clear of speed bumps.'

An office had been built along the back wall of the showroom, glass-fronted so the stock was always in view. Halfway there, however, Fleck changed his mind and walked over to one of the cars instead, opening the driver's side and gesturing for Rebus to join him. Fleck was caressing the steering wheel as Rebus closed the passenger door.

'This is a beauty. A decade old, but only six thousand miles on the clock. Being a Merc, it's not even properly run in yet.' He turned his head towards Rebus. 'Can I tempt you?'

'Who told you about Haggard?'

'Well, number one, it's all over the internet. And number two, the Crew keep me up to date. We even have regular meets. I thought you'd be on the invite list?'

Alan Fleck wasn't yet sixty and looked even younger. Rebus wondered if he'd had some work done. Maybe a tuck or a weave. He'd always liked looking good; never one to walk past a mirror without checking. Designer clothes, too, and watches that were understated but top-of-the-range. Then there were the cars – two Audis (both limited editions) and an Aston Martin in the time Rebus had known him. It had surprised no one that in retirement he had started dealing in second-hand but upmarket vehicles.

'If you do fancy joining us one day,' Fleck went on, 'I can promise you'd be treated royally.'

Rebus reached across and grabbed a handful of the man's coat. 'I'm sod all to do with any of it, Alan, got that?'

Fleck's salesman veneer melted away. The ice Rebus remembered from incidents past was back in his eyes and his voice. 'All those bottles of malt, John. The restaurant bills torn in half at the end of a blowout. Ringing any bells?'

'I did you the occasional favour as a mate. End of.'

'Well, obviously not end of or you wouldn't be here.' Fleck shrugged himself free of Rebus's grip. 'The Crew aren't too happy about Francis, I can tell you. They've tried reaching out to him but been snubbed. Lot of discontent at Tynie.'

'My heart bleeds.'

'I assume he's got as far as naming names, yours among them. Mine too, no doubt.' Fleck exhaled noisily and at length. 'So what do we do now, John?'

'You tell me. There's a warrant out for him so he's gone silent and deep.'

'Otherwise we could have one of our famous quiet words.' Fleck leaned back in the leather-upholstered seat. 'How are things otherwise? Managed to steer clear of the virus? Retirement suiting you?'

'You need to take care of this, Alan,' Rebus said quietly but determinedly.

'Plenty other actors involved, John, some of them still on the force. I reckon you'll be a footnote if you're anything at all.'

Rebus was shaking his head. 'The high-ups are taking an interest. They've brought a DI called Fox in from Gartcosh.'

'I know Fox.'

'Thought you might. Well, he's no longer Complaints, but he still has the mentality, and that means he loves nothing better than using the likes of you and me as his personal crapper. Police Scotland want minimal collateral damage from this. Best way to achieve that is to zero in on a few old warriors. That way they can say lessons have been learned, we don't work like that these days. We'll be statues they can pull down to appease the mob.'

'Point taken.' Fleck was running his fingers up and down his clean-shaven face, staring through the windscreen as if studying a multi-routed signpost. 'I can try phoning him again – though he's taken to not answering. You're sure he's not at the flat?'

'He's renting a place on Constitution Street. There are eyes on it.'

'Constitution Street? Why there?'

'Family home's off limits.'

Fleck thought for a moment. 'His best mate at Tynie is Rob Driscoll. Could be sleeping on his sofa. I can ask.'

'Now?'

'Don't think I've got his number on me, but I can find it easily enough. Leave it with me.' He took out his phone. 'Give me yours so I can let you know the upshot.'

'It's the same one I've always had.'

Fleck watched as Rebus held up his own phone. 'Same handset, too.' He gave a snort, but his smile quickly faded. 'The Crew think of themselves as just that, John – a crew. United we stand, et cetera. The thought that Francis might start grassing them up . . . Could get very ugly, that's all I'm saying.'

'I'm relying on you to stop that happening.'

'You say that, but I can't help wondering . . .'

'What?'

'You, me and everybody else – best result all round is if Francis Haggard just stops talking. Giving him a fright might do that. You know I'm right, I can see it behind your eyes. I don't suppose we're the only ones thinking that way either. I've seen people try to cross the Crew before. It never turns out well for them.' Fleck paused. 'But then I don't need to tell you that, John, do I?'

Rather than answer, Rebus got out of the Mercedes, leaving the passenger door open and walking along the row of covetable vehicles towards the relative safety of his old Saab.

8

Having led the two detectives up the staircase, Stephanie Pelham raised an open bottle of wine and gave it a waggle.

'Bit early for me,' Siobhan Clarke said with a meaningful glance towards Christine Esson.

'How about a pot of tea?' Esson said, taking the hint. 'I'll make it.' She headed for the kitchen while Clarke walked towards where Cheryl Haggard was seated, knees tucked under her chin, arms wrapped around her legs, as if in an attempt to make herself as insignificant as possible. The chair she sat in was big and squishy and lacked arms. It sat in a corner of the room by the window, though she showed no interest in the panorama beyond.

'You doing okay?' Clarke asked her, receiving a slow nod of reply.

'Neither of us got much sleep,' her sister said. 'Every hour I was checking the doors and windows. You've not found him yet?'

'I wanted to take another look at the footage. Maybe you could talk me through what we're not hearing?'

'Swear to God, I'm getting someone in to wire the system for sound.' Pelham looked around for her iPad, eventually spotting it under a TV remote. 'To think that when James ordered it, I told him he was wasting his money.' She sat at the table and busied herself finding the recording. Esson appeared carrying a tea tray.

'Couldn't find any sugar,' she said.

'Neither of us takes it,' Pelham said.

'Then we're fine.' Esson took a mug over to the chair. When Haggard showed no interest, she placed it on the floor next to her.

At the table, Pelham angled the iPad towards the two detectives.

'This is from the outside camera. He climbed over the bloody

81

gates while the four of us were in here. Hid himself behind the bins. Hang on, I'll fast-forward.' She did so, but overshot and had to go back. 'That's you and Gina leaving.' She looked at Clarke. 'He walks to the door, tries it, and then rings the bell. I thought you'd forgotten something, so I didn't even check the spyhole. I won't make that mistake again.'

She talked them through the home invasion, her jaw tightening as she relived the incident.

'He seems to be listening at the bedroom door,' Clarke commented at one point. 'Is Cheryl talking to him?'

'Telling him to sod off,' Pelham stated. But Clarke had noticed Cheryl Haggard raise her head slightly to look in her sister's direction.

'Are you sure about that, Stephanie?' Clarke asked.

'Of course.'

'I told him we'd talk – not right then, but sometime.' Cheryl's voice caused all three of them to turn towards her.

'Which would be a huge mistake,' Pelham stressed.

Cheryl unfolded herself, picked up her mug and joined them at the table. She seemed interested in the iPad.

'You sure?' her sister asked solicitously, receiving a nodded reply. Not that there was much more to see. The whole drama had lasted only a couple of minutes.

'What's happening now?' Clarke enquired as Francis Haggard stabbed his finger towards his sister-in-law.

'He's warning me off,' Pelham said, her free hand reaching to her neck. 'I thought he was going to attack me. It had my stomach doing somersaults. I thought I was going to throw up on the spot.' She drew in a deep breath. They all watched as Haggard wrenched the phone from her grasp, Stephanie touching her wrist at the memory of it. 'And then he leaves,' she said. 'Back down the driveway and over the gates. So much for security, eh?'

'Have you tried calling your phone?'

'Goes straight to voicemail.'

'Could he unlock it if he wanted to?'

'Facial recognition, so I doubt it.'

'Tracking?'

'Never bothered setting it up.' She saw that Clarke was looking at the phone lying on the table close to the iPad. 'A trick I learned from my ex – keep your business and personal lives separate.'

'Which phone did Francis take?'

'Business. Which is a blessing, I suppose, since I've put work on hold.'

'Stephanie did a wonderful job of our flat,' Cheryl said quietly.

'Yes, about your flat.' Clarke pulled back her shoulders. 'Bit of additional bad news – neighbours reported a break-in.' She watched Cheryl's mouth fall open. 'It's a bit of a mess and there are some breakages. Plus you'll need a locksmith.'

'What happened?' Stephanie demanded.

'From the CCTV, two delivery drivers got in. We reckon they just kept pushing buttons until someone unlocked the door. They were carrying pizza boxes and wore motorbike helmets, visors up but mouths and noses masked.'

'I don't understand,' Cheryl said, her voice trembling.

'How much damage did they do?' Stephanie added.

'Broken vase,' Esson recited, 'some art that will need re-framing . . .'

'Bastards.'

'Mostly stuff just needs picking up and put back in drawers.'

'One thing they did do,' Clarke added, 'was strew the place with a powder that I'm pretty sure is cocaine. Would they have found it in the flat, Cheryl?'

'I don't . . .' She looked to her sister for guidance.

'Francis used the stuff,' Stephanie answered. 'Not my sister, though.'

'Ever partake yourself?'

She stared at Clarke. 'Very occasionally.'

'Would Francis's stash have been easy to find?' Clarke asked Cheryl.

'I don't think he kept any at home. It was just for nights out, maybe at a party.'

'You're sure about that?'

Cheryl nodded.

Clarke signalled to Esson and began to rise to her feet. 'If you're worried about security,' she told Stephanie, 'we can maybe make officers available. No promises, though, we're hellish stretched.'

'Gina Hendry said the same. She was here first thing.' Stephanie's focus shifted to her sister, who was cupping both hands around the mug as she held it up to her mouth. 'You can't go anywhere near him, Cheryl. You know that, right?'

'Of course,' Cheryl Haggard said quietly, blowing across the surface of the liquid and studying the ripples her breath made.

Clarke and Esson had almost reached the front door when a buzzer sounded. Stephanie Pelham checked the screen on the wall. It showed a man standing at the gates to the driveway. She pushed the intercom button.

'James, what the hell do you want?'

'I heard about Cheryl. Just wanted to know if I can help.'

'You can help, as a matter of fact – sign the bloody divorce papers and get this over and done with. Now sod off back to wherever you crawled out of.' She lifted her finger from the intercom button and turned towards the two detectives. 'If I open the gates for you, he'll take it as an invitation.'

'We'll soon disabuse him,' Clarke assured her, before turning to Esson. 'You get in the car, I'll walk to the gates.' Esson nodded her understanding.

Stephanie Pelham unlocked the door. Clarke nodded a goodbye and strode down the driveway, Esson catching her up just as the gates were beginning to open. James Pelham was sitting in a white saloon. He got out again at the sight of Clarke. She had her warrant card open in front of her.

'You're not wanted here, Mr Pelham,' she stated.

'It's my bloody home!'

'It was once.'

He looked exasperated and dragged his fingers through his hair. 'Are they okay, though, Steph and Cheryl?'

'They're fine.'

'She won't talk to me on the phone, won't meet me for a drink . . . I'm just trying to be reasonable here.'

'And the reasonable thing to do right now is leave.'

Esson had brought the car roadside, but had stopped in front of the gates, blocking any attempted entry. Clarke watched the gates start to swing slowly closed.

'Tell me,' she said, 'how well do you know Francis Haggard?'

Pelham thought for a moment. 'The girls would go off together, but our services weren't usually required. I probably met him once a month, maybe less.'

'Get along okay?'

He met her gaze. 'Not particularly. Nothing really in common.'

'Ever see signs of a temper?' Clarke watched Pelham shake his head. 'No hints that he was mistreating Cheryl?'

'Not until recently – and by then Steph and I had parted company.'

Clarke saw that Esson was drumming her fingers against the steering wheel, wondering what she was missing. 'Thank you for your help. Don't let us detain you.' She headed to the car and got in.

'He's older than he looks in the papers,' Esson commented. 'The phrase "washed-up" springs to mind.'

'It's a shame, isn't it?' Clarke said, fastening her seat belt.

'I'm practically in tears here. Back to the office?'

'Actually, I've got another destination in mind, Christine, I'm just not sure you're going to like it . . .'

Malcolm Fox was waiting on the forecourt when Alan Fleck got back from road-testing a BMW. As he locked the car, he gave Fox's Mercedes a good look.

'Bought from new?'

'I prefer getting my wheels from reputable dealers. It's been a while, Mr Fleck.'

'Long enough for you to switch from Complaints to Gartcosh.'

'Who's been whispering in your ear?'

'What do you want, Fox?'

'I want what's due.'

Fleck narrowed his eyes. 'And what's that?'

'Your head on a plate.'

'You've tried that before, remember?'

'I certainly remember Kyle Weller's death in custody – I'm sure you do, too.'

'Accidents will happen, as they say.'

'But Tynecastle was always more accident-prone than most.'

'As I recall, you did everything short of hiring a proctologist, and you still drew a blank.'

'Kyle was by no means the only one. You'll not have forgotten Tony Barlow – guy spent a month in hospital and a year doing physio.'

Fleck folded his arms. 'Never proved we had anything to do with it.'

Fox gave a cold smile and pretended to scan his surroundings. 'Did Cafferty help bankroll this place?'

'A lifetime's savings, as bank records will confirm.'

'He gave you a taste for it, though, didn't he? Fast cars, I mean. When you helped him ship all those hot ones to Europe.'

'Why don't you go waddling back to your little desk job? It's all your fat arse is fit for these days.'

Fox shook his head slowly. 'I'm here now, Fleck. And I'm not going anywhere until I've heard what Francis Haggard has to say.'

'Saying is one thing . . .'

'Only takes one to start, though, in my experience. That gets the fear going, and others soon join in.'

Fleck took a step towards him. 'I get it, Fox, I really do. You'd rather hang a history lesson like me out to dry than anyone still on the force.' He paused. 'There's some I could point a finger at – not all of them dead and buried, though at least one is well on his way.'

'You're talking about Rebus.'

'I'm just remembering the favours he did for Cafferty back in the day.' He paused. 'You should dig a bit further into the Tony Barlow case, then ask Francis Haggard about it.'

'Should I ask him about the cars shipped to Zeebrugge, too?'

Fleck offered a shrug. 'Feel free, but it'll get you nowhere. Road I'm pointing down is the one you should be taking.'

'I'm not sure I trust your GPS. You know where to find me if you want to come in for a chat.' Fox turned towards his Mercedes.

'Mind if I ask how much you paid for it,' Fleck called out to him. Instead of answering, Fox climbed in behind the steering wheel. When Fleck approached, he lowered the window. 'Whatever it was,' Fleck said, his teeth bared, 'I'd have charged you a fuck of a sight more.'

Fox revved the car hard as he headed out of the compound, hitting every pothole, Fleck visible throughout in his rear-view mirror, waving and grinning.

9

'You absolutely confident about this?' Esson said from the driver's seat of Clarke's Astra.

'It's practically on the way back to base, Christine.'

'Which doesn't mean it's a good idea.'

Having cut through from Corstorphine, they were on Gorgie Road, heading towards Tynecastle police station. It was situated on a square near the Hearts football ground, hemmed in by a mixture of tenements, workshops and garages. There was no car park, and liveried vans and cars had taken every on-street parking spot in the vicinity, so Clarke ended up on a double yellow line on the far side of the square. At the heart of the square was an unloved grassy area protected by low iron railings. A gate led to a couple of children's swings and the stubby remains of what had probably been a seesaw. The police station was a couple of storeys tall, with mesh-covered windows staring blearily from the upper level. The facade was battleship grey, retouched to cover up indecipherable graffiti. Someone with a thick black Sharpie had been busy on the front door, too.

'Bit of a throwback,' Esson commented. Clarke nodded her agreement. She'd known a few stations like this in her early days on the force. They usually ended up with a nickname like Fort Apache or Precinct Thirteen. Most of them had been bulldozed and replaced. She wondered how much longer Tynecastle would endure.

The door was locked, and they had to be buzzed in. The reception area was cramped, its walls decorated with the usual public information notices and misper posters. A wall-to-ceiling clear plastic screen kept the desk officer safe, but Clarke noticed that it had been scratched with expletives and gang affiliations. She and Esson held up their warrant cards.

'Need to speak with someone about Francis Haggard,' Clarke said.

'Colour me shocked,' the desk officer responded with a world-weary smile. He was probably still in his twenties, but was experienced enough. 'CID are currently elsewhere, though.'

'Rank-and-file will do. Whoever's available.'

'Let me go and check. Why don't you take a seat?'

He disappeared through the door behind him. When Clarke looked behind her, she was unsurprised to find that there was nowhere to sit.

'Sense of humour probably comes in handy,' Esson said, studying the literature on the walls.

'Mop and bleach wouldn't go amiss either,' Clarke added, her shoes almost adhering to the black-and-white linoleum tiles.

A second door was opening to the side of the reception desk. A uniformed officer stood there, sizing up the visitors. He was in his mid to late thirties, tall and broad and with short dark hair. There were a few touches of acne on his neck, which he would probably never lose.

'In you come then,' he said, holding the door open.

'DI Clarke,' Clarke introduced herself as she passed him.

'DC Esson,' Esson added.

He nodded, then gestured down the hallway. 'Left at the end,' he said.

They entered an airless interview room, their host having the good grace to leave the door open once they were all inside. He indicated the chairs either side of the table.

'We're fine standing,' Clarke said. He shrugged and rested his backside against the table. 'I didn't catch your name.'

The day's paper was on the table. The officer twisted his body, making show of skimming it, then he picked it up and held it in front of him. The headline was *OUR LAWLESS CAPITAL*.

'"Feral youths control unpoliced streets",' he recited from memory. 'That's why this place is empty. It's why we're *running* on empty. Nobody's afraid of us any more, not the way they used to be. How do you think that makes us feel when we're out there?' He jabbed a finger towards the outside world.

'Is this what's known as getting your retaliation in first?'

'Just giving you a bit of background, DI Clarke.' He dropped the newspaper. 'My name's Rob Driscoll. I'm a mate of Francis's.'

'Then maybe you'll know where we can find him.'

'I heard you'd let the dogs loose. He went to talk to Cheryl, didn't he?'

'I didn't think that was public knowledge.'

'It's public knowledge that uniforms have been wasting their time making detours to Constitution Street since last night.'

'So you know where he lives.'

'Like I said, we're mates.'

'When did you last speak?'

'Few days back.'

'In person?'

'Phone.' Driscoll pinched the bridge of his nose and squeezed his eyes shut for a moment. He was either exhausted or doing a passable impression.

'Did it affect your friendship?' Esson asked. 'When you found out he'd been battering his wife, I mean?'

'All I know is, he's absolutely nuts about her.'

'Funny way of showing it, wouldn't you say?'

'I'm not here to defend what he did, but there's give and take in that relationship. Cheryl can get fired up, too.'

'So the bruises, the bloody nose – they just go with the territory?'

'Like I say, I'm not defending him.'

'I'm hearing different, Rob.' Clarke folded her arms. 'Has he said anything to you about what he did to Cheryl?'

'Not really. I don't think he felt proud of it, though.'

'Be a bit odd if he did.'

'Pressure's been getting to him – not that that puts him in a minority.'

'He ever mention his proposed defence?'

Driscoll shook his head. 'But that hasn't stopped word getting round.'

'So you know he's going to drop you all in it?'

'He's blaming the job for the way he changed. Maybe he's got a point. I've no idea if he's planning to name names.'

'Trust me, he is.'

'He'll do what he has to do.'

Clarke gave a thin smile. 'Are your colleagues managing to be as phlegmatic as you about it?'

'Dunno – I'd have to look up "phlegmatic" first.'

'Oh, I think you know what it means. Any chance we can see his locker?'

'I don't see why not.'

'Opened, I meant.'

'That'll require a search warrant.'

'He's absconded, Rob.'

'Maybe he has and maybe he hasn't. Depends if he realises he's broken his bail conditions. Guy's in a heightened emotional state, his head's out of the game.'

'You seem to know a lot about it.'

Driscoll's phone was buzzing, alerting him to an incoming call. He checked the screen.

'Take that if you need to,' Clarke said, but he shook his head and waited for the caller to give up.

'I know Francis,' he said. 'As I told you, he's one of my very best buds. And he *does* love Cheryl to bits, I promise you.'

'So you'd reach out to help him, maybe even cover for him? That's what mates do, isn't it, especially at Tynecastle? And maybe in turn he'd keep your name out of things . . .' Her voice tailed off. She'd been trying not to think about her own relationship with Rebus – trying and failing.

'I've got nothing to hide.' Driscoll looked from Clarke to Esson and back again.

'Your accent's not local,' Clarke commented.

'Neither is yours.'

'I grew up south of the border.'

'And I grew up north of the border – just a different border.'

'Northern Ireland.' Clarke nodded her understanding. 'Driscoll's a Catholic name?'

'So?'

'So what nickname did you get given?'

'It's all perfectly innocent, DI Clarke.'

'Just banter?' Esson interrupted.

'That's right.'

'If you hear from Francis, tell him he'd be wise to come see us,' Clarke said. 'Meantime, who else should we be talking to?'

'Nobody's going to tell you anything.'

'Closing ranks, eh? Might not serve you so well these days as it has in the past. Try contacting him, will you? Tell him he needs to come in.'

'If you like.'

'We've just been to his home, actually,' Esson said. 'Someone had kicked the door in, made a real old mess.'

'Our lawless capital,' Driscoll echoed.

'Rather than take anything, though, they left something.'

'What?'

'Cocaine, spilled all over the floor.'

'What a waste – and I keep being told it's in short supply.'

'Funny way for mates to behave, isn't it?' Clarke asked.

Driscoll stared at her. 'You think *we* did it?' He gave a snort. 'Why?'

'A shot across his bows?' Clarke speculated.

'Dream on.' Driscoll levered himself up from the table. 'Now if you don't mind, there's proper policing some of us need to be doing, so . . .' He gestured towards the door.

'We can find our own way,' Clarke told him.

She led Esson back down the corridor, pressing the button to unlock the door. Three uniformed officers filled the reception area, one slightly older than the other two, none of them sporting welcoming looks on their faces. They didn't say anything and didn't clear a space, meaning Clarke and Esson had to squeeze past. One of them gave a long, loud sniff, as if trying to pick up a scent.

'You'd have to be desperate,' Clarke heard one mutter to another.

'I'd do you before I'd do them,' a second voice replied in the same stage whisper.

For a moment, she considered confronting them and taking badge numbers. But she knew they would consider that a win. Instead, as she hauled open the door to the outside world, she half turned towards Esson.

'I can never remember,' she said, voice raised loud enough to carry, 'if they're called Tynie because of their brains or their dicks.'

'One doesn't necessarily rule out the other,' Esson replied, closing the door after her.

Two patrol cars were arriving, officers piling out. 'I see we're too late for the strippers,' one of the uniforms said.

'Thank Christ,' his colleague replied.

There were six of them, all male, all in their twenties or early thirties. They knew damned well who Clarke and Esson were, doubtless alerted by the officer at the desk. Which also meant they knew why they were there.

'Any of you particularly close to Francis Haggard?' Clarke asked.

'Give me a kiss and I'll tell you.'

Amidst the laughter, Clarke caught the words 'Nice one, Chris.' She fixed the man with a look. 'We'll have a proper chat later,

Chris, yes? See how chirpy you are away from your carers.'

The laughter started up again, and someone thumped the officer called Chris on the back. They began to file into the station, giving last appraising looks as they went.

'What century is this?' Esson muttered, following Clarke to the Astra.

'They'll be dangerous if they ever learn to make fire,' Clarke agreed.

Driscoll summoned them all to the locker room. They arrived armed with fizzy drinks cans and chocolate bars.

'What did they want?' he was asked almost immediately.

'It's as we've been hearing,' he explained. 'Francis has gone rogue. He's out there somewhere, nobody knows where. He can't hide for ever, though, and when they find him, he's going to start shooting his mouth off. Anybody catches a whiff of him, we need to know. I'd love for that to happen before we all rendezvous at the pub later. But there's something else.' He paused, his eyes landing in turn on every man in the room. 'His flat in Newhaven was turned over, coke dumped on the floor.'

'Just paying our respects, Rob.'

Driscoll stared at the speaker. 'Was that the wisest move, Chris?'

'He needs to know we've got as much on him as he has on us.'

'Well, that's probably backfired nicely. See, he's not allowed within half a mile of the family home, so he's highly unlikely to walk into your scenario. Instead, someone phoned it in, and that brought CID here, sticking their noses in. And the cherry on the top is, they now have more dirt on Francis than was previously the case, since you've just flagged up that he likes a bit of hokey-cokey. Giving him even more reason to grass on us to save his neck.' Driscoll's voice had been rising throughout, while Chris had seemed to be physically shrinking.

'So what do we do?' someone asked into the silence.

'We talk tactics, maybe with a wiser head than I seem to be seeing around me here. Now bugger off, the lot of you, and give me some peace to think.'

As he watched them leave, he saw that Chris was busy on his phone. Driscoll snatched it from him. The message hadn't quite been completed. All it said so far was *How you doing?* Chris grabbed it back.

'I'm not even going to ask,' Driscoll said.

'Keep it that way,' Chris said, making his exit.

Driscoll sat down heavily on one of the benches that lined the room, staring at his lap for a moment before digging his own phone out of his pocket and returning the call from earlier.

'Catch you at a busy time?' he heard Alan Fleck enquire.

'Couple of visitors.'

'To do with Francis?'

Driscoll pressed the palm of his hand against Haggard's locker. 'You've had them too?'

'Not yet, but John Rebus paid a visit, swiftly followed by someone from Gartcosh. Seems we might be in a queue to get to Francis. But they don't have *you*, Rob. If Francis will listen to anybody . . .'

'I'm trying. You know the flat at Newhaven is off limits to him?'

'Stands to reason.'

'He's renting a place on Constitution Street.'

'Rebus told me.'

'Did he tell you which building, though?'

The silence on the other end of the line lengthened. 'You're kidding me,' Fleck eventually said.

'What if I told you the flat number?'

'I'd say that's one hell of a coincidence.'

'You might even say we shouldn't be discussing it on mobile phones.'

'That's a good point. Are the Crew still due to meet later?'

'Four o'clock onwards. You didn't invite Rebus, by any chance?'

'You know what, I nearly did.'

'Lucky you didn't. Might need to turn it into a council of war.'

'Wouldn't be the first time, Rob. I'll be there on the dot of four. Still haven't found you an M4, by the way, but I've got feelers out. Sure you don't want to go hybrid? Petrol's going to be red-flagged in the city centre sooner rather than later.'

'Just keep looking, Alan. I'll see you at four.'

Driscoll ended the call and made another, but it went straight to messaging. 'I want to help,' he said, holding the phone in front of him, his eyes reflected in its glass. 'And I *can* help. But not if you keep avoiding me, Francis. The Crew's meeting at the usual place, but I'll be free from six onwards. So let's do this – you say when and where. It'll just be the two of us, swear to God. I really do want to see you, mate. And I really do want to help.' He tried to think what else to say, ending the call when he couldn't come up with anything. Was it worth having eyes and ears on Constitution Street? Maybe even the Newhaven flat, despite what he'd said to Chris? Where the hell else would Francis go when he was busy burning bridges? He brought out the little packet of powder from his pocket, snorted some of it off the back of his hand right there and then.

Constitution Street . . . I'd say that's one hell of a coincidence. It wasn't, though, was it? It couldn't possibly be . . .

10

There was no one at the Oram home when Rebus got there. He walked around to the back door and peered through the kitchen window: a sink half filled with dishes, and a cat staring back at him from above the plate it had been licking on the drop-leaf table. The garden itself was tidy enough, and a new-looking barbecue sat under its covering on the patio. The garage was locked and there were no windows for him to look through. He had just finished retracing his steps to the pavement when he saw Ishbel Oram and her distinctive orange hair heading his way, two bags of shopping hanging heavily from her arms.

'You again,' she said.

'The proverbial bad penny.'

'Still ghost-hunting?'

'Just for as long as the spirit is willing.' She made to pass him. He followed her along the path to her front door, wondering how different her life would have turned out if her husband hadn't been made to run. 'It's Tommy I was looking for,' he said to her back.

'He's at work.'

'What time does he finish?'

'Can you not just leave us in peace?'

'Jack's been spotted, Mrs Oram. By more than one person. He was even seen on the pavement here. You're telling me you don't know anything about that?'

'I'm telling you you're wrong. And if I see you here again, I'll toss a coin. Heads I call the polis, tails I grab a hammer from the kitchen drawer – is that clear enough for you?'

'Why would he be watching the house but not come in?'

She had found her keys and unlocked the door. She closed it after her without saying anything. Rebus took out his phone and called QC Lettings. Eventually, Marion answered.

'Marion, it's John Rebus again. You mentioned a lock-up where Tommy keeps his bits and bobs. If I absolutely promise this is the last time you'll hear from me, any chance you could save me some time and give me the address?'

It was in Burnhill, a few turnings off Calder Road into a maze of low-quality housing, mostly of 1960s and '70s vintage. Three-storey blocks, the palette drab, the roadway spattered with litter mulched by car tyres. Rebus knew this area from the day job. It was a place where residents, whatever their hardships, closed ranks, protecting their own. If you lived in Burnhill or the neighbouring estates, you were part of an ever-evolving tribe with its own unwritten rules, rules you were best advised to learn and abide by.

The row of six lock-up garages was down a dead-end street. Rebus didn't like his chances so sat in his car for ten or so minutes, just getting a feel for the terrain. He wished he'd brought Brillo with him, not as a deterrent but because no one really thought twice about a dog-walker.

'You're an old geezer,' he told himself. 'Nobody looks twice at you anyway.'

But he locked the Saab when he got out.

One of the lock-ups belied its name, having lost both lock and whatever door was attached to it. It had become an open-sided skip, doubling as a lavatory judging by the aroma. The other garages boasted a serious array of padlocks. Even then, dents and scrapes showed where attempts had been made to breach their defences. Rebus had no way of knowing which belonged to Tommy Oram, so retreated to the car and, for want of anything else to do, sent Clarke another text:

Nothing?

He had brought the misper case notes with him and reached under the passenger seat to retrieve them. There had been interviews with friends and associates of Oram's. Rebus knew he could try questioning them himself, but he got no sense that the man had a close confidant or best pal. According to his wife's statement, he'd been regular in his habits – at the Potter's Bar from midday until nine or ten, five or six days a week, leaving his staff of four to make

96

up the other hours. The staff had been questioned and had proved as forthcoming as any breeze-block wall.

He turned the radio on while he read, but couldn't find anything he wanted to listen to. He slid a CD into the player instead. It had been playing up recently, skipping or refusing to work altogether, but today it seemed in a more generous mood. Peter Green-era Fleetwood Mac, which would do Rebus just fine. He leaned back in the driver's seat, eyes on the outside world. There were days in winter when the sun barely seemed to rise above the rooftops before running out of juice. On those days, the lights stayed on in his flat from when he woke up until he retired for the night – same went for the heating. They were saying on the news that bills were about to shoot up. Rebus reckoned he would be okay, but others wouldn't. Politicians would say the usual things while wringing their hands. Whole bloody country seemed to be fraying, and its inhabitants along with it. He wondered where Jack Oram had spent the last four years.

Wondered, too, why he'd bothered coming back.

A black van, maybe a Citroën Berlingo, was crawling towards the lane. Rebus had parked a few yards along from the entrance. His was still the only vehicle in the vicinity, and he could feel the driver's gaze on him. But eventually the van trundled down the lane and stopped. Rebus was just out of its eyeline, but he heard the handbrake being applied. He got out of the Saab again and closed the door as quietly as he could. A young man had emerged from the van and was standing in front of one of the garages, a set of keys in his hand but eyes peering up the lane to the figure sauntering towards him.

'Not opening up?' Rebus asked.

'Who are you?'

'Name's Rebus. Your mum might have mentioned me.'

'I don't think so.'

'Probably doesn't want to stir up memories.'

'Memories?'

'Of your dad. He's who I'm looking for.'

Tommy Oram – Rebus was sure it was him – angled his head downwards, suddenly very interested in the outline of each key he was holding. He had a wavy mop of dark hair and a long, sharp face with pronounced cheekbones. Rebus could imagine him fronting a band. He had enough presence to pull it off.

'My dad's gone,' the young man said, blood rising to his neck.

'Look, Tommy – it is Tommy, isn't it? – he's not in any trouble, if that's what you're thinking. I just need a quiet word with him.'

'I told you he's gone.'

'And I'm telling you he's back.' Rebus slid his hands into his pockets and offered a shrug. 'We've met before, in the Moorfoot, when I was showing everyone his photo. You did a pretty good job of looking oblivious.'

'What else was I going to do?'

'Who was the lassie you were with?'

'Just a pal.'

'Gaby Mackenzie?'

'No.' Tommy Oram paused. 'How do you know about Gaby?'

'I'm good at my job.'

'There's nothing I can tell you.'

'You sure about that, son?'

'Who the fuck *are* you?'

'I told you, my name's John Rebus.'

A light went on behind Tommy Oram's eyes. 'He talked about you. I used to play pool after school, and I remember that name being mentioned around the tables. Cafferty had some cops in his pocket, kept them sweet, and you were one of them.' He broke off as he studied Rebus. 'You look too old, though.'

'I've been out of the force a while. And I was never in Cafferty's pocket.'

'He had my dad bumped off – did you know that?'

Rebus took a moment to form a response. 'It's actually Cafferty who asked me to find your dad – so he can apologise.'

'Oh aye.' The young man sounded rightly disbelieving. 'Like that makes sense.' Rebus was almost ready to agree with him, though he didn't say as much.

'Who do you think sent that envelope of cash to your mum?'

'Not my dad, that's for sure.'

'Cafferty, then?'

'That's what Mum says. Didn't stop her spending it, though.'

'If you do see your dad—'

'*I keep telling you!*' The young man's voice had risen so much that a dog somewhere nearby sent up a complaint.

'Easy, son.'

Tommy Oram's eyes had gone glassy, as though he might be near to tears. 'You say you're not Cafferty's man, but here you are working for him.' His face twisted. 'Apologise to my dad? He had him killed for skimming a few lousy grand. *That's* who your boss is, and I'm done talking here.' He opened the van again and got in, slamming the door shut after him. Jammed the key into the ignition but didn't turn it. Instead, he took out his phone, checking for messages or sending one.

Discretion being the better part of valour, Rebus retreated to his car. He decided Oram would be watching for it, so he made sure his headlights were on as he drove past the top of the lane. He took a right when he could, then another, doubling back on himself. This time he parked a hundred yards short of the lock-ups, again closing the door as quietly as he could. He wouldn't exactly call it tiptoeing, but he kept his footsteps light.

The garage next to the van had been unlocked. Rebus could hear someone inside; sounded as if they were rifling through boxes of screws or nails. A light had been switched on, and music too – a dull, repetitive thump such as he heard from car and van windows a dozen times a day in the city. Tommy Oram was standing sideways on, busy at a row of shelves, each one containing boxes and trays filled with the bits and pieces he needed to do his job.

Rebus saw, however, that there was more to the lock-up than mere storage. A camp bed had been unfolded, a duvet draped across its thin mattress. There was a lamp next to it and a compact music system next to that, everything plugged into an extension cable that stretched to the wall.

Sensing movement, Oram's head jerked round.

'Get out!' he barked.

'In a minute,' Rebus said, settling himself on the bed and switching the music off. 'This where he sleeps?'

'It's where *I* sleep.'

'No, Tommy, you sleep in your own bed under your mum's roof.' Rebus angled his head. There were discarded fast-food wrappers under the bed alongside a drained bottle of whisky. 'Will he be back soon?'

When he spoke, the fight had gone out of the young man's voice. 'I told you, he's gone. He was here, but not any more.'

'What happened?'

'He just left. Couldn't bring himself to . . .' His voice had thickened. He cleared his throat and swallowed. Rebus saw it all in an instant: how hard it was to lose your father in your teens, how hard to then start dealing with his sudden return.

'What?' he prompted.

'He wanted Mum to know without either of us having to tell her. Don't ask me why – I think he thought it would soften the impact.'

'Might explain why he was hanging around Craigmillar. How long have you known?'

'He phoned me last year, said he was missing us. He wanted to hear how we were doing.'

'Up until then you thought he was . . .?'

Tommy nodded.

'That must've been hard, son.'

'Too right.'

'Why didn't you tell your mum?'

'He made me promise not to. He wanted to get himself straightened out.'

'Meaning off the booze?'

'Aye. Last few years he's been hitting it pretty hard.'

'All paid for by the money he took from Cafferty?' Rebus touched his toe against a box of empty spirits bottles. 'He still had a ways to go by the look of things.'

'That money you mentioned – Dad was skint when he came back. Even borrowed from me, though I could see how much it embarrassed him.'

'Do you ever see your aunt?'

'Which one?'

'The one your dad's brother Paul married.'

'Auntie Joanna? Not in years. Uncle Paul and my dad had a falling-out decades back. Dad wouldn't even let us go to the funeral.'

Rebus's eyes narrowed. 'I heard your dad gave her a bunch of cash after Paul passed away.'

Tommy Oram gave a snort. 'I very much doubt that.'

There was sudden movement at the mouth of the lock-up. Two lads not yet in their teens had stopped their bikes and were straddling them, toes on the ground. The hoods of their jackets were up, and one of them had a hand in his pocket, as if ready to pull something out.

'It's okay,' Tommy assured them. 'Nothing to worry about.'

Nothing more was said. But as the two kids cycled away, a squat monster of a dog appeared, licking its lips.

'Hiya, Buster,' Tommy cooed. The dog gave a short growl and made to rejoin its owners. 'They keep an eye on the place,' he explained.

'For a fee, I dare say.'

'Not necessary. What's worth nicking?'

'Everything has its price.' Rebus pressed his hands down against the mattress. 'Why this place rather than a flat or a B&B?'

'Didn't cost anything, and the bed was already here. There's another one folded up over there. It's in case one of the flats needs them.'

'You like your job, then?' Rebus got up and approached the workbench. The shelves above it held rows of five- and ten-litre paint pots.

'It's better than nothing.'

'Your employer's okay? I suppose he must be, keeping you on after you were suspected of thieving.'

'That was a renter who was being booted for non-payment. Just stirring things up.'

Rebus made show of remembering something. 'I know you know the daughter. I hear she helped get you the job. I'm not saying I'd have thought she's out of your league . . .'

'On a dance floor, doesn't matter which school you went to.'

'So that's how you met?'

'I kept putting in requests – obscure stuff, showing I knew what I was talking about. And eventually she played one.'

'So she's a DJ?'

'It's allowed these days, you know.'

'I'll take your word for it.' Rebus rested one hand against the worktop.

'Careful,' Oram said.

He lifted his hand and saw spots of pale blue paint on the tips of his fingers. Oram handed him a rag from a pile further along the bench.

'I've got some white spirit if you want.'

Rebus shook his head. 'It'll come off. Nice colour, though.'

'Posh paint for the premium lets.'

He put the rag back on the bench and took out a card with his number on it. 'When you next talk to your dad, tell him to give me a bell.' He placed the card on top of the used rag. 'By the way, how long ago did you last see him?'

'Three weeks, more or less.'

'I know he was trying to get off the booze, but did you ever take him to the Moorfoot?' He watched Oram shake his head. 'Not even for sentimental reasons?'

'He hated the fact it wasn't his pool hall any more.'

'You like the place, though?'

Oram offered a shrug. 'It's round the corner from the house.' He looked around him. 'I've got work I need to be getting on with.'

'Aye, me too.'

'What will you tell Cafferty?'

'As little or as much as I think he needs to know. And Tommy, if I thought Cafferty meant your dad any harm, I wouldn't be doing this. Tell Jack he's safe – I'll be there to make sure.'

Oram picked up the card and slid it into his pocket. 'I'll tell him,' he said. Rebus wanted to believe him, but he wasn't sure that he did.

Back in his car, he wondered about the young man and what he'd already had to deal with in his young life. Maybe his future would be brighter. The two kids were pedalling hard across the rutted playing field towards their own futures, their dog trotting behind them. Rebus sounded his horn in farewell as he passed them.

Jack Oram hadn't been close to his brother and didn't attend his funeral. Unlikely he'd have sent money to the widow, using it instead to tide him over during his time on the run.

'Hell's going on here?' Rebus muttered to himself as he drove.

11

Cafferty's assistant was waiting at the door.

'Andrew, right?' Rebus said.

'No dogs,' Andrew said, eyes on Brillo.

'He's house-trained, unlike your boss.'

'They spread germs.'

'Okay, in that regard maybe he is like your boss, but if I leave him out here, he'll howl the place down.'

Andrew stared at him, then disappeared back inside, the door clicking after him. Rebus checked, but it was locked.

'Clever boy,' he muttered. Brillo looked at him expectantly. 'Yes, you too.'

A minute later, the door reopened, Andrew standing back to let dog and owner in. 'Still need to frisk you,' he announced.

'Just me, or the dog too?'

'Just you.'

Rebus stretched his arms out to either side. 'I used to be in the army, you know. They showed us how to kill someone with a rolled-up magazine to the throat. Maybe you should sweep the premises for potential weapons.'

Andrew patted him down without saying anything. Once he'd finished, he met Rebus's eyes. 'You were probably a piece of work in your day.'

'I held my own against your employer, if that's what you mean.'

'Changed times, though.'

'As a man called Dylan once sang.'

'Who?'

Rebus gave a theatrical sigh before starting down the long hallway.

'I want him kept on the leash,' Cafferty warned. He was seated by the window. A trolley table had been placed in front of him, a newspaper open on it alongside a hot drink and his phone. 'I take it there's news,' he said, his focus on the day's headlines.

'Oram's been seen,' Rebus obliged, 'though not for a few weeks. His son seems to think he got wind you were looking for him and headed for the hills again. Makes me wonder if I'm the first person you've had working on it.'

'How wounded would your pride be if you weren't?' Cafferty paused, hands resting on the newspaper. 'What makes you so sure the son's not spinning you a story?'

'He wouldn't be the only one, would he?'

'How do you mean?'

'There was no love lost between Oram and his brother. The son reckons his dad wouldn't have handed over a bean.'

Cafferty made a noise at the back of his throat. He folded the paper closed and focused on Rebus. 'You've been busy, I'll grant you.'

'I even went to QC Lettings, your old stamping ground. Nobody there seems to have had dealings with Jack Oram, though there is *one* Oram they know – the son works for them.'

'News to me.' Cafferty's fleshy brow furrowed. 'He never gave that money to the family?'

'Who told you he did?'

But Cafferty wasn't about to answer. Brillo had stopped sniffing his immediate surroundings and sent up a quiet mewl of complaint.

'Mind if I give him some water?'

It took Cafferty a moment to make up his mind. 'One of the yellow bowls, cupboard above the sink. I never use them.'

'Dinner parties only?'

Cafferty was studying the back page of the paper, filled with sports coverage. 'Siobhan still a Hibs fan?' he asked.

'Far as I know.'

On his way to the sink, Rebus passed the coffee table. A pile of mail sat there, a larger envelope at the bottom. He could make out the words *MGC Lettings* on its corner. He angled his head towards Cafferty, but the man was still reading – or putting up a decent pretence. Rebus filled the bowl from the tap, placing it on the floor next to the coffee table. The slurps that started coming from Brillo covered any sound as he lifted the letters above the larger envelope. Its contents had been removed – a single sheet of paper, a photocopy of a blurry photograph, no writing. The profile of a man in a living room, patterned wallpaper behind him, shot from the doorway, one edge of the door coming into frame.

'Noisy little bastard,' Cafferty grumbled, starting to turn his chair around. The trolley didn't make it easy, and he had to reverse away from it, giving Rebus plenty of time to step away from the envelopes and gaze instead at Brillo.

'So what's next on the agenda?' Cafferty asked.

Rebus gave a shrug. 'If he's gone, he's gone.'

'You said it yourself, though – the son works for the lettings agency. Good reason for his dad to go there, yet nobody seems to have seen him? Tell me you don't think that's a bit skew-whiff?'

'You didn't take me on to look at the lettings firm.'

'The son must know more than he's telling,' Cafferty persisted.

'I drove past the Gallery of Modern Art earlier. They've a huge neon sign outside –"There Will Be No Miracles Here", it says.' Might be art, but that doesn't mean it's wrong.'

'I'm not asking for a miracle, just another day or two of your time. His old allies, his old haunts . . .'

'I already tried the Potter's Bar.'

'And?'

'Yet another dead loss. How much did he take from you anyway?'

'Hard to say. Fifteen, maybe twenty grand.'

Rebus had crouched down to give Brillo a pat.

'There's something else bugging you,' Cafferty said, edging his wheelchair closer. The movement spooked Brillo. Rebus scooped the dog up into his arms, cradling it. 'You been painting?' Cafferty had noticed the smears of blue on Rebus's fingers.

'Man needs a hobby,' Rebus told him. 'And yes, something else *is* bugging me – it's called Tynecastle.'

'Cop shop rather than stadium, I'm guessing.'

'Skeletons are about to come tumbling out of closets.'

'Unfortunate for some.'

'Present company included.'

'We're old men. We'll be well down the list, no?'

'I wouldn't be so sure. Malcolm Fox is in town.'

'Never liked that man.'

'Didn't stop you trying to tuck him into your pocket.'

'I tried that with you too, if I remember correctly.'

'Plenty still reckon you succeeded.'

'Which amounts to more or less the same thing, while saving me a packet.' Cafferty's smile was as frosty as the top of the Pentlands.

'Fox isn't exactly on my pall-bearers list,' Rebus said, 'and there's nothing he likes better than getting to grips with bent cops. No shortage of those at Tynie, some of them with ties to you – everything from nicked cars to Tony Barlow.'

Cafferty was on the move again, back to his trolley and his newspaper. 'This is all because of that cop knocking his wife about?'

'You've heard.'

'Not much in the paper, but Andrew gets his news online. All the juicier when the victim's brother-in-law is a weel-kent face, and James Pelham is definitely that.' Cafferty paused, lost in thought for a moment. 'The cop plans to cut a deal, is that it? And he's got you rattled, which means Alan Fleck is probably rattled, too.'

'I hope I'm not putting thoughts in your head.'

'Thoughts are about all I've got left.' His eyes met Rebus's. 'Another day or two, a bit more digging, that's all I'm asking. Otherwise, I'd say a partial refund is due. What's your outlay been so far – a couple of beers and a quarter-tank of petrol? Allies and old haunts, John – just to humour me.' He peered into his mug. 'Andrew!' he bellowed. 'I need a top-up!'

'Floor could do with a wipe, too,' Rebus commented. 'Brillo's not the most refined drinker.'

'Tony Barlow,' Cafferty mused. 'There's a name I've not heard in a while.'

'Maybe we should add him to your apology list?'

'Don't tell me it still rankles?'

'Francis Haggard was working at Tynecastle back then, Cafferty. Probably not much wrong with his memory.'

'Stress can take years off your life, you know. You need to learn how to switch off.' Cafferty noticed Andrew hovering in the doorway. 'Mr Rebus and his mutt are just leaving. I'll have my tea after.'

Once he'd seen Rebus out, Andrew brought the fresh mug to Cafferty, who was at the window, eye pressed to the telescope.

'Not that you're obsessed with the guy or anything,' Andrew said. Cafferty turned, noting that Andrew had put a jacket on.

'Off out?'

'You know me. But I've got my phone and you've got your panic button.'

'I never panic.'

'Okay, your *alarm*, then.'

'Nightclub, is it?'

'Bit early. Might go for a drive first, check out the town.'

'Send me photos if anything stands out.'

'I always do, don't I?'

Cafferty peered through the telescope. 'There he goes,' he said. 'Not yet quite KO'd, but well on his way.'

'It's all working out, then?'

'It's all working out,' Cafferty confirmed with a nod. He would wait until Andrew had left the room before attempting to pick up the mug. He didn't like people noticing the slight tremor in his hands.

Christine Esson was driving home when Ronnie Ogilvie called her.

'How are you doing?' she asked him.

'Minimal discomfort.'

'Need anything bringing?'

'I think I'm fine for tonight. Just bored.'

'So you're going through your contacts and you've reached E?'

'Is that you finished for the day?'

'Thank God.'

'A hard one?'

'Thanks to half the force putting their feet up like you.'

'So what have you been doing?'

'Driving around looking for Haggard.'

'He's gone AWOL?'

'Seems so.'

'Edinburgh's a small city. His options are limited.'

'Thanks, Sherlock.'

'Though I suppose some brethren aren't going to bust a gut hunting down one of their own – present company not included, obviously.'

'Obviously.'

'How's it working out with Siobhan?'

Esson gave a sigh she knew would be audible. 'We seem to be cut from different cloth, Ronnie. I never used to think that, but I do now.'

'You joined a profession, Christine. With Siobhan, every case is more likely to turn into a crusade.'

107

Esson nodded along as she signalled to turn right. 'We had to visit Tynecastle. Could have done with some armour and shields.'

'Did they close ranks? Only to be expected.'

'Except we also suspect they broke into Francis Haggard's home and trashed it.'

'Because of what he did to his wife?'

'Because his defence is that working at Tynecastle is what drove him to it. And now he's scarpered and could be anywhere.'

'He's scared they'll come after him?'

'Maybe.'

'Work's finished, Christine. Go home, forget about it for a few hours, maybe watch a film.'

'I dare say you can suggest some.' She signalled left. Five more minutes and she'd be at her front door. Ronnie was right: the job was just that to her, a *job*. Once upon a time it had maybe meant more, but not these days. The uniforms at Tynecastle might be pigs, but they were pigs with a sense of purpose, while she was beginning to doubt, beginning to coast.

'First thing I'm doing after quarantine,' Ogilvie was saying, 'is hitting a wine bar.'

'I hope I'm invited.'

'Of course. And maybe Haggard will be done and dusted by then.'

'I wouldn't bet on it.'

'Do you think Siobhan will hand it back to me?'

'I wouldn't bet on that either.'

'She's found herself another crusade?'

'Something like that. Bye, Ronnie.'

'Wine night is coming, Christine. Hang in there.'

She ended the call and drove the final few hundred yards in silence, Ogilvie's words echoing around her brain.

Hang in there ... hang in there ... hang in there ...

12

As usual, the Crew had convened in a pub in Fountainbridge, its back room set aside for them by dint of a sign on the door saying *Private Function*. Rob Driscoll had tried his best to keep things focused, but his colleagues didn't make it easy. Chris Agnew had started flicking foam from his pint at those nearest him, who'd retaliated in kind. Then the first beer mat had come whizzing across the room, and the place had become a school playground until Alan Fleck appeared through the door. Everything had calmed down fast after that. Three-plus years a civilian, but there was still something about the guy that made them behave themselves, and for the next hour they were good as gold.

Driscoll was the first to leave, being in dire need of a cigarette. Outside, he sparked one up and angled his head, sending the smoke skywards, feeling the knots of tension in his neck and shoulders. The rush hour was winding down, though a procession of crawling buses kept the thoroughfare noisy. People trudging past him on their way home had their heads lowered, unwilling to engage. He wished more of them would take off those bloody masks. He liked studying faces. They were like pages a life was written on. He had studied his own reflection half an hour back in the mirror above the sink in the men's toilet. Handsome enough, though age was creeping up. 'Single, solvent and fancy-free,' as his mum had said recently. She'd never liked his ex, had phoned him on the day of the divorce and sung Cliff Richard's 'Congratulations' down the line to him. He exhaled more smoke and was reaching into his jacket for his phone when a hand landed heavily on his shoulder.

'You know smoking affects your insurance premiums?' Alan Fleck said.

'That's why I always say I've never smoked. Sorry about tonight.'

'It's your job to rein in the numpties. That little pantomime in Newhaven was reckless.'

'Nothing to do with me.'

'Chris Agnew doesn't have your brains. You need to control him.'

'I do what I can, Sarge. You left a pair of pretty large shoes behind.' Driscoll took another draw on his cigarette.

'You need to dig deeper.' Fleck prodded the younger man's chest.

Driscoll nodded slowly. 'You reckon our arses are covered, though?'

'Like I said in there, you all need to clean up your phones and computers. It's probably okay to send texts, but make sure and delete them after.'

'Bit drastic.'

'Malcolm Fox is a complete bastard, but he's also forensic. If there's something there to find, he'll find it.' Fleck watched as Driscoll studied the screen on his phone, as if evaluating its potential to become a grenade. 'He's not been in touch yet?' he asked.

'I was just about to check again.'

'Don't let me stop you.'

A moment later, a slow smile spread across Driscoll's face. 'We're on,' he said, turning the screen towards Fleck.

'No where or when, though,' Fleck commented, having read the curt message.

'I reckon he won't give much notice – less chance of me bringing a posse.'

'Well done anyway. I'd buy you a drink if I hadn't just had a skinful.' A taxi with its orange light illuminated was approaching. Fleck lifted his hand towards it. 'Treat you to a lift somewhere instead?'

'My car's around the corner.'

'After the amount you've put away?'

'I'm teetotal, though – says so on all those insurance forms.'

Fleck gestured towards Driscoll's phone. 'Sooner rather than later, eh, Rob? And if a carrot's not going to tempt him . . .'

'Don't worry, I know how to wield a stick.'

Driscoll watched Alan Fleck climb into the back of the black cab, starting up some chat with the driver as the vehicle eased into the flow of traffic, just another businessman on his way home at shift's end. He wondered if that might be his own future, too. Full pension, out of the job while still young enough, new vistas and experiences waiting. Fleck had even dropped a hint about a possible partnership. He hoisted his phone again, began composing a reply to his old comrade Francis Haggard. The smile was back on his face, though there was no trace of humour in his eyes.

Though he lived in Edinburgh, Malcolm Fox's daily commute took him far to the west, to where the Scottish Crime Campus had been built on industrial land next to the village of Gartcosh. The place was a modern-day fortress styled as a college and housing everything from forensic labs to Inland Revenue fraud inspectors, Major Crimes to Anti-Terrorism. Fox's remit was Specialist Crime, which gave him access to every database going, including Internal Affairs, known in his day as the Complaints.

The building around him emptied as Fox sat at the computer terminal in his glass box of an office. He had removed his jacket and draped it over the back of his chair. A half-eaten cheese and ham baguette sat forgotten next to two emptied coffee beakers. He had already run checks on Francis Haggard and Alan Fleck, but had widened his search to include other officers currently serving at Tynecastle, as well as those who had retired in the past decade. Then there was John Rebus, though the paperwork on him was so voluminous that Fox almost lost heart at the prospect of wading into it.

Almost.

For now, though, as day turned to night, he was reading about Tony Barlow. Eight years back, Barlow had been the victim of a sustained and brutal beating on some parkland close to where he lived. He had been walking home from the pub when, as he had put it in his witness statement, 'they came out of nowhere'. Four or five men, he believed, armed with pickaxe handles or metal bars.

'Cops,' he said. 'I'd swear to it.'

Not that they'd been in uniform. Dark, unbranded hoodies, denims and trainers. But Tony Barlow had had enough dealings with the law to know police officers when he saw them, even if they were in mufti. He was a petty criminal with a lengthy string of convictions, and the immediate reaction of the investigating officers to his claims could best be described as healthy scepticism. Much more likely surely that this was the result of a falling out amongst thieves, Barlow too savvy to grass up his actual assailants while happy to point the police towards their own.

'Said I was to stay away from kids,' he told the investigators from his hospital bed. 'Or else worse was coming. I told them I don't have kids. "You know what we mean," they said.'

A CID detective called Bobby Wilson had proposed a theory of mistaken identity. A paedophile ring had been operating in Edinburgh's Old Town at the time. Police were on to them, but no arrests had yet been made, insufficient proof having been offered to the procurator fiscal. The notion that officers might have taken the law into their own hands was discussed, but nothing came of it.

But now Alan Fleck was hinting at Rebus's involvement, and that interested Fox mightily.

Tony Barlow had spent weeks in hospital and many months afterwards undergoing physio to help him walk again without pain. Eventually he'd gone back to his regular source of income and been arrested and charged several more times. When pressed as to why he thought his attackers had been policemen, he'd said that they 'spoke like the filth and smelled like the filth'.

Fox could understand why no great effort had gone into probing his accusation.

He'd found a phone number for Bobby Wilson – now himself retired – and had discussed the case with him. Wilson had no doubt that if it had indeed been a punishment beating, the most likely source was Tynecastle police station.

'Alan Fleck wouldn't have liked it,' he'd told Fox, 'if he thought a bunch of paedos were getting away with it.'

Fox's brief conversation with Wilson had brought another name bubbling to the surface – Josephine Kilgour. He'd not thought about her for a while, and wondered if she was still at the same address. He jotted down her name as a reminder, then stared at his screen and tapped his pen – a chunky Montegrappa, a little treat to himself – against the pad. He could see how Tynecastle might well have been involved in the Barlow beating, but where did Rebus fit in? Was Fleck putting up a smokescreen? Any amount of time Fox spent taking the wrong road was time not used in pursuit of Fleck and the Crew.

He glanced at his Omega wristwatch, then stretched his spine, pulling back his shoulders. He hoped Francis Haggard would re-surface soon. If he was in the mood to tell some stories, maybe Tony Barlow could become a significant chapter.

112

He shut down his computer and put his jacket back on. He was halfway down the stairs when he saw someone he knew coming up. Colette Newman worked for HMRC, fraud inquiries her speciality.

'Working the late shift?' he asked her.

'Justice never sleeps, Malcolm,' she replied with a smile. She was carrying a folder under one arm, which she patted with her free hand. 'Furlough scams,' she explained.

'All the glamour all the time,' he commented. 'We should grab another drink one of these days.'

'So many choice spots in Gartcosh – were you thinking cappuccino from the kiosk?'

'I'd say a West End wine bar is more your style. Before or after a spot of dinner.'

'I'll get back to you, Malcolm.'

'We could call it a work meeting and charge it to the public purse,' he teased.

'I reckon HMRC would take a dim view of that, don't you?' Her smile was widening as she passed him and continued to the top of the stairs.

Rather than drive straight home, Fox, having hit the outskirts of the city, started following the signposts to Edinburgh North and East. Newhaven was right on the coast, looking out across the Firth of Forth. It still boasted a harbour, one side of which was lined with restaurants, though only a few hardy souls were out and about. It was practically on Leith's doorstep, but didn't have the same buzz. Still, the views would have been the selling point for the block of flats developed by James Pelham. Some had uninterrupted views towards the three bridges across the Forth, while others looked towards Inchkeith and the other islands out on the firth.

Fox got out of his car long enough to smell the air. There was a party on one of the balconies, just three or four people laughing at their good fortune while jazz played somewhere inside the flat. It was the sound of moneyed security. He thought of his own modest Oxgangs bungalow. Here was what he could have won. He could see through a glass door at ground level to where a concierge sat in front of a bank of screens, though the man seemed far more interested in his phone, feet up on the desk, knees bent. Above, Sinatra was singing about being flown to the moon. But if there was a moon up there somewhere, Malcolm Fox couldn't see it.

*

When Clarke arrived on Rebus's doorstep that evening, she found the door opening before she could announce her presence. Rebus was readying to take Brillo to the Meadows, accompanied by his daughter and granddaughter. Turned out Carrie took dance lessons somewhere nearby, and they sometimes caught up with Rebus afterwards for a bite.

'I had fish fingers,' Carrie announced.

'And did Grandad cook them?'

The child gave Clarke a look like she might be suffering from some form of mental illness.

'Come with us,' Samantha said, sliding an arm under Clarke's elbow. 'Been ages since we caught up.'

So they talked as they walked, the conversation remaining light. Clarke skated over the surface of her recent workload, while Rebus looked relieved throughout that there was no opportunity for her to grill him further about Francis Haggard and Tynecastle police station. When Brillo dropped the ball at her feet, Clarke gave a mighty swipe, sending it flying.

'Working off some of that tension?' Rebus enquired.

'You could play for Scotland!' Carrie added excitedly.

Clarke smiled, then noticed that Rebus was looking up in the direction of Cafferty's penthouse. The main room was in darkness. 'Can't let him go, can you?' she commented.

'No idea who you mean,' Rebus answered.

'Aye, right.'

'Dad's favourite expression,' Samantha interjected, taking his hand and squeezing it. 'Two positives but meaning the exact opposite. *Very* Scottish.'

'Probably him who taught me it then,' Clarke said. Samantha was looking at her.

'Have I thanked you for helping Dad during lockdown?'

'More than once.'

'I'm not sure he deserves you.'

'He doesn't make it easy sometimes,' Clarke answered, her voice falling away. She noticed Rebus almost lose his balance, taking a step to correct it.

'It's an inner-ear thing,' he explained when he saw that she'd noticed. 'Doctor says it'll sort itself out.'

'Not that he's *been* to the doctor, you understand,' Samantha

114

announced. 'You can maybe try, I've given up. He gets chest pains, too.'

'Indigestion,' Rebus muttered. 'Couple of Rennies and I'm right as rain.'

'You're not, though,' Samantha chided him.

Clarke was checking the time on her phone. 'I'd best be off.'

'News?' Rebus demanded. She shook her head.

'Just tired,' she explained.

'Hard to believe he's not turned up yet.'

'We've looked all over. I want to request his phone records, but my DCI says I've insufficient grounds. How about you – any progress with Jack Oram?'

'Apparently he's in a smoky room playing hand after hand of poker with your guy.'

'I'll take that as a no.'

Rebus took a step closer. 'There's something I want to say. Coming from me, you'll probably burst out laughing, but I'm going to say it anyway.' He looked over towards his daughter and granddaughter. 'There's more to life than the job, Siobhan. When I think of the energy I put into it, usually at the expense of folk who should have been important to me . . .'

'Be a shame to lose them then,' Clarke replied. 'Go see a doctor, John.'

'Come on, angel,' Samantha was telling her daughter. 'Time to give Grandpa his freedom back.'

'I will,' Rebus told Clarke. For once, she almost believed him.

On her way home, she stopped at a pizza place, no cooking required. The parking gods were gentle with her and she found a space further along her street. She half expected Fox's Merc to be there, but it wasn't.

Inside her flat, she dumped her coat and bag and placed the pizza box on the kitchen worktop, sliding a couple of glistening slices onto a dinner plate. She thought of the break-in at Newhaven. Nobody looked twice at a food delivery. Any neighbour would have opened up, even after checking. She switched the TV on for company and got comfortable on the sofa. Good thing about a pizza was there'd be some left for breakfast. She would up the ante in the morning, make Haggard's disappearance public, whether her DCI agreed or not. Although his particulars had been issued to every cop working the beat, she wondered how hard they would try. Christine Esson probably had a point: he was one of their own, whatever he had done. Not all of them would think that way, but some definitely would. Those same cops would have been the type to turn a blind eye to Rebus and his ilk back in the day. Should she include herself in that group? Probably. She'd been warned what Rebus was like from the first day she'd worked with him.

'But he gets results,' was always the excuse.

If past sins were about to catch up with him, how would she handle that? Malcolm Fox would be watching for any sign of a cover-up. Could she protect Rebus, even if she wanted to?

After an hour or two's mindless TV, she considered closing her eyes and napping on the sofa, but knew she'd probably wake up in the middle of the night feeling like crap.

'You can do this,' she told herself as she swivelled her feet onto the floor.

She was in bed, dead to the world, when her phone started ringing.

Esson looked every bit as alert as Clarke felt, but had managed to conjure up two beakers, at least one of which contained coffee. Clarke accepted it with a grateful nod. Uniformed officers were constructing a cordon of blue-and-white tape. A scene-of-crime vehicle had arrived, finding a way through the roadworks and parked on the emerging tram line. Clarke recognised the man in charge, Haj Atwal, so knew things would be handled properly. Gawkers had appeared at the windows of the tenement across the street. Inside Haggard's building, neighbours were being ushered back behind their doors.

'Do we know who reported it?' Clarke asked Esson as they began to ascend the stairwell.

'Anonymous.'

'How anonymous?'

'Not very.' Meaning the switchboard had a record of the caller's number.

One of Haj's team was keeping guard on the second-floor landing. Clarke and Esson signed in and got suited up in protective overalls and shoe covers.

'Doctor been?' Clarke checked, receiving a nodded reply. Then, to Esson, 'Shall we?'

'After you, boss,' Christine Esson said.

Clarke paused in the hallway. Surfaces were being dusted, a

hand-held UV scanner checking for blood. Lowered voices were coming from the living room. Rather than interfering, Clarke and Esson stopped in the doorway. Clarke turned at a rustling sound behind them. Haj Atwal had returned.

'What can you tell us?' Clarke asked.

'Doctor estimates time of death at between seven and eleven p.m. Phone call was logged at eleven twenty. He's been stabbed. Twice in the back and once in the abdomen. Seems to have bled out right where he's lying.'

Clarke forced herself to focus on Francis Haggard's face. His eyes and mouth were open, tongue visible. The scene was vividly illuminated by the SOC team's own freestanding lamps. A photographer crouched down for a closer shot, obscuring the view. Blood had pooled around the body.

'A violent struggle?'

'No signs of defence wounds on the hands or arms. And as you can see, the furniture is pretty much where you'd expect to find it. One thing we've done is close the shutters. No curtains or blinds, and we didn't want anyone across the way being able to look in.'

'Means someone over there could well have seen something,' Esson commented. 'Were the lights on in here when the body was found?'

'Yes.'

'Immediate neighbours didn't hear shouting?' Clarke added.

'That's very much your department, Siobhan. We've not found the murder weapon as yet. I'd suggest a search team.'

'A knife, right?'

'Doctor reckons a fairly small blade. Centimetre and a half in width, at least eight centimetres long. Autopsy will tell us more.'

'If you wanted to chuck a knife,' Esson broke in, 'the tram works would be as good a place as any. Lots of nice deep holes.'

'Look on the bright side,' Atwal commented. 'MIT office is just around the corner. Couldn't be handier.'

MIT: Major Incident Team, who would gather whenever a serious enough crime took place. In Edinburgh, a suite of rooms had been set aside in Leith police station for use whenever the MIT needed it. Not even a five-minute walk. But it wasn't a given that Clarke and Esson would be chosen. Esson seemed to be reading Clarke's mind.

'They'd be mad not to.'

Clarke gave a slow, uncertain nod and began studying the living room again. 'We got the victim's phone and computer?'

'Yes to both,' one of the SOC team piped up from behind her mask and visor. 'Plus a second phone.'

'Probably the one he took from Stephanie Pelham,' Esson commented.

'Anything else of interest?' Clarke asked.

'There's a holdall in the bedroom,' Atwal answered. 'Half filled with clothes. I'm guessing he hadn't been living here long. Police uniform hanging up in the wardrobe along with a couple of nice suits. Bottles of vodka and tequila in a carrier bag on the worktop, fast-food containers in the fridge and the bin.' He paused. 'Oh, and some cannabis and cocaine.'

'Where?' Clarke asked.

'Bedside drawer for the cannabis, coffee table and bathroom sink for the coke.'

'Do we start talking to the neighbours or await further instructions?' Esson was asking Clarke.

'I reckon we won't have long to wait. All sorts of alarm bells are going to be ringing . . .' Clarke broke off, staring past Esson's shoulder. 'And speak of the devil . . .'

Esson turned her head and saw Malcolm Fox march into the flat, suited up like everyone else, eyes fixed on the figures in the doorway. He shared a nod of greeting with Haj Atwal, who then headed into the living room. Fox's gaze shifted to the body on the stripped wooden floor.

'Doesn't exactly help matters, does it?' he stated. 'There's at least one citizen journalist outside already, by the way, filming everything that happens.'

'And a murder victim in here who's now become our client,' Clarke replied. Then, 'You got here quick.'

'ACC phoned me. Soon as I heard the address, I knew who it would be.' He exhaled noisily.

'Christine and I know more about Francis Haggard than anyone, Malcolm. You need to make sure your boss is aware of that.'

Fox fixed her with a look. 'The T in MIT stands for Team, Siobhan. Egos left at the door and no room for hidden agendas.' He stopped when he saw she was about to erupt. 'Anyway, this is hardly the place . . .'

'You really don't want me outside the tent, Malcolm,' Clarke warned him, before setting off down the hallway.

'And don't forget to pick up your ego from the coat rack before you leave,' Esson added, following Clarke into the stairwell.

Stripped of their coverings, they exited to the busy pavement. A fair-sized crowd had gathered and was growing. Some held up phone cameras. Others were shuffling their feet to try and get warm. The shutters on the window of Haggard's flat were closed tight, just the thinnest blade of light visible.

'MIT wouldn't thank us for trampling all over their nice new shiny inquiry,' Esson commented. 'I reckon that means we can stand down till morning.' She had picked up the two drinks from the foot of the stairs. Clarke took a sip from hers.

'You reckon you'll sleep?' she asked.

'Whale-song app on my phone – it never fails.' Esson saw that Clarke was not to be appeased. 'Whatever happens, Siobhan, Fox can't just make it all go away, not now.'

'I wouldn't be so sure of that. Hence my crack about needing me inside the tent rather than out. He'll see it as a threat, and he'll want to keep a close eye.'

'Me rather than us?'

'That depends, doesn't it? Are you on my side or his?' Clarke watched Esson's face darken. 'This was your case before it was mine, Christine,' she said, her tone conciliatory. 'Fox knows that.'

'So we'll probably both be MIT tomorrow?'

'If Malcolm gets his way.'

'And will he?'

Clarke looked at her over the rim of her cup. 'In my experience, his sort inevitably do.'

Day Four

13

The text arrived at 6.53 a.m.

Leith police station, 0800 sharp. Sent from Malcolm Fox's telephone. Clarke checked that Christine Esson had received the same summons.

Yep. See you there.

Clarke parked her Astra next to Leith Links at quarter to eight and walked from there to Queen Charlotte Street. It struck her that she'd no idea who Queen Charlotte was or why a road in Leith had been named after her. The police station was situated in what had at one time been the town hall and sheriff court. The building was a couple of hundred years old and showing its age. An imposing staircase led up from ground level, but Clarke was unsurprised to see plastic buckets dotted about, ready to collect the rain that sometimes breached the leaky roof. She knew the MIT office, having worked a couple of cases there, and even dated her boss at the time. But he had moved north to Inverness and ceased communication. She wondered who would be in charge today.

'Anyone but Fox,' she prayed under her breath as she reached the top of the stairs.

She saw him immediately, standing at the far end of the corridor in quiet conversation with a woman Clarke didn't recognise. He beckoned for her to join them.

'This is DI Siobhan Clarke,' he said by way of introduction. 'Siobhan, this is DCI Katherine Trask.'

'But Kathy will do fine,' Trask said, shaking Clarke's hand.

Clarke had heard of her. 'From Stirling?'

'That's right.'

Trask was Clarke's height and a few years older. Her hair was black and shoulder-length, the lines around her eyes the only part of her face giving any real indication of her age.

'You've been working the domestic abuse case against Mr Haggard,' Trask continued. 'That makes you a valuable commodity.'

'Me and DC Christine Esson both,' Clarke corrected her.

'Well, any time either of you thinks there's something the rest of the team should know, don't be shy.'

'Understood.'

'And you're okay with the sudden turnaround? From offender to murder victim, I mean?'

'I think I'll be fine, but we can't forget that he was a seasoned abuser.'

'Yet,' Fox broke in, 'there's plenty of evidence that he regretted his past and was preparing to atone.'

'He was desperate, Malcolm,' Clarke snapped back at him. 'A bent and violent cop who was going to blow the whistle to avoid jail.'

Trask held up a hand, palm outwards. 'Can we maybe focus on *our* job, which is identifying and charging his murderer?' Her eyes were on Clarke, maybe having second thoughts about her selection.

'Of course.' Clarke tried to look contrite.

'Rest of the team should be here any minute,' Trask said. 'Neither of you is new to MIT, so you know the drill. Autopsy is scheduled for eleven thirty. We need to get uniforms organised to search for the weapon.'

'Victim's phone and computer?' Clarke asked.

'Undergoing forensic examination.'

'Stephanie Pelham can almost certainly ID the second phone found at the scene. Francis Haggard took it from her forcibly.'

'We'll get to that in good time, Siobhan,' Trask stated.

'If the victim's phone and computer are at Howdenhall,' Fox commented, 'be warned that they sometimes promise more than they deliver.'

'Then I'm making it your job to chivvy them, Malcolm.'

Trask broke off at the sound of footsteps on the stairs. Christine Esson was leading two other detectives towards the MIT office. They could have been mistaken for a tour group, the two new faces admiring the relative grandeur of their surroundings.

'Looks like we can get started,' Trask said, giving a slight tug of her buttoned jacket's hem, after which she was ready.

'There should be enough desk space,' she announced to the room at large as she strode in, leaving Clarke and Fox in her slipstream. 'I'll let you get acquainted and set up. Couple more faces still to join us, but they're currently stuck in traffic.' She walked to a door at the far side of the room and flung it open. 'Not the stationery cupboard but apparently my inner sanctum – lucky me. The door will stay open, mostly. If it's closed, there'll be a compelling reason.' She saw that Esson was over at the kettle, adding supplies from a carrier bag. 'Excellent show of initiative. Let's hope for more of that over the next few days and weeks. DI Fox here, on secondment from Gartcosh, will be doling out your various tasks – just as soon as I've told him what those tasks are.' She crooked a finger, signalling for Fox to join her in her cramped office.

Clarke walked over to Christine Esson. 'Has Malcolm been on to you at all?'

Esson started peeling the cellophane from a box of tea bags. 'How do you mean?'

'Just that some of the things he's saying about Haggard could have come straight from you.'

Esson had moved on to shaking the kettle, then peering into its depths as if to ascertain how long the contents had been sitting there.

'He has, hasn't he?' Clarke said.

'Does it matter?'

'I said last night, I need us to be on the same side, Christine.'

'We are, if you hadn't noticed.' Esson made a sweeping motion, taking in the whole office.

'So if it comes down to me versus Fox . . .?'

Esson was saved from answering by two more arrivals, both of them known quantities. Clarke was surprised to find that DS George Gamble had not yet quite retired. He was as stout and red-faced as ever, breathing heavily after surviving the flight of stairs. DS Tess Leighton could not have been more different, pale, tall and willowy, as if she shunned both sunshine and nourishment. They waved a greeting before approaching the DCI's doorway in order to introduce themselves. Meantime, the two faces new to Clarke were being drawn as if by a magnet to the vicinity of the kettle. They introduced themselves as DC Colin King and DC Jason Ritchie.

'It's Jason's first murder case,' King said. 'He's like a kid at Christmas.'

King was probably only two or three years Ritchie's senior, but he had about him the air of an older, wiser brother, a role Ritchie seemed happy enough to play along with. Both were sandy-haired, probably early to mid twenties. Ritchie's cheeks had a pink glow to them, making him appear even younger. He was wiry, while King was bulkier, his shirt straining over his stomach. Clarke and Esson introduced themselves in turn.

'Have you seen the *Courant*?' King asked, waving his phone. 'The murder's mentioned there already, including who the victim is.'

'Someone's been blabbing,' Christine Esson said.

'It's on Twitter, too,' Ritchie added.

'Not surprised,' King said. 'I mean, it's got everything, hasn't it?'

'I don't know, has it?' Clarke retorted icily.

King began holding up his fingers in turn. 'Cop turned abuser ... police station with a reputation ... victim related to tycoon experiencing messy and very public divorce ...' His voice tailed off as he saw the look Clarke was giving him.

'We're not here to entertain the public, Colin. Keep that at the front of your mind. Any journalists come sniffing – amateur or professional – you direct them to our media office.'

'Got it,' King said, reddening slightly.

'Do the mugs need a wash?' Ritchie blurted out, seeking an escape route.

'Sink is in the gents', end of the corridor,' Esson instructed, Ritchie nodding as he scooped up the chipped and tarnished crockery.

When he was gone, Clarke focused on King. 'Where are you usually based, Colin?'

'St Leonard's.'

'And this isn't your first MIT case?'

He shook his head, regaining some of his composure. 'DCI Trask must have been satisfied last time round.'

'You've worked with her before?' Clarke tried not to sound too interested. 'What's she like?'

'She's brilliant.'

Clarke nodded in apparent agreement. 'She's been a DCI for a while?'

'Five years, maybe a bit more.' King looked from Clarke to Esson, wondering where this was going. Clarke knew Esson was probably thinking the same.

'So is she stuck, do you think?'

'Stuck?'

'I mean, could she go further?'

'Siobhan's just playing with you,' Esson said, digging a finger into King's shoulder. 'We'll bring your tea over when it's ready.' He started walking back to his desk in obvious bemusement. Esson glowered at Clarke.

'See, here's the thing, Christine. Fox is already nice and cosy with her. If she wants further promotion, she needs the bosses on her side, and she knows who it is Fox ultimately reports to. Makes her more likely to listen to his theories and play by his version of events.'

'It's hour one of day one, Siobhan. You wanted to be here and here you are. What do you say we just try doing our job?'

Ritchie was coming back with the mugs. 'Clean as I could get them,' he apologised.

'In which case, we'll make do,' Esson told him, her eyes never leaving Clarke's.

King was approaching again, phone held out in front of him. 'Latest from the *Courant*,' he said.

Clarke took the phone from him, making sure Esson could see the screen. Most of it was filled with a grainy night-time photo, shot on a well-lit city street. She recognised Rob Driscoll, but not the man he was talking to.

'"Shortly before their banished colleague was killed in cold blood, Tynecastle's finest were enjoying a night on the bevvy at their usual clubhouse. A sign on the door of the pub's back room warned outsiders to steer well clear, but the mutterings from within didn't sound exactly celebratory – what could have been worrying them? And what might they have been planning to do about it?"'

She handed the phone back to King.

'Should I take it to the boss?' he asked.

'If a pat on the head's important to you,' Clarke answered. 'Otherwise, it's just a sideshow.'

He considered for a moment before stomping back to his desk.

'Important to rid them of all that puppyish enthusiasm,' Christine Esson commented. Then, to the waiting Ritchie, 'Kettle needs filling.'

Clarke meantime was exiting the room. She headed down the stairs and out into the crisp cold air. Tapped at her phone and pressed it to her ear.

127

'Thought I might be hearing from you,' Laura Smith said.

'I'm not a fan of one-way streets, Laura. How did you know where and when the Crew meets?'

'Would it shock you to learn that you're not the only member of Police Scotland who talks to me? Besides which, I thought it was common knowledge. They meet there regular as clockwork.'

'Who was the other man with Rob Driscoll?'

'You mean you've never bought a car from Alan Fleck? Big discounts for serving officers.'

'Why was he there?'

'You tell me.'

'Anything you find out, you need to let me know.'

'I assume you've been assigned a role? Who's in charge? Anyone I'll have heard of?'

'Media office will give you what you need.'

'Is that how we're playing it?'

'Until you give me good reason not to.'

'I told you, Siobhan, the more clicks I get, the more revenue.'

'It's not going to win you any friends at Tynecastle – you need to be careful, Laura.'

Clarke ended the call and stood for a moment breathing deeply. When she looked up at the first-floor windows, Malcolm Fox was staring down at her. She kept her face impassive, but she knew Fox would be wondering. Pocketing her phone, she headed back indoors.

Rebus heard the news from a fellow-dog walker who knew he was ex-CID.

'Something happening in Leith,' the man said while his dachshund exchanged greetings with Brillo. 'They've got Constitution Street cordoned off.'

The nod Rebus gave was impassive, but his mind was racing. He got Brillo back on his lead and marched him home, grabbed the keys to the Saab and set out. He parked on the edge of Leith Links – recognised Clarke's Astra parked half a dozen cars further along. He wasn't sure what he'd say to her, but he cut through to Constitution Street anyway. Sure enough, the pavement had been blocked by strands of tape marked *POLICE*. A cold-looking uniformed officer provided an extra disincentive to ghouls. Rebus smiled a greeting and slipped his lanyard around his neck.

'Meeting DI Clarke,' he announced. The officer checked the list he was holding.

'She's not here,' he said.

Which meant she was at Queen Charlotte Street, which in turn meant she had been recruited by the Major Incident Team.

'I'll take a look anyway,' Rebus said, running his fingers down the lanyard.

'All that bit of card tells me is that you're exempt from wearing a mask. Nice try, though.'

Rebus stared towards the doorstep where he'd had his run-in with Fox only two nights back. Looked like the SOCOs hadn't yet finished. A pair of them were having a dialogue, still wrapped in white protective suits and masks.

'Haj!' Rebus called out, giving a wave. Haj Atwal recognised him and walked towards the cordon.

'Hiya, John,' he said.

'Any chance I could have a word? Might have something useful for you.'

Atwal gave him a long, searching look, but eventually nodded him through, the uniform lifting the tape with obvious reluctance so Rebus could duck beneath it.

'How have you been keeping, John?' Atwal enquired.

'Never mind that. It's Francis Haggard, right?'

'Right.'

'I was here a couple of nights back with Siobhan Clarke. He wasn't home.'

'Would have been better for him if he'd kept it that way.'

'There was supposed to be surveillance on him.'

'They did what they could.'

'Busy times, eh?'

'Been a while since I had so many crime scenes flying at me. I'm almost nostalgic for lockdown.'

Rebus nodded his agreement. 'So tell me again, how was he killed?'

Atwal gave him a look. 'Something useful, you said?'

'Whatever got me past the cordon,' Rebus replied with a wink. The door to the tenement had been wedged open, and he walked in, Atwal at his heels.

'Crime scene, John. No place for a civilian.'

'So give me some overalls.' Rebus was already climbing the

stairs, gripping the banister for assistance. He paused at the first-floor landing, turning to face Atwal.

'Word to the wise, Haj – steer clear of COPD.'

'Get your breath back. Last thing I need is another body.' Atwal headed to the second floor and returned with a white suit for Rebus to wear. 'So what connects you to the victim?'

'He was a wife-beater, or whatever the term is these days.' Rebus started struggling into the overalls, Atwal helping. 'Siobhan had the bit between her teeth.'

'Which doesn't really answer my question.'

Rebus looked at him. 'Were you really expecting it to? Okay, how do I look?' He zipped the suit up.

'Just don't bend down or breathe out.'

'I could have you for body-shaming.'

'Why do I get the feeling this is going to come back to bite me?'

They climbed to the next storey, Rebus stopping at the doorway of the murder flat. 'Door's not been forced,' he commented.

'It was open a few inches when the first responders got here.'

'Did a neighbour call it in?' He watched Atwal shrug. 'How did he die?'

'Stabbed, bled out.'

'Somebody must have heard.'

'These flats are mostly rentals, not all of them occupied. Good solid walls, too.'

Rebus had entered the flat, pausing halfway down the corridor.

'Did you know him, John?'

'If I did, you really shouldn't have let me in.'

'You're telling me I'm better off not knowing?'

Rebus stood in the living room doorway. There wasn't much to see. If Haggard had been lying on a carpet, it had since been removed for analysis. The bloodstain on the wooden floor beneath was dark and large, but nothing a sander and some varnish couldn't do something with. Rebus's attention, however, was on the wallpaper. It covered only one wall – abstract squiggles and spirals against a silver background – the others painted pale mauve. He swallowed, his mouth suddenly dry.

'Has the weapon been found?' he asked, not really interested in the answer.

'Teams are out and about just now.'

'Who's leading the MIT?'

'No idea.'

130

'Could it be Siobhan?'

'Is there any reason you're asking me rather than her?'

'You're far more charming and approachable. Still traipsing down to Anfield for the occasional match?'

'I need to be getting back to work, John.'

'Hint taken. Thanks for the tour.' Rebus peered into the other rooms: galley-style kitchen, bathroom, three bedrooms. 'Bit excessive for one person, no?'

'I had the same thought. Plus the fixtures and furnishings are a cut above. Only oddity is that wallpaper in the living room. I saw that you noticed it too. Pretty antiquated, I'd say.'

'Anyone from the lettings agency been for a look?'

'Not as far as I know.'

'They will.' Rebus winked and shook Atwal's hand. 'Thanks again,' he said, turning to go.

But Atwal insisted on accompanying him to the ground floor, helping him remove his protective suit.

'I really am leaving,' Rebus assured him.

'I trust you implicitly, John,' Atwal answered, 'but all the same . . .'

As they stepped outside, they saw that an argument was taking place at the cordon. Rebus offered Atwal another wink. 'Told you,' he said.

Fraser Mackenzie recognised him and broke off from remonstrating with the officer on guard duty, pointing a finger at Rebus instead.

'How come *you* get to be that side of the tape? It's my bloody property!'

'The whole tenement?' Rebus asked.

'Two flats, but they're among my best.'

'Probably in demand, then?' He pretended to muse.

'Always.'

'Francis Haggard seemed to have acquired his at short notice.'

'It was available.'

'Lot of space for a single tenant. You knew he was police?'

'What does it matter?'

'Not only police, but suspended from duty and charged with slapping his wife about.'

Mackenzie tried to compose himself. 'I had no idea. And you still haven't answered my question.' He shifted focus to Haj Atwal. 'Surely the owner of the property is allowed to gain entry? To size up any redecoration that'll need doing.'

131

'You got off lightly, Mr Mackenzie,' Rebus answered. 'Shouldn't need much more than Tommy Oram and some elbow grease.' He lifted the tape and stepped to Mackenzie's side of it, resting his eyes on Atwal. 'Your choice if you let him through or not, Haj. I wouldn't.'

He strode off in the direction of Leith Links and his car. He hadn't got far when he heard Mackenzie behind him.

'What *are* you doing here? What has any of this got to do with Jack Oram?'

Rebus stopped and turned to face him. 'You tell me.'

'What is there to tell?'

'Do you often do favours for police officers, Mr Mackenzie? Or maybe just for ones based at Tynecastle? Is that something else you acquired from Cafferty?'

'I've no idea what you're talking about.'

'The flat you put Haggard in, it belonged to Cafferty before you, yes?'

'It was part of the original portfolio,' Mackenzie agreed.

Rebus had caught a glimpse of someone in the distance, over Mackenzie's shoulder. The man turned a corner and was gone while he was still trying to focus. Same build and hair as Cafferty's helper Andrew. Rebus brushed past Mackenzie and headed to the end of the street, but whoever it was had vanished. Now Mackenzie was coming towards him.

'Maybe a phone call to my lawyer will get me past that cordon,' he was saying. He had the device in his hand and was already dabbing at it with a finger.

'Interesting choice of decor,' Rebus said. 'The living room wallpaper, I mean.'

'Beth's department,' Mackenzie commented.

'Judging by the state of your office,' Rebus added, 'that's probably no bad thing.'

He was almost back at the Saab when he changed his mind and began walking towards Leith police station instead. He stood across the street from the building and took out his phone, wondering how much to tell Siobhan. His call wasn't answered, but thirty seconds later, a text arrived.

Bit busy here. I suppose you've heard.

Changes things a bit, Rebus messaged back. *Please tell me Fox isn't in charge.*

He had to wait only a few moments for her reply.

Not quite.

132

He wasn't sure he liked the sound of that. He decided he would try to catch up with her properly later in the day. Instead, as he walked to his car, he called Cafferty.

'News?' Cafferty barked when he answered.

'A question,' Rebus said.

'Fire away.'

'That photo on your table, the one showing a man in a living room . . .'

'Snooping behind my back, Strawman?'

Strawman – Cafferty's nickname for him. It usually meant Rebus had drilled into a nerve.

'It came in one of your own envelopes – MGC Lettings. Since sold to Fraser Mackenzie. The flat in the shot belongs to him, too. Very distinctive wallpaper.'

'So?'

'So why send it to you?'

'Who the hell knows?'

'Have you asked?'

'What's this all about?

'You've not heard about the murder on Constitution Street? In one of the flats run by QC Lettings? Rented out to the victim, who happened to be a cop?'

'Anyone we know?'

'In a manner of speaking. He's one of the Crew, or was until he was suspended from duty.'

'The abusive husband?'

'Looks to me like someone sent a picture of him to you, and now he's on a mortuary slab.'

'You sure it's him in the picture?'

'I dare say the inquiry team will want to check.'

'What the hell is this? You trying to stir up shit?'

'Where you're concerned, there's never a spoon far away.'

'This has got the square root of *nada* to do with me.'

'You might want to tell the inquiry that.' Rebus paused. 'So what have you done about it?'

'The photo? Not a damned thing.'

'Mind if I ask why?'

'I do mind, yes. You're not CID any longer, Strawman. I think sometimes you forget that.'

It took Rebus a moment to realise that Cafferty had rung off. Sitting in his Saab, he texted Clarke again.

133

The murder flat is owned by QC Lettings. I've had dealings with them about Jack Oram. Could there be a connection?

She called him back almost immediately.

'What sort of connection?' she demanded.

'As of right now, I've no idea. But there's something else.'

He heard her sigh. 'What?'

'Has to be done face to face, Siobhan.'

'Why?'

'Because it does.'

She considered for a moment. 'I can drop by the flat this evening.'

'Yes, you could. On the other hand, I can be with you inside of a minute. And back when I was working cases, we didn't let a gift horse go to waste.'

It took her a few moments to decide. 'I'll meet you at the front desk,' she said.

14

True to her word, she was waiting for him inside the police station's front door.

'MIT would have been daft not to bring you on board,' Rebus said. He gestured further into the station, but Clarke stood her ground.

'Something that needs saying face to face?' she nudged.

'What is it with everybody guarding their territory today?'

'What do you mean?' She rolled her eyes as the truth hit her. 'You went to the crime scene. Of course you did.'

'Which makes this your lucky day. It's the whole reason I've got something for you.'

'You don't get to do this, John. It was bad enough when you carried a badge. Number of times I had to lie through my teeth for you ...'

'Buyer's remorse, Siobhan?' He didn't sound completely unsympathetic.

'Just spit it out, will you?'

'I would if my throat wasn't parched. Blame the medication.'

She fixed him with a look before turning a hundred and eighty degrees, Rebus following as she unlocked the inner door.

'Same old Leith,' he said as he followed her upstairs.

'My boss isn't here right now, so let's keep this low-key, eh?'

'Your boss being ...?'

'DCI Katherine Trask.'

'Can't say I know the name. So where's she off to?'

'Autopsy. Took Fox with her. They're updating the fiscal after.'

'For which absence we are truly grateful.' Rebus broke off as he saw that Clarke had walked straight past the MIT door and was leading him towards an interview room. 'Really?' he queried.

'Really,' she confirmed, ushering him inside. 'Time to remember you've not been CID for a while.'

'Fair enough, I suppose.' He pulled out a chair and sat down. 'Okay if I take my coat off?'

'Fine.'

'And the tea?'

'I thought that was just a ruse?' She watched Rebus pull a blister pack of tablets from his pocket. 'Milk, no sugar?' she said.

'If it's not too much trouble.' He looked and sounded suddenly weary, shoulders slumped.

'I'll be right back.'

Rebus nodded slowly as he held the strip of tablets between both hands. Once she'd left, he counted to five, then opened the door, peering along the corridor. Clarke was marching out of the MIT room, carrying the empty kettle in the direction of the toilets. He stuffed the tablets back into his pocket, grabbed his jacket and made his escape.

'Gang's all here,' he said, making his entry. 'Christine, George, Tess . . .'

'Nice surprise, John,' Esson said, waving from her desk. 'We wondered who the mystery visitor was.'

'Who's missing?' Rebus asked, indicating the vacated desks.

'Couple of kids called King and Ritchie,' Tess Leighton answered. 'They're at Howdenhall. DCI's taken DI Fox to . . .'

'The mortuary,' Rebus said, nodding. 'Professor Quant doing the honours?'

'You and her still winching?' George Gamble said, his face almost a leer.

Rebus concentrated on Leighton. 'How about you and Fox?'

She shook her head, the blood rising to her neck.

'You're well shot of him,' Rebus told her. 'I see the diet's working, George.'

Gamble ran both hands down his distended stomach. 'A healthy appetite. *You've* shed some weight, though. Not cancer, is it?'

'I'm touched by your concern.'

All the time Rebus had been conversing, he had also been making a circuit of the room, taking in paperwork on desks and the notes and photos that were beginning to be placed on the murder wall.

'Anybody got a pic of the victim *in situ*?' he asked.

'Think Siobhan would want us to show you?' Esson lobbed back.

'Show you what?' Clarke herself enquired as she brought in the filled kettle. She froze when she saw Rebus, a low growl forming at the back of her throat.

'Whole team needs to hear what I've got to say,' Rebus explained. 'But before that, I need to see the victim's face.'

'Any particular reason?'

He was at her desk now, studying her computer screen. Having switched the kettle on, she shoved him aside and settled in her chair. Rebus headed across the room and made himself comfortable at the desk next to a closed door.

'DCI's office?' he speculated. 'Making this Fox's little acre of land?'

'How did you guess?' Leighton wanted to know.

'Malky's always going to want to be as close to the boss's arse as possible without a restraining order needing issued.'

'Milk, no sugar?' Esson checked, busying herself with mugs and tea bags.

'Nothing wrong with your memory,' Rebus replied.

A phone rang and Leighton answered.

'DS Leighton.' She listened for a moment, then rolled her eyes. 'All requests have to go through media liaison. There'll be a news conference later today. If you're on the list, you'll be welcome to attend.' She put the phone down. 'Another bloody citizen journalist,' she commented. 'Anybody with a keypad thinks they're Woodward and Bernstein.'

'Showing your age there, Tess,' Rebus said.

'Two words, John – Robert and Redford.'

'Even the proper journalists – the ones still left – are led by the rumour mill,' Esson said as she went about making their drinks. 'One or two voices online even saying cops like Tynecastle get the job done so where's the problem?'

'You were ahead of the curve there, John,' Gamble said with a chuckle.

'While we're waiting for the tea to brew,' Clarke interrupted, her voice stony, 'why not entertain us with a story, John?'

'If you insist.' Rebus leaned forward, resting his elbows on the desk. 'I happened to be visiting our old friend Morris Gerald Cafferty yesterday and I spotted a letter that had been sent to him. Actually, a printout of a photo rather than anything written. But it arrived in a branded envelope with the words MGC Lettings top left.'

'Cafferty's company as was,' Clarke said.

Rebus nodded. 'The photo looked like it was shot on a phone. It showed the profile of a man. He was standing in a room and behind him was some fairly distinctive wallpaper, identical to that found at the murder scene.'

'You visited the locus?' Leighton asked.

'Let's not go there,' Clarke warned her. Then, turning to Rebus, 'You're saying it's Francis Haggard in the photo?'

'I can't be certain, Siobhan. You've seen him recently, not me.'

Clarke took the hint and summoned him over. Esson handed them a mug of tea each while Leighton retrieved two more for her and Gamble. On Clarke's screen was a shot of the murder scene. As Rebus watched over her shoulder, she found one from close range and zoomed in. Rebus studied the face, not that he really needed to.

'I'm pretty sure,' he said.

'So why was Cafferty sent a photo of Francis Haggard?' Esson asked.

'And who sent it to him?' Leighton added.

'If only there were detectives in the room who could establish answers to these excellent questions,' Rebus said, taking a slurp of tea and heading back to Fox's desk.

'What were you doing at Cafferty's?' Esson asked.

'I pick up his pension from the post office.'

'Really, though?' she persisted.

Rebus glanced in Clarke's direction. She didn't seem in the least bit surprised when all he did was offer a shrug.

'Does Cafferty know you know?' she asked.

'Might have slipped out in passing,' Rebus admitted.

'Bang goes any element of surprise.' She paused. 'It's him, isn't it? Cafferty? He's got you looking for Jack Oram?'

'Who Cafferty says was seen in the vicinity of the QC Lettings office and whose son just happens to work for them,' Rebus said.

'Hang on,' Gamble broke in. 'I know that name – Cafferty had him topped four or five years back.'

'Turns out not to be the case,' Rebus enlightened him. 'Jack Oram was living and breathing right here in Edinburgh three weeks ago. And by the way, the guy who owns QC Lettings, Fraser Mackenzie, was trying to get past the cordon earlier so he could check his property. Haggard was renting one of the best flats on the company's books.'

'Food for thought,' George Gamble concluded, drumming his fingers against his shirt front.

Clarke checked a text that had just arrived. 'On their way back from the fiscal's office,' she announced to the room. Her eyes fixed on Rebus.

'Time to skedaddle, eh?' he said. 'Thanks for the tea, Christine. Keep practising.' He rose to his feet, Clarke following him from the room.

'What do you think it all means?' she asked once they were out of earshot. He pursed his lips and shook his head. 'Jack Oram,' she persisted. 'What is it Cafferty wants with him exactly?'

'I thought I had half an idea, but now I'm not so sure,' Rebus confessed.

'What is it you thought you knew?'

'He said he wanted to say sorry for making the guy's life hell.'

'Doesn't sound like Cafferty.'

'A tick-box exercise so he can show St Peter he's tried his best.'

'That's the version he wants to sell you – are you still in the market?'

'I'm thinking there has to be more to it.'

'So are you sticking with it to track down Oram or to get to the bottom of why Cafferty asked in the first place?'

'You're not as daft as you look, are you?'

'I have my moments. So Jack Oram connects to QC Lettings through his son – which is why you had me run a check on him?'

'That's about the size of it.'

'And where does Francis Haggard fit in?'

'Right now, I'm not sure he does.'

She stopped in front of him. 'You know what I'm going to say next?'

'I need to leave it to the professionals, not get involved, not take a stick to any wasps' nests?'

'I knew I could save my breath, just as I know you won't pay any heed. But John – just ca' canny, eh?'

'How do you think I've lived so long?'

'Sometimes I think the answer to that is a vast amount of sheer bloody luck.' She dug her phone out, opened a page, and held the screen towards him. 'Taken last night, outside a bar in Fountain-bridge. This is one reason why we're fielding so many calls. I'm assuming you'll know both faces.'

'I know them,' Rebus said, scanning the accompanying paragraph. 'Let's catch up for a drink later if you've got time.'

'There's a line in the sand, John, remember that. I'm the cop here, not you.'

'I don't know why people feel the need to keep reminding me.'

'Don't you?'

He gave her a parade-ground salute as he headed back down the staircase.

As Elizabeth Mackenzie turned into her street in Cramond, she reached down towards the storage area below the central console, her fingers picking out the little black box that opened her gates. When she looked up, however, a car was parked across her driveway, blocking entry. She stopped in front of it, knowing better than to get out. Instead, she watched as a tall young man emerged from the driver's side. He wore an unthreatening demeanour and casual clothes, and approached as if their meeting like this was the most natural thing in the world, leaning down so his face was level with hers. Then he tried the door handle, but she had already engaged the locks. He gestured for her to lower the window. Eventually she slid it down a couple of centimetres, nothing like enough for an arm to reach in and grab her.

'Mrs Mackenzie?' he enquired politely.

'What do you want?'

'Mr Cafferty would like a word.'

She relaxed a little. 'He can have several. I'm just not sure he'd want to hear them.'

'You'll appreciate that he's not as able to get out and about as he once was, so I said I'd bring you to him.'

'And how do you plan to do that?'

'By being courteous?' The smile slipped from his face. 'At least to start with.'

Elizabeth Mackenzie narrowed her eyes. 'I know who you are now. You used to work for Darryl Christie. When he got put away, you sold yourself to a man he loathes.' She moved her face closer to the glass. 'Does Darryl know you belong to Cafferty now? I hear he's pretty well informed for a man spending life behind bars. Andy – that's your name, right?'

'Andrew,' he corrected her.

'Is that because you're all grown up these days?' She shaped her lipsticked mouth into a pout.

'Mr Cafferty only needs five minutes of your time,' Andrew persisted.

'Then tell him to call me.'

'He'd rather meet.'

'Are you going to move that heap of junk?' She gestured towards the car blocking the gates.

'Only once you're in the passenger seat.'

'We're going to be here a while then.' She heard the noise of an approaching vehicle and glanced into her rear-view mirror. 'Or maybe not,' she said with a smile.

The Range Rover pulled to a halt behind her, her daughter emerging from the passenger seat. A couple of seconds later, the driver climbed out. He was broad-shouldered and shaven-headed, and he examined the man in front of him the way a predator would its prey, alert to any weakness.

'What's going on?' Gaby Mackenzie asked. She was a good foot shorter than the man who was now backing away from her mother's car, his eyes on her companion, who was moving with seemingly infinite slowness towards him, hands clenching and unclenching in anticipation. Elizabeth Mackenzie unlocked her door and stepped out.

'It's fine, C,' she said, causing the shaven-headed man to pause. All three of them watched Andrew retreat into his car and reverse it onto the roadway. He didn't give them so much as a glance as he drove away.

'Mum?' Gaby asked, brow furrowed.

'It's nothing,' Elizabeth Mackenzie answered.

'Oh, it's definitely something.'

She touched her daughter's cheek. 'Let's keep it between us for now, eh? No telling your father.' She got back into her car, clicked the button, and waited for the gates to do their thing.

'I know him,' the man called C told Gaby Mackenzie as he stared along the road. 'I've seen him around.'

'Who is he?'

'I'm not sure.'

'Can you find out?' She stared at him intently as he slowly nodded.

'Good,' she said, striding back to the car and climbing in.

*

141

Rebus had tucked the Saab in between two anonymous grey vans in the mortuary car park. Staff joked that the building was sited in the dead centre of Edinburgh, and they weren't far wrong. Cowgate was central and yet easy to ignore, being a canyon over which both South Bridge and George IV Bridge passed, the mortuary itself an anonymous modern slab flanked by clubs and pubs. No one staggering late at night from any of these establishments could know that so many corpses lay in chilled stillness close by. The older Rebus got, the less he relished being in its vicinity. He was starting to think he might have to head inside when the staff door opened, Deborah Quant rummaging in her bag for her Lexus key fob.

Bingo.

'Fancy seeing you here,' he said, climbing out of his car. She'd had her red hair cut short since they'd last met, a drink at a wine bar where she'd told him there was someone else in her life. 'The new style suits you,' he added, nodding towards her head.

'Fresh start all round,' she replied, checking the time on her phone. 'I've got a class to teach, John.'

'I'll get to the point then: I miss you a lot.' He paused. 'And I'm wondering how the Francis Haggard post-mortem went.'

She stared at him in silence as cars crawled past on Cowgate, some of them about to learn that access to Grassmarket had been blocked to allow Richard Branson to build a new hotel.

'You're unbelievable,' she eventually stated. 'How many years is it now since you left the force?'

'I'm a private eye these days, though.'

'A private eye?' She was trying not to smile. 'Working for who? The widow?' She watched him shake his head. 'You know I can't tell you anything, John. It would be unprofessional.'

'I know he was stabbed, so that's the cause of death established, but was there anything else? Did he defend himself? Were there bruises? Was he even conscious when it happened?'

It took her a moment to decide to throw him a scrap. 'There was a lot of alcohol in his system, lager and tequila mostly. As far as I know, no empty cans or beer bottles were found in the flat. There was one tequila bottle, mostly finished, only the victim's fingerprints on it. He wasn't a complete philistine, though – there was orange juice in both his fridge and his stomach.'

'So the lager had been consumed elsewhere? A pub, maybe?'

'Or a friend's house. He hadn't eaten at all that day, though.'

'Nothing?'

Quant shook her head. 'Then there were the narcotics in his system – cocaine and hash.'

'What do you make of the stab wounds?'

'Don't get greedy, John.' She opened her car and slung her bag in.

'I'm serious, you know. I do miss you.'

'We still speak on the phone.'

'I get the feeling that's just so you can reassure yourself I'm not yet ready to end up in one of these.' Rebus slapped the side of the nearest van.

'I'd be grateful if you kept it that way. Bye, John.' She leaned towards him, pecking his cheek.

'Bye, Debs,' he said, watching her reverse out of her space and drive off.

15

Driscoll and Agnew knew the officer manning the cordon. There were a couple of ghouls on the opposite pavement, and Driscoll gave each of them a hard stare, as though committing their faces to memory. Neither tried snapping a photo. If they had, he'd have pounced. The uniform on guard duty was getting his clipboard ready. There was a list of visitors there. Agnew placed a meaty paw on it.

'We don't need to bother with that,' he said.

'It's procedure,' the officer managed to blurt out.

'Not necessary, okay?'

Driscoll wrenched the clipboard from the officer's hand and studied the names. 'Anyone in there just now?' he enquired, receiving a shake of the head in answer. 'How about the flat – is it locked tight?'

The officer dug keys from his pocket and handed them over.

'Good lad,' Driscoll said. 'Where do you normally drink?'

'The Starbank.'

'Nice place. There'll be a few in the tap for you next time you visit. Our treat.' He turned away, but then stopped. 'Starbank's not far from where Francis lived – he ever come in?'

'Not that I know of.'

'Fine,' Driscoll said, filing the information away. He walked to the tenement's main door, unlocked it, and held it open for Agnew.

'Remind me what we're doing here,' Agnew said in a lowered voice.

'Don't tell me you're not interested?'

'Just feels a bit creepy.'

'Afraid he's going to fly through the walls at you and say boo?' Driscoll started climbing, Agnew a few steps behind. Their blood was pumping by the time they reached Haggard's landing. Driscoll unlocked the door to the flat and stepped inside. 'In you come then,' he said.

'Is this by way of a punishment, Rob? For Newhaven, I mean?'

'There's nothing to be scared of, Chris.' Driscoll walked into the living room and stared at the floor. 'We're just paying our respects to one of our own.'

He could sense that a death had taken place here. The whole aura had changed. It was the same out on the stairwell. He reckoned a few flats might end up going on the market, neighbours not happy sharing their lives with a news story. The room was freezing, the heating switched off – probably the landlord's doing, eager to save a few quid. The floorboards creaked under his weight, and he thought about the downstairs neighbours. Had they heard anything? A body dropping to the ground, perhaps? Well, this was Edinburgh; nobody wanted trouble or to make a fuss. The shutters had been closed across the large window, deepening the gloom. Had they been open the night Francis had died? The building across the street looked lived in, making for yet more potential witnesses. He'd not bothered trying to access the statements gathered so far, knowing how it would look to the MIT if he were rumbled.

Interviews with the Crew would be in the offing, of course. Stories would need to be got straight.

His phone was vibrating, so he lifted it to his face.

'I have to take this,' he said, heading for the landing. 'You stay here, maybe say a few words.'

'Like what?'

Driscoll closed the door after him, pressing the phone to his ear as he descended half a flight. He took up a position that would alert him if Agnew emerged from the flat.

'What's up, Alan?' he said.

'You tell me, son. What the hell have you gone and done?'

'Absolutely bloody nothing. How about you?'

'That's not the tone you should be using, Rob. I'm not the one Francis texted shortly before his demise – think MIT won't pick up on that?'

'Everything deleted, like you said.'

'Just because it's gone from your phone doesn't mean it's gone from Francis's. We need another pow-wow.'

145

'After getting papped at the last one?'

'If I ever get my hands on whoever did that . . .' Driscoll heard Fleck expel a breath.

'Let's leave the pow-wow one more day, wait to see if they come for us.'

'Oh, they're coming for you.'

'Not "you", Alan, *us*. You need to understand that.'

'This is why we need a meeting. Has to be somewhere new, though.'

'Why? I reckon the cat's out of the bag there. Another photo would be stale news. Besides, we don't have anything to hide, do we?'

'I know I don't.'

'Unlike our anonymous blogger.'

'Can we find out who it is?'

'I'm working on it.'

Fleck seemed to calm. 'You at work?'

'In the office, aye.' He checked that Agnew was still out of earshot.

'Meet tomorrow, then?'

'Same time, same place. Maybe I'll send the *Courant* an invite. Set a trap and ID them.'

'Not the worst idea you've ever had.'

'Not that you know of.' Driscoll managed the trace of a smile. Downstairs, a buzzer sounded, meaning one of the flats had unlocked the door to someone outside. The door clicked open, then clattered shut again.

'You sure you're at—'

Driscoll ended the call and listened as heavy footsteps started coming up the stairs. He could see a man's hand on the banister, but nothing else until Malcolm Fox reached the landing below. Spotting Driscoll, he offered a brief nod.

'Funny, that,' he said as he continued to climb. 'Officer outside doesn't have you listed. Doesn't have a key, either, though he should have. Had to get a neighbour to buzz me in. Remember me, Rob?'

'More's the pity.'

Fox had stopped a couple of steps shy of Driscoll. 'I'd ask what you're doing here, but you'd only give me some pish in return. We both know, though.'

'Do we?'

'Well, if I were in your shoes, I'd probably be fretting just a tad.'

'You're not Complaints any more, are you?'

'Moved up a rung to SCD, and now on secondment to the Francis Haggard inquiry – I don't need to tell you why.' Fox climbed another step. 'Police corruption, Rob. It taints us all. Vast majority of the force wants the stables cleaned, even if they're too scared to say so out loud. So here I am with a pail and shovel. But here's the thing – my bosses reckon your pal got himself killed because of something he was about to tell us. That puts your whole station under suspicion. Any scandal, it has to be managed – that's my role here.'

Above them, a door opened, Chris Agnew peering down.

'Join us, why don't you?' Fox called up, before refocusing his attention on Driscoll. 'The crap will end up in that pail, Rob – maybe not all of it, but enough to keep my bosses satisfied. Could be officers like yourselves,' he gestured towards Agnew, who had appeared at Driscoll's shoulder, 'could be a previous vintage. I'm not fussed, to be honest, but you probably should be. Bit of chat between us, and your conscience would be clear. I'm at the end of a phone when you want me. Now, I'm just going to reacquaint myself with the locus. If you give me the keys, I'll lock up after.' He held out his hand, and Driscoll dropped the keys into his palm.

'No grasses at Tynie,' Driscoll stated, jaw jutting. Fox brushed past him and Agnew both.

'Sorry for your loss, by the way,' he said.

They watched the flat door close after him.

'More trouble?' Chris Agnew demanded.

'More trouble,' Rob Driscoll was forced to agree.

It was near-dark on the Meadows, especially away from the lamp-posts that lined the various footpaths. When Brillo went bounding up to a shadowy figure, it took Rebus a few seconds to realise it was Siobhan Clarke.

'I tried at the flat,' she said. 'Once upon a time, my second choice would have been the Oxford Bar.'

'A dog can ruin your social life.' Rebus watched her rub a hand along Brillo's eager back. 'But then so can CID.'

'Outside of work we're still friends, I hope,' Clarke said. 'But I have to be professional. If I'm not, then I'm nothing.'

'I get that. And I'm sorry for sneaking into the MIT office like that.'

'No, you're not.'

'No, I'm not,' Rebus confirmed.

Clarke took a deep breath and exhaled. 'Fox has started a list of everyone who could've known where Francis Haggard was holed up.'

'That's another circle round my name, then. But then Fox himself knew too – do we know how that came about?'

'When Haggard contacted the ACC, he added his address.'

Rebus nodded. 'Lettings agency will be on the list, of course. I wonder who else.'

'It'll all be gone into, John.'

'Murder weapon turned up yet?'

'Teams have been out all day – the length and breadth of Constitution Street, plus Leith Links. The contractors digging up the roads have told their workers to be on the alert.'

'Anything useful from the post-mortem?'

'He'd been drinking heavily, not eating.'

'Plenty vitamin C, though.'

She gave him a look. 'I might have guessed you would run straight to Deborah Quant.'

'Who was every bit as cagey as you. He'd been drinking elsewhere as well – pub or a mate's.'

'I don't get the sense he had many friends outside the force.'

'Well, I doubt he'd have found a welcome from anyone in the Crew, which makes it more likely he'd been to a pub or club.'

'We're putting word out.'

'And his phone and computer?'

'We're promised news tomorrow. I called Cafferty, by the way. That's why I'm here.'

'Well?'

'Denied ever receiving a photo or anything like it. He reckons you might be in the early stages of dementia. Hasn't seen you in weeks and says his PA will back him up on that.'

'Surprise, surprise.'

'He didn't seem too enamoured of QC Lettings, though. Reckons they'll rent a flat to anyone, up to and including bent cops. Not above using a bit of muscle when those same renters start to default.'

'As if Cafferty didn't do the selfsame thing when he was in the game.'

'He got me thinking, though, so I did a bit of digging. Turns out he dated Mrs Mackenzie for a time before she was whisked away by her current husband.'

Rebus angled his face skywards. 'Thought I recognised her from somewhere, that somewhere being Cafferty's arm.'

'This is going back twenty-odd years, mind, but it might explain the grudge.'

Rebus thought for a moment. He knew why Clarke sought him out like this sometimes: she needed both a sounding board for her own theories and someone who might spot what had so far been missed. But then other times, she produced a perfect nugget herself, a nugget such as Elizabeth Mackenzie. 'How's DCI Trask shaping up?' he asked, filling the silence while his synapses got to work.

'I've no complaints so far.'

'You mean she's not being unduly swayed by Malcolm Fox?'

'Something like that, despite him clinging to her like a limpet. Oh, nice work there, by the way.'

'What?'

'Fox's notebook – the cock and balls you doodled on it while seated at his desk. He thinks it was one of us, and telling him the truth would mean admitting we allowed you the freedom of MIT.'

'Simple pleasures, Siobhan. Has anyone listened to the 999 call?'

'Woman's voice, pretty shaken. Didn't give a name when asked. Just described what she'd seen and added the address, rang off straight after.'

'But there's a log of the number she rang from?'

'We've tried. No answer, but it's a man's voice asking the caller to leave a message. We'll get a name and address eventually, but it takes time.'

'So far it all sounds textbook, Siobhan. I suppose the widow will have to be questioned again. Far as we know, her and her sister were the last people to see him.'

'Caller wasn't a voice I recognised, if that's what you're asking.'

Rebus nodded. 'Are the media behaving themselves?'

'Just about. Though online is a pain. There was a press conference this afternoon. The DCI did fine.'

'When do you start pulling in Haggard's fellow officers?'

'Probably tomorrow. I'm assuming you'll warn your pal Fleck?'

'He's bound to know what's coming.'

'It's not going to go away, John. Whatever stories Haggard was planning to tell at his trial, they'll come out one way or another.'

'Things don't always, you know. People have gone to their graves taking their secrets with them.' He stooped and fastened Brillo's lead. 'Fancy coming back for some tea?'

She shook her head, stuffing her hands into her coat pockets. 'I should get back to the office. Might manage another couple of hours.' She locked her eyes onto his. 'Are you ready to face whatever's coming, John?'

'I'm like Billy Joel, Siobhan – an innocent man.'

'Haggard seemed to imply that plenty of those had been put in prison on his watch.'

'His watch, Siobhan, not mine. You parked outside the flat?'

'More or less.'

'Walk back with us, then. Here, you can take charge of Brillo.'

'What for?'

'It's what detectives do, isn't it? Follow leads?'

Clarke gave a groan, but she couldn't help grinning too. It felt like the first time she'd cracked a genuine smile all day.

'Mr Cafferty's up on the roof terrace,' Andrew told Rebus as he opened the door to him. Rebus nodded and made show of spreading his legs and arms, but Andrew shook his head. 'You're no longer perceived as a threat.'

'You might want to reconsider that,' Rebus said. Then, 'What were you doing down Constitution Street?'

'What do you mean?'

He affected a shrug. 'Thought I saw you there. Just wasn't sure if it was me or Fraser Mackenzie you were interested in.'

'I've no idea what you're talking about.'

'Must be a case of mistaken identity.' Rebus met the taller man's eyes. 'But if it *was* you and you were trying not to be seen, you need to sharpen up. Same goes for that stunt you and your boss pulled with DI Clarke and her team. Haven't seen me in weeks and reckon I must be going senile? I'm guessing the security cameras in the concierge office will tell a different story. If you're going to lie to a murder inquiry, it has to be watertight. Wee tip for you there.' He patted Andrew's shoulder. 'Now let's go see the cripple before he turns into Jack Nicholson at the end of *The Shining*.'

The roof terrace stretched the length and width of the building, hemmed in by waist-high glass panels and accessed by a glass-walled stairwell that had been fitted with a stairlift.

'Mr Cafferty says you can use it if you like,' Andrew commented as they passed the machine.

Rebus took each subsequent step with more determination. He patted his jacket pocket, making sure he had his inhaler, before stepping out onto the roof into something not far short of a gale. A few contemporary sculptures and a lot of potted plants had been added to the space. The plants looked lifeless, hunkered down until spring. Rebus was tempted to join them, but instead he zipped his jacket up to the chin and hid his hands inside the sleeves.

Cafferty was in a portable wheelchair rather than his electric. He sat at the very centre of the terrace. Rebus did a slow turn, the city and its rooftops spread out around him.

'Impressive, no?' Cafferty said. His mittened hands were pressed down against the tartan travel rug covering his lap and legs, stopping it from flying away. He wore a plain maroon beanie on his head and a scarf of the same colour around his neck. The only lighting was at floor level, so that his face remained largely in shadow.

'How many days a year can you come up here, though?' Rebus queried. 'Without the fear of hypothermia, I mean?'

'I told them there's no picture,' Cafferty stated, his eyes on the view eastwards towards the university and the dark hump of Arthur's Seat.

'I was just telling Andrew how stupid that was.'

'Maybe so, but I like my business to remain my business.'

'So you've worked out what the photo means?'

'Enquiries are ongoing, as you might say.' Cafferty's gaze drifted towards Andrew for a moment. Rebus looked too. Andrew had taken up position by the top of the stairs. He was a decent distance away, but Rebus reckoned he'd still be able to hear every word. Cafferty turned his attention back to Rebus. 'So what's got you so het up that we needed to meet?'

'Apart from my annoyance at you saying I've got dementia?'

'Ageing is a cruel process, no shame in starting to forget things.'

'One thing I did forget – but it came back to me – is that you and Elizabeth Mackenzie used to be an item.'

'For about five minutes.'

'A bit longer than that, I think. Then along comes the bold Fraser and sweeps her off her feet.'

'Water under the bridge.'

'Twenty years' worth of water.'

'Are you coming to a point any time soon?'

'You still sold the agency to him.'

'I've never let the personal get in the way of business. And I still don't see what it has to do with the little job I gave you.'

'No? When the first thing you handed me was QC Lettings?' Rebus made show of studying the vista again. 'City like this,' he said, 'things tend to connect, visible or not. You connect to Elizabeth Mackenzie, her daughter knows Jack Oram's son, Jack Oram connects back to you.'

Cafferty stared at him. 'Are you going to find Jack Oram or not? Seems to me you're sticking your nose into everything but.'

'If he's not done another runner, I'll find him. His son seems to think that's what happened.' He paused. 'But I'm not at all sure I'll hand him over to you.'

Cafferty stretched out a hand, palm up. 'Then give me back my money.'

'Why were you sent that photograph, Cafferty? And what are you doing about it?' He watched Cafferty shake his head. 'A cop killed in cold blood in a flat you used to own – a photo of the victim sent to you, either to taunt you or to alert you to where you could find him. No details, but a patch of wallpaper they knew you'd recognise. You had dozens, maybe even hundreds of flats on your books. Unlikely you'd remember all of them. Somehow you were expected to recall that one, though. And how about Francis Haggard himself? Don't tell me the two of you never met back in the days when you were passing weekly brown envelopes across to Tynecastle?'

Cafferty's face had grown stonier, his jaw clenched. He managed to loosen it, angling his head so he could make eye contact with Andrew.

'Take this bastard downstairs – and keep an eye on him until he's out the door. Then get your arse back here pronto so I can go indoors and start thawing out.'

Rebus stared at him a moment longer, knowing there'd be no more conversation. 'You're not getting that money back,' he said. 'And I'll keep on digging – to get the answers *I* want rather than whatever it is you're after.' He could sense Andrew standing behind him. 'Another hour or two up here and you'd be doing the world a favour,' he added.

In place of an answer, Andrew took him by the arm and started marshalling him towards the stairwell. As they passed through the living area, Rebus wrenched himself free and headed for the coffee table. He got there three seconds before his minder. The grip on his arm was tighter this time as it steered him to the front door. Rebus was content to let it happen. He'd seen what he'd expected to see.

Both the photograph and the envelope it had come in were gone.

Day Five

16

As Clarke entered the MIT office, she saw that Trask was hovering by her desk. When she spotted Clarke, the DCI stomped towards her, guiding her back into the corridor.

'You're late.'

'Maybe five minutes – I was here till almost ten last night.' Clarke saw that they were heading in the direction of the two interview rooms. 'What's going on?'

'Not enough space in my office,' Trask said, pulling open the door to IV2. Two men were seated within. Clarke recognised Fox, but not the other. They could have been cut from the same cloth, though. She knew Gartcosh when she saw it. The man she didn't know rose to his feet and offered his chair, there being only three in the room. But Trask waved his offer aside and nodded for Clarke to take the one remaining seat while she stayed on her feet.

'I'm Geoff Dickinson,' the man told Clarke by way of introduction. He was in his forties, well fed and with sleek salt-and-pepper hair. He looked to Clarke like a middle-ranking executive or politician.

'Serious and Organised Crime,' Trask explained.

Clarke wished she'd picked up a coffee en route. She had slept almost too deeply and still felt leaden. 'Busy enough these days?' she asked Dickinson.

'One hundred and twelve active criminal gangs currently working in Scotland, comprising around two and a half thousand members – what do you think?'

I think you've had a sense-of-humour bypass, she didn't quite say out loud.

'Malcolm here,' Trask explained, sounding not altogether happy about it, 'has been keeping ACC Lyon up to speed on the case, and she felt inclined to pass word on to Geoff.'

'That word being . . .?'

Dickinson's eyes met Clarke's again, as full of warmth as one of Deborah Quant's fridges. 'Mackenzie,' he stated.

'As in QC Lettings?'

'It transpires,' Trask said, folding her arms, 'that Fraser Mackenzie might do more than simply rent out some flats.'

'He's a drug dealer,' Fox added, loath to be left out of the conversation.

Dickinson cocked his head to one side. 'No hard evidence as yet, but we're getting there.'

Clarke tapped her chin with the knuckle of her thumb. 'I suppose Cafferty's health issues left a vacuum that needed filling. I spoke with him yesterday and he didn't sound like a fan of QC.'

'Spoke with him about what?' Fox asked, shifting in his chair.

'We had a tip-off,' Clarke improvised. 'A photo of Francis Haggard sent to Cafferty.'

'Sent why?'

Clarke shrugged. 'It showed Haggard at the murder scene some time before he died.' She paused. 'However, Cafferty denied receiving it.'

'You saw it, though?' Dickinson asked.

'No,' Clarke admitted.

Fox's eyes were drilling into her. 'Who tipped you off?'

Clarke, however, was keeping her attention on the visitor. 'QC Lettings used to be owned by Cafferty. You reckon he sold his dope empire to Mackenzie too?'

'There's no evidence of that.' Dickinson was checking the impeccable crease down his left trouser leg.

'Is it going to have any bearing on the murder investigation?' Clarke was looking to Trask for guidance. Trask in turn looked back at Dickinson.

'You might well turn something up in the course of your enquiries. If that happens, we'd like it brought to our attention. We've been gathering information for the past several months and don't want anything to jeopardise imminent or future proceedings.'

He talks like a textbook, Clarke thought. But at the same time, he had her hooked.

'We've managed to stop several big shipments arriving into the

UK,' Dickinson went on. 'And Brexit plus COVID have made it harder than ever to ship product anyway. That has led to constriction. We believe another delivery is due from the Continent, but right now, the harder drugs are proving difficult to source.'

'Hence the upsurge in antisocial behaviour,' Trask said, nodding to herself. 'Pharmacies attacked, people lashing out on the Royal Mile and elsewhere . . .'

'Of course,' Dickinson said, clearing his throat, 'there's no sign of a general breakdown of law and order.'

'If anyone asks, you mean?' Clarke enquired.

'If anyone asks,' he confirmed.

She thought for a moment. 'How does it work, though, Mackenzie's operation?'

'Many of his properties are rented to damaged people. I'd say that gives him a ready market. It's mostly mephedrone, MDMA and speed – the usual "party" drugs. A bit of crystal meth, too.'

'Plus coke and hash?' Clarke wanted to know.

'Plus coke and hash,' Dickinson agreed.

'We know Haggard was a user of both – does that make him one of Mackenzie's customers?'

'I can't say, but it's interesting that a police officer just happened to go to QC Lettings, isn't it?'

'And was immediately given one of Mackenzie's better properties,' Fox added, gaining a look of approval from Dickinson.

'Is that so?' he said.

'Definitely worth checking if Haggard was paying the market rate.'

'Let's not bungee-jump to conclusions,' Trask broke in. 'As of now, we don't know that this will have any bearing at all on our case.'

'It should also be noted that I'm telling you this in strictest confidence,' Dickinson added. 'Fewer people who know we've got eyes on Mackenzie the better.'

'But you've nothing so far linking him to any officers at Tynecastle police station?' Clarke asked. 'Haggard's name in particular hasn't come up?'

Dickinson considered the question for a moment before shaking his head. 'There is something else, though. One of Mackenzie's oldest friends is a man called James Pelham.'

'I've met him,' Clarke stated. 'He was Francis Haggard's brother-in-law until the separation.'

'Well, he's being investigated for furlough fraud,' Dickinson said. 'Says it's an accounting error, but I dare say HMRC will have a view on that in the fullness of time. None of which has stopped Mackenzie investing in a few of Pelham's recent projects.'

'You reckon he's using Pelham to launder money?'

'I'd say it's a racing certainty.' He brushed at his trousers again.

'Well, we appreciate you making the trip from Gartcosh,' Trask said, readying to bring the meeting to a close. 'And I'm sure Malcolm will keep you apprised of developments.' She almost managed to make it sound like a rebuke, not that Fox was really listening, being too busy assuring Dickinson with a nod that he would be only too happy to help. Clarke meantime was wondering if it meant anything that her question about Tynecastle and Haggard had led to a silent head-shake from Dickinson rather than a spoken denial.

As they left IV2, Clarke noticed that a couple of chairs had been produced from somewhere in the building. Seated on them, just outside IV1, were Stephanie Pelham and Gina Hendry. She told Trask and Fox that she'd catch them up, then watched as Fox began escorting Dickinson down the stairs, reluctant to let go of him just yet.

'Cheryl's giving her statement,' Hendry explained, nodding towards the interview room door. Stephanie Pelham looked pale and tired.

'You doing okay?' Clarke asked her.

'It's just such a bloody shock.'

'And Cheryl?'

Pelham puffed out her cheeks and expelled a blast of air.

'Cheryl's doing her best,' Hendry answered. 'But it's going to take time.'

'You know she had to identify the body?' Pelham said. 'I went with her, but I bottled it. Poor love had to do it all by herself. I keep thinking,' her voice rose shakily, 'should we maybe have been a bit more . . . I mean, if we'd let him stay, calmed him down . . .'

Hendry took one of her hands and gave it a squeeze.

'None of this is your fault, Stephanie,' Clarke said quietly. 'Nor is it Cheryl's.'

'Then why drag us here?'

'It's just a formality. You can get through it, the pair of you. Gina will keep you right.'

Hendry leaned forward a little, angling her head to get Pelham's attention. 'Tell DI Clarke what you told me, Stephanie.'

'It's nothing.'

Hendry turned towards Clarke. 'A few days back, we were chatting over a glass, talking fabrics and interiors, and Stephanie mentioned that she'd done a bit of work for QC Lettings. That's the company Francis was renting from, isn't it?'

'I just did a few of their more upmarket properties,' Pelham qualified.

'So you know the Mackenzies?' Clarke asked, glancing towards where Dickinson and Fox had been standing.

'My ex and Fraser go back a ways,' Pelham admitted. 'We used to wine and dine together, the same parties and charity bashes – you know how it is.' Clarke nodded so she would keep talking. 'Beth got me to do a bit of work on her house. That went well, so then she got the idea of adding a bit of value to some of the flats.'

'Including the one where Francis . . .'

She gave a vigorous shake of the head. 'I was busy elsewhere when that came up.'

'So Francis would have known the Mackenzies too, would he?' Clarke nudged.

'To talk to, yes, I suppose so. He wasn't one for black-tie events, though – or dinner parties, come to that, not unless they involved half a dozen of his pals from Tynecastle. Cheryl often had to come along on her own – on those rare occasions he'd let her out of his sight.' Pelham stared at the interview room door. 'What are they doing in there?'

'I'm sure she's being looked after,' Clarke said, gesturing to Hendry that she had to get back to work. Hendry offered a smile of thanks, while Pelham glanced down at the blank screen of her phone, which she was clutching in both hands as if it was a prayer book. 'We have your other phone, by the way,' Clarke informed her. 'We'll get it back to you soon.'

'Christ, no thanks.' Pelham gave a shudder. 'Everything I need from it I can transfer from the cloud.'

'I know you said it required facial recognition, but I assume there's a passcode too?'

'Cheryl's birthday.' Pelham was studying Clarke. 'Why?'

'The footage of the home invasion,' Clarke explained. 'It'll have audio, unlike the CCTV.'

'Fill your boots.'

She gave a little nod of thanks and walked the short distance back to MIT. Looking around the room, she was relieved to find that Tess Leighton and Christine Esson had been assigned IV1.

'Just the menfolk, eh?' she said, glancing through the doorway towards where the DCI sat at her desk, busy with a phone call. Jason Ritchie was making tea and waved a mug at her. She rewarded him with a thumbs-up. Colin King was on his phone while at the same time working his computer's trackpad. George Gamble, meantime, had slouched towards the shared printer and plucked a sheet of paper from it, wafting it in front of him as he began to approach Clarke's desk.

'Got a name and address for the phone's owner,' he crowed. 'It's not a woman, though.'

Clarke registered that he meant the source of the original 999 call. She took the sheet from him.

'Kenneth Lloyd,' she recited. 'Flat on Canongate.' She looked at Gamble.

'Probably the top floor,' he responded, his whole face wrinkling at the thought of the climb.

Malcolm Fox entered the room, looking pleased at having carved out some private time with Dickinson.

'Bit of proper police work for us,' Clarke said, handing him the address. Then, to Ritchie, 'I'll have that tea when we get back.'

As Clarke switched on the ignition, her phone synced and music blared out of the speakers. She scrabbled to turn it off.

'What in God's name was that?' Fox asked.

'Manics.' He looked at her. 'As in Street Preachers.' He looked none the wiser and she just shook her head.

They travelled in silence for a few minutes. 'Put it on again if you like,' Fox eventually said. Then, 'I thought you maybe wanted me along so you could give me a grilling.'

'Why would I want to do that?'

'Because you reckon I've a foot in two camps – Gartcosh and here.'

'And do you?'

'The ACC is obviously taking an interest.'

'And you're only too happy to help.'

He tried swivelling towards her, not easy in the cramped confines of the car. 'I think we're after the same result, Siobhan.'

'I'm not so sure.'

'I'd hate you to prove me wrong.'

She took her eyes off the road for a second to meet his stare. 'What do you mean?'

'Your little chat with Cafferty. First I'd heard of it was in that interview room.'

'Sorry for not reporting to you personally, Malcolm. Do you want updates just once a day or on the hour?'

Her tone told him to back off. He twisted in his seat and stared at the passing city. 'Geoff is a good guy. It was decent of him to brief us.'

'Under orders from ACC Lyon, I presume?' She watched Fox consider his response and then offer a brief nod. 'The stuff about Mackenzie and Pelham was interesting,' she conceded, watching as Fox reacted to a ping from his phone. He dug it out and studied the screen.

'Some right-wing news site,' he explained to her. 'They're having a dig at the *Courant*. "Maybe the heroes *are* the bad guys",' he recited.

'What does that mean?'

He read on. '"Sticking to the letter of the law means criminals go free. What we need right now are more Gene Hunts and less Sam Tylers."'

'They mean "fewer",' Clarke said, 'and maybe more subeditors.'

'I don't get the reference.'

'That TV show from a few years back, *Life on Mars*.'

'Never watched it.'

'Cop goes back in time and basically finds himself surrounded by the cast of *The Sweeney* – I'm assuming you used to watch that?'

'When I was a kid, sure. Never liked the way they did things.'

'You were born for Complaints, Malcolm.'

'Sometimes I think I was. Cops who go off piste are anything but heroes in my book.'

'Social media says otherwise.'

'Social media, as you well know, is a complete bear pit.'

'Is that why you get alerts every time a right-wing news site adds a story?'

'Know your enemy, Siobhan.'

'I can't work you out, Malcolm.' He looked at her. 'You come across as a mahoosive prick half the time, but the other half I sometimes find myself agreeing with and even almost liking you.'

'I wonder which half I need to work on.' He thought for a moment. 'The photo sent to Cafferty – what's that all about?'

163

'Beats me.'

'Where was I when this tip came in?'

'Swanning around town with the boss.'

'And Cafferty says it never happened?'

'Which means it definitely did.'

North Bridge was shut off to traffic heading north – long-standing repairs – but they were heading south. As she made to signal left onto Canongate itself, however, Clarke remembered that more repairs had blocked the road at the St Mary's Street junction. Cursing, she turned down Blackfriars Street, then left on Cowgate and left again, rejoining Canongate just past the roadworks.

'Glad you're driving,' Fox told her as he busied himself with his phone.

A few hardy tourists were out and about, gift shops reopened and ready to welcome them. The road was surfaced with setts, increasing the noise level in the Astra's cabin and giving Clarke and Fox an excuse to stop conversing. They were halfway to the Parliament building when Clarke pulled up onto the pavement and stopped the car. She reached under her seat for the sign that told the parking attendants police business was being undertaken.

'This where he lives?' Fox queried.

'Yes.'

'He works at the Parliament, though.' He turned his phone towards her, showing the results of his Google search.

'Tell me he's not an MSP,' Clarke muttered.

'Special adviser,' Fox elucidated. So they stayed in the car and Clarke phoned the parliament.

'Mr Lloyd?' she checked when the call was answered. 'I'm Detective Inspector Siobhan Clarke. I'd appreciate a few minutes of your time. In person if possible.' She listened for a moment. 'We're not far away, if that helps. Can we meet outside the main entrance? Saves the hassle of security . . .'

There was a car park alongside the Palace of Holyroodhouse, so they left the Astra there. For a change, no demonstrations were taking place outside the Parliament, and only a few people were around. The security guard at the entrance looked bored, and Clarke didn't blame him. The young man who appeared through the doors sported a trimmed beard, black-rimmed glasses and a checked shirt. Multiple lanyards swung from his neck, each holding a laminated pass of some kind.

'Mr Lloyd?' Clarke held up her warrant card.

'What's this about?'

'Two nights ago, your phone was used to make an emergency call. That phone has since gone missing, is that correct?'

'Not missing as such, she just didn't give it back to me.'

'"She" in this case being the person who actually made the call?'

Lloyd nodded. 'It's the murder, isn't it? You don't even have to answer, I saw it on the news.'

'Maybe we can rewind a bit,' Fox interrupted. 'Who is this woman?'

'I didn't catch her name. I mean, she must have told me, but I'd had a skinful.'

'So we're not talking about an acquaintance?'

'It was a party at a flat on the Shore. In Leith?'

'We know where the Shore is.'

'It all got fairly boisterous. Like we'd survived the apocalypse or something. I was dancing with her and then we were drinking in the kitchen and then we were . . . well . . .'

'You didn't take her back to your place, so I'm assuming you went to hers?'

'Sort of. I don't really know.' He saw that the two detectives were happy to wait in silence for him to clarify. 'She said she knew a flat we could use and it was walking distance, so off we went.'

'To Constitution Street?'

Lloyd nodded. 'When we got there, she unlocked one of those key box things and took the keys out, and that was us inside. I was chatting away – probably too much, knowing me – and then I noticed she wasn't there any more. She'd disappeared into one of the flats. I started to follow, but she burst out again, grabbed my phone, demanded to know the passcode, and started heading down the stairs like the devil was on her tail.'

'You didn't happen to look inside the flat?' Lloyd shook his head. 'And just so I'm clear, the flat she came out of wasn't your intended destination?'

Lloyd blinked a few times as he considered Clarke's question. 'I don't think so. I'm pretty sure we had one more flight to climb.'

'Okay, so you followed her back out onto the street?'

'Yes.'

'And?'

'And she was still running. Took me a few moments to work out what was happening. The main door had clicked shut, so I couldn't get back in. And she was disappearing round the corner with my bloody phone.'

'In your shoes, I'd probably have given chase,' Fox said. 'Not least because I'd imagine there might be security implications, with you being an adviser at the Parliament and everything.'

Lloyd looked chastened. 'Maybe if I hadn't been so drunk . . .' He rallied a little. 'I reckoned I could talk to the party host, get some contact details for her. But first I had to source a replacement phone, then today I had work . . .'

'The one thing you should have done was talk to us,' Clarke reprimanded him.

'I didn't think I had any real information.'

'Not your decision to make, sir,' Fox said coldly. 'You've just told us that at some point you realised you'd stumbled on a murder scene.'

They watched Lloyd give a little shiver. 'We need a description,' Clarke added.

'Of my phone?' Lloyd seemed puzzled.

'Of the woman you planned to have anonymous sex with,' Clarke corrected him.

'Christ, yes, of course.' He closed his eyes for a moment. 'Short, slim, dark hair cut in a spiky style. Red leather skirt, black top, black leather jacket, boots.'

'Age?'

'Mid twenties, maybe a little older.'

'Local accent?'

'Yes. Educated, I'd say.'

'Anything else?'

He shook his head. Clarke handed him a card. 'In case she gets in touch,' she said.

'How would she do that?' He saw the look on their faces and made show of slapping his head. 'She has my phone and passcode,' he answered, looking like the bright kid in class who's suddenly been found wanting.

One phone call got Rebus the address he needed. Laura Smith was a reporter who used to be her newspaper's crime correspondent but now, as she told him, was doing general and local news as well. Cutbacks, she'd explained with a sigh, seeming to perk up when Rebus asked if she could get him a home address for Fraser Mackenzie.

'Something cooking, John?'

'If there is, you'll be the first person invited to the table.'

Her text had arrived ten minutes later. An address in Cramond. Rebus took Brillo with him, in case he needed to pose as a man walking his dog.

Cramond Village boasted a harbour and waterfront walks, but Cramond itself blended in with neighbouring Barnton. The Mackenzies lived on a wide street of large detached Edwardian houses, the very definition of Edinburgh des res. As Rebus approached the address, he caught sight of a small red sports car pulling out of the driveway ahead, two women in the front. He recognised Elizabeth Mackenzie and reckoned the younger passenger must be her daughter. He did a three-point turn and began to follow as they headed for Ferry Road, soon signalling to turn into a car park belonging to a gym and health club. As he stopped kerbside, he saw both women emerge, toting brightly coloured backpacks and rolled-up yoga mats. After a brief exchange the daughter headed inside, her mother lingering in order to spark up a cigarette. Despite the slate-grey sky, she wore large sunglasses and a short jacket that prized fashion over practicality. Leaving Brillo to peer through the window, Rebus got out of the Saab and headed towards her.

'Mrs Mackenzie?' he said. 'My name's John Rebus.'

'I know who you are. I saw you at the office that day, asked Fraser about you when he got home.' She narrowed her eyes behind the billowing smoke.

'And I know *you* from when you were going out with Big Ger Cafferty. I was CID back then.'

'He sometimes mentioned you – never in hugely flattering terms.'

'I'll take that as a compliment.'

'You're looking for someone, Fraser said.'

'Jack Oram. One of Cafferty's associates.'

'Well after my time.'

'You know who he is, though?'

'Tommy's father. Gaby told me.'

'Your daughter?' Rebus gestured towards the gym door.

'Who'll be waiting for me in the changing room.' She studied what remained of her cigarette.

'She and Tommy are friends, eh?'

'Not the way you seem to be suggesting.'

'Must have been weird, taking him on.'

'Why?'

'Big Ger having done away with his dad – that's what a lot of people reckon happened. And QC used to be Big Ger's business.' Rebus paused in case she had anything to say, but she was managing to look increasingly bored. 'Ever see him these days?'

'Big Ger? Not in years.'

'So you've not been in contact with him? Sent him anything?' Rebus watched as she shook her head. 'Not even a Get Well Soon card after the shooting?'

She slid her sunglasses down her nose with her free hand and looked at him over the rims, her eyes vividly blue. 'You think Jack Oram's still alive?' she asked.

'Witnesses confirm it.'

'I can see how that might make you want to talk to Tommy, but I don't see what my family's got to do with any of it.'

'Jack was seen entering or leaving your office.'

'And both Fraser and Marion told you you've been misinformed.' She granted him a smile that had had all possible warmth removed from it. 'Big Ger always called you thrawn. Said even when you were wrong about something, you just kept ploughing away.'

'You'd be amazed at what even a rusty plough can turn up.'

The smile evaporated as she stubbed out the remains of her cigarette under the toe of her shoe. 'Time for me to go get supple. People should look after themselves, don't you think?' Her eyes took him in, from top to bottom and back again. With her sunglasses back in place, she pushed open the door and went inside. Rebus caught the scent of eucalyptus as the door closed. He realised he'd been sucking in his gut throughout the meeting.

'Really, John? At your age?' he chided himself as he walked back to the car.

Having not yet given Brillo his promised walk, he took him to Bruntsfield Links before depositing him in the flat. Then it was back in the Saab and Lasswade Road. He parked close to the QC Lettings office and waited. At 12.30 on the dot, he watched Marion step out, locking the door after her. There was a row of shops across the street, and she headed in that direction. Some workmen were milling about on the pavement next to their van, eating hot pastries from paper bags. Marion squeezed between the van and a white car with tinted windows, emerging from the bakery a couple of minutes later clutching a beaker of soup and a white bag of her own. As she crossed the road, Rebus got out of the Saab. She saw him and her face tightened.

'Just a quick question,' he said to her back as she got the office keys out of her handbag.

'You promised me I'd heard the last of you.'

'Circumstances have changed.'

'Nevertheless.'

'I promise I'll do better in future.'

'It's my lunch break.'

'Mine too, which is why I'll be quick.'

She gave a theatrical sigh and turned sharply towards him. 'Well?' she snapped.

'There's a photocopier in the office, yes? I'm assuming it's shared?'

'It is.'

'Do you remember your boss – or anyone else, for that matter – printing out a photo? A man in profile, standing in a living room?'

'No. Now if you don't mind . . .' She had turned away from him again and was sliding the key into the lock.

'The photo was of Francis Haggard. He had just started renting a flat on Constitution Street. He was murdered there a couple of nights back.'

'I know. We're all in shock.'

'Someone took his photo and sent it out in an MGC Lettings envelope.'

'We threw those away years back.'

'All of them?'

'All of them. I dare say the old owner might have kept some for himself . . .' She was opening the door.

'Francis Haggard must have come here, yes? You'll vet every new client?'

She nodded.

'So you met him?'

'Just the once, very briefly.'

'He was here to see Fraser Mackenzie?' He watched her nod again.

'One question, you said – my soup's getting cold.'

'Did Fraser take him to see the flat? Someone must have?'

'I think it was Gaby. Gaby or Beth. Not for an inspection. He'd already made up his mind to take it, a month plus deposit paid up front. So it was just a courtesy really, a handing-over of the keys.'

'Gaby works for the firm?'

'If no one else is available to show a prospective client a property.'

'Does Tommy ever fulfil that role?'

'Tommy?' She sounded almost aghast. 'Repairs and maintenance are all he contributes.'

'Did anything need doing at Constitution Street?'

'Something always needs doing in that building. But this was a premium let, fixtures and fittings in perfect order. Now if you'll excuse me . . .' She pushed open the door and made sure it was locked behind her. Rebus tapped on the glass, gaining her unenthusiastic attention. But all he wanted to do was offer her a mouthed thank-you for taking the trouble. Then he crossed the street, reckoning he deserved a pie, or maybe a bridie, with an extra one as a treat for Brillo. The workmen and their van were still there, but the white car had gone.

17

The cordon was still being controlled by an officer in a high-vis jacket. He took Clarke's name for his clipboard, but seemed to know Fox's, the two men sharing a look that Clarke couldn't quite read. Protective coverings were no longer needed, the scene-of-crime team having packed up and left. There'd been a stabbing in Gorgie, and Clarke reckoned that was where they'd be right now. She examined the key boxes fixed to the door jamb. Just the two of them, both locked tight. She unlocked the door using the key from the high-vis and started climbing, Fox right behind her. A postman passed them as he descended.

'Nothing for the flat you're interested in,' he commented. Clarke reached out a hand to stop him.

'Did you ever see the tenant?'

'No.'

'Did he get much mail?'

'Bills and flyers, same as everyone else.' He offered a shrug and continued on his way.

Rather than pause on the murder landing, Clarke and Fox hauled themselves up a further storey to the top floor. It was brighter up here, thanks to a large skylight. Just the two doors, one dark blue and the other yellow. Clarke rang the first bell, then crouched to peer through the letter box. From what she could see, the place was furnished, but without showing much sign that anyone actually lived there. The yellow door further along had no bell, just a traditional knocker. She tried it and stepped back. The door was opened by a woman in her seventies or eighties, a cat draped across her shoulders. A faint smell of litter box wafted out onto the landing. The cat's owner hadn't stinted with the make-up this morning – applied with more enthusiasm than skill – and was dressed in frilled, colourful layers.

'I've already given a statement,' she said in a refined Edinburgh accent. Clarke had a sudden image of girls' schools and spinster teachers.

'Just wanted to ask about next door,' Clarke said. 'It's a rental, yes?'

'I suppose so. Nobody seems to stay very long. Last couple of faces were tourists, I think.'

'Have you ever seen a young woman use it?'

'Not too tall,' Fox added. 'Slim, with dark spiky hair.'

'Sounds like the daughter.' She noted their lack of comprehension. 'The owners' daughter.'

'The owners being . . .'

'The Mackenzies – QC Lettings. Cheeky lot put a note through my door a while back asking if I was thinking of selling. But we like it here just fine, don't we, Horatio?' She gave the cat's forehead a stroke. 'Or we did until the tram works arrived.'

'How do you know the Mackenzies' daughter, if you don't mind me asking?'

'She shows tenants around.' She pursed her lips, and Clarke sensed there was more.

'And?' she prompted. It was all the encouragement the woman needed.

'Well, I'm not one to talk, but she sometimes uses that flat,' she nodded towards the door next to hers, 'or the one downstairs – you know, where *it* happened – when she needs to . . . let her hair down, shall we say.' She took a deep breath. 'I've never complained, though Mr Arbuthnot on the first floor has. Mind you, he's never *not* complaining about something.'

'His complaint in this instance being . . .'

'The front door banging at all hours. Loud music and whoops and squeals. You know, young people having a bit of fun. We were all that way at some time, weren't we?'

Clarke tried not to look at Fox. 'We were,' she confirmed.

'Did you know the victim at all?' Fox asked, shifting his feet.

'Never set eyes on him. Can't say I heard a peep either. Terrible thing to happen. You hear stories, but you never think . . . well . . .' The woman's hand went to her throat, as if to clutch at a string of pearls that weren't there. 'The officer who questioned me said he could arrange for someone to come and discuss home security with me.'

'That's certainly true,' Clarke confirmed. 'I can give you a number to call.'

'The other officer already provided me with one. Maybe I'll do something about it. I don't get many visitors these days, and we always have biscuits in the tin, don't we, Horatio?'

DCI Trask had gathered them in the MIT office for an update. The lab at Howdenhall had got into both Haggard's computer and his phone. His phone service provider had promised by day's end to have a list of calls sent and received.

'So even if he's deleted them from the device,' Fox added, 'they'll be visible.'

'Thank goodness you cleared that up for us, Malcolm,' Esson cooed.

'We're also checking,' Trask went on, 'how many keys there were for the flat. Apart from the one found in the victim's pocket, the answer seems to be at least two – both kept in a wall cabinet in Fraser Mackenzie's private office. Both have been accounted for, meaning the killer gained entry without a key.'

'Though keys can be put back after use, ma'am,' Jason Ritchie piped up, receiving a steely look for his troubles.

'Still,' Trask continued, 'the more likely scenario – by far the more likely – is that Haggard himself allowed his killer access, either by buzzing them in or by taking them home with him. We still don't know where he'd been doing his drinking, and I'm keen for us to get that timeline a lot clearer, so I hope you all like visiting bars and clubs. But do try not to get yourself papped coming out of too many of them.'

'Speaking of which,' King said, 'online media's getting pretty restless.'

'Malcolm's already flagged up that article from this morning,' Trask said, nodding. 'I dare say there's more to come. But here's the thing – we're not the Met, nothing like the Met. We do things differently up here. This inquiry gives us the opportunity to prove that.'

'You're saying we shouldn't bury bad news?' Clarke asked, trying to make it sound like an innocent question and managing not to look in Fox's direction.

'Correct,' Trask answered. 'Scrutinising Tynecastle and its officers – as we're about to do – might bring about changes for the better. We just need to maintain focus on doing the job ahead of us.' She scanned the room, checking that heads were nodding in agreement.

'What's the thinking on the murder weapon?' Tess Leighton asked, breaking off from writing in her notebook.

'I'd say the trail had gone cold if there had been any trail in the first place. No bloodstains on the stairwell or the handle of the main door. Knife had probably been pocketed, meaning bloodied clothing if nothing else. Communal bins have been checked.'

'Worth a dive team heading to the docks?' Gamble enquired.

'You volunteering, George?' Trask asked back, raising a much-needed smile from the room.

'Be honest, ma'am, you just want to see me in my parrot-smugglers.'

'They're called budgie-smugglers, George,' Leighton corrected him.

'I know what I'm talking about.' Gamble seemed pleased someone had taken the bait, and the smiles around the room became quiet groans. Trask didn't look put out by the moment of levity – it was sometimes needed, especially if a team was to feel like a team.

'On a more serious note, though,' she added, 'Siobhan and Malcolm think they've got our 999 caller.' She indicated for Clarke to take over. Fox insisted on joining her when she stepped forward, the two of them ending up flanking Trask.

'Gaby Mackenzie,' Clarke began, 'short for Gabrielle. Daughter of the owners of the lettings agency. She met a special adviser at a party in Leith, knew there was an empty company flat nearby so took him there.'

'We think,' Fox butted in, 'she noticed the door to the murder flat was open, knew it was owned by her father, so took a look. When she saw what was inside, she grabbed the spad's phone and called it in. Then she ran, taking his phone with her.'

'We got a description from the spad,' Clarke took over, 'and though fairly vague, it's a match for Gaby Mackenzie, who has been known to visit the tenement on occasion.'

'She's been summoned?' Trask checked.

'Should be here any minute,' Clarke confirmed with a glance at her phone.

'Progress of a sort,' Trask said, 'which is of course to be welcomed.

But let's not lose sight of everything else. We've got a police officer suspended from duty, charged with domestic abuse; he worked at Tynecastle and was about to tell a few tales out of school; he was a frequent drug user. Plenty avenues to follow, and hopefully not too many dead ends.'

'We're bringing in his fellow officers?' Gamble checked.

'We are,' Trask confirmed.

'All of them?'

'All of them. Phones and computers checked – anyone who refuses gets prioritised as a potential suspect. We need to know who he was in touch with, any online communities he was part of. But we can't just depend on his phone and computer for help. I know it won't be easy to convince his friends and colleagues to hand over evidence of their calls and texts to him, but we still need to try. He was active on Facebook, Twitter and Instagram, but I wouldn't mind knowing about any other use of social media.'

'There's also the break-in at the victim's home in Newhaven,' Christine Esson added. 'Our strong suspicion is that it was carried out by officers from Tynecastle in an attempt to warn him off talking to us.'

From the corner of her eye, Clarke sensed someone standing in the doorway. It was the officer from the front desk. He nodded in her direction.

'Looks like the daughter's on the premises,' she announced to Trask. 'If we can be excused, ma'am?'

Trask's gesture left Clarke and Fox in no doubt that they could.

Both interview rooms were empty, so they opted for IV1.

'Do I need a solicitor?' were the first words out of Gaby Mackenzie's mouth as she was ushered in by the desk officer.

'We're just gathering information,' Clarke said. 'You're not in trouble or anything.'

'Well,' Fox interjected, 'apart from the possible theft of a phone ...'

She winced as she sat down. 'I feel bad about that. If you have his details, I'll get it back to him.' She was indeed petite and slim, elbows and knees prominent. Her short tartan skirt led to fishnet tights and chunky-looking boots with extraneous straps and chrome buckles. Her eyebrows had been plucked to thin arcs, eyeshadow plentiful. The haircut was choppy and probably expensive. Clarke reckoned she was wearing the same zippered leather jacket Kenneth Lloyd had described.

'I'm sorry I didn't . . .' She left the apology unfinished.

'Why keep the call anonymous?' Clarke asked.

'Didn't want it getting back to the 'rents.'

'Your parents, you mean?'

'Right.'

'You didn't want them knowing you sometimes used their empty flats to entertain friends?'

The young woman shrugged, the gesture made awkward by the large headphones clamped around her neck. 'I don't suppose they'd mind, really, except of course that it would indicate their daughter has a fuller sex life than they might wish.'

'You work for the family firm?' Fox asked.

'Not really.'

'But now and again,' he went on, 'you show someone round if nobody else is available?'

'As a favour, yes. It's not like I'm on the payroll.'

'So what do you do at other times?'

'I'm a DJ.' If her chair had been of the swivel variety, she would have been rotating from side to side. She seemed to Clarke all barely contained energy and life force. A tattoo crept out from just below one cuff of her jacket. Clarke would take bets it didn't feel lonely. 'Ever go clubbing?' the young woman asked.

'Believe it or not, I sometimes do,' Clarke answered. 'I can't speak for DI Fox here.'

'Where do you go?'

'Cowgate mostly.'

'Might have danced to one of my sets, then. I call myself Gabz – with a z. DJ Gabz.'

'I'll look out for you next time.'

'I'm doing a set tonight. The Elemental Club on Blair Street.'

Fox cleared his throat, patently feeling sidelined. 'Did you snatch Kenneth Lloyd's phone for the same reason you didn't give your name to the switchboard – to try to remain anonymous, in other words?'

'Maybe. But actually I just think it was closest.'

'And you ran off with it because . . .'

She stared at him. 'I was freaked out. I'd just seen a dead body.'

'A body you recognised?' Fox persisted. She shook her head. 'You'd not been to the flat before? Maybe shown the victim round?' Another shake of the head, though she had stopped making eye contact and was busying herself with her jacket zip.

176

'You knew the flat belonged to your parents, though?' Clarke asked quietly, receiving a nod of agreement.

There was a tapping at the door. Clarke rose to answer. The desk officer was there, and he wasn't alone. Clarke recognised Michael Leckie, Francis Haggard's lawyer.

'I believe you have Gabrielle Mackenzie here,' he said. 'I've been asked to represent her. Can I see her, please?'

'We're just gathering information, Mr Leckie.'

'All the same.'

Their staring contest lasted a few seconds. 'Be my guest,' Clarke eventually conceded.

Leckie refused to meet her eyes as he brushed past. The desk officer just shrugged and retreated to the stairs. By the time Clarke went back in, Gaby Mackenzie was on her feet.

'But how?' she was yelling. 'I don't fucking believe this! How did she know?' She looked to the two detectives. 'Did you tell her?'

'Tell who what?' Clarke asked.

'My fucking mother, of course – that's who sent him here. But since I didn't tell anyone I was coming . . .' She broke off and picked up her phone from the table. 'Bloody tracker – that's what it is, isn't it?'

'Your parents just think,' the solicitor said, keeping his voice level, 'that proper representation might help you avoid falling into any traps.'

'No traps here, Mr Leckie,' Clarke said.

'Unless we're missing what they might be,' Fox added. 'Maybe you'd care to enlighten us?'

'It's merely precautionary,' Leckie said.

'We're done anyway,' Clarke said. 'Ms Mackenzie was just on her way out. A wasted journey for you, Mr Leckie.'

'But still probably costly for your clients, eh?' Fox added. 'Don't let him give you a lift home,' he advised Mackenzie. 'One of those tourist rickshaws would be cheaper.'

'What do I do about the phone?' Mackenzie asked, regaining her composure.

'Hand it in here when you can,' Clarke advised. 'We'll see it gets back to its owner.'

Mackenzie nodded, looking around to check if she'd forgotten anything.

'What about prints and DNA?' Fox was asking Clarke. 'Even if Gaby doesn't think she touched anything at the crime scene.'

'That's true,' Clarke said, keeping her focus on the young woman. 'A hair might have landed on the floor without you knowing, or maybe even a bit of saliva. I dare say you gasped when you saw the body. A quick dab and pluck would help to eliminate you.'

'Right now?'

She shook her head. 'We'd send someone to you.'

'To be discussed,' the lawyer said, holding up his hand.

'Best tell Gaby's parents we'll need samples from them too, assuming they've visited the flat in living memory. That goes for anyone else working at the agency.'

Leckie stared at the table's surface, listening intently as if memorising her words. 'Is that us done?' he enquired after she'd finished.

'Thanks for coming in, Gaby,' Clarke said, extending a hand for the young woman to shake. 'Some Boards of Canada will suit me fine if you ever spot me on the dance floor.'

'Not easy to dance to,' Mackenzie said with a flicker of a smile.

'Trust me, I know . . .'

Five minutes later, the desk officer was back again.

'Keeps you fit,' Clarke commented.

'He's wanting to see you downstairs.'

Her first thought was Rebus, but as she entered the reception area, she saw Michael Leckie waiting for her. He gestured towards the outside and she joined him on the pavement.

'What was that all about?' she asked.

'Overly protective parents?' He hazarded a guess.

'There were no traps, you know.'

He shrugged his acceptance. Clarke noticed him glance to left and right, as if wary of being seen.

'What's up, Michael?'

'You know I can't discuss Francis Haggard – client confidentiality and all that. You're working his murder, yes?'

'That's right.'

'So I suppose he's not really my client any longer. Thing is, it can't be official, Siobhan – any conversation you and I might have, I mean.'

'Understood. We could have a drink, though, couldn't we? Talk off the record?'

'We could do that, yes.'

'Always supposing neither of us had anything else keeping us busy this evening.'

'It might almost be an accidental meeting.'

'It might. Somewhere quiet where people keep themselves to themselves. How about the Oxford Bar?'

'I've only ever been there when the Six Nations is on.'

'Well there's no rugby tonight, and it's not long reopened – I reckon we could find a private corner. If not, we'll head elsewhere. Seven o'clock suit you?'

'Eight would be better.'

'I have plans later.'

'Seven it is, then.'

Clarke turned to head back inside, but paused. 'Did you put her in a cab?'

The lawyer shook his head. 'Range Rover sounded its horn and she got in. I could hear her arguing with the driver as it pulled away.'

'Mother at the wheel?'

'Father, I think. Big guy, shaved head.'

'See you at seven, Michael.'

'I look forward to it, Siobhan.'

The office felt more animated than when she'd left it. Fox was first to give her the news.

'The white coats at the lab got into the victim's phone,' he announced, leading her to the printer, which was churning out copies for everyone. 'Last text he sent was to Rob Driscoll.'

'His pal from Tynecastle.'

'Driscoll was after a meet, and Haggard agreed.'

Clarke looked at the transcript of the exchange. It was fairly one-sided, Driscoll asking eight or nine times for Haggard to talk to him, eventually eliciting a short reply:

I'll get back to you when I've had a think where.

Timed at 6.40 p.m. on Francis Haggard's last day alive.

'Nothing after that?' she checked.

'One further nudge from Driscoll.' Fox pointed it out to her. 'Sent just after midnight.'

'By which time Haggard was already dead?'

He nodded.

'Anything else?'

179

'A bunch of unanswered calls and texts to his wife, some of them from the hours after he burst into her sister's house.'

'Any chance we can find out where he was when he made them?'

'Phone company reckon they can triangulate, but it's not likely to give us much more than a general area.'

'It would still help cut down the amount of pubs we'd otherwise have to contact.'

Fox nodded again. 'If we're about to start pulling in the Crew for interview, looks like Rob Driscoll should be our primary focus.'

Clarke locked eyes with him. 'You told me Complaints have had Tynecastle on their radar for years – we need access to those files.'

He puffed out his cheeks. 'My ex-colleagues can be wary of sharing.'

'Understandably so, but a word from the ACC might prise open the vault.'

'I suppose I could suggest it.'

'A quick result would be in her interests; make sure she understands that.'

'Okay, but I want a favour in return.'

'What?'

'Something tells me you'll be going out tonight.'

Clarke was pulled up short, wondering how he knew. But then she realised he didn't mean Michael Leckie. To reinforce the point, he did a little shuffle, wiggling his hips, elbows jutting.

'That's not how human beings dance,' she told him.

'I'm right, though, aren't I? You want a look at DJ Gabz in her natural environment.'

'Which is very far from *your* natural environment, Malcolm.'

'I'm sure I've got a party shirt somewhere in my wardrobe. What time are you thinking of going?'

'I doubt anything much will happen before ten.' She saw doubt enter his mind. 'Maybe even eleven,' she added, hoping to strengthen the deterrent. Instead, he shrugged his acceptance.

'We need those files today,' she stressed.

'I'll get on it,' Fox answered, heading to his desk.

Clarke sat down at her own desk and noticed that Christine Esson was glaring at her.

'What?'

'He seems to be taking up a lot of your time.' Esson glanced in Fox's direction so her meaning was clear.

'Plenty to keep you busy, Christine – and a heap more about to land on our desks.' Clarke held up her copy of the printout. 'What do you make of it?'

'Driscoll seemed pretty open when we met him, comparatively speaking. But this definitely needs explaining. DCI's already told Jason and Colin to start talking to people listed as recent calls.'

'Any contact with the lettings agency?'

'Should there be?' Esson watched as Clarke shrugged. 'The suit who paid us a visit this morning, who was he?'

'Gartcosh. Just had some background to offer.'

'Something that's got you interested in QC Lettings?'

'Daughter of the owners discovered the body – wouldn't you say that's a bit of a coincidence?'

'I sense there's more.'

'I'm sworn to secrecy, Christine.'

'So there *is* something.'

'Soon as I can tell you, I will, I promise.'

'And to think you were accusing *me* of getting too close to Malcolm Fox.'

Clarke opened her mouth to respond, but Esson had put her head down, concentrating on her keyboard.

Tess Leighton noticed something was off, but that didn't stop her approaching, eyes on her phone. 'The *Courant* has got a quote from an unnamed source at Tynecastle,' she announced. 'Apparently we're conducting a witch-hunt that won't end until "policing itself and everything that underpins it becomes untenable, after which all that awaits society is anarchy, full stop".' She looked up. 'It's almost as if they know we're coming for them.'

'It almost is.' Clarke's eyes moved to where King and Ritchie were hunched at their desks, jackets off, phones pressed to their ears. Noting her interest, Colin King placed his hand over his phone and mouthed something neither Clarke nor Leighton could catch. He resorted to the pad of A4 paper in front of him, writing something and then lifting it so they could see the capitalised message:

THEY'RE ALL TYNECASTLE!

Meaning every call and text to Haggard's phone.

'He had them rattled, didn't he?' Leighton commented.

'He really did,' Clarke agreed.

Leighton was looking at Clarke's monitor. 'What's that?'

'I finally worked out how to transfer stuff from a phone.' Clarke started the video. 'It's Haggard forcing his way into his

181

sister-in-law's house.' She turned the volume up. The two detectives watched the confrontation.

'And he's the reason we're now putting in a hard shift?' Leighton enquired.

Malcolm Fox, having weaved between the various desks, joined them.

'Couple of hours for the Complaints stuff,' he informed Clarke.

'Fast work, Malcolm.'

'Some of it will be sent to my computer – and only my computer. But there are box files too. To be kept under lock and key and not leave this office.'

'Understood. And thanks again.'

'I'll make sure my shirt's freshly pressed.' He retreated to his desk.

'Freshly pressed?' Leighton echoed.

'Don't even start,' Clarke said with a sigh as Leighton moved off. Ignoring the scowling Esson seated across from her, she typed the name Fraser Mackenzie into Google and pulled up a screen's-worth of images, starting at the top and scrolling down. Unless the man had had a drastic makeover, he didn't in the least fit the description given of Gaby Mackenzie's chauffeur.

'Do you want me to send you the stuff from Stephanie's phone?' she asked Esson.

'If you can bear to share.'

'I reckon I can force myself.'

With a few clicks, it was done. Some things were easy, others not.

'Thanks,' Esson said, slightly less grudgingly than Clarke had been expecting.

'Always welcome,' Clarke replied, their eyes meeting across the wide expanse of desk. She was about to add something, but Esson had plugged her earphones in, the better to listen to the footage.

'Always welcome,' she repeated under her breath.

18

Gaby Mackenzie was at the place she felt most comfortable and safe, The Elemental Club, setting everything up for later in the day. Downstairs from her DJ rig, staff were restocking the bar. Someone had decided that a bit of Bach cello suited the mood, and it was playing softly over the speakers. Gaby didn't mind. She'd borrowed from classical music plenty of times, and she had an ear open right now, wondering if there was anything worth sampling. When her phone buzzed, she almost didn't answer, but it was her mum, finally getting back to her. She slipped off her headphones and raised the device to her ear.

'I left a hundred messages,' she complained.

'So I see,' her mother purred. 'Everything's all right, though? C told me you were in a bit of a state. We can probably lodge a complaint.'

'It's not the police I was pissed off with. You've done something to my phone. I want it undone today, or else it goes in the bin and I make sure you don't get anywhere near its replacement.'

'What did the police want, Gaby?' Her mother's tone had changed, hardening several degrees. 'You were there, weren't you? Francis Haggard's flat, I mean?'

'You tell me, you're the one bugging my phone.'

'What happened, did you meet someone?'

'As it so happens. And I was headed to the flat upstairs, where I could have mindless sex with a man whose name I hadn't even caught.' There was silence on the line for a moment.

'And that's all you've got to tell me?'

'Yes.'

'So you didn't know Francis Haggard?'

183

'What makes you think I did?'

'He worked at Tynecastle.'

'So?'

'So some of his colleagues frequent Elemental, no?'

'I didn't know Francis Haggard.' Gaby paused. 'You did, though, didn't you, you or Dad? One of you had to give him the tour of the flat.'

'I suppose so.' Her mother gave an all-too-audible sigh. 'Reckless behaviour isn't good for business, Gabrielle.'

'I'm not reckless, I'm young – there's a difference.'

'Why *that* tenement, though?'

'It was closest, that's all. And now, if you don't mind, I have to get my set ready for tonight.'

'Will you eat with us first?'

'Only if you promise to debug my phone.'

'I just want you to be safe, darling. We all need to be careful.'

Gaby felt her shoulders slump. 'I know.'

'So I'll see you later?'

'Just make sure it's vegetarian. And remember – chicken doesn't count.'

'It so nearly does, though, doesn't it?'

'Nearly,' Gaby conceded with a tired smile. Then she put her phone down next to her, reattached her headphones to her ears, and concentrated on her music.

James Pelham was rising to his feet, readying to leave, when Fox arrived at the restaurant. Fox had been biding his time, not really wanting to sit down with the man. When he'd called ACC Lyon to ask for the Complaints files, she'd told him his timing was perfect and there was someone she wanted him to meet. She was having a drink with him that very afternoon at Peacock Alley.

'It's in the Waldorf Astoria,' she had informed him.

'Edinburgh folk still call it the Caledonian,' Fox had countered.

'Well, I'm not from Edinburgh, Malcolm . . .'

The man she wanted him to meet was her old friend James Pelham, which was why Fox hadn't exactly rushed to the scene. Even after arriving, he had lingered in the lobby, watching discreetly as Lyon checked her watch and phone and craned her neck in an effort to locate him. Finally Pelham had risen to his feet and given her hand a squeeze, which Fox took as his cue.

184

'Malcolm, at long last,' Jennifer Lyon said coolly. 'Meet James.'

Fox shook the proffered hand and managed something approximating a nod of greeting. Pelham, however, didn't even bother making eye contact. He had extracted two crisp twenty-pound notes from a wallet and, despite Lyon's protest, placed them next to his glass.

'Another time,' he said. 'I have a meeting I need to get to.' And with that he was gone. Lyon fixed Fox with a scowl as he sat in what had been Pelham's chair.

'He would have been a useful man for you to meet,' she said, tipping the dregs of her drink into her mouth. A waiter arrived, but Fox shook his head and he retreated, eyes on the banknotes.

'Would he have been useful to me, or am I useful to him?' Fox enquired. He noted that Lyon had a fresh glow about her, and she'd had her short, blonde-highlighted hair restyled, too. He realised there was a history here that went beyond old friends.

'James is worried,' Lyon said. 'With some justification, he feels.'

'Oh?'

'You know his wife – soon to be ex-wife – was related to Francis Haggard?'

'It hadn't escaped my notice.'

'Well, James being James, he's worried the media might try to make him the story.'

'What does he think we can do about that?'

'Not give them any additional ammunition, to start with,' she stated.

'With respect, you need to step away from your old friend.'

'That doesn't sit well with me, Malcolm.'

'Nonetheless, James Pelham happens to be close to Fraser Mackenzie – and I'm assuming you're not unaware of SOCD's interest in the latter? On top of which, Pelham's company is being investigated for fraud and he's going through a very public and messy divorce.'

Lyon took all of this on board without her face showing any trace of emotion. Eventually she stared past Fox's left shoulder towards the well-stocked bar. He didn't think she was focused on anything in particular; quite the opposite. She was lost in some memory.

'James has always had a thing for the ladies – that's pretty much word for word how he would put it. A romantic from the old school, all charm and guile. Plus roses, champagne and getting his own way. I felt duty-bound to agree to meet him, even though I knew he was after a favour.' Her eyes settled on his. 'Those files you asked for are on their way. Don't worry, I'm not petty like that.'

'I never doubted it.'

'And Siobhan Clarke?'

'Time hasn't been quite right as yet.'

Her demeanour had become more businesslike. 'How much trouble are we likely to be in, Malcolm?'

'Police Scotland, you mean? I'll do what I can.'

'But?'

'Tynecastle should have been dealt with generations back.'

'And if a handful of the worst offenders end up being brought into the light . . .?'

He gave a thoughtful nod. 'Maybe,' he eventually said.

Lyon leaned forward across the small circular table. 'It would be a personal favour to me if, despite your reservations, you did whatever's possible for James.' She paused. 'You know there's talk of a place at the top table for you? Higher even than DCI. Positions are about to become vacant, and your name is being mentioned.'

Fox just managed not to lick his lips. 'Message received, ma'am,' he said.

'Call me Jennifer, Malcolm,' the assistant chief constable purred.

Rebus had made sure his Saab was parked in a conspicuous spot. He didn't walk down the lane to Tommy Oram's lock-up straight away, but lingered by the car, not really doing anything, just standing there. Eventually he approached the lock-up, rattling the handle. The large metal door shook slightly without giving any indication that it would yield without a good deal more force than Rebus could apply. A couple of bikes passed the top of the lane. Two minutes later, they passed again. Rebus knew eyes were on him. After a few more minutes, two different bikes arrived. He recognised both faces from his last visit. Though not yet in their teens, they had learned to act older and meaner.

'You need to beat it,' the leader said, feet on the ground, hands wrapped around the handlebars of his bike.

'Dog not with you today?' Rebus said. Then, 'You don't remember me? Tommy will be disappointed – he pays you to be sharp.'

'You were here a couple of days back,' the second kid said.

'Seeing my old pal Tommy.' Rebus lifted his foot and gave the door of the lock-up a kick. 'You know Tommy's dad was sleeping here until recently?' The kids stared at him without answering. Rebus brought a twenty-pound note from his pocket and held it up, taking a step closer to the obvious leader. The note was snatched and trousered. 'You knew it was his dad?' he asked again.

'Aye.'

'You spoke to him?'

'He got us to fetch stuff from the shop,' the second kid said.

'That was good of you, Tommy must have been pleased.' Rebus paused. 'Any idea why his dad left?' He watched them shake their heads. 'And he's not been back since?'

'We'd know,' the leader stated.

'I don't doubt that.' He almost asked why they weren't in school, but it would have been a stupid question. Either they'd given up on education or education had given up on them. 'Tommy been around today?' More head-shakes. 'Did he seem to get on okay with his dad?' The head-shakes switched to shrugs. Neither boy looked especially warm, despite their thick black hoodies. Their bony fingers had turned a raw-looking pink. Their denims were cheap and ill-fitting, their trainers well worn. Heads shorn sides and back, left longer at the front. There were hundreds if not thousands just like them spread across the city. Rebus nodded towards the graffiti on every available surface.

'Which tags are yours?' But they weren't about to answer that. 'Twenty doesn't buy much around here, does it?'

'Your car's not been touched,' the leader corrected him.

'There is that, I suppose.'

He watched them turn and pedal back the way they'd come, then returned to the Saab, unlocking it and getting in. He sat for a moment, then turned the ignition, got the heater working, and started driving around the streets. It didn't take him long before he passed a hatchback with racing stripes and a modified exhaust. It was idling kerbside, making a racket. Rebus's two young friends had stopped alongside, next to the open window on the driver's side, while an exchange of some kind took place. A few streets further on, a different bicycle had stopped in front of one of the terraced houses, the occupier opening his door just wide enough for another transaction.

'Home deliveries,' Rebus said to himself. Well, why not? In his CID days he'd known school-age children used as couriers, but never as young as these. These were kids who should have been at home with their games consoles and loving parents. At one time

Cafferty had controlled most of the trade in the city, but he'd never used kids, not as far as Rebus knew. But then this was a different world, a less furtive culture. You could hardly walk down a pavement these days without catching a whiff of blaw. Bedrooms and attics were being turned into hothouses for growing the stuff. One such property had gone up in flames a while back and neighbours had been warned to keep their windows shut if they didn't want to feel the effects. Users and dealers had stopped fearing law and order because law and order had stopped being overly bothered about a bit of weed or a few pills or wraps of powder.

When his phone buzzed, he saw that the incoming call was from Alan Fleck. He let it ring without answering. Fleck tried again a minute later, but Rebus still wasn't in the mood. Instead he drove the relatively short distance to Tynecastle cop shop. He had to double-park, but that was okay, he wasn't planning on getting out of the car. The place had the same soul-crushing air that it had always had. Inside, however, with Fleck and his ilk running the show, the staff had acted like princes and soldiers in some grand fiefdom. Rebus had been treated like a valued emissary, gifted bottles of malt and promises of bills waived in some of the best of the city's restaurants.

'Just give them my name,' Fleck would say with a wink or a tap of the nose. He would pat Rebus's chest or arm, and at some point Rebus would realise a wad of banknotes had been added to that day's wardrobe.

He'd never said no, rationalising that to do so would be to give offence. He was reminded of a sign that used to be widespread in business premises: *Please do not ask for credit as a refusal often offends*. And besides, Fleck was a good cop, wasn't he, the kind that got results? Loved by those who served under him, admired by those higher up the tree. Rebus had once, after a drink too many, wondered aloud why he stayed stuck at sergeant.

'I keep turning them down when they offer,' Fleck had answered. 'Nothing beats where I am now, John, nothing. You and your CID pals, I wouldn't swap with you if you offered me a diamond mine.'

Was it because he enjoyed being close to the front line? Rebus had often thought about that. He reckoned now that it had more to do with the strings that could be pulled and the power he wielded. When Alan Fleck walked down the street, everyone knew him, or else they wanted to know him. What he said and did mattered. And when some graffiti had gone up not too many streets from the police station stating in metre-high capital letters that *SGT ALAN FLECK = BASTARD*, Fleck had insisted on being photographed next to it. He'd then had the photo copied, framed and wrapped as Christmas gifts for every person, cop and non-cop, who worked at Tynecastle. There had been one for Rebus, too, though he wasn't sure now what he'd done with it.

And yes, he'd granted Fleck and his crew a few favours along the way, of course he had. Because to say no was to become an outsider, and maybe even the enemy, no longer trusted, no longer part of that seemingly charmed circle.

Whisky and cigarettes, dinners and bungs – Rebus guessed people had sold themselves for less. And better Alan Fleck than the likes of Big Ger Cafferty. Fleck had always framed it as if it were a question of us and them, two teams in polarised competition.

'But you have to watch out for the goalposts, John,' he'd said. 'Those sleekit damned things have a way of shifting, and they can do it in the blink of an eye.'

The initiation ceremonies had maybe been challenging and demeaning, but that was often the way with institutions. Rebus remembered plenty of attempted humiliations from his days as an army recruit. The name-calling, the sabotaging of equipment, the cruel practical jokes, all of it could be construed as character-building, couldn't it? Besides, those days were definitely numbered. Everyone now was a potential whistleblower, everyone had a phone to help gather evidence. If the *Courant* and its brethren had been around during Rebus's heyday ... well, he shuddered to think. But actually he would bet that whatever the scale of misbehaviour pointed out to them, the general public even now would be accepting, just so long as the police continued to stand firm between them and the bogeyman.

When a dog, out for a walk with its owner, paused to sniff and cock a leg against a lamppost, he remembered Brillo was waiting at home for him. He put the Saab into gear, and had just started moving when a uniform emerged from the police station. He didn't recognise the face that held up a phone to take a photograph of vehicle and driver.

He only knew his presence had been noted.

Clarke was ten minutes early at the Oxford Bar, but Leckie was already waiting in the back room. He rose to his feet, ready to go fetch her a drink, but she waved the offer away, arriving at the table a couple of minutes later with a gin and tonic. The bar was busier than she'd hoped, but there was still a decent distance between their table and the others. Moreover, everyone seemed too interested in their own conversations to be bothered to eavesdrop. Nevertheless, she had requested that the TV be switched on. The owner, Kirsty, did the honours with the remote. Foreign football, the commentary not obtrusive but helping mask anything being discussed at the tables. Clarke nodded to let Kirsty know the volume was fine.

'This your local?' Leckie asked, hoisting his pint glass in a toast.

'Once upon a time.'

'I know John Rebus haunted the place – maybe still does, for all I know. And yes, I know you and him used to work together.'

'You've been checking up on me?'

'Lawyers like to know who they're dealing with. Your name and his have been mentioned on the odd occasion.'

'I'm not entirely sure I like the sound of that. Cheers.' She touched her glass to his and took a sip.

'How's the case going? Am I allowed to ask?'

'Of course you are.'

'And?'

'It's confidential.' She watched him eventually smile. 'But let me ask you something – were you surprised when you heard?'

'That he was dead?' He thought about this for the best part of a minute. 'I suppose I was and I wasn't. I'd asked his analyst if he considered him a suicide risk. He told me it was sixty–forty against.'

'Men like Francis Haggard rarely top themselves. Or if they do, they wait until they've killed their partner first.'

'I don't think that was ever going to happen.'

'This analyst of his,' Clarke said, 'it was a ruse, wasn't it? Started seeing him after the first recorded assault?'

'If you go back far enough into his phone records, I think you'll find he tried several times to book sessions with psychotherapists prior to that incident. Mostly they were booked solid. Eventually he found one. So to answer your question, no, I don't think it was a ruse.'

'He seriously wanted to change?'

'I'm sure of it.'

'Really?'

'He grew up in the Catholic faith, did you know that?'

190

'He said it got him teased at Tynecastle.'

Leckie nodded. He was slowly revolving his glass on its coaster. 'He was talking about seeing a priest, not just for confession, but as a way back into his faith.'

'Psychoanalysis and religion – he was trying every angle, wasn't he?'

'That's not what it felt like. I sensed him opening up after a lifetime of hiding emotion and weakness.'

'Because those would have been seized on at Tynecastle?'

'Seized on and ridiculed.'

'So when he was opening up, did he mention any enemies to you, people he had reason to be afraid of?'

'I think the person he was really scared of was himself. He hated how he'd stopped being able to control his temper.' He met her gaze. 'I genuinely believe that, and I know whereof I speak.' He broke off long enough to take a sip from his glass. 'My father abused my mother for years and we all turned a blind eye. Grandparents knew, uncles and aunts, family friends, neighbours . . . Nothing was ever said.'

'I'm sorry.'

'Never any contrition either, just lies and denials and those occasional rages, right up until a stroke turned him into an invalid. My mother nursed him until the day he died, can you credit that? I was in my mid teens by then, and when I was alone with him, I vented. Nothing he could do but lie there and take it. But I attended his funeral, same as everyone else, and we all went back to pretending again.' He released the breath he'd been holding and blinked away the flashback. 'When Francis spoke about how the job had coarsened him . . . well, it seemed to make sense.' He looked at her. 'Did I mention my dad was a cop?'

Clarke nodded her understanding. 'So you think the job played a part in Francis's death, but is there anything specific we should be looking at?'

'Client confidentiality, Siobhan.'

'Strictly off the record, though.'

Leckie thought again. Clarke realised that she was warming to him. He seemed to her one of those people who lived a considered life – weighing up pros and cons; empathetic; looking for the positives.

'He used recreational drugs with a fair degree of regularity, but since he could afford them, I don't suppose that's an issue.

191

He wasn't thrilled at the prospect of going to jail – he knew that inmates don't take kindly to disgraced police officers. I dare say it didn't help that he had helped put away innocent men.'

'He told you that?'

'He told me these men were guilty of crimes, just not the ones ascribed to them.'

'Specific cases?'

Leckie shook his head.

'What about the names he was planning to name?'

'We hadn't got that far.' He thought for a further moment. 'He mentioned several times that police officers are often placed in a prison's sex offenders wing – harder for the general population to get access to them. He said he'd rather be knifed in the food queue than have to hang out with that sort.'

'He definitely said "knifed"?'

'I think so.'

Clarke had taken out her phone. She held up a finger, meaning she needed a minute. Then she walked outside onto Young Street. The setts gleamed in the street light, slick from recent rain. Christine Esson eventually answered.

'Sorry about earlier,' Esson said.

'Forget about it. Air sometimes needs clearing, and you were right – you've been on this case from the get-go. You deserve not to be shoved in a corner.'

'So why aren't you here, festooning me with apologies and caramel bars?'

'I'm in a meeting with Haggard's solicitor. I take it you've started on those Complaints files?'

'You saw them arrive, right? You know how much there is to wade through?'

'I'm trying not to think about it.'

'Should you even be talking to the lawyer?'

'Probably a grey area. But it got me thinking – Tynecastle has a history of fitting up suspects. I'm wondering how many of those Haggard played a part in and whether any of the guilty have been released recently.'

'So we'd be looking for a criminal mastermind then, the sort who'd know that he'd just moved into a rented flat?'

'They could have followed him.'

'Rather than stabbing him as soon as they laid eyes on him?'

'You're right, it was just a thought.'

'It *is* a thought, though. Maybe we could give it to Liam and Noel.'

'You mean as in Oasis?'

'My new name for King and Ritchie. King does everything but call him "our kid".'

Clarke smiled. 'What's Fox up to?'

'He's just gone home – early for him. The DCI's clocked off, too. Just us worker bees left. Should I let you get back to your grey area?'

'See you tomorrow, Christine.' Clarke ended the call and went back inside. Fresh drinks had appeared on the table.

'Work,' she explained, sitting down again.

'Here's to it.' They clinked glasses.

'Let me ask you something else,' she said. 'Do you do much for the Mackenzies?'

'Personally, no. The commercial side of my practice does. That's who sent me to look after Gaby.'

Clarke was checking her phone, finding photos of Fraser Mackenzie. She turned the screen towards Leckie. 'The man who picked her up in the Range Rover?'

'God, no.' Leckie took the phone from her as he studied it. 'The driver looked more the sort you'd cross the street to avoid.'

'That's what I thought,' Clarke said, taking her phone back. She lifted her drink in silence and took a sip.

'Maybe,' Leckie said, 'we can draw a line under the shop stuff and just talk instead.'

'You mean like normal everyday people?'

'You don't think it can be done?'

Clarke met his gaze. 'I suppose we can try,' she said. 'Are you a football fan?'

'More rugby.'

'Music?'

'Modern classical.'

'Books?'

'Maybe the occasional thriller.'

'You're not making this easy, are you?'

He copied her smile. 'How about you?' he said. 'What brought you into the police?'

'Doesn't that qualify as shop talk?'

'Not if it's telling me more about you.'

'How long have you got?'

'You're the one with a later engagement.' He eased back in his seat, readying himself to listen.

'Just don't let me drink any more of these,' Clarke said, gesturing towards her glass. Then she began to tell him.

19

Fox was waiting for Clarke outside the Elemental Club, standing slightly apart from the cluster of young smokers and looking more like a concerned parent ready to escort his daughter home than someone ready for a loud and sweaty dance floor. He was wearing a jacket suited to woodland walks, beneath which Clarke could make out a pale blue polo shirt.

'What?' he said.

'Your party shirt?'

'It's got short sleeves. And look.' He hoisted one leg. 'Jeans.'

'Nicely pressed, too. Come on then, let's see how you blend in.'

The two burly doormen, dressed in regulation black, checked them out but saw no reason to stop them going in. A steep staircase led down below pavement level. There were plenty of these underground venues on and around Cowgate. It made sense, Clarke supposed, in that it provided a level of natural soundproofing. The bass grew more insistent as they paid at a makeshift desk and allowed the staff member to stamp their wrists.

'Do you want us to track and trace?' Fox enquired.

'If your phone can get a signal,' she told him with a shrug.

'Vaccine passport?' This time she shook her head.

The corridor eventually led them to a single cavernous room, lights strobing from recesses halfway up its bare stone walls. There was a bar in one corner, a few tables on a raised platform, and a long ledge down one side of the room where most of the clubbers seemed content to sit. The dance floor was only half full, with what looked like students keen to get the night started.

'It's still early,' Clarke explained to Fox.

'Wonder if they've put a cap on the capacity.'

'If you catch COVID, I promise I'll do your shopping.'

'In that case, drinks are on me.'

'I'll stick to orange juice.'

'You sure?'

She nodded and took the only empty table, looking around. There was no sign of any DJ, so she craned her neck and noticed a minstrels' gallery immediately above her. It faced the bar but couldn't really be seen from where she sat, so she got up again, slipped her mask on, and joined Fox in the queue. Now she had a better view of the upstairs. Behind a waist-high glass panel there was a long table arrayed with boxes and flashing lights, and behind it all stood Gaby Mackenzie, shoulders hunched as she listened to her headphones, fingers busy teeing up the next track. It looked as if her main aid was a small silver notebook computer, though she also rifled through some CDs, pausing to sip from a plastic beaker with a fixed straw.

'When does the actual music start?' Fox asked from behind his mask, handing Clarke her drink. His seemed to be identical. He nodded towards the tables, but Clarke squeezed herself into a space on the ledge, leaving him with no option but to stand in front of her. As they removed their masks, she gestured over his shoulder and he turned, clocking Gaby Mackenzie and giving a nod of understanding.

When the next tune arrived, Clarke recognised it from the first few notes: Boards of Canada. It quickly morphed into something else, however, as the DJ added her own elements. A rapper joined the fray, appearing seamlessly. Clarke was quietly impressed. When she looked up at the gallery again, Mackenzie acknowledged her by raising her beaker.

'We've been spotted,' Clarke told Fox. He had removed his jacket and loosened the last of the three buttons on his short-sleeved shirt.

'She's playing your song?'

'In a manner of speaking. You really didn't have to come, you know.'

Fox gave a shrug. 'Nice to have a break from the files.'

'Anything there leap out at you so far?'

'Just that the worst excesses – albeit unproven – I'd classify as historic, carried out by officers long retired or in some cases even deceased.'

'I thought you might say that, since that's the result you're after.'

'Doesn't matter what I want, it's there in black and white. I lost count of how many times John Rebus's name came up, usually in cahoots with a sergeant called Alan Fleck.'

'I've heard of him.' Clarke lifted her drink to her lips. The orange juice tasted cheap, not helped by the addition of three ice cubes. But then no matter how cheap the juice, ice was cheaper. 'John never actually worked at Tynecastle, though, right? So he was never a member of the Crew?'

'Honorary status. He was still their go-to guy.'

'For what exactly?'

'If they needed a message passed on to Cafferty or one of the other thugs John seems to have enjoyed rubbing shoulders with.' Fox paused. 'You can't tell me that all of this is coming as news to you. Those files show you covering Rebus's arse more than once when the two of you worked together.' He paused again, but Clarke wasn't minded to add or admit anything. 'Look, there's something I want to tell you . . .'

'I'm listening.'

He leaned in further towards her. 'It's Fleck I want. Every time we tried in my Complaints days, he somehow wriggled free. So for me it's not strictly about deflecting attention from anything currently happening.' He paused. 'If the ACC knew this, she'd probably pull me from the case. See, it doesn't really bother me if the walls of Tynecastle come tumbling down.'

'And how about John?'

Fox shrugged. 'Difficult to take Fleck down without Rebus falling too. Too much shared history.'

'Then we might have a problem.'

'Despite which, I get the feeling it leaves a bad taste in your mouth, the way this stuff keeps being covered up year after year, decade after decade. Tell me I'm wrong.'

Clarke concentrated on her drink again, determined not to give him the satisfaction of agreeing with him. She noticed that someone had joined DJ Gabz behind the decks. Looked like one of the doormen. His mouth was close to her ear, telling her something. She nodded before slipping her headphones back on and getting back to her job, the visitor disappearing into the darkness around her. The same doorman appeared in the main room a few moments later, but lingered just long enough to satisfy himself that there was no trouble in the offing. The soundtrack had shifted gears, becoming louder and edgier, the students growing ever more animated.

'Is this techno?' Fox asked, a brief look of pain crossing his face.

'Been a while since I checked the various categories,' Clarke answered, realising after a moment that he could no longer make out what she was saying. The dance floor was filling, people moving their hips and feet, holding drinks aloft. It was hard to tell if Gaby Mackenzie was pleased by the reaction. She was checking the screen of her phone, the bottom half of her face illuminated by its display. Clarke noted the arrival of another figure next to her, a different doorman though almost identical to the first in size and uniform. She thought of Leckie's description of the driver who'd collected Gaby from Leith. Her parents had found her a solicitor PDQ – Clarke wondered if they'd sent the chauffeur too, or had it been someone Gaby herself knew and trusted?

'She's a popular young woman,' she said. Fox cupped a hand to his ear, but Clarke just shook her head, the gesture telling him it wasn't important. She rattled her drained glass instead and motioned towards the bar. He accepted the offer with a thumbs-up.

As she queued, Clarke saw a sign atop the bar alerting clubbers to a number they could text with requests. She added it to her phone before sending a message: *Thanks for the BoC. See you around.* Having collected her drinks, she turned towards the gallery and saw the nod Mackenzie gave in her direction.

Message received.

'Can we go after this?' Fox yelled in her ear as she handed him his drink.

'The party shirt isn't enjoying its outing?'

'I just don't want to get blood on it.'

'I doubt there'll be any trouble, Malcolm. Place looks well policed.'

'I meant from my ears.' He drained his drink in one go and waited for Clarke to do the same. She threw a wave towards the gallery as she followed him out of the room.

At the entrance, a party of young men was arriving. Despite the cold, they had no jackets, their tight short-sleeved shirts showing off gym-toned biceps. Clarke recognised a couple of faces from her visit to Tynecastle.

'No fucking way,' one of them barked, giving a harsh laugh.

'Bit of powder still in your left nostril,' Clarke advised him.

'Who's the lumberjack?' another voice enquired, meaning Fox.

'Seems you let all sorts in here,' Clarke said to the nearest doorman.

'Should have a policy on ugly tarts, though,' one of the Crew said.

Fox tried to shove his way past Clarke to get to the speaker. She made sure he didn't. A couple of the cops looked ready to square up to him, the doorman intervening.

'They're from Tynecastle,' Clarke informed Fox.

'Then I look forward to making their acquaintance in a Leith interview room,' he said, teeth gritted.

A queue had formed behind the Tynecastle contingent, including a hen party armed with satin sashes, fake tan and deely boppers. They started to complain about the wait. Another clubber stood off to one side, filming with his phone. Clarke shook her head at him, but he ignored her.

'We don't want any trouble,' one of the doormen was saying.

'Relax, C,' one of the cops reassured him. 'We're just measuring cocks here.' He made eye contact with Clarke. 'Got to say I think hers is winning.'

There was more laughter as the Crew began to filter through the doorway. Clarke watched them descend the stairs, offering each other slaps on the back. One of them punched the air. They seemed already to have pushed Clarke and Fox from their minds – they had a dance floor they now needed to own. Clarke turned her attention to the doorman they'd called C.

'Regulars?'

'They can sometimes get a bit exuberant.'

'Especially after a few lines.'

'I wouldn't know anything about that.'

'That's good,' Fox added. 'You won't mind the drugs squad coming and checking your toilets then?'

'Not if they don't mind patting down half a dozen of their own.' The doorman looked at him without blinking.

Clarke took Fox's arm and led him away. She could no longer see the clubber who'd been filming, didn't suppose it mattered anyway. One thing she knew was, he wasn't the *Courant*. A little further up Blair Street, she noticed a parked Range Rover. She broke away from Fox and walked around it. A sticker on the back window told her it had been bought from High End Motors.

'More my style than yours,' Fox commented.

'True enough, Malcolm. Especially if you're thinking of an expedition to fell some trees.'

He glanced down at his jacket. 'It's not that bad, is it?'

'It's fine,' Clarke assured him, taking out her phone and snapping a shot of the Range Rover's licence plate.

'You're lying, aren't you?'

'Of course I am,' Clarke said, taking his arm again. 'Let's go find ourselves a nice quiet bar.'

Back home, Clarke poured herself another orange juice and popped two ibuprofen tablets into her mouth. There wasn't much in the fridge, so she settled for an apple and started charging her phone. She found herself thinking about Michael Leckie. Why had she opened up to him? Poor bugger now knew enough to pen her obituary. She reckoned it was because of the way he'd taken her into his confidence, telling her about his father. It struck her that maybe he'd made it all up, just so she *would* open up. He'd said he didn't work for the Mackenzies, but maybe that was a lie, too.

You have to trust someone sometime, girl, she told herself.

Fox, too, had opened up, telling her things she wasn't supposed to know. Maybe they were on the same side and maybe they weren't. She reckoned Malcolm's ethics might be prone to shifts as and when required. He lived for advancement. Offer him that in exchange for Rebus and she doubted he'd think twice. Whatever an idealist was, Malcolm Fox was probably the opposite.

Then again, at least he had goals, and achievable ones at that. *It leaves a bad taste in your mouth . . . Tell me I'm wrong . . .* She thought of John Rebus, who had bent every rule to breaking point in pursuit of results, regarding every unsolved case as an affront. Illicitly, he'd taken copies of many of those case files home with him on his retirement. Every morning and evening they were there, taunting him with past failure. Did that make him an idealist or just an obsessive? Those cases would never be closed – he knew it and she knew it. Maybe it was guilt he felt, guilt at having let the victims down.

Had Francis Haggard too felt guilt? His lawyer certainly thought so. His confession would have incriminated those he'd worked with and called friends, possibly the only real friends he'd had. You didn't go to those lengths in the hope of a lesser sentence or even no sentence at all. Talking entailed losing everything for only relatively minor gains. There had to be a compelling reason. Atonement was the only thing she could think of. Past sins acknowledged and paid for.

She picked up her phone again and was googling Haggard's namesake, St Francis, when a text arrived. It was from Laura Smith.

There's someone outside.

She stared at the three words for a moment before making the call.

'Are your doors locked?' she checked.

'Yes,' Laura told her.

'Who is it, do you know?'

'It's a man in a car. He was here last night, too. I thought maybe he was a minicab or something.'

'The same car, you're sure?'

'Can you come take a look?'

'I've had one drink too many, but leave it with me. Meantime, keep your lights off, stay away from the windows, okay?'

'Am I being paranoid?'

'There's only one way to find out . . .'

Clarke hung up and called it in, requested a patrol car and stressed the urgency. Her one caveat: nobody from Tynecastle. Then she phoned Smith again.

'Officers are on their way,' she told her. 'You'll probably see the blue light.'

'Like Roxanne?'

'Except I think her light was red, wasn't it?'

'Thanks for doing this.'

'What are friends for?'

'Is there any news, by the way?'

'Christ, Laura, you never stop, do you?'

'I can't afford to.'

'Reckon you'll get a story out of this?'

'I've already considered it.'

'Do you have any idea who's outside?'

'No.'

'Or why?'

'Too many suspects, Siobhan.'

Clarke thought of something. 'You don't use a stringer, do you?'

'How do you mean?'

'Taking pictures for you.'

'People send me stuff, but as yet I can't afford to pay.'

'Anything arrive tonight?'

'Like what?'

'A nightspot called the Elemental Club on Blair Street. Tyne-castle's finest on the randan.'

'Oh, I know they go there, or some of them do, the ones with no wives and cash to spare.'

'Someone was taking pics as they trooped in.'

'Meaning you were there too – hence the alcohol intake?'

'I was working.'

'Do tell.'

'I don't think so.'

'Oh – here's that light you were talking about. What will the neighbours think? Is it safe to go to the window now?'

'Probably.' Clarke listened as Smith rose from her chair and crossed the living room.

'Patrol car's in the middle of the road, meaning I can't see the other car.'

'It's still there, though?'

'Does that mean he's probably got nothing to hide?'

'We'll know soon enough.'

Clarke waited in silence, her eyes on her phone in case she got either a text or an incoming call. After ninety seconds, Smith came back on the line.

'Car's leaving. Will the police want to talk to me, do you think? Wait – one of them's coming up the path.'

Clarke heard Smith's doorbell ring. Then the sounds of her walking to the door and unlocking it. A brief muffled conversation and the door closed again, Smith lifting the phone to her mouth.

'It was James Pelham,' she said, a fresh tremor in her voice. 'He told them he stopped to make a call.'

'On his way where?'

'I didn't ask.'

'I assume he's not a neighbour?'

'Nothing like.' Smith paused. 'He knows, doesn't he?'

'Knows what?'

'That I'm the *Courant*. Meaning the one who flagged up his adultery for all the world to see.'

'You're sure it was the same car last night?'

'What am I going to do? Why was he here?'

'I don't think he'll come back, Laura, not now. Try to get some sleep and we'll talk tomorrow.'

'Thanks, Siobhan.' Clarke could hear her taking a deep breath. 'And if anything does happen regarding the Francis Haggard story . . .'

Clarke ended the call. Her phone rang almost immediately. The patrol repeated the version they'd told Laura Smith.

'She says he was there two nights running,' Clarke informed the officer. 'Reckon he always stops there to make late-night calls?'

'Don't know,' was the eventual reply. 'But this is James Pelham we're talking about. It's not like he was casing the joint.'

'Well, thanks for keeping an open mind. Maybe ask patrols to cruise that street the next night or two just in case.' She paused. 'You took note of the licence plate, yes?'

The silence on the line was as telling as any spoken answer.

'It was a white saloon,' the officer blurted out.

'That's hugely helpful,' Clarke said.

'Maybe a Volkswagen,' the man was stumbling on as Clarke hung up.

James Pelham. Not just Stephanie's ex, but also friend to Fraser Mackenzie. Businessman and charity donor.

Should she add stalker to that list?

Day Six

20

They met at an early-opening café near Tollcross. The booths were tight, Rebus just about managing to fit. He was halfway through a bacon roll when Clarke arrived.

'Yours might be cold,' he said. 'Wanted it ordered before they got busy.'

She nodded and sat down, looking bleary. 'I'll take it with me,' she said, focusing instead on the mug of sepia-coloured tea.

'Late night?' he asked.

'Probably a few more of those in my future – we've got hold of about two decades' worth of dirt on Tynecastle.'

'Gathered by the Complaints?' Rebus guessed. 'Fox must be like a pig in shit.'

'Your name seems to be a constant refrain.'

'Oh aye?'

'A conduit between the Crew and gangland. Any truth in that?'

He chewed silently for a few seconds. 'Maybe some,' he eventually conceded.

'Some truth?'

It was his turn to nod. 'But I don't see where any of it gets you – I didn't top Haggard. Stands to reason if it was a cop, it was someone still serving.'

'Or else with something in their past that has to stay hidden at all costs.'

'Such as?'

'You tell me.'

'I would if I could, Shiv.' Rebus took another bite of roll. Brown sauce oozed from it, causing him to put his fingers to his mouth to clean them. The café had filled with workmen queuing for take-away. Bacon sizzled and spat in the kitchen. The radio behind the counter was tuned to a local station with an excitable presenter.

'There's something else,' Clarke said. 'We're questioning everyone with access to keys to the tenement. That includes anyone who works for QC Lettings. What can you tell me about Thomas Oram?'

'I can tell you I doubt very much he killed a man he didn't know.'

'And you're sure he didn't know Francis Haggard?'

'I don't think he's kept much from me so far. Even told me about his dad.'

'What about him?'

'Tommy gave him a bed in a lock-up just off Calder Road.'

'Why?'

'Jack wasn't quite ready to go home.'

'Couldn't his son have got him a cheap deal with QC?'

'Even cheap deals cost money.'

Clarke paused, as if trying to make her mind up about something. 'Spit it out,' Rebus said.

'Francis Haggard used recreational drugs from time to time.'

'Not exactly front-page news.'

'But it might connect him more firmly to Fraser Mackenzie.'

Rebus stopped chewing. 'Mackenzie's dealing dope?' He thought of the kids on their bikes, delivering to cars, delivering to homes, kids befriended by Tommy Oram . . .

'What is it, John?' Clarke demanded.

'Nothing.' He hoisted his mug and drank from it.

'I worked that misper case, John. Tommy Oram's dad used to work for Cafferty, so how does the son end up working for the man Cafferty sold his lettings business to?'

'He knows the daughter.'

'Tommy knows Gaby Mackenzie?'

'I think that's what I just said.'

It was Clarke's turn to be thoughtful. Rebus kept his eyes on hers until her brain re-entered the room.

'It's nothing,' she said, anticipating his question.

'Whole lot of nothing going on around here,' Rebus commented, wiping his hands on a serviette.

'Gaby's a DJ, did you know that? I watched her do a set last night at a club on Blair Street.'

'Any good?'

'Pretty popular.'

'Anything I'd know – a bit of Jeff Beck or Rod Stewart?'

'Music's moved on.'

'Got worse, you mean, like everything else.' He looked at Clarke's plate. 'Apart from bacon rolls. You can trust a bacon roll.'

Clarke started to wrap hers up. 'We got into a bit of a scrap as we were leaving the club.'

'We?'

'Malcolm was with me.'

'That's some choice of dance partner.'

'On our way out, some of the Tynie lot were heading in.'

'I'm sure Malcolm proved equal to the moment.'

'He didn't back off, if that's what you're thinking.'

'The world is full of surprises.'

'One of the doormen calmed things down. Seemed pretty pally with the Crew.'

'Doormen can be a good source of information. I had a few on my books back in the day.'

'They can be sources of other things too, though?'

Rebus saw what she was getting at. He gave a slow nod.

'You'll probably be pulled in for questioning,' Clarke went on, changing tack, 'if only so that Malcolm can have some fun. We'll be talking to Alan Fleck, too. He's a car dealer now. Must have required a chunk of start-up money. Lives in a big house in Gullane – that wouldn't have come cheap either.'

'And Haggard had a swish flat on the Newhaven waterfront – what's your point?'

'Funding must have come from somewhere.'

'The Scots are canny, Siobhan, don't tell me you've forgotten that?' Rebus started to manoeuvre himself out of the booth. He had popped two indigestion tablets from their blister pack and was crunching down on them. 'I just hope you don't find my Caribbean hideaway and SLP.' He straightened up, angling his gaze down towards her. 'I do appreciate the heads-up, though.'

'It's Fleck Malcolm wants. He told me himself – not that he'd thank me for adding you to the circle of trust.'

Rebus mimed zipping his mouth closed and started to make his way out of the café.

'And go see a doctor,' she called out to him. As she stuffed her bacon roll into her bag and made to follow suit, the owner called her back.

'Eight pounds fifty,' he announced.

209

Clarke squeezed past the line of workmen, listening to their tuts of disapproval. Well, of course John Rebus had left her with the bill. What else was he going to do?

Out on the pavement, she called Laura Smith. Rebus was walking towards Bruntsfield Links. His shoulders were hunched, and he seemed to be finding each step ponderous. Her heart sank slightly, remembering him as he had once been.

'I'm okay,' Smith assured her.

'Are you going to do anything about it, though?'

'I'm writing it up right this minute for the *Courant*. It'll go live in about an hour. No names, obviously, but at least it's on the record.'

'Meaning Pelham will probably see it. You're sure he knows? If he doesn't, you're not leaving him in any doubt.'

'That's why the wording's important. So what have you got on today?'

'Interviews mostly.'

'The victim's friends and associates? That'll be fun.' Clarke could hear Smith typing as she spoke.

'It's given you your mojo back, hasn't it?' she asked. 'The *Courant*, I mean.'

'It really has. Sooner I can monetise my way out of print journalism, the better.'

'Any blowback from that photo of the Crew?'

'An email from a certain car dealer's solicitors, sent via the website.'

'Cease and desist?'

'The way they worded it, they might as well have been using a quill.'

'You're going to ignore it?'

'Yep.' Smith seemed to hit one final key of her computer with a flourish. 'Worth my while heading to Leith to get a shot of the Tynecastle lot when they start arriving?'

'My guess is, they'll be on the lookout for exactly that.'

'Good point. I'll maybe stay here with my coffee and biscuits then.'

'Just don't get too comfortable, Laura. Ask yourself how James Pelham found out who you are. If he can do it, others can too.'

Leighton and Esson had been dispatched to interview Tommy Oram. When Clarke found out, she phoned Esson and told her to bring him in instead.

'Isn't the station going to be busy enough with the Tynecastle interviews?'

'Always room for one more,' she said, ending the call.

Fox stuck his head around the office doorway. 'Ready when you are,' he announced.

She was ready.

Rob Driscoll sat slouched in the interview room, legs splayed.

'Interesting,' Clarke said as she pulled out the chair alongside Fox.

'What?' Driscoll asked.

'Francis Haggard sat in that chair the exact same way as you.' She paused and watched Driscoll slowly draw himself upright, knees closing, unhappy perhaps to be too closely compared to his friend.

'Everyone must be in shock,' Clarke eventually said. 'At the station, I mean.'

'Obviously.'

'And with this being a murder inquiry, we got the permission we needed to empty Francis's locker.'

'Find anything juicy?'

Fox extracted a sheet of paper from the file in front of him. 'Couple of dodgy DVDs – nothing you'd classify as legal. And a passport belonging to a tourist who reported it lost three months ago. I hear there's a bit of a market for those?'

'I wouldn't know.'

'We've also looked at Francis's phone,' Clarke continued. 'DI Fox has a printout of his recent text messages. The very last one was to you, time-stamped the evening he was murdered.'

'Aye?'

'You didn't think to mention it earlier?'

Driscoll shrugged. 'Can't see how it's relevant.'

'The meeting under discussion never took place?'

'He failed to get back to me, as you'll also know from his phone.'

'And you'd no idea where he was staying?'

'No.'

'Absolutely sure about that?'

'Categorically sure, DI Clarke.'

'You seemed to think the meeting was urgent,' Fox added.

'You know as well as I do he was talking about making spurious claims about his workmates. Only natural we might want to discuss that.'

'In a frank but friendly manner, I'm sure.'

Driscoll turned his head from Fox to Clarke. 'Me and DI Fox have a bit of history – did he tell you that?'

'Your Professional Standards file is in the next room. I've looked at it.'

A fresh wariness crept across Driscoll's face. 'Thought you'd moved on from Complaints,' he said to Fox, who answered with a thin smile.

'Look,' Driscoll eventually said, 'of course we wanted him to change his mind. We don't piss on each other's chips.'

'What was your biggest fear?' Fox asked.

'In other words,' Clarke added, 'when he did start talking, who had most to lose?'

'I think I need a lawyer,' Driscoll said after a moment's consideration.

'Is that because you want to do a deal?' Fox asked.

'It's because I wouldn't trust you as far as I could throw you, DI Fox. And right now, I'd throw you over a fence at the fucking zoo.'

'I assume you've got a solicitor in mind?' Clarke asked. Driscoll nodded and took out his phone.

'Enjoy yourselves at Elemental?' he asked them as he made the call.

Clarke and Fox left the room without replying.

They stood next to the kettle, each holding a mug of instant coffee. Most of the desks around them were piled high with box files, those that had been dealt with consigned to the floor by Jason Ritchie's desk.

'Tell me about Driscoll and you,' Clarke said.

'He rules the roost now, anointed by his old mentor. He's probably never done anything without Fleck's say-so. Every time we interviewed him, he'd been coached. But he was never exactly a firebrand – the break-in at Haggard's, for example, I wouldn't say that was his style.'

'So is he losing control?'

'Maybe.' Fox paused. 'I meant to thank you for last night, by the way. My ears won't forget it in a hurry.'

'Any time, Disco Stu. We ended up getting to Driscoll, didn't we?'

'Hopefully the first of many.'

212

'Speaking of which . . .' Clarke had noticed Christine Esson passing the doorway. Just behind her came Tommy Oram and Tess Leighton. Esson was back a minute later.

'Promised him a drink,' she said, switching the kettle back on. 'Three sugars – who on earth takes three sugars these days?'

'Mind if I sit in?' Clarke asked.

'You're the boss. Should I tell Tess to stand down?'

'If she's okay with that.'

'She might not be.' Esson gave a glance in George Gamble's direction as he part-stifled a belch. 'Longer she spends away from her desk, the better she seems to like it.'

'She can have mine,' Fox offered. 'Next bunch of files are waiting on the screen there.'

Clarke took her coffee through with her, Esson carrying one for Tommy Oram. A quiet word with Leighton and she left the room. Oram played with the mug after it was set in front of him, but didn't seem inclined to drink from it.

'This is really just us filling in the blanks, Mr Oram,' Clarke began. 'Nothing for you to worry about.' He nodded his understanding. 'Do people call you Thomas or Tommy?'

'Tommy.'

'So, Tommy, how long have you worked for the Mackenzies?'

'Three years, three and a bit.'

'You're a general handyman? Replacing light bulbs, fixing broken locks?' He nodded again. 'Making you a bit of a locksmith?'

'Not really.'

'The flat where Francis Haggard died, when was the last time you were inside?'

'Before he moved in. Socket in the kitchen needed replacing, new batteries in the smoke alarms – just a general maintenance check.'

'So you didn't know him at all?'

'No.'

'And you'd no need for the tenement keys?'

'No.'

'There's a key safe attached to the door jamb, isn't there? I suppose you know the code.' Clarke watched him shake his head. 'Really?'

'If I need a key, I get it from the office. Needs to be okayed with the Mackenzies or Marion.'

'Marion being Mr Mackenzie's assistant?'

'She works reception.'

213

'And I notice you said Mackenzies plural – are you meaning Mrs Mackenzie or your pal Gaby?'

'Mrs Mackenzie,' he answered. Then, 'How do you know about me and Gaby?'

'We're detectives, Tommy. It's our job to know.' Clarke paused for a beat. 'Been to any of the other flats in that building recently?'

'Not since the maintenance check.'

'And that's all you do for the Mackenzies? Maintenance, I mean? It's just that you're young and you look pretty fit. You're never asked to collect rent, maybe talk to anyone who's fallen behind?'

Oram gave a snort. 'They don't need me for that. Plenty out there more qualified.'

'Qualified how?' Esson asked, sounding genuinely curious.

'Just people who don't take any nonsense.'

'Like nightclub bouncers?' Clarke guessed.

Oram shrugged. 'Wasn't much else for them during lockdown, was there?'

'That's a good point,' Clarke told him. Ever since her breakfast with Rebus, she'd been thinking of the doormen last night and how they'd cosied up to Gaby Mackenzie. 'Do you see much of Gaby these days?' she asked, trying to make the question sound casual.

'Now and again.'

'Known her a while, though? She got you the job, didn't she?'

'It's what pals do.'

'Still, her dad must have interviewed you? I mean, it's a pretty trusted position when you think of it.'

'We met in his office.'

'And he'd have known you're Jack Oram's son?'

Clarke could sense Christine Esson tensing a little, not knowing what she was on about. Across the table, Tommy Oram hadn't so much tensed as gone completely rigid. The knuckles around the coffee mug had turned white.

'Jack Oram who used to be close to Big Ger Cafferty,' Clarke went on, 'the man who sold his lettings company to Fraser Mackenzie.' It was statement rather than question, and intended for Esson as much as Oram.

'What of it?'

'I just think it's—'

'It's a coincidence, that's all,' Oram snapped. 'I knew Gaby and Gaby put in a word – she'd no idea who I was related to.' His eyes went from Clarke to Esson and back again. 'Coincidence,' he said, spreading out the syllables.

'You'll appreciate that detectives aren't too fond of those,' Clarke said, smiling with her mouth but not her eyes.

'I can't help that.'

'There was an accusation against you a while back . . .'

'Pack of lies. Your lot cleared me.'

Clarke nodded her apparent agreement. 'Any idea why Francis Haggard merited one of your premium properties?'

'I assume he could afford it.'

'See, that's the thing. We've got hold of his bank debits, and it looks like he was being charged way under the market rate.'

'You'd have to take that up with Mr Mackenzie.'

'We intend to. One last thing then, Tommy . . .'

'Yes?'

'Has Gaby ever taken you back to one of the vacant flats? Seems to be a regular thing with her.'

'I told you, we're friends – just friends.'

His voice was level enough, but Clarke could tell that behind his eyes he was seething.

'Ever go to the Elemental Club on Blair Street?'

'Sometimes, sure.'

'Is that how the two of you met?'

'Yes.'

'Where were you working back then?'

'Building sites mostly.'

'And suddenly you're rubbing shoulders with a wealthy and attractive young woman from the right side of the tracks.'

Oram looked from Clarke to Esson and back again. 'Is this going anywhere?'

'It was Gaby who found the body – did you know that? Door was open when she passed it with a guy she'd picked up at a party. Another coincidence, you reckon?'

'World is full of them,' Oram said, folding his arms.

Clarke glanced at Esson, who gave a slight twitch of the mouth, indicating she had nothing to add. There was a knock at the door. Malcolm Fox's head appeared.

'That's Driscoll all lawyered up,' he said. Clarke nodded that she was on her way. She turned back to Oram as the door closed.

'Know who DI Fox is talking about?' she asked. 'Rob Driscoll?'

215

Oram shook his head. 'He's a uniformed officer at Tynecastle police station. Staff there seem to be regulars at Elemental.'

'Are we done here?' Oram demanded.

'I'd like you to stick around for a bit, if you don't mind. In case we think of anything else . . .'

Rob Driscoll's solicitor was a steely-haired woman in late middle age, dressed in an immaculate trouser suit. Her name was Susan Jones, and she favoured an iPad over a pad of paper. The device's blue protective cover was folded open so that it could sit propped on the table in front of her. She puckered her mouth to let the detectives know she was ready, while her client sat next to her with his hands in his pockets. With Tommy Oram stewing in IV1, they had taken possession of IV2, Fox commenting that more rooms might be needed if they were going to bring in the whole of Tynecastle.

'You were Francis Haggard's friend as well as a co-worker?' Clarke began.

'Yes,' Driscoll said.

'Ever visit his flat in Newhaven?'

'Plenty times.'

'Did you do drugs there with him?'

'No comment.'

'Or see him do drugs himself?'

'We're none of us angels.'

'Is that a yes?'

'It's a no comment.'

'What about the break-in at his home?' Fox added. 'Anything to tell us about that?'

'No comment.'

'We were asking you earlier,' Fox went on, 'if you knew who stood to gain most from his death . . .'

'No comment.'

Clarke leaned forward. 'Is that how we're playing this, Rob? I mean, it's up to you, obviously, but as of right now, you are our main suspect. You were the one he was planning to meet the night he was killed. You were the one he trusted.'

Driscoll stared across the table at her. 'You've got his phone, right? So you must know I tried calling him again at midnight, by which time his body had already been found.'

'How do you know what time the body was discovered?'

'I'm a cop.'

'Classic alibi technique,' Fox said nonchalantly. 'Make it look as though you couldn't have known he was dead. I've seen it before, maybe you have too – after all, you're a cop.'

'Fuck you, DI Fox.'

Susan Jones decided it was time to intervene. 'Is my client being charged with anything, or is this just a fishing expedition?'

'Oh, it's a lot more than that, Ms Jones,' Clarke answered. 'The procurator fiscal is very interested in Rob here. *Very* interested.'

'We'd like to examine your client's phone,' Fox added. 'Phones plural if he has more than one – plus his home and work computers. We also have CCTV evidence from the Newhaven break-in, so it might be that PC Driscoll is required for an identity parade.'

'I was nowhere near the flat,' Driscoll growled. 'Is this you trying to fit me up?'

Fox studied him for a moment. 'Now you know how Tony Barlow must have felt.'

'Are you a detective or a bloody archaeologist?'

'Probably a bit of both. It's amazing how often history can come back to haunt those involved.'

'I'd like to consult with my client,' Jones stated, needing the gaps in her knowledge filled in.

'Knock yourself out,' Fox said, closing his folder. In the hallway, he turned to face Clarke. 'I don't suppose we've grounds to hold him.'

'Not really, not yet at least. But who the hell's Tony Barlow?'

'Misidentified as a paedophile, given summary justice by the Crew, headed by Driscoll under orders from Fleck.' Fox gestured towards the MIT office. 'Another coffee?'

'You get started, I'll catch you up.'

She turned the handle and pulled open the door to IV1. Tommy Oram was up on his feet, pacing the floor, under the watchful eye of a uniform from downstairs. He stopped and looked at Clarke.

'Off you go then,' she said. 'But be warned that you might be hearing from us again. And if there's anything you think we should know . . .'

'Half my bloody day wasted,' Oram said, grabbing his jacket from the back of his chair. 'Thank you very bloody much.'

'I'm sure your employer will be sympathetic. If he isn't, send him along and I'll have a word with him. Saves us summoning him ourselves.'

21

Rebus recognised the passenger first. He tugged at one of the car's rear doors and threw himself in. The two men in the front seats flinched and turned towards him.

'All right, Alan?' Rebus said to Fleck, reaching out to give the man's shoulder a squeeze.

'Rob,' Fleck said to the man in the driver's seat, 'you remember John Rebus?'

'Heading indoors, are we?' Rebus pointed towards Leith police station, fifty yards further along the street.

'Rob here's already had his grilling,' Fleck said. 'It's us oldies next, John, eh?'

'They've been going through the Complaints files,' Rebus stated. 'My name's come up more than I'd like. Apparently I was some kind of broker between Tynecastle and the likes of Cafferty.'

'They didn't mention that to me,' Driscoll said, studying Rebus in the rear-view mirror.

'So what did you chat about?'

'They brought up Tony Barlow,' Fleck answered.

'They?'

'Two DIs, Clarke and Fox,' Driscoll replied. 'But specifically Fox. He was Complaints, now Specialist Crime.'

'Rob was the last person Francis was in contact with,' Fleck said, all his earlier fake heartiness gone. 'MIT have zeroed in on that.'

'I'll bet they have.'

'It won't go anywhere – there's nowhere for it *to* go,' Driscoll said.

'Which is presumably why they've added Barlow to the pot.'

'You know this bastard Fox?'

'We've had dealings, haven't we, Alan?'

'Never got very far,' Fleck countered. 'We were far too canny to let that happen.'

'One loose link in the chain is all it takes,' Rebus said. 'And with Francis Haggard, Fox thinks he has his link.'

'Pity the chain seems to have fallen down a grating.' Fleck was smiling quietly. Rebus got the feeling it was a performance meant to bolster Driscoll, who was gripping the steering wheel as though ready to choke the life from it. Fleck even patted the younger man's arm, as if to calm him. 'You did the right thing, Rob. Bringing your lawyer in and then saying as little as possible. Here's hoping the others are half as wise.' Then he half turned towards Rebus. 'Best not keep them waiting, eh?'

He opened the passenger door and climbed out. Rebus followed suit, the two men striding towards their destination.

'Nice motor,' Rebus commented. Driscoll was still gripping the steering wheel, staring straight ahead without seeing.

'He'll be selling it soon, if you're interested.'

'What I'm interested in is keeping my name out of this.'

'Sounds like it's too late for that, John.'

'*One* meeting I set up, just one.'

'Sure your memory's not going?'

'I did it as a favour, nothing more – and I stayed the other side of the door.'

'I'd be disappointed if you weren't listening in, though?' Fleck watched Rebus shake his head. 'Or if Cafferty didn't fill you in afterwards?'

'Not that either.'

'And I suppose the ton I gave you as thanks went to good causes?'

'I probably used it to prop up local businesses,' Rebus said.

Fleck came to a stop and faced him. 'You really don't know what that meeting with Cafferty was about?'

'I really don't.'

Fleck sought something in Rebus's eyes and body language, failing to find it. He shook his head slowly and opened the door to the police station, Rebus following him inside. Fleck gave his name to the front desk and was handed a visitor pass.

'They want me too,' Rebus told the officer. He signed in and clipped his own pass to his jacket. A young man in a suit opened the inner door.

'Mr Fleck?'

Fleck held out a hand for him to shake. The officer stared blankly at Rebus.

'I'm John Rebus,' Rebus informed him. 'DI Clarke invited me along for a chat.'

'I'm DC King,' King said by way of introduction. 'If you'll follow me . . .'

'How long have you been in CID, son?' Fleck asked as they were led towards the stairs.

'Long enough.'

'I was stationed here for a while when I was about your age. Place was falling down then, and nothing seems to have changed.'

'Attitudes have,' King offered.

'Did you hear that, John?' Fleck said. 'That's us being put in our place.'

Malcolm Fox was standing at the top of the stairs. He ignored Fleck, his attention fixed on Rebus.

'What's he doing here?' he asked. Colour began to flood King's cheeks.

'Said he has a meeting with DI Clarke.'

'In a manner of speaking,' Rebus offered. 'You'd be summoning me eventually, so I thought I'd save you the trouble. Siobhan in there?' He gestured towards the MIT office. 'I'll leave you to get acquainted with Mr Fleck, then.'

'You can't just . . .'

But Rebus already had. His eyes took in the box files, and the drawn looks on the faces of Gamble, Leighton and Esson. The murder wall had been added to. He studied it briefly, then turned his attention to Clarke's desk. He could see her through the open doorway of the DCI's private office. She had her back to him and was blocking any view of him the DCI herself might have. From the paperwork on her desk, she seemed to have been checking Francis Haggard's finances. Flat worth half a million with no mortgage outstanding. About seventy K in various bank accounts, not including his accumulated pension.

As Clarke emerged from her meeting, she froze, turning her head to check her boss was busy on her computer. Then she pulled Rebus by the sleeve out of Trask's line of sight.

'How was your roll?' he asked her. 'I hope you didn't waltz off without paying?'

'What the hell are you doing here?' she hissed.

'Waiting for my interview.'

'You can't just—'

'Malcolm Fox said the exact same thing.' He gestured towards her desk. 'Haggard wasn't exactly hurting, was he? Have you asked the widow where it came from?'

'She reckoned he was just well paid – told her he did a lot of overtime.'

'What as – a bank robber?'

'We know plenty of the Crew were on the take.' She waved a hand towards the box files. 'Luxury holidays, flash cars and watches, designer clothes.'

'My old Saab becomes my alibi,' Rebus commented. 'Who else have you been speaking to?'

'We brought in Tommy Oram.'

'Did he give you much?'

'Not as such.'

'But?'

'His employer might have been using club doormen as muscle on anyone falling behind with their rent. One way for them to earn a crust when lockdown was at its height.' Rebus nodded but stayed silent. 'Remember I told you I watched the daughter do a DJ set last night? Doormen kept going up to talk to her.'

'She's the one doing the recruiting?' he guessed.

'Stands to reason.' Clarke checked the time on her phone. 'Your old pal Fleck should have been here by now.'

'Malcolm's got him in one of the interview rooms.'

'How do you know that?'

'I arrived the same time as him.'

'You shouldn't *be* here.' She took him by the arm again and led him into the corridor.

'But you do need to question me?'

'At some point, yes.'

'Whenever you like, Siobhan – I won't even demand a lawyer.'

Clarke gave a sigh. 'And *of course* you've been talking to Rob Driscoll, too.' She glanced in the direction of the two interview rooms.

'You should be in there,' Rebus advised.

'Once I've seen you off the premises.'

'I've not lost my sense of direction.'

'You do have a tendency to wander, though.' She gestured to the stairs with one hand. Rebus headed down.

'You won't get anything from Alan Fleck, you know,' he told her. 'He's as savvy as they come, and he's got a hide like a rhino.'

'He's also mentioned on every other page of those Complaints files. Maybe if we promise to go easy, he'll become a bit more amenable.'

'Fox has no intention of going easy on the likes of Fleck – you told me so yourself.'

'Which is why I'm going to make my presence known in the interview room, just as soon as you're safely off the premises. Don't want Malcolm ignoring the bigger picture.'

She opened the door to the reception area, noticing two uniformed officers standing there shuffling their feet. She recognised one of them.

'You still wanting that kiss?' she demanded of him.

'Thought you were Gayfield Square,' he shot back.

'I'm everywhere – and I'm particularly looking forward to asking you some questions.' She saw another face she knew. 'The queue at the nightclub last night?' she said, pointing at the man. 'I hope you're as chatty today.' The officer's face began to colour. 'Won't keep you waiting longer than we have to.'

Clarke made eye contact with Rebus for a moment before heading back through the door. Rebus stood in front of the two uniforms.

'All right, Chris?'

'Long time, John.' Chris Agnew angled his head towards his red-faced companion. 'This is Deek Turnbull. He's fairly new to the game. Deek, this is John Rebus.'

Turnbull's eyebrows rose perceptibly. 'It's an honour,' he announced, his hand shooting out to meet Rebus's.

'Don't believe half the stories,' Rebus cautioned. 'Any relation to Billy Turnbull?'

'My grandad.'

'Good copper in his day, took no nonsense.'

'He still likes to go look at the police box at the foot of Canongate. Says he spent more time there than at home.'

'Probably some truth in that.'

Rebus turned to Agnew. He hadn't seen him in four or five years, during which time the younger man had added too much weight around the middle and his hairline had started receding. He'd never been blessed with the best skin, and his face was blotchy and had an unhealthy sheen to it. Even back when Rebus had seen him on a more regular basis, he'd wondered if Agnew's nickname – 'the

Swordsman' – was ironic. Alan Fleck had sworn, however, that he had a knack for finding willing women. Rebus saw no sign of a ring on his wedding finger.

'Still with Rosie?' he asked.

'You've a good memory, but I chucked her three years back.'

'Watch out for this one,' Rebus advised Turnbull. 'He's better at chat-up lines than actual policing.'

Agnew's mouth twitched, his eyes on the door Clarke had disappeared through. 'I heard they'd brought in Rob, and even Alan – didn't know their net was being cast any wider.'

'Anyone and everyone, it seems like.' Rebus looked at Turnbull. 'You've been briefed, have you?'

'We've had team talks,' Agnew answered for Turnbull. 'Deek here knows when to keep his gob shut.'

'Same goes for you, I dare say, Chris.' Rebus paused. 'Sounds like the pair of you have already managed to rub DI Clarke up the wrong way, though – that's not a great start.'

'Just a bit of banter, John. Surprised she couldn't take it on the chin.'

'Maybe it wasn't her chin you were trying to kiss?'

'It's true I'm not the fussiest, but she's not particularly my type.' Agnew rubbed the underside of his jaw. Rebus didn't like to think what scenarios he was imagining.

'She happens to be a friend of mine,' he said coldly. 'She's also fucking good at her job. So if you're thinking of employing a charm offensive, take it from me – she won't be charmed, and she *will* find it offensive.'

'Roger that,' Agnew said, stiffening his shoulders.

'I assume there'll be a debrief this evening? You still using that pub on Fountainbridge?' Rebus watched Agnew nod, then looked around as if taking in his surroundings. 'Shame there are no chairs. If I know Siobhan Clarke, you're in for a long stand.'

Agnew reached out and touched Rebus's arm. 'Word outside, John?' After Rebus had nodded, he turned towards Turnbull. 'Don't let them take you upstairs without me.'

'Understood.'

He led the way out onto the pavement. Rebus asked him what was on his mind.

'You knew Francis, John,' Agnew said, checking no one else was within earshot. 'We all thought we knew him better than we did. Never thought he'd be one to squeal.' He shook his head slowly. 'I didn't see that coming at all. This was a guy I'd hang out with – dinners with the wives and girlfriends; nights at the boxing; trips to the football. We were *mates* – him, me and Rob. Proper buds, not just work mates.'

'These parties and nights out, who else would be at them? Alan Fleck?'

'Alan, aye, and a few others.'

'Any bad boys invited? Or were they maybe the hosts?'

'Ach, you know what it's like. You're getting a box at Ibrox, you don't always want to know whose wallet's responsible.'

'Cafferty sometimes, I'm guessing.' Rebus paused. 'And latterly, maybe Fraser Mackenzie?'

Agnew studied Rebus's face. 'What's going on here, John?'

Rebus held up his hands in a show of innocence. 'Nothing up my sleeves, Chris. I'm a civilian these days, remember? It's just that some of your lads were at a nightclub last night where the resident DJ happens to be Mackenzie's daughter.'

'Gaby?' A smile spread across Agnew's face. 'Tried to have a wee go there myself one time, but she wasn't having it. And I suppose you could call her the resident DJ, if you were feeling ungenerous.'

Rebus's eyebrows contracted. 'Well, what is she then?'

'The owner,' Agnew told him. 'Lock, stock and profit-making barrel.'

'Should I have asked Rob Driscoll's lawyer to stick around?' Alan Fleck asked Clarke as she settled on a chair across from him in IV2.

'Depends how guilty you want to look.'

Fleck shrugged. 'Rob knows the score. He was angling to meet Francis and Francis had agreed. Stands to reason he's a person of interest. I'm just not sure I qualify.' He broke off as the door opened and Malcolm Fox strode in carrying a mug of coffee for himself. Fleck managed a wry smile. 'How many times have you rehearsed that entrance?' he asked.

Fox ignored him, sitting down and placing a hand on the two bulging and antiquated manila folders on the tabletop.

'You know DI Fox here has already been to see me at my place of work?' Fleck informed Clarke before either detective could say anything. 'Almost counts as harassment, the way he carries on, same as when he was Complaints.'

Fox had been busying himself on his phone. He found what he was looking for, Fleck making show of peering at the screen.

'This is you and Rob Driscoll,' Fox stated, 'after you'd convened a meeting of the Crew, yes?'

'I didn't "convene" anything.'

'I'm sure it was Driscoll's idea, but he takes his cue from you, doesn't he, "Sarge"?'

The smile returned to Fleck's face, though he looked anything but amused. 'You think you're Prince Golden Balls, don't you? But the way I hear it, you're nothing but Jen Lyon's poodle. Everyone at Gartcosh says so.' He turned to Clarke. 'You know as well as I do, in any big institution shite tends to get hoisted upwards.'

'None of this is going to get us very far,' Clarke commented, keeping her tone neutral.

'She agrees with me,' Fleck said to Fox. 'And she should know – she learned from one of the best.'

'Why did you have this little get-together?' Fox said, unwilling to be diverted. He waggled his phone in Fleck's face.

'Francis was readying to tell a pack of lies about his colleagues. Stands to reason those colleagues might want to talk tactics.' Fleck studied the ceiling. 'No air in this place. You sure it's COVID-safe?'

'COVID is the least of your worries,' Fox said. 'You'd tried talking to Francis Haggard yourself, hadn't you?'

'Had I?'

'According to his phone.' Fox made show of studying the list in front of him. But Fleck had turned his attention back to Clarke.

'You know Wee Malky here tried to kick your old friend John off the force on more than one occasion? John's in bad enough shape as it is, but can you imagine him stripped of his pension? That's the type of slug you're sitting beside right now.'

'When we spoke at your showroom,' Fox countered, 'you seemed pretty keen that I look at John Rebus's past exploits rather than your own.'

'That's not my recollection, DI Fox.'

'Francis Haggard's phone.' Clarke nudged Fleck, hoping to avert a staring contest.

'Yes, all right.' He seemed to concede. 'I tried getting in touch. I was concerned about him.'

'About what he'd say?'

'About what he was going through,' he corrected her. 'His life had turned from bed of roses to field of pish in an absolute bloody instant.'

'So you reached out to him, but he ignored you – that can't have

225

made you feel good.' Clarke paused. 'Tell me, when you found out he was abusing his wife, did you similarly reach out to him – or was it only when you got wind that your past exploits were to be his defence?'

'Does it matter?'

She took the list from Fox. 'Seems you only started trying to contact him after he'd begun talking to us.'

'What was I supposed to do – slap him about for hitting his wife?'

Fox cleared his throat. 'You've slapped people about for less.'

'So how come I retired with an unblemished record, DI Fox? Despite your frenzied efforts, I mean?'

'You had the Crew backing you up and repeating your lies. But now with Francis Haggard in the mortuary, they've got a lot more to lose. Are you confident you can still depend on them? I know I wouldn't put money on it.'

Fleck cupped a hand to one ear. 'I'm not hearing any evidence here that puts me within half a city's distance of Francis when he got topped.' He paused, meeting the stare Fox was giving him. Fox slapped his palms against the tabletop and, leaving them there, pushed himself upright, leaning across towards Fleck.

'That smug self-satisfaction of yours is about to get a hefty dose of paint-stripper. The car-smuggling, the death of Kyle Weller, the crippling of Tony Barlow and everything else – you're going to be made to pay for the lot.'

'I look forward to seeing your evidence. I get the notion I might be six feet under first, though.'

'Are you forgetting we've got Haggard's computer? His killer wasn't sharp enough to take it. I'd like to say that narrows down the possible suspects, but Tynecastle's brimful of halfwits who'd have done what you told them. Then there are the notes he left behind in a drawer in Newhaven – whoever broke into the family abode only did half a job, messing the place up rather than searching it.'

'We've got those same men on CCTV,' Clarke improvised. 'You'd be amazed what modern technology can do with just a pair of eyes.'

Fleck seemed to be chewing the inside of his cheek.

'Feel free to do a line if you think you need one,' Fox said, lowering himself back onto his chair. 'Your boys seem to be reliant on the stuff. Shame the supply's been choked off recently.'

'*Do* you use narcotics, Mr Fleck?' Clarke asked, keeping the question casual.

'No comment,' Alan Fleck said.

It was Malcolm Fox's turn to smile. 'Took you long enough,' he said.

After they'd let Fleck go, Clarke and Fox lingered in the corridor, breathing in lungfuls of slightly fresher air.

'One thing he wasn't wrong about,' Clarke commented. 'That room *is* a COVID risk.' Then, her eyes on Fox, 'Computer files and written notes?'

Fox gave a shrug. 'I was winging it. Definitely got to him, though. That was a nice line about the drugs, too.'

'Thanks.'

'*Can* we ID suspects from just the eyes, though?'

'Given the right budget and a friendly face at Special Branch . . .'

Christine Esson appeared in the office doorway. 'We think we've got something,' she told them, drawing them inside.

Trask waited until she had the team's full attention. 'We have a name for at least one bar where Francis Haggard might have spent some time on the afternoon before he was killed. A regular saw his photo in the *Evening News* and called it in. We need to go talk to the staff and the witness. So far it's an ID from a grainy newspaper photo, so I'm not pinning up any bunting, but it's as good a lead as we have right now.'

'What's the name of the bar?' Gamble asked.

'Drifter's. It's on Great Junction Street – basically walking distance from here.'

'And from his flat,' Clarke added.

Trask nodded. 'Take Christine with you. Let us know what you find.'

'Will do.'

'Colin and Jason, go see the caller. I've got his details here.' She held out a slip of paper, which King took from her with the eagerness of a seagull snatching a chip.

They all grabbed their jackets, Clarke glancing in Fox's direction to see if he felt snubbed. But he was at his desk, peering at the screen of his computer. Downstairs, the two uniforms from Tynecastle were still waiting, propped against a wall and passing the time on their phones. Recognising Clarke, they began to shift their feet. She shook her head.

'Someone will be with you shortly,' she said, opening the door and making her exit. Once outside, Esson turned to her.

'That was a lie, wasn't it?' she asked.

'Obviously,' Clarke said with a thin smile.

King and Ritchie barrelled out through the door after them, Ritchie giving a thumbs-up.

'They'll learn,' Esson smirked.

'It's still nice to see, though,' Clarke mused.

The day wasn't bad, and they knew they'd be quicker walking than taking a car. Drifter's was trying to make itself look like a Hawaiian tiki bar, with fake straw on its facade and pedal steel guitar music playing over the speakers. There was just the one server, dressed in a loud shirt and with a pink plastic lei around his neck. The half-dozen drinkers seemed resistant to the theme and were sticking to pints of lager. Clarke showed the barman her warrant card and then a photo of Francis Haggard.

'He was in here three days ago,' she said.

'Afternoon or evening?'

'Afternoon, we think.'

'Well, that was my shift.' The man studied the photo again and nodded. 'Think he'd had one or two before he arrived. Didn't cause any trouble, but looked like he might.' He glanced over to a table where two men sat talking. 'Hey, Colin,' he called out, 'you spoke to him, didn't you?'

The man called Colin, tall, skinny and probably retired, got up and walked over to join them.

'Oh aye,' he said, looking at the photo. 'He's the one that died, aye?'

'That's right.'

'He was in a bit of a mood. I happened to be passing his table and told him it might never happen.' He kept his eyes on the photo. 'It did, though, didn't it?'

'We would have appreciated you coming forward with this information, sir,' Esson scolded him.

'What information? That a guy sat in a pub and had a drink?'

Clarke tried to keep her tone light. 'Did he happen to say anything else, maybe where he was headed next?'

'Don't think so.' The man paused. 'No, hang on – he saw that I had the paper folded open at the racing pages, asked me if I was a betting man. Well, I do like a wee flutter and I probably said as much. He told me he preferred casinos. Higher stakes, I think he

228

said. Which is fine for those who can afford it, but he looked to me like he'd slept in a hedge.'

'What time was this?'

'Maybe four or five o'clock.'

'My shift finishes at six,' the barman commented.

'And he'd left by then?'

Both men nodded. 'Don't ask me to swear on it,' Colin said, 'but he might've flagged down a taxi. He went out, and next thing a black cab pulls up. Unmistakable engine they've got. You can hear it above a ukulele, which can be a blessing in here.'

'You love it really,' the barman told him. Then, to Clarke and Esson, 'He paid cash, I remember now – bit of a rarity these days. He told me to have one for myself. Speaking of which, drink on the house?'

Clarke shook her head. 'We'll have something, but we'll pay our way, thanks all the same.'

They ordered fruit juices and took them to a table, sitting opposite one another.

'Casinos?' Esson speculated.

'More likely he just went home,' Clarke said.

'He wouldn't have needed a taxi for that.'

'After a skinful he might.'

'Sounds to me like he was steering clear of the flat, though, waiting for the heat to die down. He probably did sleep rough the previous night.'

'How many casinos in the city?' Clarke asked.

'These days, fewer than half a dozen. Wouldn't take us long to check.'

'Start by phoning around with his description?'

Esson nodded. 'But maybe take pity on those poor sods stuck in the waiting area,' she said.

'Why?'

'Because we're better than them.'

'I suppose that's true,' Clarke said. 'But all the same, let's not rush our drinks, eh?'

22

Rebus opened the door to the pub's back room, carrying his pint of IPA with him.

'This the party?' he said. He recognised Fleck, Driscoll, Agnew, Turnbull and a few other faces, but by no means all of them. The space wasn't large, three narrow tables forming a U shape. There was a frosted window with vertical bars at the far end, and padded benches rather than individual chairs. Every one of the dozen or so heads turned towards him, conversation paused.

'Bunch up a bit, lads,' Fleck said with affected levity. 'Nice of you to join us, John.'

'I'm not staying,' Rebus declared. 'Just passing and thought I'd say hello.'

'Just passing.' The speaker gave a disbelieving snort. Rebus knew the face. Jimmy Callan. They'd retired around the same time.

'Heard you were dead, Jimmy,' Rebus said, raising his glass to his lips.

'In better health than some.'

'Well, you can probably afford to go private, with all those back-handers you took.'

'You'd know more about that than me.'

'Time was, I'd probably have agreed with you – I thought I knew every scam going, along with who was pulling them. But now I'm not so sure.'

'We learned from the best,' Agnew said, eyes flitting between Rebus and Fleck as he raised his glass.

'The best or the worst,' Rebus replied. 'Sometimes it's hard to tell them apart.' He looked around the room again. 'How many have been grilled so far? I assume the ones who have are here to pass their wisdom on to those still waiting.'

'Talking of waiting,' Turnbull said, 'your wee pal Clarke kept us hanging around almost the whole day. Waste of time and the taxpayer's money.'

'When we're so many bodies down from the 'rona,' someone else piped up.

'Oh aye,' Rebus said, 'I can see how seriously you all take public health. There's probably more germs than oxygen in this room. In fact, I'd bet on it.'

'You calling us germs?' one of the younger drinkers growled.

'If the diced cap fits,' Rebus answered with a shrug.

'Careful, John,' Fleck said in warning. 'Some of us know we've got things to be grateful to you for, but goodwill goes only so far.'

'If you mean Kyle Weller's death in custody, I know the feeling is I magicked the evidence away, but I really didn't. Stuff gets lost, it's a fact of life.'

'Not just Kyle Weller, though,' Fleck stated quietly.

'Well then, let's talk about Cafferty. But that requires some chat about Fraser Mackenzie first. Your old colleague Francis Haggard needed a place to stay, and he went straight to Mackenzie. I've been pondering why, and the simplest answer is that he knew he'd get a good deal. All he had to do was say he was a cop from Tynecastle. Now, I've started hearing some stories about Mackenzie, and things are clicking into place. Same sort of deal you had with Cafferty you now have with Mackenzie. But here's the thing – someone took a photo of Francis Haggard in that flat on Constitution Street and sent it to Cafferty. Why would they do that? Is it to do with Haggard or the flat? Or maybe a bit of both?'

Rebus waited in silence, biding his time, until Alan Fleck rose to his feet, seemingly with infinite slowness, and nodded towards the door.

'Best take this outside, John,' he stated, leading the way.

By the time Rebus joined him, he was ten yards along the pavement from the pub, standing by a low wall belonging to a car wash. The car wash itself was closed, its forecourt unlit. Fleck had pulled up the collar of his coat. As soon as Rebus arrived, he began to talk.

'Before we start, I need to know this goes no further. We're clearing the air here, putting your mind at rest. If it gets back to Fox, Clarke or anyone else, I'll know the source.'

'Say what you've got to say.' But Rebus saw that Fleck was

prepared to wait. 'Okay, just between us, then.'

'You'd swear on your granddaughter's life?' Fleck saw Rebus's face turn stony. 'Theoretically, I mean.'

'I'm giving you my word. Time was, that would have been enough.'

'Things have changed, though, haven't they, and people with them?' Fleck paused, looking to left and right. 'It was seven years back,' he began. 'You remember that meeting I had you set up with Cafferty? What I didn't tell you was I wanted you there as protection.'

'Protection from what?'

'There was this addict we'd pulled in; a spell behind bars loomed. But he had something to trade, a rumour about where Cafferty stashed at least some of his ill-gotten gains.' He paused again. 'An everyday flat in a tenement on Constitution Street. The one property he owned that was never rented out. So we went and took a look. The door it had on it was like something out of Fort Knox. That's when we knew we weren't being spun a line. How to get in, though, that was the question. Wait until someone came along and unlocked it? Francis had a better idea. We went around the back of the building. Nothing much there but a shared drying green and a lot of bins. Francis took one look at the drainpipe and knew it was the route in. He was bloody fit, I'll give him that. Said he'd always been a dab hand with the climbing ropes in the school gym. Up he went, pulled on a glove and punched the window in. We kept lookout, but you know what it's like – nobody saw or heard anything. Francis clambered inside. He told me after, it was candy from a baby. Bin bags stuffed with banknotes. He dropped them down to us, then shinned back down the pipe.'

'How much did you get?'

'Plenty. We all decided when we split it that Francis should get a bit extra for his efforts. And that was that.'

'It wasn't, though, was it?'

Fleck exhaled loudly through his nose. 'I'm not sure how, but Cafferty started hearing who it was that might've ripped him off. I knew I had to go have a word.'

'With me riding shotgun?'

'I suppose that's one way of putting it. I made it clear to him that any reprisals would be very bad news for him. He should think of it as a business write-off. Chalk it up to experience and maybe put some bars on that window.'

'He couldn't have been thrilled.'

232

'He wasn't.'

'No payback, though?'

'The junkie, the one who told us? Someone tipped off Organised Crime that he had a stash of weapons in his flat. There was a raid. Half a dozen shonky handguns retrieved. He went down for it, swearing they'd been planted. He'd only been inside a couple of weeks when someone walked into his cell and tried cutting his throat.'

'Tried?'

'He pulled through. Got himself cut again a few months later, survived that too.'

'Cafferty taking it out on the one person who couldn't retaliate?'

'I always thought you knew,' Fleck mused.

'About the money?' Rebus shook his head.

'I reckoned that was why you never felt the need to ask about it.'

Rebus grew thoughtful. 'Would the Mackenzies have known?'

'About Francis specifically? I don't think so.'

'But they know the flat's history?'

'Well, Cafferty owned that flat for a long time, so one of them probably does.'

'Beth, you mean?' Rebus watched Fleck nod. 'And is it true that Tynecastle now has an arrangement with Fraser Mackenzie?'

'I'm a car dealer these days, John.'

'But Mackenzie's business is a front for dope-pushing – your pals in the Crew won't have kept that nugget from you?'

'I probably hear the same stories you do.'

'Thing is, I hadn't heard *any* stories, not until a few days back.'

'City was just lying there legs open after Cafferty got shot. Someone was bound to take advantage.'

'So what's this photo all about?' Rebus asked.

'I'm every bit as intrigued as you are.'

'Someone who reckoned Cafferty would recognise Haggard and decide to make him pay for what he'd done?'

Fleck seemed to consider the possibility. 'One more thing, John,' he eventually said. 'You might not have helped us with Kyle Weller, but there's still the Tony Barlow case. It was you who gave us the guy's name. We went after him thinking he was a paedo. He wasn't, though, was he? He was just someone Cafferty wanted to see get hurt. He had us in his web after that – you as much as me and everyone else. That pissed me off. In fact, it's probably why I sanctioned the break-in. Some of the cash we took went towards

Barlow's physio.'

'You're all heart, Alan.'

Fleck was looking over Rebus's shoulder. Rebus turned and saw that Driscoll and Agnew were on the pavement outside the pub, Driscoll's face illuminated by his lighter as he lit a cigarette. The two men began to saunter towards Rebus and Fleck, trying to look casual for the benefit of passing traffic.

'Everything all right, Sarge?' Driscoll asked.

'Tickety-boo,' Fleck assured him. 'Wouldn't you agree, John?'

'I'd say I'm probably a thousand light years away from agreeing,' Rebus countered. 'Because chances are, when I stepped into that little cabal of yours, I was in the presence of whoever murdered Francis Haggard, and that realisation gives me whatever the opposite is of a nice warm glow. Now I learn that you stole a slab of cash from Big Ger Cafferty . . .'

Driscoll looked at Fleck. 'You said he knew.'

'I thought he did.'

Driscoll turned his attention back to Rebus. 'Stands to reason Cafferty told you.'

'He didn't.'

'But you were his—'

Rebus grabbed the front of Driscoll's jacket, shaking him. The cigarette flew from the corner of Driscoll's mouth.

'I was never his anything!' Rebus snarled.

'Easy, John,' Fleck said.

'Loosen that fucking grip, old-timer,' Driscoll said, baring his teeth. His eyes were glassy and there was rum on his breath.

'Or what?'

The answer dawned on Rebus a moment too late as Driscoll's forehead drove into the bridge of his nose. He reeled backwards, eyes brimming with tears. He could feel the warm blood begin to run from his nostrils down towards his chin.

'Christ's sake, Rob.' It was Chris Agnew who spoke, hauling Driscoll a few steps away from the fray. Driscoll ignored him, pointing at Rebus instead.

'Just keep the fuck away from us! We're fighting fires in all directions and the last thing we need is an interfering old bastard like you!'

'VIP welcome, I think you told me I'd get,' Rebus said for Fleck's benefit. Driscoll meantime was looking around for his cigarette. Having decided it couldn't be saved, he dug another from the packet, all witnessed by Rebus through blurred vision. While he wiped at his eyes, Fleck produced a large white handkerchief, which he pressed to Rebus's nose.

'This isn't how we go about things, Rob,' Fleck declared.

'It's *exactly* how we go about things. I've known you do a lot worse in your day.'

'What sort of worse?' Rebus asked.

A blast of laughter escaped Driscoll as he arched his face skywards. 'He just won't give up, will he?'

'I really won't,' Rebus confirmed. He had taken control of the handkerchief with one hand and was pinching the bridge of his nose with the other.

'Come on, Rob,' Agnew was saying, tugging at his colleague's arm.

'Keeping you from something, are we, Chris?' Driscoll teased. 'Or should that be some*one*?' He jabbed a finger into Agnew's chest as he spoke. 'You're looking for people who didn't get on with Francis, here's exhibit one.'

'I've had enough of this,' Agnew said, releasing Driscoll's arm. 'You're well out of order.' He began to march back towards the pub.

'Tell me something I don't know!' Driscoll called out to him, before turning towards Rebus and Fleck. 'There goes a bastard who can't take a joke.'

'Probably because he didn't think you were joking,' Fleck responded.

'Alan, you've got a face like a skelped arse.'

'Whose fault is that, do you think?'

'Oh aye, blame me. Is that where this is all headed? You don't think it's enough I've got a murder inquiry on my back?' When Fleck failed to respond, some of the fire seemed to leave Driscoll, and he turned his attention to Rebus. 'Lost it there for a second, John. No hard feelings, eh?' He held out a hand, which Rebus studiously ignored until Driscoll took the hint and retracted it. 'I won't be anybody's fall guy, Alan,' he said, his voice low and controlled. 'If anyone tries, they're dead meat, understood? You old fuckers can plot all you want between you, but you're not taking me down, not without a fight that'll make you wish you'd never started it.' He nodded to himself as if to stiffen his resolve, then, finally lighting the cigarette that had been bobbing in his mouth, he began to follow Agnew back towards the pub.

Rebus lifted the handkerchief away and studied the blobs of

scarlet. The flow had slowed to a trickle. He kept up the pressure with his thumb and forefinger.

'Just a silly laddie, John,' Fleck commented. 'Francis's death, it's got us all ...' He broke off. 'I'll see to it that he apologises properly.'

'Will he try fobbing me off with a ton?'

'Why? Do you need it?'

'What I need is not to have short-fuse merchants getting in my face.'

'You've got to understand, Rob was Francis's best friend – or at least assumed he was. He's been feeling the betrayal more than most.' Fleck was staring at the retreating figure. 'He's a good kid really.'

'They're not kids, though, or laddies. They're fully grown men who know what they're doing.'

'As if you never did anything daft when you were young.'

'Nothing as stupid as ripping off a gangster.'

'Some of which *you* took for organising the meet with Cafferty.'

'I wish to hell I'd never set foot inside Tynecastle, or let you worm your way into my life.'

Fleck's face darkened. 'Remember, nothing you heard tonight goes anywhere, or there'll be payback.'

Rebus bunched up the handkerchief and stuffed it into Fleck's breast pocket. 'One last question,' he said. 'What happened to the guy in jail?'

Fleck thought for a moment. 'Did his time and broke free of the drugs – Christ knows how. Runs a pub these days and gives Cafferty a cut.'

'Which pub?'

'The Moorfoot in Craigmillar. He's called Kenny Beecham.'

'That wasn't the name of the licensee last time I was there.'

'Ex-cons tend not to get alcohol licences, John. There'll be a second party involved.' Fleck was holding out a hand towards Rebus, same as Driscoll had done. Rebus stared at it.

'Is this you telling me it's either truce or consequences?' The hand was still there as he turned away, digging a tissue from his pocket and tearing it into clumps, which he shoved into either nostril. 'Worth it, though, all the same,' he told himself, wiggling his nose a little. It wasn't broken, which counted as a bonus under the circumstances. Chris Agnew had told him he'd been close mates with Francis Haggard, but Driscoll seemed to think otherwise. Rebus

236

thought of Agnew's reputation and nickname – the Swordsman. Maybe he'd tried turning on the charm for Haggard's other half. Either that or there was some other reason for their enmity – always supposing Driscoll had been telling the truth. Had Agnew denied it? He had not, though Driscoll himself had called it a joke.

If so, no one had been left laughing.

Clarke met Gina Hendry at a wine bar on George Street. The liaison officer already had the dregs of one cocktail in front of her and was being served another as Clarke arrived.

'As bad as that?' Clarke said, ordering a G and T from the waiter.

'Just felt like it,' Hendry explained. 'I've spent most of the afternoon with Cheryl and Stephanie.'

'Cheryl's still at her sister's?' Clarke shrugged off her coat and got comfortable.

'Can't bring herself to go back to her flat. She says the break-in just adds insult to injury. Meantime there's a funeral to arrange.'

'Though we won't be releasing the body just yet.'

Hendry nodded. 'I made sure she knows. Then I broke the news that my role was done and dusted.'

'How did she take it?'

'She said she'd miss me. Stephanie tried to press a bottle of wine on me.' She peered at Clarke above the rim of her glass. 'Anyway, how's your day been?'

'Lots of interviews with the deceased's erstwhile colleagues. I don't suppose any of them have offered condolences?'

'There *was* a wreath left at the gates – I took it in with me. Card was from someone called Rob. Stephanie screwed it up and tossed it in the bin.'

'Rob Driscoll,' Clarke stated.

'Tynecastle, right?'

'Did the wreath go the same way?'

'How did you guess? Can I assume you're treating all those colleagues as suspects? Stephanie seems to have made up her mind that it has to be one of them.'

'We're ruling nothing in and nothing out.'

'This isn't a journalist you're talking to, Siobhan.'

Clarke's drink arrived. She thanked the waiter and stirred the wedge of lemon around the glass. 'Constitution Street wasn't a break-in,' she said. 'Nothing taken. Probably someone he knew and trusted.' She concentrated on her drink for a moment. 'Cheryl's never mentioned drug use to you?'

'Hers or his?'

'Either.'

'I got the feeling alcohol was their fuel of choice. Did he dabble?'

'He definitely dabbled.'

Hendry looked thoughtful. 'One thing I've been feeling the past couple of visits . . .'

'What?'

'A bit of edge between the sisters. Just a slight crackle, like static.'

'The trauma of death rubbing up against the trauma of divorce?'

'Not much sign that Stephanie is suffering. A few more weeks and she reckons she'll be loaded. I know we're not supposed to get attached, but I did enjoy hanging out with the pair of them.'

'They do seem very close, edge or no edge.'

They focused on their drinks for a bit. The room was growing busier and noisier as more offices emptied and shops slid down the shutters.

'You having another?' Hendry asked. Clarke shook her head. 'I shouldn't either. Quiet night at home will make a change.'

'I'll probably head back to the office.'

'You're a glutton for punishment. Unless . . .' Hendry paused for effect, 'someone there has you smitten?'

'No such luck.' But Clarke's phone was letting her know she had a message. It was from Michael Leckie. *Fancy dinner some time? I categorically promise no shop talk.*

'Good news?' Hendry nudged.

'Might be,' Clarke said, her fingers busy on the screen. It didn't take long to compose her two-word reply.

Why not?

23

Ishbel Oram didn't seem to recognise Rebus when she opened the door, which was fine by him.

'Is Tommy in?' he asked. She drew on her cigarette before replying.

'He do that to you?' She watched Rebus shake his head. From her reaction, he knew there must be swelling and bruising. His eyes felt puffy and there were still probably smears of dried blood on his upper lip and chin. 'Didn't think so, he's not the type.'

'Any idea where I could find him?'

'Have you tried phoning?'

'No reply,' Rebus lied. Because phoning was what a friend would have done. Because a friend would have had Tommy's number.

'Pub maybe. Tell him to remember the pizza – and no bloody olives.'

'No olives, right,' Rebus said to the closing door. He walked around the corner to the Moorfoot and headed in. All three TV screens were tuned to the same football match, and the place was busy. Tommy Oram was in front of the one-armed bandit, not that they had arms these days. He was slapping at the flashing buttons as if his life depended on it.

'No girlfriend tonight?' Rebus enquired.

Tommy seemed to recognise the voice, but wasn't about to take his eyes off the prize.

'I told you, she's not my girlfriend, she's just someone I see.'

'Your mum says no olives, by the way.'

This elicited a smile. 'I only do it to piss her off.'

'Fetch you a drink?'

'Rum and Coke.'

'You sure?'

'Why wouldn't I be?'

'I'm just not a fan of rum, that's all.'

Rebus headed to the bar. The barman had already clocked him. He bided his time while the orders before him were dealt with. Then it was his turn.

'Forgot to bring some records,' he said. 'Next time for sure, and for now I'll have a dark rum and Coke and a Highland Park – always supposing that's what's in the Highland Park bottle.'

With a scowl, the drinks started to be poured.

'You're Kenny Beecham?' Rebus tried to make the question sound casual. 'I hadn't noticed the scar before.'

Unable to stop himself, Beecham's fingers went to the pale raised line just below his jaw. 'So what if I am?'

'Still handing over a cut of the proceeds to Big Ger Cafferty?'

'Drink your drink and get the hell out,' Beecham said, snatching the twenty-pound note Rebus was holding out to him. Although Rebus's palm was ready when the change arrived, Beecham slapped it down onto the bar instead.

'Nice shooting the breeze as always,' Rebus said.

Over at the machine, Tommy Oram's luck had run out. Rebus placed the two drinks on a nearby table and pulled out a stool, Oram taking the one next to him.

'What happened to your face?'

'Nose job.'

'I'd ask for a refund.'

'Know why I'm here, Tommy?' Rebus asked, not bothering to wait for an answer. 'Those kids you use as lookouts at your lock-up. Turns out you're far from their only source of income.'

'Oh aye?'

'It can't have escaped your notice that they're being used to shift drugs around the estate. Probably further afield, too, thanks to those bikes.'

'News to me.' Oram gulped from his glass and looked around the room. Rebus did the same, and noted the barman over in one corner, talking to the bald heavyweight who'd been the only other customer last time Rebus had been in. He was seated alone at a table with no view of any of the TVs.

'Somebody must be in charge of them, though,' Rebus pressed. 'Strikes me you're the ideal candidate. You know your boss Fraser

Mackenzie is at the top of the pecking order? How about his daughter? She in on it too?'

'I don't know what you're talking about.' Oram had taken his phone out and was tapping the screen.

'Calling the cavalry?'

He turned the screen towards Rebus. 'Ordering the pizza, if you must know.'

'Whole point of me coming here is to stop you getting in any deeper than you already are.'

Oram stared at him. 'Why?'

'I just think maybe that slot machine isn't the only thing in your life that's left you short-changed.'

'Not your fault, is it?' Oram broke off as he noticed a shadow falling across the table.

'Everything all right, Tommy?'

It was the ogre from the corner. Oram managed a nervous smile. Not that the man was paying attention. His eyes were drilling into Rebus's. 'Yeah, fine, fine. Cheers, man. Might see you later?'

The heavyweight was pulling the hood of his dark fleece over the dome of his head. Rebus probably looked to him like one of his easier KOs.

'You should see the other guy,' Rebus commented.

The man seemed unwilling to pull his stare away, but eventually he left, letting in a blast of cold clear air.

'Who was that?' Rebus asked Oram.

'Crosbie,' the young man answered. 'Most folk call him C.'

'This is his pub?'

'Sort of, I suppose.'

'Him and Kenny Beecham are buddies?'

'Since school.'

'He's a doorman, aye?' Oram looked up at Rebus from his phone. 'I saw what he was clutching in that paw of his,' Rebus explained. 'One of those armbands they all wear these days. He'll be working Gaby's nightclub, then? That's why you might see him later?' He leaned in towards Oram. 'I know Gaby owns the club as well as doing the DJing.' He started holding up his fingers one by one. 'Gaby – doormen – enforcers – drugs – the Mackenzies.' His palm was now splayed. 'You're the webbing between them, Tommy. And if I've worked it out, maybe your dad did too . . .'

A hand snaked between Rebus and Oram, scooping up the empty

241

glasses. Beecham waited for Rebus to give him his undivided attention.

'I told you to offski,' he announced.

'It's not even half-time,' Rebus complained, nodding in the direction of the screens.

'Game's over for you, pal. All the floodlights are going dark.'

'I need to fetch the pizza anyway,' Oram explained, rising to his feet and starting to zip up his thin jacket.

'Maybe see you at that club, eh?' Rebus said. Then, to Beecham, 'Your mate Crosbie's putting me on the guest list.'

'Shit list more like,' Beecham said.

Drinkers waiting to be served had started yelling about the drought conditions. He headed off in their direction. Rebus focused on Oram.

'Remember what I said – don't get in more trouble than you can handle.'

'You're not my dad.'

'He'd want what's best for you.'

'Maybe that's not what *I* want, though.'

Rebus shrugged. 'Be nice to your mum – no olives for a change.'

'You were joking about the club, right? You're not going there?'

'Not a chance in hell, son,' Rebus said, the bar erupting as the ball went into a net.

Rebus had walked Brillo, fed both dog and owner, and then poured himself into the armchair in his living room alongside a second whisky. The hi-fi system was playing Jackie Leven at barely discernible volume. Even so, as Siobhan Clarke answered his call, she recognised the song.

'"Single Father"?' she said.

'I taught you well.'

'In some respects maybe. What can I do for you, John?'

'Who said I want anything?'

'I think I just did.'

'Well, now that you mention it . . .'

'Hang on, let me find my mug.'

'Home or office?'

'Still at MIT. I had a meeting with Gina Hendry earlier.'

Rebus took a sip of his drink. 'I think I've found part of the reason Francis Haggard could afford the good life.'

'He was on the take,' Clarke stated.

'On top of that, though.'

'So tell me.'

'I can't go into details yet, but I do have something for you – Chris Agnew.'

'What about him?'

'He had a bit of a barney earlier with Rob Driscoll.'

'You've been hanging out with Tynecastle?'

'Maybe I happened to stumble into them.'

'Well, isn't that just great?'

'I never liked it, you know.'

'What?'

'The way I was held up as something they should aspire to.'

There was a sharp burst of laughter in his ear. 'Oh, I think you did, John. I think you lapped it up. You forget how long I worked with you and saw you in action trading on that reputation of yours.'

'Maybe you've a point,' he eventually conceded. 'But only because it worked. I collected a few scalps, didn't I?'

'And didn't they look fetching, draped around your neck?' The silence stretched between them until she sighed. 'Chris Agnew, you say?'

'Not Haggard's biggest fan, according to Driscoll.'

'I don't think Haggard had many cheerleaders at Tynecastle.'

'This seems to go back further though, something more personal.'

'Meaning what?'

'The widow, maybe?'

'Playing away from home? I get no whiff of that at all.'

'Maybe the sister, then? The two are close, right?'

'Absolutely.' Clarke paused. 'Though Gina did mention a bit of friction.'

'If there *is* a connection between Agnew and one of them, and then Haggard gets violent against Cheryl . . .'

'Violent against both of them, actually. When he shoved his way into Stephanie's house, he ended up jabbing a finger at her. She reckons he was warning her that worse was to come.'

'But worse didn't come, did it? Instead, he ended up in the mortuary.'

The silence stretched again until Clarke broke it.

'Is this Tynecastle's doing? Pushing for a domestic so we stop digging into stuff they need kept hidden?'

'By sacrificing one of their own? How does that make sense?'

'Because they're not so much a crew as a pack of wolves – leave the weak and the wounded behind; always look out for number one.'

'This is me, Siobhan. Telling you what I saw and heard.'

'So tell me how Haggard came by all that cash.'

'Not yet.'

'You could be put on a charge for obstruction.'

'Well, that would *definitely* loosen my tongue.'

'I'll bet.' She gave another sigh.

'Still working your way through the Complaints files?'

'There's a good reason no action's ever been taken.'

'Lack of corroborating evidence?'

'There are times I hate Scots law.'

'Well, that's something we can agree on.'

'That and Jackie Leven,' Clarke said.

'You'll take a closer look at Chris Agnew? He has a bit of a rep as a ladies' man. They call him the Swordsman at Tynecastle.'

'And they tell me the Scottish male lacks romance.'

'I'll let you get back to your files,' Rebus said.

'And I'll let you get back to your music.'

'Hey, I'm working here,' Rebus said. 'Oh, one last thing. That bit of bother you and Fox had at the nightclub – one of the bouncers wasn't called C or Crosbie, was he?'

'Yes, as it happens.'

'He owns the Moorfoot, meaning the Potter's Bar as was.'

'He might also drive a Range Rover bought from your pal Alan Fleck.'

'Someone mentioned a web to me earlier tonight,' Rebus said. 'This feels an awful lot like that.'

'I'll add Chris Agnew to my shopping list, John.'

'I'm sure he'd be delighted to come in for another interview. Thanks, Siobhan.'

He ended the call, sat back and thought about that burst of laughter. Yes, he'd collected some scalps, but at the cost of a higher number of disciplinary hearings. Yes, there were pats on the back from the rank and file, who wished they could get away with the stuff he did. He knew none of that made him a good cop, not in an age of brains rather than brute force. And yes, buried in his past there were probably enough booby-traps to blow him to smithereens – most months he thought about them, wondering if and when. Scots law – that need for corroboration – had probably saved his skin. He did still feel bad about Tony Barlow, too, though Alan Fleck had been right – the actual blame went back to someone else.

'I'm not a *real* criminal, am I?' he asked Brillo, who lay on the floor next to the radiator, eyes closed. One of the dog's ears pricked up. 'Would I be living like this if I was, eh?' He got up and refilled his glass, adding a decent drop of water. Then, once he'd settled himself in his chair again, he made the second of his planned calls.

'If you would move just a couple of streets,' Cafferty drawled, 'I could see right into you.'

'What makes you think I'm not out on the Meadows?'

'You're playing music. Now, what the hell do you want?'

'I know who sent you that picture.'

'Good for you.'

'You know too, don't you? Beth Mackenzie?'

'Ah, you're getting warm.'

Warmer than you know, Rebus thought to himself.

'I also know why,' he continued. 'Wallpaper's the same as when you owned the place, left there as a memento of the time you were royally shafted by a bunch of cops.'

'Is that a fact?'

'And it just so happens the man in the picture is the one responsible – it was Francis Haggard who shinned up the drainpipe.'

'I didn't know that.'

'You sure?'

'I had nothing to do with Haggard and whatever happened to him. If I'd wanted anyone punished, it would have been your good pal Fleck. Christ knows how I stopped myself.'

'Meantime the Mackenzies have taken over your turf, the illicit along with the legal. Your old flame's done well for herself, considering.'

'What has any of this got to do with the job I gave you?' Cafferty was trying not to sound rattled. 'You just can't help yourself, can you, Strawman? Have to keep sticking your neb in.'

Rebus touched the sides of his nose, feeling the rawness there.

'I'm not going to deny it,' he said.

'But there's no photo any more, is there, which means nothing for any CID team to get their teeth into.'

'The photo was taken on a phone, Cafferty. It's not like the old days when you could torch a negative.'

'Is this your way of stalling because you're no nearer finding Jack Oram?'

245

'I'm on his scent, don't you worry.'

'Never shit a shitter, Rebus.'

'As God is my witness.'

'Some trial proceedings those would be.'

'It might all connect to the Moorfoot – you'll know the place, of course?'

'The Potter's Bar as was?'

'Now run by an ex-con of your acquaintance.'

'You've lost me.'

'Kenny Beecham, the man who sold you out and lost you all that money. You saw to it he went away. Now he runs the Moorfoot and pays you no doubt handsomely for the privilege of not having his throat cut again.'

'My, my.'

'Starting to wish I'd done a bit more slacking?'

'You've been busy, granted.'

'A friend of Beecham's called Crosbie has his name above the door to fool the licensing board. Crosbie works as a doorman at a club owned by Beth Mackenzie's daughter. Now did I forget anything . . .? Oh yes, Jack Oram's son Tommy is a regular fixture at the Moorfoot and owes Gaby Mackenzie for his job at QC Lettings.'

'Okay, you lost me somewhere back there.'

'I'm not sure that I did,' Rebus said quietly. 'But even so, all you need to know is that I've got my headlights on. Doesn't mean the whole road's visible, but I can see enough.'

'If the whole road isn't visible, you might want to trade up to a new car. Maybe you even know someone who has them to spare.'

'It must sting that he convinced you not to retaliate?'

'It was business, Rebus. One storage facility out of dozens, one night out of thousands.' Cafferty paused. 'They never told you or cut you in?'

'The sum total of a ton for setting up the meeting.'

'Bloody hell, you came cheap. You might have been the only thing that day that stopped me wrapping my hands around Alan Fleck's windpipe.'

'I take it as a compliment that you didn't.'

'It would have led to complications, though – Fleck was right about that.'

Rebus drained the whisky from his glass and swallowed.

'Something nice?' Cafferty enquired.

'At my age, you have to treat yourself. Never know if your eyes will open tomorrow.'

'Come over and have a nightcap.'

'I'm fine where I am.'

'When you find Jack, make sure he knows I'll meet him anywhere he likes. Five minutes is all I'm asking.'

'Even though he didn't give the money to his brother's family?'

'You should maybe ask him about that first, just in case I'm not going to like the answer.'

'I'll do that then,' Rebus said, as Cafferty ended the call.

The CD hadn't quite finished yet. He sat back and let it wash over him, eyes staring towards the darkness.

'Like hell I will,' he muttered, as Jackie Leven sang about a morning that never comes.

24

'You at home?' Geoff Dickinson asked when Fox answered his phone.

'Yes. And no serious and organised crime to report.'

'Knock knock, then.'

Fox went to the door and unlocked it. Dickinson was on the doorstep, placing his phone back in his pocket.

'Bungalowland suits you.'

Fox looked past him to the black Vauxhall Insignia parked kerb-side. 'I expected something flashier.'

'Flashier gets you noticed – not my style. Besides, that's not a car, it's my office.'

Fox ushered him inside. 'Must be urgent,' he said.

'Actually, I was just passing.' Dickinson saw the look of disbelief Fox was giving him. 'In a manner of speaking, anyway. Just been out to East Lothian. Small-time dealer by the name of Guy Strathairn. Privileged background and all that, reduced to dealing hash and pills from a caravan.'

'What happened?'

'He met the acquaintance of a baseball bat or similar and is now relaxing in one of the wards at the infirmary. They torched his caravan, too. Our thinking is, Mackenzie is tightening the screws on any and all opposition. And by the way, the latest attempted shipment never even made it across the Channel. Expect to see a lot of very strung-out people real soon.' He had settled on the sofa in Fox's living room. 'This is nice. Tidy for a bachelor pad, too.'

'Can I get you something?'

'Everything I need is in my office out there. He looked at Fox. 'How's the case going?'

'We might have had a breakthrough regarding Haggard's movements in the hours before he was killed.'

'And how does that get you closer to catching his killer?'

'We won't know that till we get there.'

'Still applying pressure to Fleck and his minions?'

Fox nodded. 'My sources say we should be looking at Tony Barlow.'

'You have sources? Good for you.'

'Fleck says John Rebus played a role. My thinking is, that's by way of a diversion.'

'Could be, but it's a good sign if they're turning against each other.'

Fox thought for a moment. He was perched on the lip of the armchair, as if ready to act. 'Mackenzie sells drugs to his tenants, but he sells them elsewhere, too. Tynecastle seem to take their share, and they're pretty pally with the security staff at the club where Gaby Mackenzie DJs.'

'What are you saying?'

'I'm saying the daughter might know more than we think.'

'Oh, I don't doubt it.' Dickinson took out his phone again, found what he was looking for, and turned the screen towards Fox, who had to stand and cross to the sofa to get a better look. 'We think this is Guy Strathairn's assailant.'

'I know him,' Fox said, catching Dickinson by surprise. 'I was at the nightclub where he works, saw him in action.'

'Unless he was pummelling someone, I don't think you can really say you saw him in action. His name's Crosbie. You definitely do not want to get on the wrong side of him.'

'Are you going to arrest him?'

'Case isn't solid enough yet.'

'So he's muscle for Fraser Mackenzie?'

'Certainly seems that way.'

'Recruited by the daughter?'

'It would make sense.' Dickinson put his phone away again, and Fox retreated to his armchair. 'One other thing I picked up at Gartcosh about the furlough fraud,' Dickinson continued. 'James Pelham used Francis Haggard's name on his list of bogus employees. Makes it a lot less likely it was somebody else's mistake. His wife's name was there too.'

'Haggard's wife?'

'Pelham's. He left Haggard's wife out of it – maybe he liked her better than her husband, or his own ex-wife, come to that. He probably enjoyed typing their names in.'

'Could Haggard have found out?'

Dickinson offered a shrug. 'I'm not sure it's any sort of motive for murder, but it's given HMRC fresh hope of nailing Pelham. If I were him, I'd be unravelling as fast as most of his businesses.' He glanced at his wristwatch. 'I'd best be off – any chance I can use your loo first? It's the one thing my office lacks, and it's a long drive back west.'

Fox showed him the way and waited in the hallway by the front door. He wondered if it was too late to call Clarke and share the news of the man called Crosbie. He decided it probably was. He had someone he was due to see tomorrow, and he planned to take Clarke with him. He could tell her then. He took out his phone and checked there were no texts. The person he'd arranged to visit had got cold feet several times in the past. So far so good, though.

He heard the cistern flush, the taps run, and then the toilet door click open. Not everyone would have bothered locking it in the first place, but then Geoff Dickinson was the cautious type. It came with the territory.

He was rubbing his hands together as he emerged. 'Time to saddle up,' he said. 'I swear there are nights I'd be as well parking up and sleeping behind the wheel.' He studied Fox again. 'Might be one of the pitfalls of that promotion that's in your future.'

'No pitfall,' Fox said, pulling back his shoulders.

'At ease, soldier,' Dickinson said with a smile.

Morris Gerald Cafferty had his phone held out in front of him as he sat by his telescope. He was dressed in his pyjamas and watching – by no means for the first time – the snippet of video Andrew had forwarded to him. It showed Clarke and Fox and some cops from Tynecastle police station. They were outside Gaby Mackenzie's club. It was impossible to make out most of what was being said. The voices of others in the queue closer to the phone were too loud. Cafferty, not too long after they'd met, had told Andrew always to follow the money, and Andrew had taken the advice to heart. In fact, he'd gone further – he just liked following people full stop. Once or twice, peering through the telescope towards the Meadows, the young man had spotted someone he fancied the look of, for whatever reason. He'd then dashed out and started trailing them.

Later, he would report back, now knowing where they lived, or where they met friends, or where they shopped. And that, seemingly, was enough for him, his itch scratched until the next time.

He had followed Fraser Mackenzie to the murder scene the morning after it had happened, had seen him meet John Rebus, and had reported back. He'd also gleaned information about Beth and Gaby Mackenzie, and about some of the city's cops, especially the ones at Tynecastle and Leith. Cafferty wasn't sure how he did it. He himself had never managed the feat of remaining inconspicuous. It wasn't just to do with physical heft – Cafferty was nothing if he was not feared, so he had learned to look like someone who merited that fear. Whenever he walked into any situation, he made sure he looked pissed off from the get-go. That way, people were more minded to appease him.

He found himself rubbing one arm of the wheelchair, resenting how it had become such a part of his life. But then what was the point of living in the past when the present was so interesting? He wondered where Andrew was right now. Somewhere out there, stalking streets Cafferty had once controlled, learning them the way an actor learned lines for a role.

When the recording stopped, he started it again from the beginning. And there were Fox and Clarke, looking like a capable enough team. He wondered what they had learned in the nightclub. They would have seen Gaby, but had they spotted anything else? He noticed one of the Tynecastle cops rub at his nose after Clarke had said something to him. Ah yes, of course.

Just for a moment, Cafferty grew wistful. What if he had put his energies into Siobhan Clarke rather than John Rebus? How might things have turned out if he had?

But Rebus remained the prize, dangling just short of him. Maybe not for much longer, though. Maybe the ending he wanted was coming . . .

'Why am I not surprised?' Siobhan Clarke muttered to herself when her phone awoke her. It was three in the morning, according to the screen. She recognised the caller's name and wrinkled her brow.

'Ronnie?' she said, answering. 'Where are you?'

'It's my first night back,' DC Ronnie Ogilvie said.

'And you thought that news worth sharing with me? Got the COVID all-clear, I take it?'

'Despite which, I'm at the Royal Infirmary. A house got fire-bombed. Owner's being given the once-over. She wanted you to know.'

'Who is it?' Clarke asked, pivoting her legs out from beneath the duvet.

'Laura Smith.'

'Tell me she's all right.'

'Just a bit of smoke inhalation.'

'I'll be there in thirty minutes. And Ronnie?'

'Yes, boss?'

'Welcome back.'

The way Laura Smith told it, she'd been lucky, in that she'd still been awake and downstairs rather than upstairs in bed when the petrol bomb came crashing through her living room window. She kept a fire blanket in her kitchen, and had done what she could with it and some pans of cold water while waiting for the fire brigade to arrive.

'They told me that if I'd run outside, I wouldn't have breathed in so much smoke. But then if I'd done that, I might have lost the whole ground floor.'

'Instead of a carpet and some damage to the ceiling,' Ronnie Ogilvie added. He looked perfectly healthy to Clarke. They were seated either side of Laura Smith's bed. There were still specks of soot on her face and in her hair, and she had been coughing some gunk into a paper towel on Clarke's arrival.

'You know what I'm going to ask,' Clarke said.

Smith nodded. 'I've plenty enemies, Siobhan, including one who's already shown his hand.'

Clarke turned to Ogilvie. 'James Pelham was hanging around outside Laura's home yesterday evening.'

'Whatever for?' Ogilvie asked.

'It was Laura who exposed the affair he was having.'

'I thought that was the *Courant*?' He saw the look both women were giving him. 'Ah,' he said as the truth dawned.

'Then there are the cops from Tynecastle,' Clarke continued, 'photographed by the *Courant* and flagged up as an example.'

'Alan Fleck and Rob Driscoll,' Smith said, nodding.

'Should I be making a note of this?' Ogilvie asked.

'You seem to be in charge, Ronnie,' Clarke told him. Then, to

252

Smith, 'Where will you go? There's a spare bed at mine if you need it.'

'I was thinking of a hotel.'

'I come cheaper.'

'Just for a night or two then, thanks.'

An exhausted-looking doctor, probably not yet out of medical school, arrived on the ward and approached the bed, telling the patient she was free to leave.

'Can we drop by mine and pick up some stuff?' Smith asked Clarke.

'You sure you want to?' Clarke watched her nod.

'Should I tag along?' Ogilvie asked.

'Of course you should,' Clarke told him. 'It's your crime scene, after all.'

Laura Smith lived in a terraced two-storey house in Bellevue, only a few streets north of Siobhan Clarke. The engine had departed, but a fire investigator remained. He was conferring with the scene-of-crime team. Despite it not yet being dawn, lights were on in the adjacent properties and, recognising Smith when she stepped out of Clarke's car, a couple of doors opened, the neighbours approaching to ask if she was all right and was there anything they could do to help. While Smith reassured them, Clarke checked that the house was safe to enter. The fire investigator was holding a clear plastic evidence bag containing the neck of a shattered bottle, charred wadding stuffed into it.

'Pretty basic stuff,' he commented.

Ogilvie touched Clarke on the arm to get her attention. 'Might start asking a few questions while memories are fresh.'

Clarke nodded her agreement. She watched Smith as she walked slowly towards her home.

'You okay to do this?'

'Takes more than an arson attack to scare me.'

'No such crime in Scots law,' the investigator interrupted. 'We refer to it as fire-raising.'

'I'll remember that when I write it up.'

The front door stood gaping. Inside, the floor was sodden after a dousing from the fire engine's hose. The ceiling had been blackened, as had the walls. Clarke doubted Smith would ever get the

253

smell out of her sofa; it would have to be replaced. Same went for the large flat-screen TV, which was dripping water.

'I use an upstairs room as my office,' Smith said, 'so my computer should be fine. Notebook and iPad are in my bedroom.'

Clarke nodded. 'I'll stay here,' she said, as Smith headed for the stairs.

She did another circuit of the living room, then headed through to the kitchen. Dishes still sat on the worktop, waiting until there were enough of them to merit the dishwasher being run. Clarke did the same thing at home. She tried to think what she might have to buy to meet the needs of a house guest. The spare bedroom – never previously used – had become a dumping ground. The ironing board and mound of laundry would need moving and the floor area around the bed clearing of boxes and bits of junk. For want of anything better to do, she stepped outside again. The fire investigator was taking photos of the shattered living room window.

'Been a spate of these recently,' he informed her. 'But mostly happening to people not unknown to Police Scotland.'

'I'm not sure there's a connection,' Clarke told him.

'Lab will examine the material used, that could give us a clue. In at least two that I've worked this past month, the cotton was from the same batch of cloth. Spirits bottles, too, same as tonight. Petrol could have come from anywhere, obviously.'

'Prints from the glass?'

'We've not been having much luck there.'

'So whoever did the others wore gloves?'

He nodded and took another photo. The SOCOs were readying to pack up. An emergency glazier had parked his van and was measuring up for temporary boards in front of the broken window. Clarke headed across the street, to where Ogilvie was chatting with a couple in their thirties.

'Alistair here,' he said, indicating the man, 'heard a car leaving at speed. This was just after one a.m., so the timing is right.'

'Weird that the breaking glass didn't wake me. Though maybe it did, and that's how come I heard the engine.'

'A throaty growl,' Ogilvie repeated for Clarke's benefit.

'Terrible thing to happen,' the man's partner added. 'Laura's such a lovely person. Will they come back, do you think? I mean, are we safe in our beds?'

'Perfectly safe,' Clarke assured her, leading Ogilvie a few paces away. 'So what happens next?' she asked him.

'I'll check the council's CCTV for traffic in this area. Doubt there'll be much of it after midnight apart from minicabs and taxis. Sounds like it was a big car, too, maybe a van.' He looked at the houses either side of them. 'I might try a few doors, in case anyone saw anything. Could get lucky with one of those video doorbells; might've captured the car or driver.' He looked at her to see if he'd forgotten anything.

'Laura will be at mine if and when you need her. That's not something I want widely known, though.'

'Understood.'

Clarke indicated the fire investigator. 'Make sure you get his details before he leaves. If this ties into any other incidents, we need to know.'

'What about compiling a suspect list?'

'I'll get Laura started on that in the morning.'

'One last thing,' Ogilvie said. 'Is this an attempted murder? I'm just wondering how I frame it to the boss.'

'Attempted murder until the fiscal says otherwise.' Clarke was thinking of how different the outcome could have been if Smith had been dead to the world in bed.

She watched Ogilvie nod his understanding, then walked back to the house and stepped through the doorway. Smith was in the living room, tapping something into her phone.

'Just putting a photo on Twitter,' she explained.

'Are you sure that's wise?'

'Maybe not wise, but necessary.'

'Are you posting as Laura Smith or the *Courant*?'

'The *Courant* is reporting an attack on Laura Smith's home.'

'You're basically outing yourself.'

'Time to step from the shadows, Siobhan. My employer will either be okay with that, or they won't. But as the *Courant* gets more hits than their own website . . .' She shrugged, then picked up the backpack and shopping bag that had been sitting at her feet.

'There's only toast for breakfast,' Clarke warned her. 'Unless one of us wakes up early.'

'No way I'm going to be able to sleep. Plus I need to get this written.'

'Just remember it's a police matter, Laura. Don't trample over our inquiry.'

'Wouldn't dream of it.'

She locked the front door after them, and didn't look back once as she headed to the car.

Day Seven

25

'It's five in the morning,' Alan Fleck said, answering his phone. He was in the kitchen of his home, his wife asleep upstairs. Two or three times a night he got up for a piss, and the third time he usually didn't bother going back to bed. Instead he would settle at the kitchen table with a mug of tea, or maybe go for a walk around the garden if the weather allowed. He might read the news online or switch on the radio. He might think about cars he'd like to have on his books. Just now, as the phone buzzed, he'd been remembering a vintage Aston Martin, sold too cheaply, just before the market for them went mega. No power steering meant the thing had been a pig to drive, otherwise he might have hung onto it for himself. Still, everyone had regrets, didn't they?

'I took you for an early riser,' Rob Driscoll said.

'And it just so happens you're right – didn't think you were a fellow traveller, though.'

'I get alerts on my phone. Have you heard?'

'Heard what?'

'Laura Smith got firebombed a few hours back.'

Fleck narrowed his eyes. 'The reporter?'

'The same. And here's the thing – the *Courant* had it before anyone else. Had it suspiciously quickly, if you ask me.'

'Smith is behind the *Courant*?'

'Tell me I'm wrong. I'm not, though. And when I think of the tip-offs I've given her in the past . . . then she goes and shits all over us.'

'Is she hurt?'

'Her living room's a mess, but that's about all.'

'One of our lot?'

'None of us knew she was the blogger, did we?'

'If you say so.' Fleck lifted his mug and sipped from it. 'So who was being targeted, the journalist or the blogger?'

'I'm just happy some bastard's got her in their sights. Might keep her off our backs for a while.'

'Like she's our biggest problem.'

'You're thinking John Rebus might be, after last night?'

'He's not the sort to take kindly to his nose getting mashed.'

'What do you suggest?'

'I suggest you keep everyone focused. More MIT interviews with the Crew today, aye? Pep talk for each one of them before they head in. I'll do some thinking about everything else. Who's in charge of investigating the fire-raising, do we know?'

'I can find out.'

'Might be an idea to do that then. If it's a friendly face, so much the better.'

'No way they can tie it to us.'

'That won't stop fuckers like Fox trying. Once everybody knows it was Smith who snapped that photo outside the pub, there'll be fingers pointing our way.' Fleck paused. 'You're sure none of your boys could have worked it out?'

'Fairly sure.'

'Say one of them did – who would your money be on?'

'Chris Agnew,' Driscoll said after only the slightest hesitation.

'Me too, probably. Let's talk again later. And Rob?'

'Yes, Sarge?'

'No more losing your head, okay?'

'Yes, Sarge.'

Fleck ended the call. His tea was a bit cooler than he liked, so he poured it away and made a fresh mug. It was still too early to take one upstairs, so instead he wandered through to what his wife always termed his den. There was a desk there, and a fairly antiquated computer, plus a leather chesterfield sofa where he could stretch his legs out and read. But this morning he was more minded to pace the floor, rubbing at the stubble on his chin with his free hand.

One thing and one thing alone mattered to him: his own neck. He would save it at all costs. He had already waved Tony Barlow in front of Fox in the hope of ensnaring Rebus, but he wasn't sure Fox had fallen for it. He knew that Fox wanted a sacrifice, and ideally that would be Fleck himself. But the man was a pragmatist – they all were, once they got high enough up the greasy pole. He would settle for less. The only thing almost certainly unacceptable to him was no result at all. Fleck knew he could offer a result. Rebus for one, Driscoll or Agnew for another. Others too, if it came to it.

But John Rebus first, obviously.

Fraser and Elizabeth Mackenzie always tried to have a family breakfast. At first it had been a way of corralling the teenage Gaby so they could at least check she still had a pulse. These days, however, Gaby tended to eat on the move, comparing herself to a shark. If they were lucky, they had her company for the length of time it took to swipe a banana from the fruit bowl and juice from the fridge. Today she was elsewhere, meaning they ate in a silence that outsiders might have thought companionable.

There was always good coffee, and Fraser always drank too much of it, Beth sticking to green tea. She was dressed for the gym and managing to force down some slices of kiwi fruit and mango. Her husband had made himself porridge, a hangover from childhood. He had his phone out, as did Beth.

'The word online,' he said, 'is that the *Courant* is actually a reporter called Laura Smith.'

'I could have told you that,' his wife stated.

'You didn't tell James when he asked.'

'Which is why he went and asked Gaby instead. She wasn't quite so circumspect.' She peered at him above her phone.

Mackenzie closed his eyes briefly. 'How did you know it was this journalist?' he enquired.

'Stephanie told me ages back, when the photos of James and his floozy changed hands.' She paused. 'There are some things you're better off not knowing. Your side of the business is yours and mine is mine. Best if it's kept that way.'

'So there's no point asking you about Tommy Oram's father?'

'What about him?'

'I did a Google search. Theory still seems to be that he's long dead, yet that man Rebus swore he was alive.'

'He is,' Beth stated. 'I've seen him.'

'Where?' Mackenzie put his phone down and pressed his hands together.

'The lock-up.' She spooned more fruit into her mouth and chewed.

'What lock-up?'

'Where Tommy keeps the tools of his trade.'

'What were you doing there?'

She gave him a stare before replying. 'Jealous, are we?' She smiled and sniffed. 'Anyway, I told him to beat it. His son had turned the place into a bloody pied-à-terre – can you imagine?'

'The man who was looking for him – did you tell him any of this?'

'Rebus? Don't be stupid.'

'You know him?'

'He stuck pretty close to Big Ger back in the day. I never knew whether to be envious or worried.'

'How do you mean?'

'It was like they hated that they couldn't live without one another. Speaking of which . . .'

'Yes?'

'You and James. I know you go back a long way, but he's about to crash and burn, we both know it. This fraud thing's going to see him in court.'

'He says not.'

'That's because he can't have his investors getting the jitters, but the clever money is already deserting him and I don't want anyone thinking we're idiots.'

'He's Gaby's godfather, for Christ's sake.'

'And yet we're the ones who seem to have done him all the favours down the years – and that includes Gaby.' She paused. 'If you can't bring yourself to cut the ties, I'll be happy to.'

Mackenzie had closed his eyes again. It was as if he were exhausted by the world and everything in it, while Beth only felt more energised with each new day.

'Okay, I'll talk to him,' he eventually said.

'And to your money men, too. Sooner the better, Fraser.'

'What is it you know, Beth?'

She lifted a final spoonful of fruit to her mouth. 'Drink your coffee, love,' she said.

Rebus got to Ferry Road early, pulling into the gym's car park and turning off the ignition. He was hoping Beth Mackenzie was a creature of habit. Commuters paraded past, heading by bus and car, on bike or on foot, to jobs in town. As a bus came to a halt in the traffic, Rebus got a better view of its passengers, most of them

262

plugged into their phones. None looked particularly thrilled with the way their lives had worked out.

He recalled his early days on the force. He'd joined in his twenties, by which time a stint in the army had scraped away any youthful idealism. He knew from the start that he was destined to shore up defences that would always remain permeable. His mentors had all been from the old school. The station at Summerhall – one of his very earliest postings – hadn't been too dissimilar from Tynecastle in its culture. You either clicked or you didn't stick around. Rebus hadn't minded bending rules and crossing lines. Everybody knew that the real trouble started when there was no one at the top of the criminal heap. Petty rivalries and vying to fill the vacuum caused all manner of problems. Better by far to have a Big Ger Cafferty keeping order and stability – even if that meant doing him the occasional favour. Rivals had come and gone, having found Cafferty to be a formidable mix of the shrewd and the ruthless. Rebus wondered how the man was feeling now, perched in his penthouse, weakened and isolated. He knew Cafferty hardly went out, didn't want people to see him in a wheelchair, his physical heft diminished. New players had run onto the field, and all Cafferty could do was watch.

'Aye, maybe,' Rebus said out loud.

Siobhan Clarke had once told him that he shared more with Cafferty than he liked to think. And maybe that was true. Could old men affect the world around them, play a part, still make their mark? The world itself might not want them, but sometimes that could make you all the more determined not to be shut out. You *would* be heard. You *would* be seen. Rebus was aware of how nobody looked at him twice these days as he walked down the street, queued to pay for a newspaper, stood at a bar waiting for his eye to be caught. He was nobody special, just one among multitudes. Sitting there in his Saab, he felt more than anonymous. He felt invisible.

Beth Mackenzie, on the other hand, drove into the car park as if launching an attack. Her cherry-red sports car was meant to be seen, as was the person who eventually climbed out. Make-up and hair immaculate; large sunglasses; a coat pretending to be an animal pelt; two-inch heels. She had tucked her rolled-up yoga mat under her arm. Having locked the car, she noticed Rebus walking towards her.

'They have an off-peak rate for pensioners,' she said, indicating the gym's door. If she had noticed his bruised face, she wasn't about to mention it.

'No Gaby today?'

'She doesn't have my dedication. What the hell do you want, John?'

'Why did you send Big Ger that photo?'

She removed her sunglasses and folded them. 'Still harping on?'

'Francis Haggard was one of the cops who turned him over that time.'

'What?'

Rebus nodded. 'Shinned up a drainpipe at the back of the building, threw the bags of cash down to his mates.'

'I didn't know.' She blinked a few times, as if to digest the news.

'You knew the story, though? The flat's history?'

'When Ger and me broke up, I stayed friends with some of his lads. They always liked to tell me things.'

'Is that why you kept the wallpaper the way it was? If Cafferty ever had reason to see it, it would remind him?'

She considered for a moment, then took a deep breath. 'I took Francis Haggard to look at the flat. He'd already told Fraser he was police, based at Tynecastle. I suppose it brought out the devil in me.'

'You saw a chance to get Cafferty's back up?' Rebus watched her give a slow nod. 'No love lost, eh? It's some journey you've been on, Beth.'

'How do you mean?'

'From one gangster to another – no distance at all, really.'

'The difference is,' she said, baring her teeth, 'one of them I made.'

'Is that right?'

She had spun round and was starting to open the gym door.

'Still got that photo on your phone?' Rebus called out, causing her to pause. 'Cafferty got rid of the print, denies ever having seen it. If you took it to Siobhan Clarke at Leith police station, told her you sent it to him, well, he'd have a bit of explaining to do. I mean, maybe you don't want to cause him any additional grief . . .' He gave an exaggerated shrug.

'Siobhan Clarke?' Beth checked, watching Rebus nod. Her hand went to the door handle again.

'I saw Crosbie last night,' Rebus added.

'So?'

'So the name obviously means something to you – interesting.'

Her head turned slowly towards him. 'What's interesting is that you think you're smart. You're really not. Crosbie works for Gaby, so of course I know him. I know lots of people, it comes with the territory.'

'What else comes with the territory, Beth?' But he ended up asking the question to a closed door, Mackenzie having disappeared inside. He stuffed his hands into his coat pockets and stared down at his feet.

One of them I made.

One of them I made.

He knew those words would stay on a loop inside his head on the drive back into town.

26

Clarke had left Laura Smith propped up in bed with tea and iPad, earbuds in. She had placed the spare key on the duvet and told her to take things easy.

'Are you kidding? I've got enough media requests to keep me busy till doomsday.'

On her way to Leith and the MIT, she phoned Ronnie Ogilvie.

'I'm getting the road traffic CCTV in an hour or two,' he told her. 'Is Laura okay to answer a few questions?'

'You might find yourself in a queue.'

'I'm known for my sharp elbows.'

'I'm glad to hear it.' Clarke ended the call just as she reached Leith. She parked by the links and headed into the police station. Christine Esson was already at her desk.

'Laura Smith?' she prompted Clarke.

'You've heard, then.'

'Ronnie told me. How's she doing?'

'She's already working on how to turn a profit from it.' Clarke sat down and made eye contact with Esson. 'You've probably already worked out she's behind the *Courant*, but what you don't know is that James Pelham has been seen loitering outside her home.'

'Because of the divorce photo?'

'I assume so. What about those casinos – any luck?'

'One says definitely no sign of Haggard on their security footage, and no staff remember seeing him. Four more are getting back to me later.'

'Maybe give them another nudge?'

'Liam and Noel are going to be phoning round the cab companies when they get here, see if any drivers remember picking him up from the tiki bar.'

They could hear voices climbing the stairs. A moment later, Trask and Fox walked in, both toting leather briefcases. Clarke noticed Fox studying his boss's choice, which was a different design to his hard-shell. She would put money on him having ordered a similar model by day's end. Trask stopped to ask for an update, which Esson provided. Satisfied, the DCI headed into her own office, leaving the door ajar. Fox placed his briefcase on his chair and approached Clarke's desk.

'Quiet night?' he asked.

'Lovely and quiet, up until someone chucked a petrol bomb into Laura Smith's living room.'

His eyes widened slightly. 'I hadn't heard. Did we catch anyone for it?'

'Not yet,' Clarke said.

'The price petrol is these days,' Esson added, 'we're looking for someone with deep pockets.'

'She's by no means the first, is she?' Fox said. 'A dealer got hit at a caravan park yesterday.'

'I hadn't heard about that.'

'You have now.' He retreated to his own desk and started up his computer while Esson went to the kettle and switched it on.

'Looks like you could use one,' she told Clarke.

'I hardly got a wink,' Clarke admitted.

'You honestly wouldn't know it.' Esson watched as Gamble and Leighton walked in, followed by King and Ritchie. Ritchie came up to her and offered to rinse the mugs.

'Already done,' she told him. 'But there's a juicy little quest waiting next to your computer. I'll fill you in in a minute.'

'Can't wait.' He was almost bouncing on his heels as he started towards his desk. King was already there and had read the note.

'This'll take all day,' he complained, looking over towards Esson.

'All the sweeter when you get a result,' she answered.

Fox, having seen something on his phone, was on his feet again and crossing the floor towards Clarke.

'Yes, Malcolm?' she said.

'There's someone I'm seeing later. I'd like it if you came with me.'

'Your pal Geoff Dickinson?'

She watched him shake his head.

'I'd rather you had no preconceptions.'

She stared at him, but he'd said all he was going to. 'As long as it's not dogging or Scottish country dancing,' she warned him.

'I think we're probably safe then,' he said, turning away.

When Rebus heard the news, he tried calling Laura Smith, but it went to a recorded message.

'It's John. Just checking up. Get back to me when you can.' He stood in the bay window of his living room. Brillo had had his morning walk and seemed content, curled in his basket. Rebus, on the other hand, had been unable to relax since his encounter with Beth Mackenzie. He studied his phone again, then called Siobhan Clarke, who picked up on the fifth ring.

'Let me guess,' was her opening gambit.

'The hell happened to Laura?'

'Firebomb.'

'Petrol through the letter box?'

It took her a moment to answer. 'No, but that's an interesting point. It would have been a lot quieter, and a burning hallway and front door make escape that bit less likely.'

'So what was this?'

'A bottle thrown through the downstairs window. She actually got it under control pretty well by herself.'

'So she's all right?'

'Apart from still coughing her guts up.'

'I take it that means she's staying at yours?'

'Elementary.'

'Who does she think did it?'

'Well, she did post a photo online that couldn't have made your chums at Tynecastle too happy.'

'She's the *Courant*?' He rolled his eyes. 'Of course she is.'

'We've seen how downright reckless some of the Tynie lot are – breaking into Francis Haggard's flat, to give one example.'

'And getting on the wrong side of you, for another?'

'Bingo.'

'So who's working the case?'

'Ronnie Ogilvie.'

'Neighbours any help?'

'Heard a car pull away. Road cameras are being checked as we speak.'

'No one in the frame apart from Tynecastle? Must be plenty others she's pissed off in one guise or another.'

'Well, there's James Pelham. She was the one who put it front and centre when he was playing away from home.'

'Sounds like a long shot.'

'Except that she spotted him hanging around her house. Drives a white car, so if it *was* him, we'll not find proving it too onerous.'

'White car, eh?'

'Mean something?'

'I don't think so. Pelham's got everything to lose, though, no?'

'Most of which might already have slipped through his fingers. He's pals with the Mackenzies – did you know that? His ex, Stephanie, sometimes works for them, decorating their flats.' Rebus remained silent. 'You still there?' Clarke eventually asked. 'Listen, I'd better go. We're starting to get traction regarding Haggard's movements. How about you – not found your man yet?'

'I'm not sure that was ever the point, Siobhan.'

She was asking him what he meant when he ended the call. He was thinking about the white car parked across from QC Lettings when he'd interrupted Marion's lunch break. Tinted windows, meaning anyone could have been inside, up to and including James Pelham. Pelham: friend of the Mackenzies. Pelham: whose ex-wife was Francis Haggard's sister-in-law. Rebus knew the man from newspaper stories and photographs taken at high-society events. He even thought he remembered Haggard joking about how he'd married into money. Not that he hadn't married for love, too, but it didn't do any harm to have a brother-in-law who could give you investment tips.

Had Francis Haggard had money to invest? Obviously, judging by his visible bank accounts. But the messy divorce had pitted the sisters against Pelham, meaning Haggard would have had to choose a side. Stood to reason he'd stand by Cheryl and Stephanie, meaning he'd have wanted his money out. But did Pelham still have enough in the bank to repay him?

If it turned out he didn't, what would Haggard have done?

Rebus returned to his armchair and reached for his cigarettes. It took him a few moments to remember he'd stopped. His doctor had suggested chewing gum as a replacement.

'I can never get the bits to catch light,' Rebus had answered, after which his doctor, with a smile, had apologised for trying to keep him alive.

He was still allowed a drink, however, in that it had not as yet been strictly prohibited. He'd wandered down to the Oxford Bar a few times during lockdown, always finding the door bolted shut. It was open again now, though. Still a bit early, but so what? He needed to process everything he knew, half knew and suspected. A quiet corner table and a pint had always helped him in the past. But then he heard a pattering against the window and knew that the forecast rain had started. Sounded heavy, too. Brillo opened one eye, seemingly happy in the dry.

'Okay, then,' Rebus told the dog. Tea would have to do instead.

'Are we working you too hard, lover boy?'

Tommy Oram looked up from the workbench and saw that Beth Mackenzie was standing in the lane, leaning against his van with one foot crossed over the other. She levered herself upright and walked into the lock-up on precipitous heels. She was wearing over-sized sunglasses and had draped a wispy scarf around her neck. Digging into her bag, she produced a pack of cigarettes and a gold lighter. She offered the pack to him.

'Oh, I forgot,' she teased him, 'your generation doesn't like to have fun.'

'I just think there's stuff here that shouldn't meet a lit cigarette.' He lifted a jar of white spirit from a shelf and added it to the brown canvas bag he was filling. 'Was there anything in particular you wanted, Beth?'

'I'm always after something, Tommy, you know that.' She had removed her sunglasses and folded them closed, keeping the unlit cigarette between her fingers. 'As it happens, I was wondering how you got on with the police.'

'It was fine.' He busied himself looking for something.

'Fine as in . . .?'

He rested the knuckles of both hands against the edge of the workbench. 'They just wanted to know if I had a key to the flat, whether I'd met the guy, that kind of thing.'

'That tone of voice tells me you've not quite forgiven me. What can I do to repair the damage?' She had taken a step towards him, close enough that he could smell her perfume and feel her breath. He shook his head, his eyes avoiding hers. But she angled her face in front of him. 'Tommy,' she said, 'he couldn't stay here, you know he couldn't. It wasn't safe for him.'

270

'It was safe.'

'Maybe I should have offered to help, done things differently, but my temper got the better of me.' She reached out and touched the back of his nearer hand. 'I'm a hot-blooded creature, what can I say?'

He drew the hand away, grabbed the bag and took it out to his van. Once it was inside, he turned back towards the lock-up. Beth Mackenzie's demeanour had changed. She glowered at him as she lit the cigarette she'd been holding.

'You need to be very careful,' she warned him. 'I mean *very* careful. You've got a good job here and we look after you. Gaby's fond of you, too. But that doesn't mean you're indispensable. In my experience, no one is.'

'First you tell my dad to sling his hook, and now it's my turn – is that it?'

She walked towards him again, pacing each step. 'I really don't want that to happen.' She made to press a hand against his chest, but he flinched, half turning from her. 'Just remember, if you ever think of doing something stupid, it's Gaby you'd be hurting, much more than me or Fraser. I suppose I'd better let you get back to work.' She glanced over her shoulder towards the lock-up's interior. 'Might as well fold up that camp bed, eh? Doesn't look as if it's going to get much use now.' She sucked in some smoke and began walking up the lane to where her car was parked.

Tommy Oram watched her go, jaw clenched. She lifted one hand, knowing he'd be looking, and waggled her fingers in a goodbye gesture. He opened the van door and peered into the canvas bag, but couldn't for the life of him think if he had everything he needed.

Just before lunchtime, King and Ritchie leaped up from their desks and marched towards Trask's office, rapping on the already open door and heading inside.

'Looks promising,' Esson commented to Clarke. Fox was already out of his chair and listening at the doorway.

'Gold stars coming their way,' Clarke agreed.

When they reappeared a minute later, they were followed by Trask, who was holding the sheet of paper they'd handed her.

'Cab driver at Central,' she announced to the room, 'remembers picking up a drunk from our tiki bar on Great Junction Street. The passenger was memorable because he had to be woken up when

271

they reached their destination, that destination being Till's Casino in Corstorphine.' She favoured King and Ritchie with a look they soaked up like Caribbean sun. 'Colin and Jason, I want you to get a statement from the driver, see what else he can add.' Looking around the room, her eyes fell on Gamble and Leighton. 'George and Tess, you two go see the manager at Till's. We need to question all the staff who were on shift that afternoon and evening, plus check any security footage the casino has. And let's pray they don't wipe it after forty-eight hours.'

If Trask had noticed the disappointed looks on King and Ritchie's faces, she didn't let it show. Clarke knew how they must be feeling, though – a chat with a cabbie was definitely the runner-up prize.

'I know the place,' Gamble was telling Trask.

'Thought you might, George. Just don't succumb while you're on duty, understood?'

Clarke looked to Tess Leighton for an explanation. Leighton's partial nod hinted that her partner had had some issues with gambling. Clarke was impressed that Trask knew. She'd obviously vetted the team at some point.

As the four detectives prepared to leave, Esson rounded her desk and leaned down towards Clarke's ear. 'So Gamble's a gambler – I'm sure there's a term for that.'

Clarke noticed that Malcolm Fox was approaching.

'While we're waiting,' he said to Esson, 'maybe you can spare Siobhan for an hour? There's someone I'd like her to meet.'

'Maybe she feels need of a wingman,' Esson retorted.

'I think I'll be fine,' Clarke told her, lifting her jacket from the back of her chair.

27

They parked outside a row of colony flats in Shandon. Clarke had never been inside one before, but she knew the layout. You accessed the ground-floor property one side of the building, and its upper-floor equivalent via steps around the other side. She didn't know if they were unique to Edinburgh or what the reasoning was behind them, but they were usually found in what had been – and sometimes still were – working-class areas. Fox seemed to know his way, locking his Merc and leading Clarke briskly through the gate, along the garden path and up the steep stone staircase. He was obviously expected, as the red-painted door was open by the time they reached it.

'Hello again, Josephine,' he said to the middle-aged woman standing there. 'This is DI Siobhan Clarke. Siobhan, this is Josephine Kilgour.'

Kilgour led them into an overheated living room stuffed with knick-knacks. A plug-in electric heater was supplementing the radiators, yet she still felt the need for a buttoned-up cardigan, below which Clarke reckoned there were at least three further layers. The woman sat down heavily on the room's only armchair, leaving Clarke and Fox the squishy sofa. There was obviously to be no offer of refreshments. Clarke peeled off her jacket before she sat, Fox doing the same with his dark woollen coat.

'He's persistent, I'll give him that,' Kilgour said with a distinct lack of enthusiasm. Her voice was a west coast rasp.

'I just wanted DI Clarke to hear a little of the background,' Fox explained.

Kilgour's eyes fixed on Clarke. 'He thinks if he keeps chipping away, he'll end up with a statue of me in court giving testimony.'

Clarke had noticed a couple of framed photos of a much younger Kilgour in uniform. 'You worked at Tynecastle,' she commented. Kilgour's gaze shifted to Fox.

'I didn't want DI Clarke prejudging anything,' he explained. Kilgour considered this before turning her attention back to Clarke and drawing in a breath.

'Me and Tynecastle go back a ways,' she began. 'Even to before Alan Fleck was promoted to sergeant. *That's* how old I am. You'd have been in primary school.'

'Secondary maybe,' Clarke couldn't help correcting her.

'But you joined the ranks after the worst of it – the worst of it for women like us, I mean. My very first day, I turned up at the station in my brand-new uniform, blouse starched, shoes polished. I was hauled into the locker room. They pulled my skirt up, stamped me with the words "Police Property". Just one big fat joke to them, of course, and if you couldn't take it, you were a killjoy. That became my nickname, by the way – from Kilgour to Killjoy.' She paused for a moment. 'Tynecastle wasn't the only posting I had, but it left its mark, deeper than a bit of ink. We were supposed to make the tea while the best jobs were given to the men around us. It's why so many of us couldn't hack it.'

'Still seems to be the case,' Clarke said. 'When I paid a visit, I didn't see a single female face.'

'Oh, there'll be some – not allowed otherwise these days – but they'll have their heads down and most will end up requesting a transfer. That's what I did. But the job never felt the same afterwards. I quit as soon as I could.'

'The rot goes way back, Siobhan,' Fox interrupted, 'and the stories are legion. But Josephine and the others have taken the decision to put it behind them and not relive it in court or an interview room.'

'Reminds me, I forgot to check if you're taping this.' Kilgour looked at Clarke. 'He tried one time, the cheeky sod, but I was wise to him.'

'You remember what my excuse was?' Fox asked her.

'It showed how badly you wanted him,' Kilgour said, nodding.

'Him?' Clarke prompted.

'Alan Fleck,' Kilgour obliged. 'Tynecastle changed for the worse when he arrived, and worse still as he climbed the heap.'

'Josephine had left by the time of the attack on Tony Barlow,' Fox informed Clarke, 'but she knew about it all the same.'

'Didn't seem to bother them that they'd screwed up. They had a whip-round at the station and sent it to his bedside. Just another casualty of the conflict . . .' She looked at Fox, her eyes moist at the corners. 'I don't blame you for trying, but at the same time, I do, because it's me that has to relive it.'

'I know that, Josephine.'

She turned to Clarke. 'And now he's passing the baton to you, is that it? Or just bringing you on board?'

'I wanted DI Clarke to understand why it matters,' Fox answered her.

'And I do,' Clarke said quietly. She was about to add something, but when her phone pinged, she decided to check it. There was a text from Christine Esson on the screen. She frowned and locked eyes with Fox. 'We maybe need to be going,' she announced.

'What's up?' he asked.

'I'll tell you on the way.' Then, to the woman seated opposite, 'A reckoning is coming, Josephine, I promise you that.'

The smile Kilgour gave was world-weary. Her eyes drifted towards the photos of her younger self. She was still staring at them as Clarke and Fox rose to their feet and started to leave.

'So tell me,' he said as they headed across town.

'First of all, what was really going on back there?'

'I just wanted you to—'

'Yeah, but what was *really* going on?'

He was silent for a moment, pretending to concentrate on the traffic.

'Professional Standards – my old stamping ground – are about to start recruiting. ACC Lyon asked for my input, and I told her I couldn't think of anyone better.'

'Than me?'

'It'll come with a promotion to DCI, and I think it's a good fit for you.'

'It also comes with pariah status.'

'*Temporary* pariah status,' he said with a thin smile. 'The posting only lasts four or five years, but the promotion is permanent.' He turned his head towards her. 'When Jennifer Lyon knocks on your door, promise me you'll look surprised.'

'Christ's sake, Malcolm . . .' It was Clarke's turn to fall silent and contemplate the world outside the Merc's windscreen. 'And this is the trade-off?' she eventually said. 'When I say yes, I repay you by keeping up the heat on Tynecastle?'

'A small price to pay.'

She began to nod slowly. 'Fleck really got to you, didn't he?'

'More than most.'

'Why, though?'

'Because he's a virus,' Fox stated. 'And we all know what viruses can do.' He signalled to turn at the approaching junction. 'Now what was the message you got on your phone?'

'It was from Christine. Fraser Mackenzie is at Leith.'

'Why?'

'Because we asked him to explain the rock-bottom rent Francis Haggard was being charged. Christine says he's turned up with a lawyer. There being no one else in the office, the DCI said she'd sit in on the interview.'

'And you're not happy about that?'

'I'd just rather I was there.'

Fox thought for a moment. 'Can I tell you something in confidence?'

'You can try.'

'That bouncer outside the nightclub . . .'

'The one they called C?'

'Dickinson has him down for the caravan park attack. The Mackenzies are putting the frighteners on any and all competition.'

'Makes sense.'

'Dickinson wants it kept hush-hush for now. He trusted me, and now I'm trusting you.'

'Noted.'

'And the job offer?'

'I'll think about it.' She glanced at the car's speedometer. 'You sure you don't want to push it above twenty, just this one time?'

'If you insist,' Fox said, pressing down on the accelerator.

'To work Professional Standards, don't you need to be cleaner than clean?'

'You're clean enough.'

'Despite past proximity to John Rebus?'

'There were things you suspected and things you could have asked.' Fox gave a shrug. 'But nothing you should be beating

276

yourself up about – unless you know different?' His eyes were still on the road ahead. When Clarke decided the question didn't really need answering, he seemed content enough.

By the time they'd parked and were approaching Leith police station, Fraser Mackenzie was leaving, accompanied by a silver-haired lawyer who looked both distinguished and expensive. Clarke and Fox climbed to the MIT office. Trask's door was closed, Esson back at her desk.

'So what did he say?' Clarke demanded.

Esson stopped typing. 'Apparently it's a COVID thing. Anyone on the front line – NHS, police, you name it – merits a discount as a thank-you for everything they've done. I did ask who else had benefited from the offer, but he couldn't immediately think of any examples. Nor is it public knowledge.'

'A pack of lies, in other words.' Clarke looked towards Trask's door. 'How did she do?'

'She was frosty. Both Mackenzie and his solicitor commented on it. Any idea why?'

'The word from Gartcosh is that Mackenzie's taken over Cafferty's operations.' Clarke noticed the look Fox was giving her.

'As few people as possible,' he said, to remind her of Dickinson's words. All three of them turned as Tess Leighton and George Gamble walked in.

'Not every day you visit a casino and hit the jackpot,' Leighton said, while Gamble, breathing heavily, knocked on the door of Trask's office. A few seconds later, Trask emerged, her eyes on Fox and Clarke.

'Where did you two get to?'

'Just had to pop out,' Clarke said. 'Sorry you ended up having to interview Fraser Mackenzie.'

'Working the shop floor does make a change.' Trask saw that Gamble was bursting to say something. 'Out with it then, George.'

'We've got him on film,' Gamble obliged, having dabbed his face with a handkerchief. 'Seemed to be spending more on drink than at the actual tables. Took some cash out of a machine – even though the casino charges for the privilege – and eventually had to be spoken to by security.'

'Oh?'

'He was having trouble locking his knees,' Tess Leighton

continued. 'Staff called him a cab. There's footage of him outside as he's poured into it.'

'So we've got a licence plate?'

'Till's always uses the same firm. Just need to phone them and ask who was behind the wheel that day.'

Trask nodded. 'This gets us a bit further along, but there are gaps we still need to fill.' She had walked to the murder wall and was studying the timeline. 'Do we have the security footage?'

'It's on its way,' Gamble assured her.

'Then in the meantime, feel free to follow up with the cab company. And find out what's taking Colin and Jason so long.' She crooked a finger in Fox's direction. 'Malcolm, my office.'

Fox followed her in and closed the door, content to stay standing though she gestured towards a chair before sitting down across from him.

'So where were you?' she asked.

'Brainstorming,' he answered. 'Thought getting out of the office for a breath of air might help.'

'And did it?'

'Not especially.' He paused. 'Was it wise to sit in on the interview with Fraser Mackenzie?'

'Why?'

'Geoff Dickinson seemed to think it was important Mackenzie not realise we're on to him.'

She leaned a little further back in her chair and studied him. 'This is first and foremost a murder inquiry. We owe it to Francis Haggard and his widow not to forget that.'

'Absolutely, ma'am.'

'Good. Now get the hell out of my office and try to avoid wandering off again.'

'Yes, ma'am,' Fox said. As he left, he thought to himself: that was twice he'd used the term 'ma'am' and twice she hadn't said to call her Kathy. Seemed the honeymoon was over.

Which was fine by him.

Rebus took Brillo with him on the walk to Morningside Road. A wasted journey, it transpired, since the hardware shop didn't quite have what he wanted. They suggested a DIY superstore at

Newcraighall, so he untied Brillo from outside the shop and headed back to Marchmont. Before venturing out again, he sat in the living room getting his breath back. He realised his plan – such as it was – had more potential drawbacks than advantages. On the other hand, at least it would mean he was doing something, and if it worked, it would certainly shake things up.

When his phone rang, he saw that it was Laura Smith. He pressed the phone to his ear.

'I'm fine,' she said, 'but thanks for asking.'

'In your line of work, if you're not making enemies, you're doing something wrong.' He paused. '*Both* your lines of work, I should say.'

'Siobhan told you? Well, I don't suppose it matters now that I've taken off my mask.'

'Like Kendo Nagasaki.'

'Who?'

'Never mind. But just remember, the journalist shouldn't become the story.'

'Not so true these days.'

'I hear you're staying with Siobhan?'

'Which is why I've just restocked her fridge. The woman seems to eat nothing but takeaway.'

'How bad is your house?'

'Getting rid of the smell might be the real challenge.' She paused. 'If you'd heard whispers, you'd have warned me, right?'

'You think it was Tynecastle?'

'They're on my list.'

'But they're not the only names.'

'Siobhan told you about James Pelham?'

'And I told her that if someone had wanted to do you real harm, they'd have gone for stealth over spectacle.'

'So it was a shot across the bows?'

'You think otherwise?'

'John, I don't know what to think.' He heard her give a sigh. 'How about you – up to anything I should know about?'

'Shopping for tools.'

'Gardening or DIY?'

'I'm in the market for a nice big crowbar.'

'That sounds promising – will you keep me posted?'

'I imagine I will.'

'How soon till we can talk again?'

'Could be tonight, maybe tomorrow.'

'For a man your age, you give good phone sex,' Smith told him, ending the call.

Rebus looked down at Brillo, seated at his feet. 'Didn't I tell you I've still got it, eh?' he told the dog, before pulling himself to his feet and going to fetch the car keys.

They'd all had a look at the footage from the casino, including King and Ritchie, who'd returned having eventually extracted a usable statement from their long-winded taxi driver.

'Swear to God,' King had said, 'all we asked him was how long he'd been working the cabs, and he was three generations deep into his family tree before we could stop him.'

'His dad drove the cabs,' Ritchie had added, 'his grandad, his uncle Billy, his cousin . . .'

The two young detectives had become more deflated as the afternoon had worn on, their finding of the cab trumped by first the casino and then Francis Haggard's subsequent journey. But they had added their findings to the murder wall and stood there for some time admiring their handiwork.

Esson was studying the casino footage on her monitor. 'How much cash did he take out, do we think?'

'Bank statement says two hundred,' Siobhan Clarke answered, 'though with fees it cost him a bit more.'

'The statement doesn't mention Till's?'

'Not every punter wants their nearest and dearest knowing they had to make a withdrawal at a gaming establishment – the transaction was kept nicely anonymous.'

'How much did he have on him when he died?' Esson found the details for herself. 'Over a hundred. After he took the cash out, he settled his drinks bill and put some into a fixed-odds machine. Presumably the cab that took him away from Till's got paid. That doesn't leave much to spare.'

'You reckon he went straight home?'

'Was he in any fit state to do anything but? He'd been steering clear, reckoning we might be watching, ready to put him in custody. But by now his brain's too full of booze fumes – where else is he going to go? He's had one night of sleeping rough and can't bring himself to do a second.'

Esson rewound the footage. Haggard could have relied on his

various debit and credit cards, but he was old-school. He'd paid cash at the tiki bar and cash to the driver who'd taken him to Till's. She would bet he'd been the type to press tens and twenties into the hands of nightclub staff and maître d's, probably never ordering a drink, as he had done at Drifter's, without adding the words 'and one for yourself'. When the cash had appeared from the slot in the machine, he'd counted the notes a couple of times – either to check he wasn't being short-changed or because his arithmetic had been blurred by drink – before pocketing them, adding the balance slip that had popped out at the same time. A member of the casino's floor staff had been hovering at a discreet distance, but had then approached to suggest it was time for Haggard to call it a day. Haggard had held up a digit – wanting one more drink – and the employee had eventually relented, leading him to a table and indicating for a waiter to take the order.

And yes, he had tried tipping the man, but it had been refused.

'Did you talk to this guy?' Esson called across to Leighton and Gamble. 'The one who let Haggard have a last drink?'

Leighton nodded.

'Did he say why he turned the tip down?'

'He only takes gratuities from the sober.'

'Why?'

'Because drunks don't know they're doing it, which makes it meaningless.' Leighton nodded again at Esson's raised eyebrow. 'The guy's a philosophy graduate,' she explained.

'For real?'

'For real,' she confirmed.

Esson gave Clarke a look before returning to the footage. A switch of cameras now, Haggard at his table, shot from further away, the resolution less clear. Then an approach by two members of staff who were an altogether more imposing presence than the philosopher. They watched Haggard drain his drink and then helped him to his feet. He didn't put up any resistance and they didn't have to use force. Cut to the front entrance, and the taxi was already waiting there. The same two men manoeuvred Haggard inside and closed the door. The taxi didn't leave immediately, though. The door opened again, Haggard's hand emerging. One of the men who'd led him from the casino took the banknote held out to him, folding it into his pocket. No philosopher he. His companion seemed to be angling for his share as they made their way back indoors and the taxi pulled away.

Fox, who had been on his phone, stood up and started snapping his fingers, gathering everyone's attention. 'Hang on,' he said into the device, 'I just want to put you on speaker.' Then, to the room at large, 'They've just patched me through to the driver who picked him up from Till's.' Having dabbed at the icon for the phone's speaker, he held it in front of him and walked into the centre of the office.

'You were saying you didn't take him very far, Mr Bishop?'

'It was supposed to be Leith,' the broad local voice boomed. 'That's a good fare any time of day.'

'Did he specify Constitution Street?'

'Just Leith to start with. Told me he'd decide nearer the time where to stop.'

'So then what happened?'

'We'd hardly got any distance at all, and he started saying he wanted chips. I mentioned two or three places we'd be passing, but he didn't want to wait. Said he'd get out right there and find somewhere.'

'There being . . .?'

'Corstorphine Road. Like I say, he'd only been in the cab two minutes.'

'Whereabouts on Corstorphine Road?' Fox had taken a couple of steps towards the murder wall, where a street plan of the city had been pinned up. He was joined by Esson and Clarke.

'Just by Howson's – it's a wine bar. I was worried he might head in there, but he didn't. Man was a gent, mind.'

'How so?'

'Gave me a nice crisp twenty – joked that he'd printed it himself. Told me to keep the change.'

Siobhan Clarke had her finger pressed to the spot on the map where she reckoned Howson's was. It was the wine bar where she'd met Gina Hendry before their first visit to see the sisters. Esson had tapped a query into her phone.

'Nearest chippie is if he doubles back to Glasgow Road.'

'Supposing that's what he really had in mind,' Clarke said quietly.

Fox had ended the call and was taking out his posh pen so he could mark an X next to where she was pointing.

'Maybe he walked on towards Haymarket,' he suggested. 'Plenty places there.'

Clarke, however, was tracing a route with her finger from Howson's to Stephanie Pelham's house.

282

'Five, maybe ten minutes it would have taken him,' she said, more to herself than anyone else.

'We'd know if he'd been back there,' Esson commented.

'Maybe there was no fuss this time. Just a man full of alcohol whose wife had promised him they'd talk.'

Esson was shaking her head doubtfully as Clarke retreated to her desk to pick up her ringing phone. It had stopped by the time she reached it. Caller ID: Ronnie Ogilvie. She tried calling him back, but it went straight to messaging, meaning he was probably already talking to someone else.

'Bugger,' she said, as DCI Trask emerged from her office to find herself surrounded by her team, each of them wanting to be the first with the news.

28

Rebus signalled off Calder Road and drove into Burnhill. He couldn't see any bicycle sentinels or doorstep deliveries, just a couple of dog-walkers and half a dozen kids playing football on the adjacent stretch of parkland. Nobody seemed interested in his arrival, which was fine by him. He did a slow circuit of the terraces and the low-rise blocks. A few mums had gathered at the gates to a nursery, their strollers parked, gossip being shared. Most of them were dressed for the weather, one or two still wearing face masks. When one toddler waddled towards the road, a barked instruction turned the child to stone. Rebus, already slowed to a crawl, smiled at the stunned face as he passed.

Reassured that the coast was as clear as it could be, he drove past the top of the lane and studied the lock-ups. Tommy Oram's was closed tight, but the next one along showed signs of activity.

'Shite,' he muttered to himself. He brought the Saab to a stop and got out, walking down the lane with hands in pockets. As he came level with the wide-open doors, he looked in. A car had been jacked up and a man's feet were protruding from beneath it.

'Help ye?' a disembodied voice said.

'Nice motor,' Rebus answered. 'Sierra Cosworth?'

'You know your stuff.'

'Used to see a lot of them in the eighties.'

'Which is where most of them stayed.' The man rolled himself out but remained prone on the trolley. He wore a blue boiler suit, a spanner in one hand and smudges of grease on his face. 'Not seen you before.'

'I'm a mate of Tommy's.'

'He was here earlier, probably at work now.'

'Probably,' Rebus agreed. 'Car needs a bit of TLC, eh?'

'Not much gets past you. Few more hours should do it.'

'Big job?'

'She'll be brand new once I'm done.' He paused. 'I might be willing to sell if you're in the market.'

'I'll think about it. Will you be here tonight?' The man shook his head. 'Tomorrow daytime?'

'I've got work tomorrow.'

'I'll maybe leave you a note then, next time I visit Tommy.'

The man rolled himself back under the Sierra. 'If I see him, I'll tell him you were here.'

'Thanks.'

'Or I would if I had your name.'

'It's Crosbie,' Rebus obliged. 'He'll know who you mean.'

Laura Smith's presence had been requested at Gayfield Square police station, where DC Ronnie Ogilvie was waiting. He seemed surprised when Siobhan Clarke arrived at the same time.

'Been trying to reach you,' she told him.

'I was going to phone you back.'

Smith looked from one to the other. 'I asked Siobhan to come with me,' she explained. Ogilvie nodded his understanding and led them to a meeting room. It boasted a new-looking table and upholstered chairs and was usually used when giving bad news to relatives or laying on a spread for visiting dignitaries. The cream walls were bare apart from a clock that needed a new battery. Ogilvie placed a slim folder on the table and his phone next to it.

'We've been looking at footage from the road cameras,' he began, 'concentrating on Bonnington Road, Broughton Street and Inverleith Row. That time of night, as we suspected, it's mostly taxis and private hires, plus the odd delivery vehicle. But we flagged up a few cars – Volkswagen Golf, Kia, Nissan, Land Rover . . .'

'Land Rover?' Clarke interrupted.

Ogilvie woke up his phone and found the footage, talking while he searched. 'Drove the length of Broughton Street and then was caught again on North Bridge.' He turned his phone towards the two women. 'Have you seen it before, Laura?' he asked.

'I'm not much good with cars.'

'Me neither,' Clarke added, 'but that's a Range Rover rather than a Land Rover.'

Ogilvie studied the photograph. 'Pity you can't make out the driver. Number plate's not exactly clear either.'

'I might be able to help you there.' Clarke got busy on her own phone, showing him the photo she'd taken outside the nightclub.

'What are you, Derren Brown?'

'Is it the same car?' Smith asked.

'Could well be.' Ogilvie was tapping the number plate into his phone. 'I'll get on to DVLA for the owner's name.'

'Do you know whose it is?' Smith was asking Clarke.

'Not definitively – but it could be the Mackenzies'.'

'Which Mackenzies?'

'Landlords to the poor and needy. That photo was taken outside a nightclub on Blair Street where their daughter DJs.'

'But I've never run a story on them.'

'Fraser Mackenzie and James Pelham are mates, though.' Clarke was looking at Ogilvie. 'How long will it take, do you think?'

'I doubt they're back to a full office,' he said. 'Probably still mostly working from home. I'll do my best, though. Are you staying at Siobhan's again tonight, Laura?'

She nodded. 'I'm making us pasta with pesto and a salad.' Her eyes fell on Ogilvie. 'There's enough for three.'

'I'll probably be stuck here for a while,' he apologised. 'We might have ID'd one car, but there are others I want to follow up on.'

'He's a grafter,' Smith said to Clarke.

'Ronnie's just back from a bit of a break, batteries recharged.'

'Go anywhere nice?' Smith asked him.

'My sofa mostly. Sometimes the kitchen for a cuppa or a lateral flow test.'

'Ah,' Laura Smith said.

The Oxford Bar's back room was mid-evening quiet when Clarke arrived. Rebus was nursing a half-pint at one of the tables. She stared at it.

'Things that bad?'

'I brought the car.'

'Walk would have been good for you.'

'The downhill bit, yes.'

'Your face looks sore.'

'Tripped over Brillo's lead.'

'That's the best story you could come up with?'

'It'll do till I can think of another.'

She shook her head before fetching herself a gin and tonic and perching opposite him, pressing a hand to her stomach.

'Are congratulations in order?' he asked.

'Laura made me eat too much pasta.'

'Any progress on the Molotov?'

'Ronnie Ogilvie owes me a call.' She lifted her phone, checking she had a signal. 'How about you?'

'I'm ticking over. Media seems to have gone quiet on Francis Haggard.'

'There's not been much we felt like sharing.'

'Finished with those Complaints files?'

She nodded thoughtfully, her eyes meeting his. 'Can I ask you something? In confidence, I mean? *Proper* confidence rather than the usual?'

'Go ahead.'

She lifted her glass. 'There's talk of a promotion.'

'Not before bloody time.'

'It comes with strings attached. I'd be moved to Professional Standards.'

'Those are pretty big strings.' He thought for a moment. 'You'd be mad not to, though.' He watched her nod slowly. 'Is this Fox's doing? You hand him me and the others, he ensures you get a poke of sweets?'

'I'm convinced it's just Fleck he wants. He took me to see Josephine Kilgour – you know her?'

'I know the name.'

'It was such an ugly job back then, and it's not exactly a beauty contest today. If there are no consequences, nothing will change.'

'There usually *are* consequences, though – you just don't always get to see them.'

'What do you mean?'

Rebus was saved from forming an answer by the sudden buzzing of her phone. She held it to her ear.

'Ronnie? Talk to me . . .' She listened, eyes moving from her glass to Rebus and back again. 'Might make sense,' she said eventually. 'When will you lift him? . . . Well, let me know. And that's good work, well done . . . I know, but you did the rest. Cheers.'

She ended the call and turned her attention back to Rebus.

'Range Rover was seen in the vicinity of the fire. It's registered to Gareth Crosbie. He works as a nightclub doorman and lives at an address in Craigmillar.' She paused. 'In point of fact, he lives upstairs from the Moorfoot public house.'

'That's because he owns it,' Rebus said. 'I've had dealings with the guy.'

'Me too. He's pally with both Gaby Mackenzie *and* the Crew.'

'You can place him at the scene of the blaze?'

'Not exactly. But he was on Broughton Street a few minutes after.'

'Then he needs to be spoken to.'

'Which will happen at Gayfield Square in the morning. What do you think's going on?'

'Your guess is as good as mine.'

'I really doubt that.' She thought for a moment. 'I had Gaby Mackenzie pegged as the owner of the car – either her or her parents. We had the father in the station earlier today.'

'Can I ask why?'

'He told us Francis Haggard got a cheap rent as an act of charity.'

'The man's all heart.'

She was silent for almost half a minute. The only sound was muffled laughter from the front room. Eventually she breathed deeply. 'Everything's fucked, isn't it? I mean, that's how it feels to me. Brexit and COVID and Christ knows what's coming at us next.'

'Alien invasion?'

'They'd take one look and do a U-turn.' She watched him drain his glass. 'Can I fetch you a real drink?'

Rebus shook his head. 'Things to do,' he told her.

'Things like going straight home for a quiet night with the dog?'

'What else?'

'Right now, I can think of about a dozen alternative scenarios, most of them ending messily.'

'Maybe in times past, Siobhan, but not these days.'

'Promise?'

'Promise.'

'That's not a real promise, though, is it?'

He was studying her face. 'Professional Standards, eh, and you're minded to say yes? Well, why the hell not? You've not ended up in anybody's pocket, and I can't recall you lying too baldly in court. Maybe you could even disappear my files for me?'

'Don't joke about it, John.'

'Who said I was joking?' he enquired, raising his empty glass in a toast.

As he drove towards Calder Road, Rebus thought about Clarke's words: *Everything's fucked, isn't it?* Very often you'd be hard pressed to deny it. Yet he had the new Dean Owens CD on the car hi-fi, and a bottle of Caol Ila and Brillo waiting for him at home, plus a daughter and granddaughter who'd invited him to lunch on Sunday. Sometimes you had to focus on the small victories. Maybe that was what he would have told her in answer to her question. Those unseen consequences could be minor or tangential, but what mattered was that they were lying in wait. Malcolm Fox might not get Alan Fleck this time, but Fleck couldn't forget that he was out there, continually trying. The little cabal at Tynecastle would melt away too, in time, now that the sarge wasn't on hand to hold it together.

And meantime, Dean Owens was still singing.

The estate was dimly lit, half the lampposts non-functioning. He could see only a metre or so into the patch of grassland where the footballers had been. Beyond that, anything could be happening. The lane was well lit, though, nor was this the only deterrent to trespassers. The door to Tommy Oram's lock-up was open, his van parked alongside. Two youths sat astride their bikes and seemed be talking to someone inside – presumably Oram himself. A joint was passed from one figure to another, and Buster emerged, licking his chops and sniffing the ground.

'Party central,' Rebus said ruefully, placing his foot down on the accelerator.

Rob Driscoll had been getting grief all day. He was on a double shift, by no means his first this week, covering for yet more COVID cases. So much for the booster jag and all the other needles they'd been given the past year. Money pissed up against a wall. Meantime, chief among the grief-givers were Chris Agnew and Deek Turnbull. They'd even talked of going to Laura Smith's house and posing for a photo – 'Put it on our website and see how *she* likes it.' Trust the pair of them *not* to get the 'rona.

Driscoll had considered driving to the infirmary and rubbing himself up against a few of the patients. A couple of bars on his daily LFT and he could stay in bed for a week being waited on hand and foot. Instead of which he was pounding the night-time streets around Haymarket, looking for a psycho. There had been several reports, the first from the railway station itself. Male, late twenties, shaved head, baggy denims, stick-thin. Threatening people, abusive language, needing dealt with. But the suspect had headed elsewhere by the time Driscoll arrived – along West Maitland Street and into Palmerston Place reportedly. They only had one available patrol car, and it was on the prowl. Driscoll's radio kept squawking, driving him demented.

The sarge had given him a right earful earlier, too, as if everything that had gone wrong could be laid at Driscoll's door. Why couldn't he get his house in order? Why didn't the Crew all jump at his command? 'It's because you don't instil fear, son,' Fleck had told him. 'There always has to be a bit of fear.' Aye, right, phoning from his comfy office in his fancy car showroom before heading home to his twelve-room mansion and his bastard wine cellar.

'Fuck's sake,' Driscoll muttered as he strode, his loaded utility belt weighing him down. A couple of pedestrians pointed him in the right direction. Very helpful, yes, thank you very much, and did you try stopping him yourselves? Of course you bloody didn't. That's *your* job, Officer.

And there he was, had to be the guy, jeans unzipped and pissing against the doors of St Mary's Cathedral, no bolt of lightning striking him down. A few revellers had stopped nearby and had their phones out to capture proceedings, soon to be shared on social media. Having got himself presentable again, the man jabbed a finger in their direction.

'Go home and kill yourselves,' he barked. 'Cut your throats. You have to do it!' His voice, not quiet to start with, was rising steadily. 'Know who I am? I'm the devil's son. And I'm *telling* you to do it.'

'Right you are then,' one of the onlookers said.

The man took a couple of belligerent steps towards the group. 'You need to listen to me. If you don't listen to me, I'll cut you myself.'

'You're not cutting anybody,' Driscoll interrupted, causing the man to turn towards him. His eyes were gaping, the pupils dark pinpricks. Driscoll had his baton in one hand, pepper spray in the other. No taser, though – Turnbull had one, but then Turnbull was, as usual, nowhere in the useful vicinity. The urine deposited against the place of worship was now pooling around Driscoll's shoes, despite his efforts to steer clear.

'Satan is my father,' the man was telling him.

'That must be handy.'

'You'll go home tonight and kill yourself.'

'But I've a new car coming next week.'

'If you won't do it, then I . . .' The man's hand went into the back pocket of his ratty denims. Driscoll took his chance and launched the baton at him. It hit him square across the cheekbone and sent him reeling. He stayed on his feet, though, so Driscoll set about the back of his knees, buckling him. He sprayed the man's face from close range, but that only seemed to rile him further. He was trying to get back to his feet, screaming like a wild animal, when Driscoll gave him another whack to the head. Two taps used to be sufficient – more than sufficient – but tonight it wasn't working. He placed his weight on the man's back, forcing him prone, then pushed the length of his baton hard against the exposed neck, holding it in place with his knee. The man started gurgling and gasping.

'You're killing him!' a bystander cried out.

'Given half a chance, he'd have cut your face off,' Driscoll answered. He ran a hand over the pockets of the man's jeans but couldn't feel anything. The man started thrashing out with his legs.

'You just going to watch?' Driscoll called to the civilians. Not that they *were* just watching – a couple of them were still filming everything. 'Aye, get your fucking fill,' he spat. 'It's all any of you are good for.'

He heard running footsteps: Agnew and Turnbull. One took the man's legs while the other got busy with the cuffs.

'About bloody time,' Driscoll told them.

'You might want to ease off the guy's neck, Rob,' Agnew advised. 'He's going a funny colour.'

Driscoll did as he was told and started getting to his feet. The bottom third of his trousers felt damp, and he knew the reason why. Realising that he was still being filmed, he flicked the Vs at the group.

'Fuck the lot of you,' he said, scooping his pepper spray up off the pavement.

Day Eight

29

Rebus was seated in the window of a café on Duke Street, walking distance from Leith police station, when Malcolm Fox arrived.

'Five minutes,' Fox stressed, perching on the chair opposite.

'You're a busy man, Malcolm, I appreciate that.' A bacon roll and mug of tea were placed in front of Rebus, and Fox looked tempted, but he shook his head when the server asked. Rebus squirted brown sauce over the filling and closed the roll, taking a bite.

'And that's one minute gone,' Fox said.

Rebus chewed and swallowed, reaching for the tea.

'Everything okay with the inquiry?' he eventually asked.

'You know I can't discuss that.'

'Well, let's head for safer ground then – Fraser Mackenzie.'

'What about him?'

'He's in Organised Crime's sights, yes? I'm wondering how long he's been there.'

Fox gave him a stare. 'Siobhan's been talking. She shouldn't have.'

'My guess would be that it's happened only recently – around the time Cafferty emerged from hospital into a wheelchair and the pandemic shut everything down.'

'So what?'

'It's just, you've maybe got it wrong – focusing on the husband, I mean.'

Fox was probably unaware that his hands were gripping the rim of the table. 'I'm listening.'

'Beth Mackenzie used to go out with Cafferty. Ancient history, but she maybe learned a few things. Her husband owns a lettings

295

agency with what could be termed a challenging clientele. Not all of them, by any means, but enough. Her daughter, Gaby, is a club DJ – a world not averse to chemical substances.'

'I've seen her at work.'

'Clubs were closed during lockdown, meaning a lot of doormen needing a wage. Useful in all kinds of ways to an outfit like QC. Up until that point, as far as you know, Mackenzie had been happy operating as an above-board businessman?' Fox conceded as much with a shrug. 'Well, maybe he still is. Mother and daughter, on the other hand . . .'

'I always enjoy your stories, John, but so far that's all I'm hearing. Doesn't really matter if it's Fraser Mackenzie or any other member of his family, what we need at Gartcosh is some hard evidence.'

'It matters,' Rebus said quietly.

Fox was getting to his feet, seemingly impatient. 'A phone call would have done the job every bit as well.'

'But then I'd have been deprived of your company, Malcolm.'

'Come to me with evidence, John. Maybe then we can cut a deal.'

'You think I'm doing this to save my own skin?'

'I don't really care why you're doing it. All I know is there's going to be fallout and you could end up doing time.' Fox paused. 'I'm here if and when you decide to talk.'

'And if I'd prefer a more neutral face?'

'There's always Geoff Dickinson at Organised Crime.'

'You'd give him the credit rather than taking it for yourself?'

'Maybe that's because I doubt there'll be any credit to take.'

Fox left the café, marching along the pavement as if on parade.

'Same prick you always were,' Rebus muttered. Some sauce had dripped from his roll onto the plate. He looked at it, then touched it with a fingertip, transferring it to his mouth.

Hard evidence . . .

'Might be able to help you there, Malky,' Rebus said to himself, getting to grips with the roll again. Then, after a further moment's thought, 'Never even asked about my face . . .'

Katherine Trask stomped into her office from the press conference, slamming the door after her.

'Looks like it went well,' George Gamble chuckled from behind his desk.

'Should we maybe make her a coffee?' Ritchie asked.

'Only if it's from the jar marked Valium, son.'

'Besides,' Christine Esson added, 'door closed equals not to disturb, remember?' She was standing next to the murder wall, checking the timeline. They now had Drifter's, the casino and two taxis, but the thinking was, Haggard would have been unlikely to undertake the long walk home from Corstorphine. Stood to reason there was one last taxi trip still to be accounted for. Cheryl and her sister had been asked and swore he hadn't been back, so what else had he done with himself?

Esson returned to her computer and replayed the casino footage. Something had been niggling at her, and now she realised what it was. She pulled up the list of belongings found on the body. It took her a moment to realise Ritchie was standing at her shoulder.

'Look at this,' she said, showing him the footage. 'What's our victim doing?'

'Getting money from a cash machine.'

'Anything else?'

'Putting it in his pocket.' Ritchie couldn't see where this was going.

'He takes the receipt too, though, doesn't he?' Esson jabbed at the screen. 'But it's not listed among his effects.'

'Probably tossed it, same as I'd have done.'

'He pockets it along with the notes,' Esson stated, playing the footage one more time.

'And at some point he took one of those notes out to pay for something, found the receipt and got rid of it.' Ritchie shrugged at the obviousness of the explanation and headed back to his desk.

Esson watched Siobhan Clarke come back in from the hallway, where she'd been taking a call.

'Anything we should know about?' she nudged.

'Elizabeth Mackenzie,' Clarke explained, 'backing up the story about Cafferty and the photo of Francis Haggard.'

'The photo he denied ever receiving?'

'Looks like we've caught him being economical with the truth.'

'And to a murder inquiry at that. I'd say that's cause to bring him in.'

'No wheelchair access, though – and I doubt his solicitor will want him being questioned in reception.'

'I've always wanted to check out a gangster's interior design.'

Clarke watched Fox enter the office. He kept his eyes front as he walked to Trask's door, knocking and entering.

297

'Brave man,' Esson commented.

'Take Jason with you,' Clarke told her. Esson waited for enlightenment. 'I've got stuff to do, and you know as much about the photo as I do.'

'I know John Rebus's version.'

'Elizabeth Mackenzie took it and sent it to Cafferty.'

'Did she tell you why?'

'She said it would wind him up, seeing a cop in an old flat of his.' Clarke saw the look Esson was giving her. 'I know, doesn't make sense to me either. There's plenty she's not telling us – maybe Mr Cafferty will be more forthcoming.'

'You really think so?'

'Just see what you can do.'

'Fine, but while you're here . . .' Esson signalled for Clarke to look at the monitor. 'The receipt that came with the withdrawal – no sign of it among Haggard's possessions.'

'And?'

'And Jason thinks he probably threw it away. From the look on your face, I'm sensing you agree.'

'Feel free to double-check – his belongings are in the evidence cupboard. But go talk to Cafferty first.'

Clarke turned and headed to Trask's office, copying Fox by knocking and then going in without waiting. Trask was seated, popping ibuprofen tablets from a blister pack. She swallowed two with a mouthful of Fanta from a plastic bottle, then gave the bottle a little shake.

'Cheaper than water, can you believe it?'

'Journalists a bit gnarly?' Clarke asked.

'One of them knew about all the boxes we've been going through.'

'And for once it can't have been Laura Smith,' Clarke said.

Trask stared at her. 'And why is that?'

Clarke realised she'd said the wrong thing. 'Because she's currently in my flat, recuperating from a petrol bomb attack on her home.'

'Sleeping with the enemy,' Fox muttered.

'It's called helping a friend,' Clarke snapped back. Then, to Trask, 'So who was it knew about the Complaints trawl?'

'Trainee from the *Record*. He looked about fifteen, dressed in a suit he might grow into.'

'Could just be that someone saw the boxes being hauled in here from the van and thought it worth telling the press?'

'Whichever way it happened, it means the media know our magnifying glass is on Tynecastle. Speaking of which, the schoolkid also mentioned a stooshie last night on Palmerston Place, Tynecastle officers involved.' She looked to the two detectives for clarification, but they just shrugged. Trask rubbed a hand across her forehead. 'Have we finished interviewing them all yet?'

'Few stragglers to pick up,' Clarke admitted. 'Currently off with COVID.'

'Have any of these chats taken us a single step forward?'

'There's a lot still to do,' Fox said. 'Mobile phones, home computers—'

'That's why I came in, actually,' Clarke interrupted. 'Chris Agnew, I just wondered if we could go a little deeper on him.'

'Any particular reason why?'

'Just a whisper that he might have had some history with the deceased.'

'What kind of history?'

Clarke shrugged. 'A bit of bad blood.'

Trask looked across her desk again. 'Has his phone been checked?'

'Plenty opportunity to delete anything he didn't want us seeing,' Fox added. 'Same goes for all of them. It's why we've asked their service providers for call records. It might not tell us much, but it's probably worth a punt.'

'Retrieval can take time, though,' Clarke said, 'which is why I thought a word from the ACC's office might work as a booster.'

'I can certainly make the call,' Trask said. 'Anything to move this bloody case along. Speaking of which, have we got any whiff of his movements after he got out of that taxi?'

'We've put word out to the cab firms,' Clarke assured her. 'I'm confident we'll fill in the gaps.'

'Well, that's certainly a load off my mind.' Trask gestured for them to leave.

'Should I close the door after us?' Fox asked.

'You definitely bloody should,' she replied.

By the time he caught up with Clarke, she was running a Google check on Palmerston Place. A couple of clicks later, they were staring at the shaky footage. At one point the camera zoomed in on Rob Driscoll's furious, reddened face as he choked the life out of what appeared to be a helpless male approximately half his height and bulk.

'Not great optics,' Fox commented. As he walked back to his desk, Clarke called Laura Smith.

'I'm gutted,' Smith told her. 'Half a dozen bloody bloggers got there first and my fire's already yesterday's news.'

'Did you tell the *Record* that we had an MIT office full of Complaints files relating to Tynecastle?'

Smith paused for a moment. 'I take it my question got asked,' she eventually admitted. 'I'd have been there myself if it wasn't for this meeting with the insurers.'

'What I'm wondering is: who told you?' Clarke closed her eyes for a second. 'Actually, you don't even need to answer that.'

'You home for supper tonight? I can cook again if you like.'

'Only if you promise to make half as much.' She watched Fox approach her desk. 'Got to go,' she said, ending the call.

Fox was standing right next to her. He leaned down, a hand on the back of her chair, his lips almost touching her ear.

'You told Rebus about the Mackenzies, didn't you?' he whispered.

'Would I do that? I'm shocked you'd even ask.'

'His theory is, it's the mother and daughter in charge rather than the father. On the way back here from talking to him, I got thinking . . .'

'You reckon he could be right?'

'He might never have been much of a police officer, but he was always a gifted detective.'

'So you'll take it to Geoff Dickinson?'

'Wouldn't you?'

'Tell him you want something in return, though – Agnew's phone records asap.'

'You reckon he's got more clout than the actual ACC?'

'Clout, no; contacts, almost certainly.'

Fox met her eyes. 'Whispers, you said?'

'Did I?'

'Agnew and Haggard, bad blood – you've heard whispers.' He paused. 'Originating where, I wonder? Maybe best I don't ask, eh?'

He was interrupted by Esson and Ritchie, who were ready to leave.

'I'm on the end of the phone if you need me,' Clarke told them.

'The one and only Big Ger Cafferty,' Ritchie was saying, like he was off to his first pop concert.

The morning was foggy, which suited Rebus fine. While he drove, he whistled an old tune he couldn't quite name. He checked at the top of the lane, but everything was quiet, so he manoeuvred the Saab down it, stopping directly outside the lock-up. He was still whistling when he got out and surveyed the structure in front of him. He began working away at the rim of the door with the heavy-duty crowbar, pausing to take his jacket off, placing it on the passenger seat. Stealth was not exactly possible, the sounds of his efforts reverberating and rising into the air. It was a good crowbar, he'd been assured, so he had to blame the workman rather than the tool for the amount of effort it was taking. Then again, the door to the lock-up was reinforced – possibly more than was strictly necessary to protect some tools, paint pots and foldaway beds.

The first bike arrived before he'd finished the job. Rebus didn't recognise the face above the handlebars.

'Off you fuck,' he told the kid.

'You're dead,' the face said, slewing the bike a hundred and eighty degrees and speeding off.

Rebus had wrenched his shoulder but knew he could live with it. The door gave with a clank and he hauled it open, keeping hold of the crowbar as he walked in. He made straight for the workbench with the shelves of paint pots above. Lifted one down and prised it open. Pale green matt emulsion, matching some of the blotches on the bench's surface, the ones that had been tacky to the touch. He upended the can slowly, paint splattering out. When he peered inside the emptied pot, he saw something wedged against its bottom.

He took out the rubber gloves he'd bought and slipped them on before reaching in to ease out the wrapped package. A lesson learned from Cafferty, he reckoned – storing something of value in an innocuous setting. Drugs would surely be kept in a secure vault, not left lying in a lock-up in one of the less salubrious parts of town. Looking around, he found an old newspaper. He separated its sheets and placed the package on one of them before starting on the next tin.

His phone pinged with a message, Sammy checking he was still okay for Sunday lunch and warning that Carrie had a new piano tune for him to hear.

Wouldn't miss it for the world, he texted back.

When he looked up from his phone, two bikes had arrived

outside, the one from before plus backup. Still no sign of Buster or his owner. The riders tried a few blasphemous threats, but Rebus ignored them, except to pick up the crowbar, giving it a brief wave in their direction.

He had six more pots to go. It took only a few minutes to relieve them of their contents. He used more sheets of newspaper to wrap the packets, then started carrying everything out to the Saab, opening the boot and loading up. He guessed there to be a couple of kilos, maybe closer to three. If it was cocaine, that probably made it worth six figures; more if it was heroin. He would have known the going rate at one time. Had Jack Oram discovered the drugs, or had his son maybe hinted or said something? Rebus knew he'd find out eventually.

He took a final look around. There could be other hiding places, but trouble was almost certainly only moments away. His eyes settled on the box of empty spirits bottles – litre sizes, the kind you only got duty-free or in pubs and clubs. Cheap brands of vodka, gin and whisky. Then there was the mound of rags. And on the floor beneath the workbench a couple of plastic jerrycans.

Nodding to himself, he got into the car and reversed up the lane. He was halfway to the main road when he saw the bikes heading straight towards him, the dog, Buster, lagging a long way behind. Four bikes in total, spread out across the road and being pedalled furiously, the riders' bums up out of each saddle. And there at the centre was the face he knew. Their nameless leader.

He watched as the boy, teeth bared in fury, drew something from his waistband. 'Christ,' he said out loud as the pistol was aimed at his windscreen. He yanked on the steering wheel and bumped up onto the pavement, heading across a section of the muddy park, losing traction for a moment before slewing the car back onto the roadway and checking in his rear-view mirror. They had pivoted their bikes and were not about to give up the pursuit. He just hoped young angry legs were no match for the Saab's antiquated engine. But now there was a white car turning into the estate, and Rebus was on the wrong side of the road. He turned the steering wheel hard and almost shredded a tyre or two against the kerb, while the white car was forced to bump up onto the opposite pavement. The Saab growled on to Calder Road, this time almost sideswiping a black cab on the roundabout. Rebus ignored the blaring horn, and when he next checked in the mirror, there was no sign of his pursuers. He allowed himself a long exhalation. That was the easy bit done and dusted.

Now he just had to wait.

'I've been trying to get you,' Clarke said when Ronnie Ogilvie called her.

'Got a bit hectic here for a while.'

'You brought Crosbie in?'

'Lovely guy. We're meeting up this weekend to play golf.'

'But meantime, in the real world?'

'He doesn't deny it's his car or him at the wheel. But he says he was nowhere near Laura Smith's house and wouldn't know her if he saw her.'

'So what was he doing there at that time of night? He lives and works the other side of the city.'

'Not strictly true. As well as being a doorman, he also does a bit of chauffeuring for the Mackenzies. He was dropping the daughter home, meaning the family home in Cramond. After that, he drove to his flat in Craigmillar. He says the daughter will vouch for him.'

'Cramond to Craigmillar via Broughton Street?'

'You and I might choose a more direct route. He just shrugged when I suggested as much.'

'Could you get a search warrant for the car? Hard to transport a petrol bomb without a bit of spillage.'

'Probable cause, Siobhan? Plus I'm sure he'd have an explanation, plausible or otherwise.'

'So you've let him go?'

'Pending further enquiries. Any chance of you helping me out?'

'He might be involved in the local drugs trade, though that's not for public consumption. Also pally with the crew at Tynecastle police station – the ones that indulge, at any rate. Bar he owns used to be connected to Big Ger Cafferty. I'd say that gives you plenty to be getting on with.'

'And he targeted Laura Smith because . . .?'

'Someone asked or someone paid.'

'Well, I'm going to dive back into the street cameras. If he really was coming from Cramond, there'll be footage of him on Queensferry Road.'

'Keep me posted, Ronnie. And thanks.'

Clarke ended the call and walked over to the kettle, making

herself a coffee. Fox joined her. 'There's only enough milk for one,' she warned him.

'Then I'll make do with black.'

'Did you talk to Dickinson?'

'He's on it.'

'What did he reckon to Rebus's theory?'

'He didn't completely dismiss it.'

'Doorman at Gaby's club, the one they call C, looking likely he's Laura Smith's fire-raiser.'

'I should let Dickinson know.' He took out his phone.

'Tell him to liaise with Ronnie Ogilvie at Gayfield Square.'

Fox nodded and pressed the phone to his ear. Clarke finished stirring and took her mug back to her computer. Then she picked up her phone and called Rebus.

'Gareth Crosbie might have thrown that bottle into Laura's living room,' she told him. 'We can place him in the vicinity. Any idea why, though?'

'No, but I might have something for you.'

'I'm listening.'

'There's a row of lock-ups just off Calder Road, near the end of Burnhill Crescent. Tommy Oram uses it for storage. If you were to pay a visit, you'd find a case of empty spirits bottles, litre-sized ones at that, plus a pile of cleaning rags and some jerrycans.'

'Everything the well-stocked firebomber needs.'

'But if you're intending to visit, best be quick – the Mackenzies will probably gut the place soon.' Rebus described the location to her while she made a note.

'Thanks for that, John.'

'Don't mention it.'

'Have you heard about Rob Driscoll's meltdown? Happened last night in full view of a few camera phones.'

'That'll be him on suspension then. Oh, has Beth Mackenzie been in touch?'

'Officers are interviewing Cafferty as we speak. Listen, I'd better follow up on this. I'll talk to you later, yes?'

'I might be busy, but don't let that stop you.'

'Thanks again, John.'

She ended the call and considered her options. Nearest station to Calder Road was Tynecastle, but she knew better than to ask, so instead she phoned West End CID. They said they'd send a car to take a look and get back to her.

30

It took the combined forces of the ACC and Geoff Dickinson only a couple of hours to deliver the goods on Chris Agnew. Clarke and Esson sat opposite one another at their respective desks, going through the list of numbers and duration of calls. Esson's visit to Cafferty had resulted only in a further denial regarding the photo. When he'd asked his aide to put in a phone call to his lawyer, Esson and Ritchie had given up the fight.

'Some pad he's got,' Ritchie kept telling his colleagues, whether they wanted to hear it or not. 'Biggest telly I've ever seen.'

'I didn't even register it,' Esson had said to Clarke.

Clarke studied the printed sheets more closely. Calls, text and media messages, browsing and downloads. There was nothing to be gleaned from the last two. She cross-referenced the numbers called against known users. Most belonged to fellow officers at Tynecastle. Some to fast-food outlets. But the most frequently called number was one she didn't recognise. She looked again at the data they had taken from Agnew's phone when they'd asked his permission to check it. The number wasn't there.

'He's deleted every instance,' she told Esson.

'So who does it belong to?'

'One way to find out.' Clarke picked up her own phone and entered the number. After ringing a few times, it went to a chatty message.

'Not here, sorry. Leave your deets, I'll get back to you if you're worth it. I'm sure you are. Mwah.'

Clarke stared at the device for a moment, then lifted her eyes, meeting those of the expectant Esson.

'Mwah,' she said. It only took Esson a moment.

'Stephanie Pelham?'

'Definitely her voice. But just to make sure . . .' Clarke got busy on her phone again. 'Hiya, Gina,' she said when the call was answered. 'Very quick one – do you have both phone numbers for Cheryl's sister? Business and personal?' She paused and listened, nodding for Esson's benefit as she did so. 'Thanks. I'll explain later.' She tossed her phone onto her desk and leaned back in her chair.

'I don't get it,' Esson said.

'Dozens of calls and texts to her personal phone this past month, not to mention media messages.'

'Meaning photos or video?'

Clarke nodded slowly. 'Stands to reason they'd have met – maybe a dinner or a function in a pub. We already know there were regular get-togethers, showing off the wives and girlfriends.'

Esson was checking her computer. 'Agnew told us he's been divorced three years.'

'And Stephanie's own divorce is well under way.'

'With her painted as the wronged woman, meaning a big payday.'

Clarke nodded again. 'Imperilled if any naughtiness on her part were to come to light.'

Esson rested her chin on one hand. 'Who was it told you Agnew was worth a look?'

'Driscoll let something slip in front of John. Possible bad blood between Agnew and Haggard.'

'Over Stephanie Pelham?'

'Doesn't really make sense, does it? Unless . . .'

'What?'

Clarke leaned forward over her desk. 'Haggard and Stephanie? What if they had something going on and the lover found out?'

'Is it worth asking, do you think?'

'There's definitely something here.' Clarke jabbed a finger against the list of numbers. 'A relationship covered up. The Crew were a pretty tight bunch; I dare say romantic conquests were discussed. If something was going on between Agnew and Stephanie, chances are Francis knew.' She was thinking of the footage from the house when Haggard burst in, the pointed finger, the meeting of eyes . . .

'So who do we bring in first?' Esson was asking. 'Driscoll, Agnew or Stephanie?'

Clarke rose to her feet and crossed to the two desks where George Gamble and Tess Leighton sat. 'Do you think you could go fetch Chris Agnew? He'll either be working a shift or at home.'

'What's it in aid of?' Gamble enquired.

'Just keep him here, either of the interview rooms will do. Mug of tea or coffee if he wants it. I shouldn't be too long.'

'And when he asks us why?' Leighton asked.

'We just need some additional information from him,' Clarke answered. 'Tell him we're in possession of his mobile phone log. Then leave him to sweat.'

'Might not be so easy, the way the radiators are acting up,' Gamble said, rising with the usual considerable effort.

'Tea won't be straightforward either,' Leighton added, 'seeing how somebody finished the milk.'

Clarke fetched a ten-pound note from her bag. She held it out to Ritchie. 'Another mission for you, Jason,' she said. 'Milk and maybe some biscuits. The change can go on my desk.'

'One minute a penthouse, the next the corner shop,' Gamble announced with a snuffled laugh.

Clarke was already hoisting her jacket from the back of her chair. Esson didn't need further encouragement.

'Do we tell them we're coming?' she asked.

'And spoil the surprise?' Clarke shot back.

'Ah yes, silly me.'

Fox emerged from the DCI's office and looked around. 'What did I miss?' he asked.

'Serves you right for deserting the shop floor, Malcolm,' Clarke said, blowing him a kiss and striding from the room.

Tommy Oram was working on a flat just off Abbeyhill. The previous tenant had been a nightmare. It had taken a couple of Gaby's men to convince the guy he wasn't getting back in and he could whistle for his deposit. Just the two broken ribs he'd ended up with. Tommy had given the place a lick of paint and replaced some of the fittings. A rug covered some of the cigarette burns in the carpet – cheaper than replacing the whole thing – and the locks had been changed, just in case the nutjob had made copies of the keys. Earlier someone had buzzed the intercom looking for him. They'd sounded spaced out to Tommy, and he'd told them to get lost.

So when he heard the door to the flat begin to open, he feared the spaceman had somehow blagged his way in. He grabbed a screwdriver and walked into the hallway. Gaby Mackenzie was closing the door behind her.

'I wanted to surprise you,' she announced.

'You've got a key?'

She dangled one from her finger. 'Dad uses the same code on every key box – didn't you know that?' She walked towards him, following him into the living room. 'It's freezing in here.'

'Cut off for non-payment. Be a few more days before it gets fixed.'

She was studying her surroundings. 'Not too far from the club. Maybe it'll come in handy, if you and Mum aren't using it.'

'Don't start that again, Gaby.' He had begun wiring a lamp to one of the walls.

'Well, she's hardly likely to be wooed by that lock-up of yours.'

'Last time I checked, the lock-up was yours rather than mine.'

'Your name on the lease, though – you must remember signing it. So if anything ever goes wrong . . .'

He stopped what he was doing and turned towards her. 'What are you telling me?'

'I'm just saying we all need to watch out.' She paused. 'I was sorry when my mum chased your dad away – I hope you know that. I told her she shouldn't have.' She did a circuit of the room and checked the view from the small double-glazed window, not that there was much to see other than an identical low-rise across the street.

Oram's phone signalled an incoming message. He swore under his breath as he read it. When Gaby turned towards him, his eyes were burning into hers.

'Did you know?' he asked, a slight tremble in his voice.

'Know what?'

'The lock-up's been turned over.'

'What?'

'They chased the guy the length of Calder Road, but he got away.'

'Christ.' Gaby dug her own phone out, switched its speaker on and placed a call, which was eventually answered. 'About bloody time,' she shouted into the device. 'I've been taking cabs all morning – where the hell have you been?'

Oram recognised Crosbie's voice. 'I've been stuck in a cop shop,' he spat. 'That favour I did for your pal has come back to bite me on the arse.'

'How come?'

'They tagged the car on CCTV. Can't prove anything, but that won't stop them digging.'

'Why didn't you nick a motor?'

'Maybe if I'd had time, but your pal said it had to be done pronto.'

'You're a fuck-up, Crosbie, you do know that, don't you?'

'Maybe I am and maybe I'm not.'

'We're finished, you and me. I'm done with you.'

'Are you sure about that, Gaby? Because if I'm going down, I might want some company.'

Gaby was staring at Oram. He watched her features soften in front of his eyes, mouth almost forming a smile.

'You're right, C. I'm sorry – got carried away in the moment. We'll be behind you a hundred per cent. Beth knows all the good lawyers; I guarantee you'll get the best of them if it comes to it, which it won't. Like you say, all they have is your car on a night-time street.'

'When they ask, I was dropping you home, by the way. You won't mind fibbing for a pal, will you?'

'Of course not.' Her lightness of tone belied the look on her face. 'Now, are you able to come and pick me up, or should I call another cab?'

'Where are you?'

'Abbeyhill.'

'Twenty minutes. You working tonight?'

'As usual.'

'And me?'

'Wouldn't be the same without you, C. See you soon.' She ended the call and settled on the nearest chair. 'Ever fancied a job as a driver, Tommy?'

'Didn't sound to me like there was going to be a vacancy.'

The smile she gave him was colder than any of the radiators. 'I take it they got what they wanted from the lock-up?'

'Sounds like. And I think I know the bastard responsible – name of John Rebus.'

'What will he do with the stuff?'

'Hand it to the cops?'

She shook her head. 'Then why didn't he just summon them to the lock-up?'

Tommy ran a hand through his hair.

'Relax,' she told him.

'How the hell do I do that?'

She dug a small bag of pills from her pocket. 'These will turn that frown upside down.'

He hesitated for only a moment before taking the bag from her.

*

They announced themselves at the intercom and watched the gates swing silently open. Cheryl Haggard opened the door to them. She looked as pale and tired as ever, but there was a spark of renewed light in her eyes.

'Have you caught someone?' But then she saw the expressions on their faces and her eyes became opaque again.

'Just need to clarify a couple of points,' Clarke said.

'Okay, let's go upstairs.'

'Actually, it's Stephanie we need – is she here?'

Cheryl gestured towards the staircase. Esson began climbing, Clarke pausing a couple of steps up when she saw Cheryl was planning to follow.

'Maybe you could stay down here for a bit? We'll give you a shout when we're done.'

'If it's to do with Francis, shouldn't I . . .?'

'Like I say, just a couple of small things we need to clear up. I really would appreciate you leaving us to it.'

'If you say so.'

'Thank you.' She managed a thin smile before starting to climb again.

Stephanie Pelham was seated by the large windows, her phone on the arm of the chair. She didn't bother acknowledging that anyone had entered the room. While Esson closed the door, Clarke approached the chair.

'Hello there,' she said.

'Hello.'

'Want to hazard a guess why we're back?'

'Not particularly.' Pelham reached down to the floor and picked up her glass. There was an inch of white wine in it, which she drained. Only then did she meet Clarke's eyes.

'You know Chris Agnew, don't you?' Clarke began.

'Do I?'

'You're saying you've never met him?' She watched the woman shrug. 'So it's just a phone thing between the two of you?'

'We know each other,' Pelham conceded.

'I'm assuming you met through Francis?'

'How else?'

'And the two of you got friendly – friendly enough for lots of chats and texts?' Clarke unfolded and held up the sheet of calls.

'So?'

'So he was – is – your lover at a time when you're finalising your divorce?'

'Did I say that?'

'And according to witnesses, Agnew was no fan of Francis. I'm assuming that's because of what Francis did to Cheryl – stands to reason Agnew would have sided with you.'

Pelham studied her glass and readied to get to her feet. Clarke held a hand out, telling her to stay seated.

'He can't have been happy,' she continued, 'when he heard Francis had barged into your house and threatened you. I mean, I've seen the recording – he isn't physical or anything, but there's that finger-pointing he does. You did feel threatened, you said.'

Pelham's eyes narrowed slightly. 'You think Chris might have done something? Got mad and gone after Francis?'

'What do you think, Stephanie?'

She drew in a breath and widened her eyes again, as if considering the possibility.

Clarke's phone pinged and she lifted it to her eyeline. Agnew was on his way to Leith with Gamble and Leighton.

Said straight off he hasn't done anything. We hadn't even told him why we were there. Keeps mumbling about Rob Driscoll cracking up. Oh, and he wants a solicitor.

She tucked the phone into her pocket again.

'I suppose he could have,' Pelham was saying, drawing out each word.

'If we bring him in for questioning, what do you think he'll say?'

'I've really no idea.'

'He's never hinted to you that anything happened between him and Francis?'

She shook her head slowly. Clarke had bent a little, hands on knees, so her face was at the same level as the woman in the chair.

'There is another scenario, though, isn't there?' she said. 'All that money coming to you unless it became public knowledge you had a lover. We've not dug back too far into Chris's mobile phone history, but we will, and I'm betting your affair has been going on a while. Maybe you're just more skilled at hiding that sort of thing than your husband was.'

'What's your point?'

'If Francis Haggard knew about you and Chris, and if you suspected he was going to bring that knowledge into play . . . I mean, the way he pointed at you in the hall that day, as if letting you know – you'd either to persuade Cheryl to go back to him and drop the case, or he'd maybe speak to your husband, giving him some much-needed ammo. Now in *that* scenario, you'd be desperate for something to happen to Francis, wouldn't you, anything that would shut him up? You'd maybe exaggerate what happened when he burst in here, in the hope of getting Chris Agnew's blood up.'

'Isn't it Chris you should be asking, not me?'

'He's on his way to the station. Maybe I should put the two of you in a room together. As of now, he's saying he didn't do anything.' Clarke paused. 'And I'm inclined to believe him.'

'What?'

Clarke straightened up and turned towards the window as if addressing her words to it rather than Stephanie Pelham. 'There's one scenario I've left out, but I think it bears airing. That pointed finger – yes, it was a warning, and one he knew needed no words, because it was personal . . . very personal. Say you'd had some sort of fling with *Francis*, say that's the secret he was willing to expose. Now, if nobody except you and him knew, you couldn't take that to your lover, couldn't trust him to do something about it . . .'

'That's absurd. You must see you're making no sense.' Pelham had taken a grip of her phone and was squeezing the life from it. Her eyes were on Clarke, who was shaking her head.

'Ever since I saw the footage, I've known there was something about it that I wasn't getting, some history between the two of you. So no, Stephanie, I don't think it's absurd.'

The door flew open. Cheryl Haggard had obviously crept up the stairs and heard at least some of the conversation.

'I knew it!' she shrieked. 'It was that night you were pissed and he drove you home – I could practically *smell* you on him when he came back! You bitch!' She made a move towards her sister, who by now was up on her feet, but Esson got between the two women. 'Then the night he died, you said you'd run out of wine,' Cheryl went on. 'You said for me to go back to sleep and you'd head to the late-night grocer's.'

'Cheryl, I swear to God . . .'

But with a roar from deep in her chest, Cheryl Haggard had turned and was stumbling down the stairs. The front door was flung open. A moment later came the sound of an engine starting.

'She doesn't know how to drive!' her sister exclaimed as she followed Esson and Clarke down the staircase.

They got to the doorstep in time to see the yellow Porsche speed

312

towards the still-open gates. Clarke opened the door of her Astra and told Esson to stay with Pelham. She hadn't even reached the end of the driveway when she heard the sound of a sudden impact. Turning left, she saw the Porsche halfway across the T-junction. A white van had hit it side-on. Cheryl was wedged between the headrest and the airbag. The van driver and his workmate got out of their cab.

'Bloody maniac,' the driver complained, looking none the worse for wear. Cheryl meantime had raised a hand to her neck, groggy but conscious. The driver's-side door had buckled, making it impossible to open. Clarke headed to the other side.

'Better be insured,' the van driver muttered.

Clarke opened the passenger door. There were glass crystals everywhere from the shattered window. She reached across, her first thought to drag Cheryl out of there, but then she reconsidered. Some things were best left to medical professionals. The driver's workmate was already on his phone, requesting an ambulance.

'Are you okay, Cheryl?' Clarke asked. There was no blood, but then she wasn't wearing a seat belt either.

'I feel sick.'

'Help's on its way.' Clarke's eyes were on the debris again. It resembled nothing so much as a spillage of fake diamonds. But there was something else on the passenger-side floor, a scrunched ball of paper, three capitalised letters visible: *TIL*.

She reached down and took it between her thumb and forefinger, unfolding it and turning it the right way up. *TILL'S CASINO* was printed along the top. It was a receipt for a withdrawal from the casino's cash machine. Date and time made it clear who it belonged to. She held onto it as she watched Stephanie Pelham come teetering down the slope, wine glass still in hand, Esson in her wake.

'Oh my God! Is she . . .? Oh my God!'

'Best leave her be until the paramedics arrive,' Clarke said.

'Won't be long,' the workmate said. His partner was already more interested in the damage to the front of his van.

'Better be insured,' Clarke heard him repeat under his breath while the workmate shook his head in what looked to Clarke a lot like an apology.

'Get away from me,' Cheryl Haggard was telling her sister, though the earlier venom had been drawn out of her. 'I don't want to see you, I don't want to talk to you.'

'It was one time, Cher. One lousy stupid time.'

Esson saw the slip of paper Clarke was holding out towards her. She took it, and eventually turned it over, noting the words scrawled there in ballpoint pen. An address on Constitution Street. A time: *10 tonight*. And an unsigned warning: *Or else*.

Clarke took a step towards her. 'Walked to the house from the taxi. Scrambled over the gate. Left it where she'd see it. She knew then what she had to do.'

Stephanie Pelham turned towards them. Esson held up the withdrawal slip for her to see. The wine glass dropped to the roadway as Pelham screwed shut her eyes, as if hoping to block out what was to come. Her eyes were still closed as Siobhan Clarke began the process of placing her under arrest.

Clarke insisted that Christine Esson be in charge of taking Stephanie Pelham's statement. In the interview room next door, Chris Agnew filled in most of the gaps. Fox and Tess Leighton had sat with him, Fox trying to cajole a few nuggets from him about the workings at Tynecastle. Cheryl would be kept in hospital overnight for observation – miraculously they'd found bed space for her. Clarke had asked Gina Hendry to go sit with her, and Hendry had been glad to help. She'd listened as Clarke had sketched out the story.

'She's lost everything,' she'd said afterwards.

'They both have.' Clarke just hoped Cheryl had the strength to get through it.

When her phone rang again, it was Ronnie Ogilvie. 'We're another step closer,' he said. 'Teenager on his way home from his girlfriend's place. He lives one street over from Laura. Saw the Range Rover tearing away. Driver had his window down. He was pulling off a black balaclava and our witness got a good view of him. He's given me the description, and I'm pretty sure if I put Gareth Crosbie in a line-up, we'll get a match.'

'That's good, Ronnie.'

'Geoff Dickinson is on his way here from Gartcosh. He reckons this is the breakthrough he's been looking for.'

'Make sure he gives you the credit.'

'You sound tired, Siobhan.'

'Do I? Maybe I am.'

She knew she should be feeling the opposite of wrung out. In a short time, the DCI would open a bottle of something and they

314

would toast the closure of the case. The procurator fiscal was already locked away with Trask in her inner sanctum, the two of them sharing facts and discussing tactics. Getting a defendant to a courtroom was one thing, Clarke knew, but the result was never a foregone conclusion. She was wondering what precisely had driven Stephanie to do it – the thought of losing the divorce money, or the worry that she might lose the love and affection of her sister? Had she judged them equal in weight? Had she known what the outcome would be from the moment she stepped into her car?

The Porsche had been sealed and transported to the forensic facility at Howdenhall. If there was blood to be found, they would find it. Clarke had also arranged a search warrant for the Pelham home. They would check for stained clothing and attempts to clean up the same. Stephanie's computer and both her phones would be taken to the lab to be pored over.

She noticed that Fox was standing by one of the towers of Complaints boxes, staring at it as if considering giving it a kick. He seemed to sense her reading his mind, and turned his head in her direction, offering a huge shrug.

'They could be yours if you want them,' he told her.

'What could?' Jason Ritchie walked into the office, a carrier bag hanging from one hand. He reached into it, producing a bottle of white and one of red.

'I prefer beer,' George Gamble pretended to grumble. 'But for once, I might make an exception.'

Their heads turned as Christine Esson entered, followed by Colin King. Esson was nodding, letting the room know they had a result. She approached Clarke.

'Is Cheryl okay?' she asked.

'Just a bit of whiplash, I think.' Clarke held out a hand. 'Congratulations, Christine.'

Esson looked at the hand, but then ignored it, pulling Clarke into a hug instead.

31

It was gone ten when the message arrived on Rebus's phone. It was from a number he didn't recognise, but that didn't matter – it would be untraceable, a burner maybe. He knew who'd sent it.

The Moorfoot right now. Jack Oram will be there. Bring the stuff.

Brillo looked disheartened as Rebus grabbed his coat and keys. 'You've had a walk,' he chided the dog. But Brillo padded after him to the door, hoping to make him change his mind.

Outside, the Saab was parked twenty yards further up Arden Street. As Rebus walked towards it, a car came towards him, heading in the opposite direction. White Audi, driver's window lowered. He recognised the face behind the wheel. Andrew, Cafferty's lackey, actually smiled as he passed. Straight away, Rebus knew why. The Saab's boot stood gaping, Rebus obviously not the only person in Edinburgh skilled with a crowbar. The emptied interior gave him the blankest of stares. He cursed, turning his head to where the Audi was making a right turn onto Warrender Park Road. Still cursing, he slammed the boot shut, but it sprang open again. He tried once more, with the same result.

'Outstanding,' he muttered to himself, climbing into the driver's seat and checking, as suspected, that he had no visibility at all in the rear-view mirror. He started the engine anyway. He reckoned the Audi would head for Melville Drive, but would it then turn left or right? At the junction, he peered in both directions, but couldn't see any white cars. Had Andrew driven up Marchmont Road instead? There were too many possibilities – and he was expected at the Moorfoot.

When his phone buzzed, he checked the screen and then answered.

'Bit busy here, Siobhan,' he announced.

'I just thought you'd want to know we got someone for Francis Haggard's murder.'

'Chris Agnew?'

'No, though he was having an affair with Stephanie Pelham, so you weren't too wide of the mark.'

'Who then?'

'Stephanie'd had a one-night stand with Francis. He was threatening to go public. She stood to lose everything. He stuck a note on her windscreen, threw a stone at her window to alert her.'

The words were pouring out of her. Rebus remembered the feeling well. When you got a result, there was always someone you needed to tell.

'So off she went to meet him,' Clarke ran on, 'taking a knife from the kitchen.'

'Premeditated, then?'

'Her team will try arguing otherwise, but the procurator fiscal seems fairly confident.'

'And all the Tynecastle stuff?'

'Turns out not to have been a factor, meaning it goes back in the vaults, luckily for some.'

'Which counts as a result for Police Scotland, too. No embarrassing skeletons tumbling from closets. Is Fox pissed off?'

'He reckons he still might get his day, if the walls at Tynecastle keep crumbling.' She paused, tale told. Rebus reckoned the next stage would be a sleepless exhaustion. 'So what are you up to?' she asked. 'You sound like you're in the car.'

'Just a bit restless, you know how it is. Thought a night drive might help.' He glanced in his mirror and was rewarded with a view of the flapping boot. 'I had Cafferty on the phone earlier, unhappy that I'd grassed him up to you.'

'Probably not relevant now, if it ever was.'

'Probably not,' Rebus made show of agreeing.

'I assume it was you that told Laura we were digging into the Complaints files on Tynecastle?'

'Reckoned I owed her a favour. How's she doing, by the way?'

'She's fine – and the noose is tightening around Crosbie.'

'Find anything at the lock-up?'

'Plenty of prints on the bottles. They've gone for analysis, as have the rags.' She paused. 'Team said someone had been there before them, made a bit of a mess.'

'Oh?'

'Emptied paint pots everywhere. Whoever it was should have checked the foldaway bed, though – hundreds of bagged pills taped to its underside.'

'Well, isn't that something?'

'One day maybe you'll share the full story, but right now I'm off for a long soak and a fresh glass of wine. Just out driving, eh?'

'That's right.'

'It's only that when you answered, you said you were busy. To me that means you've a destination in mind.'

'Enjoy your moment of victory, Siobhan. They're few and far between.'

'Your way of telling me to mind my own business?'

'Goodnight, Siobhan.'

He ended the call and pointed the Saab towards Craigmillar.

Bring the stuff . . .

He was going to have to make something up. Stall them. Prevaricate.

Either that or tell the truth.

He tossed a coin in his mind. Made his decision.

There were lights on in the Moorfoot, but the door was locked. Rebus bunched his fist and gave a confident-sounding thump. The door opened just wide enough to allow him in. The man called Crosbie locked it again after him and gave him a shove, propelling him towards the bar, behind which Beecham stood. Untended glasses sat on tables, some of them barely started.

'All of this for me?' Rebus pretended to speculate. 'Regulars can't have been happy about early closing.' There was a glass on the bar with the dregs of a whisky inside. He sniffed it and drained it before scoping the room.

'How's the firebombing business?' he asked casually.

'Don't push it,' Beecham said. 'Crosbie's just about ready to start tearing heads off as it is.'

'I was told Jack Oram would be joining us.'

'And we were told you'd have something to trade.'

'I need to see Jack first.'

'Good luck with that.' Crosbie's voice was a low growl. He was behind Rebus, close enough for his sweat to be an issue. Rebus angled his body a little, an eye on both men.

'Meaning he's no longer with us,' he stated.

'A wetsuit and an oxygen tank, you'd be in with a shout,' Crosbie said.

'Off the coast would mean he might be washed up sooner or later,' Rebus speculated. 'I'm guessing a quarry?'

'Where's the stuff?' Beecham demanded.

'To cut to the chase, I've not got it. Car's parked outside if you want to check. Boot's been jemmied open and is now well and truly shagged. I'm amazed I made it here without getting pulled over.'

'Who took it?'

'He works for Cafferty. Name's Andrew. Drives a white Audi.'

'Fuck,' Crosbie muttered. Beecham looked at him.

'You know him? This Andrew?'

'Didn't realise he belonged to Cafferty.'

'Well,' said Rebus, trying to sound matter-of-fact, 'I'll leave you to go tell Beth Mackenzie you need to pay Cafferty a call.'

'You're going nowhere,' Beecham stated. 'Except maybe to hang out with Jack Oram.'

Rebus scratched at his chin, taking his time. 'Funny, isn't it,' he said, trying to keep his tone conversational, the words directed at Beecham, 'you working for Mackenzie so you can keep paying off Cafferty? I don't suppose you do very much other than turn a blind eye when deals are being done and hand over crates of empties for use as petrol bombs. But all that makes you is a hamster on a wheel. Reckon you've got the balls to go fetch that consignment from Cafferty, or will Beth require the big guns? And there's another thing – neither of you has mentioned Fraser Mackenzie yet. He's not even in the picture, is he?'

'What does it matter?' Beecham said.

'I don't like the idea of going to my grave with unanswered questions, that's all.' Rebus turned his head towards Crosbie. 'You're not an ex-con – you wouldn't have got the licence here if you were – so I'm guessing you were either army or police.'

'Army.'

'Ever serve in Northern Ireland? Me too. Explains why you know your way around a petrol bomb. But that was a friend of mine you nearly killed – and for what?'

'Crosbie never can say no when a skirt asks,' Beecham answered.

'Shut it, you,' Crosbie snarled.

'So the world of the nightclub bouncer beckoned,' Rebus went

319

on, 'which was fine until lockdown. Was it mother or daughter who reeled you in?'

'Fuck do you care?'

'I'm just working my way up to why you felt the need to kill Jack Oram.'

'He was drunk and mouthy,' Beecham said. 'Turned physical. Not a good combo when Crosbie is in one of his moods.'

Rebus gave a slow nod. 'One problem dealt with. Might not be so easy with me, though.'

'You think people care about a washed-up ex-cop?' Beecham asked with a sneer.

'I didn't mean it like that. Hang on, let me show you my phone . . .'

Neither man paid much notice that Rebus was taking a step back at the same time as he reached into his coat. He whipped out the crowbar and swung it at Crosbie's head. It was a glancing blow at best, but better than nothing. Beecham grabbed the record player and heaved it in Rebus's direction before following it over the bar. Rebus aimed the crowbar at his knuckles and struck gold. Beecham howled as he retreated, grabbing a bottle and smashing it to give himself a ragged-edged weapon.

Rebus turned and made for the door, but Crosbie slammed into him from behind, buffeting him against the solid wood, the air flying from his lungs. He managed to turn the lock, but had only opened the door an inch when he was dragged back into the bar, by which time Beecham had joined his partner. The crowbar was prised from his grip, Crosbie flinging it across the floor. Still winded, Rebus had little resistance to offer, every breath sending stabs of pain through him. Crosbie forced him to his knees, hands around his throat, the pressure intensifying. Rebus's own hands were clasped around Crosbie's, but no way he could loosen the grip. His eyes began bulging, choking sounds gurgling from his throat, the blood roaring in his ears . . .

Suddenly there was a fourth voice in the bar.

'Thought that was your car.'

Rebus's vision was fogged as he looked up towards the doorway. Tommy Oram stood there, aiming a pistol. Looked to Rebus a lot like the one the kid on the bike had been brandishing earlier.

'Step away from him,' Tommy ordered. Beecham and Crosbie shuffled backwards, making sure there was some distance between them. If he tried firing at one, the other would make his move.

320

Rebus was gasping as he rose shakily to his feet, one hand at his throat, feeling for damage.

'Your nose is bleeding,' Tommy informed him.

'I'm getting used to it.' Rebus swiped at the blood with the back of his free hand.

'Some mess you and your police pals made of my lock-up. Don't know what made me think I might find you here or hereabouts.'

Rebus nodded towards Beecham and Crosbie. 'They killed your dad, right here in this pub.'

'He's fucking lying!' Beecham roared.

'He's not, though, is he?' Tommy said in a quiet voice. 'It's why I kept coming in, so you wouldn't think I had an inkling. I was hoping you'd let something slip. You probably would have, sooner or later.' He glanced towards Rebus. 'My dad didn't like what I was mixed up in. He knew Crosbie worked the door at Elemental as well as owning this place, on paper at least. Stood to reason he would come barging in here and get on the wrong side of you.' His attention was focused once more on Beecham and Crosbie. 'Then he vanishes, leaving no proof, no witnesses . . .'

'There still aren't,' Beecham stated.

'Oh, I don't know,' Rebus countered. 'Not too many quarries around Edinburgh. Won't take a team of divers long to check them.' He had taken out his phone. 'Just need to call it in.'

'And what happens when they get here?' Beecham went on. 'Who's the one pointing a gun at two innocent men? Won't be us they'll be taking in. Best thing you can do, Tommy, is walk away, let us deal with this.'

'Like you dealt with my dad?'

'That was Crosbie. Nothing to do with me.'

The look Crosbie gave him was incendiary. 'Bastard,' he spat, flinging himself at Beecham, the two men starting to wrestle, twisting and turning. Rebus saw it as the ruse it was, but nothing like quickly enough, the two men suddenly launching themselves at Tommy Oram. The gun exploded into life, turning Beecham into a momentary waxwork before he angled his head down to examine the hole in the front of his shirt. Crosbie had paused too, but for only a moment. It was long enough for Tommy to take aim and fire a second time. The noise was deafening, the smell of burning powder filling even Rebus's blood-clogged nostrils. He watched Crosbie drop to his knees, hands pressed to the wound. Beecham had fallen backwards like an axed tree. Tommy was breathing

321

heavily, gun still held out in front of him. He looked resigned to his fate, nothing but jail time ahead of him despite saving a man's life.

'Thanks,' Rebus said.

When Oram spoke, his voice was unnaturally calm. 'I'll make the call, hand myself in. You best get out of here. You were never part of this.'

'They'll want to hear my side,' Rebus argued.

'Including lifting all that coke from the lock-up? That busted boot of yours tells me you didn't get to hang onto it.'

Rebus considered for a moment, a moment during which Oram switched gun for phone and began making the call.

'Cafferty has the coke,' he said. 'Make sure Beth gets to hear. And I'm sorry . . .'

'Sorry?'

'For everything,' Rebus said as he headed towards the door.

There was an underground car park opposite Cafferty's building. The lift took Rebus down to the first level, but all the spaces there were for visitors rather than residents. The private parking was a further storey down. The strip lighting overhead flickered into life when the sensors picked up movement. About half the available bays were occupied. A smattering of electric vehicles sat charging. One or two cars looked to have been there for a while, wrapped in dust sheets. The white Audi was squeezed in between two other cars, its bonnet cool to the touch. Rebus knew it would be locked, but he tried the doors anyway. He stared at the boot for fifteen or twenty seconds, gave the rear bumper a kick, then headed for the lift again.

So many lives tainted by association with Cafferty and his ilk, and it never seemed to stop, each new generation suckered in or repeating the mistakes of their elders. Tommy Oram's father had twice been snatched from him. Beth Mackenzie had learned from her old boyfriend and shared those lessons with her daughter. Rob Driscoll, like so many others, had fallen under Alan Fleck's spell. There seemed no end to it.

The night was frosty. Rebus could see his breath in front of him as he pressed the buzzer and waited. A few food delivery drivers were still plying their trade, but none stopped at Cafferty's block. The sound of exuberant singing drifted towards him from the Meadows. Young voices, female and male, a reminder that there was another world out there. He punched in the number for Cafferty's flat a second time.

'What?' Cafferty's voice eventually barked from the intercom. There was a camera there too, so Rebus knew he was being watched.

'Need a word,' he said.

'This time of night?'

'Jack Oram has surfaced.'

'Has he now?'

'And that means there's something we have to discuss.'

Rebus waited, folding his arms around himself for warmth. He wondered if he was maybe suffering a delayed reaction from the Moorfoot. Couldn't seem to stop trembling. When the door gave a click, he shoved it open and took the lift to the penthouse, all the time feeling as if he were descending rather than going up.

The door to Cafferty's flat was closed but not locked. Rebus went in and found the man in his usual place by the windows and the telescope. There was just the one floor-standing lamp illuminating a corner of the huge room, the rest left in shadow.

'Do you never go to bed?' he asked, looking around for something to drink. He found whisky and a glass, poured out a generous measure.

'Don't stand on ceremony,' Cafferty said. 'My casa is your casa, et cetera.' Then, taking a good look at Rebus, 'The absolute fucking state of you.' He watched as Rebus refilled the glass. 'Did Andrew do that?'

'All Andrew did was break into my car and lift the drugs I took from Beth Mackenzie.'

'Thought he might,' Cafferty said with a warm smile.

'Not your idea then?' Rebus looked around. 'Where is he anyway? Should I pat myself down for weapons?'

'He gets nights off – I'm not a slave-driver.'

'Before I came in, I checked the car park, saw his Audi sitting there. If I'd had any tools on me, I'd have meted out a bit of revenge.'

'My car actually, he just uses it as and when.'

'You've had him tailing me throughout.'

'Again, his own initiative.'

'Who the hell is he?'

'He used to belong to Darryl Christie until Darry got himself put away. Andrew was always sharper than most. I took him on as a pet project. He has a flat a few blocks away, though right now . . .'

Cafferty checked the time on his wristwatch. 'Yes, I suppose he could be out clubbing somewhere. He likes Elemental.'

'Probably not just for the music.' Rebus was pouring himself another drink.

'True enough, it's the staff he's interested in – he's a people person.'

'Especially if those people can come in handy after you've taken down the Mackenzies. Is that the plan – to install your protégé in their place?'

'You know as well as I do, John, there's never a vacuum. Now, you were saying something about Jack Oram?'

'He's dead, but then you already know that, don't you?'

'I still have eyes and ears in this town.'

'Funny, I remember you telling me the exact opposite. You can go to hell for telling lies, you know.'

'The owners of his old pool hall were clocked hauling something into a van at dead of night. You could say I had my suspicions.'

'And you hired me to find you a dead man because . . .?'

Cafferty's eyes were glittering. 'You tell me.'

'Even if I didn't find him,' Rebus obliged, 'I'd still be making a nuisance of myself, and probably disrupting the Mackenzies in the process. That's why you spun me the line about him being seen at QC Lettings. Did you know the son worked there?' He watched Cafferty nod. 'Not the only line you spun either – the money going to his brother's family?'

'I needed something to get you interested,' Cafferty commented.

'How about the cash you sent to his wife?'

'I thought it might flush him into the open.'

'The way I was supposed to flush out the Mackenzies? And meantime, if I got close to the truth, the men who topped him would want the same fate for me. You'd probably call that a win–win. Nearly was, too. I'd be growing cold on the floor of the Moorfoot right now if Oram's son hadn't come looking. Lucky for me, he was tooled up. Oh, and the upshot of that is, Beecham won't be giving you any more money.' Rebus paused. 'How come you took the price off his head anyway?'

'He got reacquainted with an old psycho pal of his.'

'Crosbie.'

'No way I could touch Beecham without Crosbie coming for me. I'd have to deal with both of them.'

'Messy,' Rebus agreed.

324

Cafferty looked at him. 'Messy isn't always good for business. Same went for Constitution Street. Losing a wedge hurt me for a few weeks, but I was back in the black soon enough. As for Jack Oram . . .'

'Yes?'

'If he hadn't got himself killed, I'd almost certainly have done him some damage.'

'So they did you a favour at the Moorfoot? Despite which, you sent me after them.'

'Yet here you are, luck of the devil.'

'Not so lucky for you, though.'

'You can't blame a man for trying.'

'Trying to do what? Get people killed, take back your old empire so you can start poisoning Edinburgh again?'

'If not me, then somebody else,' Cafferty snarled. 'Everybody knows the way it has to be. I just couldn't stand the thought of it being Fraser Mackenzie.'

'Fraser?' Rebus raised an eyebrow. 'You've no idea, have you? It's your old flame Beth running the show. The daughter provides muscle from her nightclub and the pair of them make quite a team, believe me.'

Cafferty's face creased as he took this on board.

'They've almost certainly been keeping Tynecastle sweet, too – another tactic Beth learned from you. Not that your relationship with the Crew was wholly amicable. After that stunt you pulled, getting them to cripple Tony Barlow—'

'With your help, Strawman,' Cafferty interrupted.

'With my help,' Rebus acknowledged. 'But that's when they decided to do the Constitution Street job, just so you'd know they weren't quite as controllable as you'd hoped.' He paused. 'So what happens now?'

'How do you mean?'

'You've got hold of the Mackenzies' stash – reckon Beth's going to let you keep what's hers?'

'She can try taking it.'

'I wouldn't bet against her. You might want to warn Andrew he's up against superior forces.'

'I'm the one in charge, Strawman!' Cafferty's voice had risen.

'I know you think you are, but from where I'm standing, you're just a greedy old man in a wheelchair.'

'A greedy old man who still pulls the strings – yours included!'

'Maybe time to cut them, then.'

Cafferty watched as Rebus poured and downed a final drink, then walked to the sofa, picking up the saltire cushion. He was carrying it in front of him as he approached the wheelchair.

'A young man's going to jail because of what you did to his dad all those years ago. A young man who saved my skin. Means I owe him, wouldn't you agree?'

'Don't be stupid,' Cafferty started to say. 'You know it doesn't—'

Rebus muffled the rest of the sentence, pushing the cushion hard into Cafferty's face. The man was strong; he got a grip of Rebus's wrists and tried to dislodge him, reminding Rebus of how close he'd come to dying on the floor of the Moorfoot. When Cafferty realised his efforts were futile, he scrabbled for the wheelchair's controls, propelling it backwards. It didn't get far, brought to a halt by impact with the heavy coffee table. The front wheels lifted off the ground as Rebus continued to press, Cafferty's muffled protestations growing weaker over time.

Rebus could still hear singing coming from the Meadows, and a dog barking, and a distant siren. Somewhere, someone needed help. Somewhere, bad things were happening. He'd spent his whole life in that world, a city perpetually dark, feeling increasingly weighed down, his heart full of headstones.

There would be frost on the paths in the morning. He would have to be careful when he took Brillo for his first walk of the day.

Now

As senior counsel readied to pronounce, Rebus looked at all the cameras situated around the courtroom, broadcasting their images to the distant jury.

Cameras: he had failed to take them into account. Bought after the attack that had put Cafferty in the wheelchair, placed surreptitiously around the airy living room, recording Rebus's assault and the eventual faltering of that assault as he thought of his daughter and granddaughter, imagining them visiting him in the prison that would be home until he died. So he had removed the cushion from Cafferty's face, watching the man taking in huge gulps of air, hoarse sounds escaping his throat. Then he had walked away, saying nothing, not looking back.

And Cafferty had died anyway, his heart giving out, leaving Rebus on a murder charge.

All at once, he felt his balance start to go and reached out for the handrail in front of him. His heart was pounding and the pain in his chest was a constant now. The judge had noticed and held a hand up to pause proceedings.

'Is the accused feeling all right?'

'Just a bit dizzy there for a second.'

'A glass of water?'

Rebus shook his head.

'Very well. Pray continue, Mr Bartleby.'

Siobhan and Sammy were right – he should see a doctor. There was one he could consult at the prison. His legal team had argued that, bearing in mind his health issues, he should not be kept on remand, but that had cut no ice with the judge. Rebus was a danger to the public, apparently, and had to be kept under lock and key.

Both Siobhan and Sammy had been to see him during visiting hours, Sammy explaining that she'd left Carrie and Brillo with a friend. He'd asked her what she'd told his granddaughter.

'That there was a bad man and you tried to do something about him.'

He'd smiled afterwards, thinking it not a bad epitaph. But then hadn't he been a bad man himself, consorting with many more devils than angels? He'd broken laws and skewed evidence and taken bungs, arrested guilty people for crimes they hadn't committed when he couldn't hold them to account for the ones they'd actually carried out. He'd used his fists and his feet as weapons of intimidation. It was all there in those Complaints boxes, including stuff he'd probably long forgotten.

Siobhan was going to take the promotion, but meantime she was kept busy with preparations for the trial of Stephanie Pelham. A lot was going to come out in court, none of it exactly beneficial to Tynecastle police station. Driscoll had already tendered his resignation. Clarke didn't think Agnew would be far behind. Jack Oram's body had eventually been recovered from a disused quarry in West Lothian. Crosbie – who had been too thrawn to die from the bullet wounds, unlike his lifelong pal – had been charged not only with Jack Oram's murder but also for his role in a spate of fire-raising incidents. Tommy, too, would appear in a courtroom soon enough. Clarke had speculated that Rebus could end up doing time alongside both Tommy and Crosbie – and potentially Fraser Mackenzie and James Pelham too. The Mackenzies, Gaby included, were under investigation for all manner of offences and conspiracies, giving Laura Smith enough material to keep her busy and solvent for the foreseeable.

'Have you seen Fox since he went back to Gartcosh?' Rebus had enquired of Clarke.

'He tells me he's got his fingers crossed for you.'

'But did you see any evidence?'

'No, now you come to mention it.' Which had caused them both to smile.

'Does he still think he can get Alan Fleck?'

'Malcolm's not the type to give up. That's one thing the two of you seem to have in common.'

'It won't be him, though, will it? It'll be *you*.'

'I suppose so.' Her face had fallen a little.

'And you'll do it right, Siobhan. Because it *has* to be done right.'

Fleck himself had asked to visit Rebus in detention, but Rebus had denied him. He knew Fleck would be after a favour: since Rebus was going away for a stretch, might he be minded to take with him some of the flak coming Fleck's way? No doubt compensation would be offered, but Rebus was done with covering his old pal's back. As soon as Siobhan had shifted to Complaints, Rebus would have her visit him. There were stories that needed to be told, and no more fitting person to hear his confession. He kept thinking of Francis Haggard, still unsure if his intention to tell all was fuelled by shame or self-preservation.

Well, hell, why not both?

He realised that time had moved on. His QC had seated himself and the advocate depute was on her feet. He had missed Bartleby uttering the all-important words.

'Are you quite sure?' Bartleby had asked him on more than one occasion.

'I've a life's worth of mitigation,' Rebus had assured him.

'Then not guilty it is,' Bartleby had agreed.

Doors were being opened to allow access to the Crown's first witness. Andrew, who had handed police the CCTV from Cafferty's penthouse, strode in. He wore an expensive suit and sported a new haircut. Dapper and ready for bigger things, he locked eyes with Rebus, and grinned.

I was a single father
But I just can't complain
Got a heart full of headstones
As I step down from the train . . .

Jackie Leven, 'Single Father'

© HAMISH BROWN

KEEP UP TO DATE WITH
THE WORLD OF

IAN RANKIN

Follow Ian 🐦 **@Beathhigh**

Follow him on Facebook **f** **@IanRankinBooks**

Find out all the latest updates
and subscribe to his newsletter:
www.ianrankin.net

**Now take a look and find your next
great Rankin read...**

The John Rebus Series

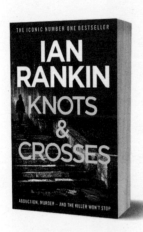

#1 KNOTS AND CROSSES

The modern classic which introduced the world to Detective John Rebus. In Edinburgh, young girls are being abducted. Soon, messages begin to arrive — knotted string and crossed matchsticks — taunting Rebus with a puzzle only he can solve.

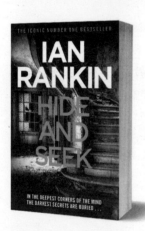

#2 HIDE AND SEEK

It starts with a dead junkie in a forgotten corner of Edinburgh. Nobody cares, but when Rebus starts to dig, he finds more than murder — and uncovers the dark heart of the city.

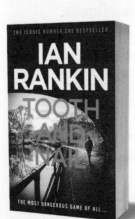

#3 TOOTH AND NAIL

A murderer targets London's East End. Rebus is called upon, due to his expertise in serial killers. But navigating the politics and prejudices of a new city is dangerous work — both for his career and his life . . .

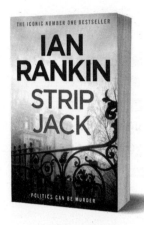

#4 STRIP JACK

A police raid on a notorious brothel ends the career of a promising local politician. But when the man's wife disappears, Rebus suspects the young MP is more than just unlucky. Someone is out to destroy him . . . but why?

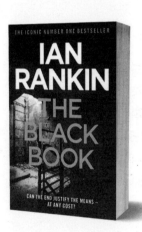

#5 THE BLACK BOOK

After a fellow officer is brutally attacked, Rebus is drawn into a case involving a hotel fire, an unidentified body, and a puzzle that not everyone wants solved – perhaps not even Rebus himself . . .

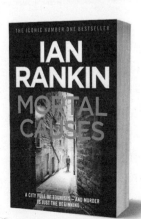

#6 MORTAL CAUSES

August in Edinburgh, and a brutally tortured body is discovered as the Festival is in full swing. When the victim turns out to be a notorious gangster's son, Rebus knows all hell is about to break loose . . .

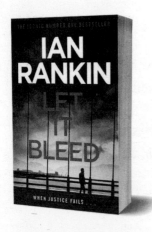

#7 LET IT BLEED

A kidnapping, a conspiracy, and an invitation . . . Far more used to investigating Edinburgh's underworld, when Rebus is invited to the home of the Scottish Office's Permanent Secretary he discovers a world in which crime really does pay – and people who are beyond justice.

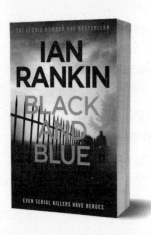

#8 BLACK AND BLUE

The award-winning masterpiece in which Rebus juggles four cases trying to nail one murderer – a copycat who may lead to the infamous serial killer Bible John. If that wasn't enough, he has to do it while being accused of a miscarriage of justice in the eyes of millions . . .

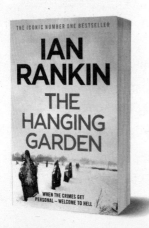

#9 THE HANGING GARDEN

Rebus is buried under paperwork, investigating the history of a war criminal now living in Edinburgh. As a turf war between two gangsters boils over – and targets his daughter – Rebus is dragged back to the present . . . ready to do a deal with the devil.

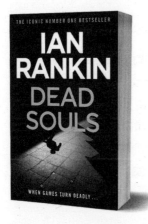

#10 DEAD SOULS

Should the past remain in the past? Rebus faces the question on all fronts: whether to out a supposedly reformed paedophile; or look into the disappearance of the son of an old friend; and whether to believe a notorious convicted killer has served their time and now walks free . . .

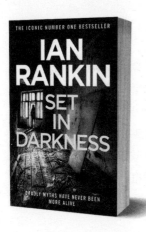

#11 SET IN DARKNESS

The new Scottish parliament opens slap bang in the middle of Rebus's patch. But when a body is discovered, a seemingly easy assignment might just turn out to be the hardest yet — and bring him face to face with Edinburgh's most notorious criminal.

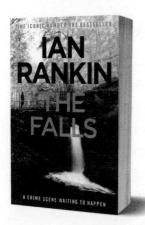

#12 THE FALLS

When a student goes missing, Rebus has a gut feeling there is bad news waiting. A carved wooden doll in a toy coffin in her home village, and clues on an internet role-playing game bring the ancient and the modern together in a cocktail of secrets, lies and murder.

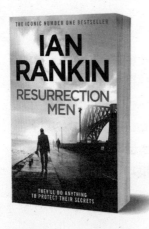

#13 RESURRECTION MEN

Following an outburst, Rebus is sent for 'retraining', where he is assigned an unsolved case alongside the other officers at the last chance saloon. While the newly promoted DS Siobhan Clarke, trying to solve the murder of an art dealer, is drawn dangerously towards 'Big Ger' Cafferty . . .

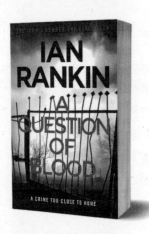

#14 A QUESTION OF BLOOD

Two students are killed by an ex-army loner who then turned the gun on himself. The mystery takes Rebus into the heart of a shattered community. Ex-army himself, Rebus becomes fascinated by the killer – who had friends in high places and enemies to spare . . .

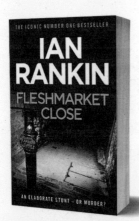

#15 FLESHMARKET CLOSE

Two skeletons discovered beneath a cellar floor in Fleshmarket Close are considered an elaborate stunt – but whose? Investigating the murder of an illegal immigrant Rebus starts to wonder if the case is linked, and just who might be hiding bodies around his town . . .

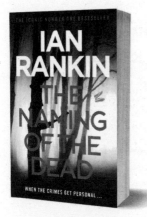

#16 THE NAMING OF THE DEAD

As the G8 summit gathers in Scotland, the apparent suicide of an MP connects to clues that a serial killer is at work. Warned off the case as protests turn to riots, Rebus was never one to follow orders – even if it sets him on a collision course with both sides of the conflict.

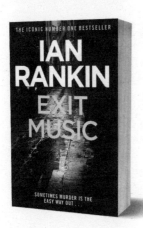

#17 EXIT MUSIC

As Rebus ties up loose ends before retirement, one last case arrives. A Russian dissident is found dead while a delegation of Russian businessmen are in town. Then, a brutal assault on Cafferty suddenly means Rebus might not survive long enough to retire . . .

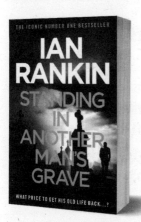

#18 STANDING IN ANOTHER MAN'S GRAVE

Rebus has been working as a civilian in a cold-case unit. When a string of disappearances stretching back decades becomes apparent, can Rebus be the man he once was and still stay on the right side of the law?

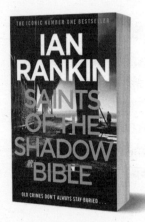

#19 SAINTS OF THE SHADOW BIBLE

Rebus is back on the force, with a chip on his shoulder and a marked card, as a case he worked thirty years ago is re-opened. Who are the saints and who are the sinners? And can one ever become the other?

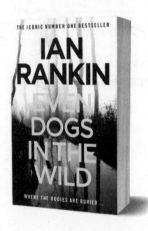

#20 EVEN DOGS IN THE WILD

Retirement doesn't suit Rebus. DI Siobhan Clarke knows what the answer will be when she asks for his help with a case. A lawyer has been murdered, a note found on the body. Across town, 'Big Ger' Cafferty gets an identical note and a bullet through his window. In the city, as in the wild, it's dog eat dog.

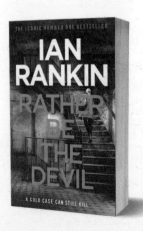

#21 RATHER BE THE DEVIL

Some cases never leave you. For Rebus, the unsolved murder of a socialite in a luxury hotel still haunts him. Meanwhile, as a dangerous young upstart muscles in on Cafferty's turf, Rebus refuses to believe his old adversary is as retired as he claims . . .

'Rebus is one of British crime writing's greatest characters: alongside Holmes, Poirot and Morse'
Daily Mail

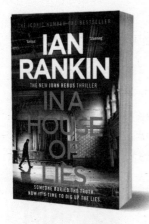

#22 IN A HOUSE OF LIES

When the body of a missing private investigator is found – in an area that police had already searched – Detective Inspector Siobhan Clarke discovers that everyone involved with the case is hiding something. None more so than her own mentor: Rebus.

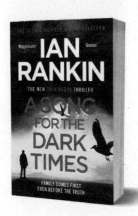

#23 A SONG FOR THE DARK TIMES

When his daughter Samantha calls in the dead of night to say her husband is missing, Rebus fears the worst and knows she'll be the prime suspect. He rushes to her aid – but is he going as a father or a detective?

The Detective Malcolm Fox Series

#1 THE COMPLAINTS

Nobody likes The Complaints – cops who investigate other cops – but that's what Malcolm Fox does. When he reluctantly takes on a new case, he soon discovers there's more to it than anyone thinks...

#2 THE IMPOSSIBLE DEAD

Malcolm Fox is investigating a simple case of misconduct – but it is soon complicated by a brutal murder and a weapon that should not even exist. When the body count rises, Fox finds himself in mortal danger.

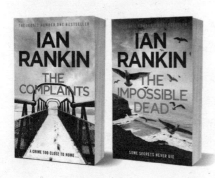

Other Novels

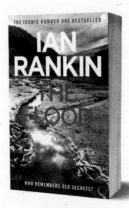

THE FLOOD

Mary has always been an outcast. Now she is a single mother, caught up in a faltering affair. Her son, Sandy, has fallen for a strange homeless girl. Their search for happiness isn't easy, as they both must face a dark secret from their past.

WATCHMAN

Bombs are exploding in the streets of London, but life has laid more subtle traps for Miles Flint — a spy who is desperate not to botch his latest case. But a trip to Belfast quickly becomes a flight of terror, murder and shocking discoveries.

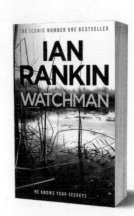

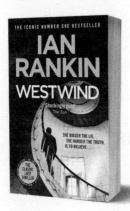

WESTWIND

After his friend suspects foul play at the satellite facility where they both work — and then disappears — Martin Hepton is determined to uncover the secret everyone is trying to keep hidden. But he isn't prepared for what he finds . . .

DOORS OPEN

Mike Mackenzie is a self-made man with too much time on his hands. When he and his friends make a plan to rip-off the National Gallery of Scotland, the real trick is make it look like there was no crime at all . . .

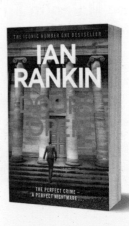